The Iron Trishula

Book Eight of the Iron Soul Series

J.M. Briggs

Contents

Dedicated to my mother who just smiles
while I bounce idea after idea off her.

1

Thoughts on Poison

Magic was still a mystery to Alex in many ways. She was aware of it and could summon it. In fact, at this point, she was aware of the soft pulse of it in the world around her all the time. There were so many invasive beings in the world that this point that the trees, earth, and even humans all seemed to be producing tiny sparks of magic at any given moment. The energy brushed across her skin, made her body stronger, and made the voices in her head a little louder.

Yet, that awareness didn't answer all her questions. Alex turned the small mason jar in her hand carefully. Inside was a thick black liquid that had a slight purple sheen to it in the light. On her lap was a pillow just in case it slipped from her hand, and she was seated on Merlin's sofa. Nothing about the contents of the jar screamed poison, but that's what it was. The most dangerous poison on Earth that wouldn't just kill, but strip away all magic. Even Merlin wasn't sure how it worked, and it was a mystery Alex doubted she'd ever get an answer to.

She shifted and caught her foot on the edge of the coffee table. Alex flinched at the sound and waited. There was some noise further down the house in the bedroom. Flexing her fingers, Alex pulled on the spark of magic in her gut. Dark silver sparks flared around her fingertips, and she waited silently. There was another, much softer sound down the hallway.

"It's me, Merlin," Alex called. "Just Alex."

The eldest of the mages appeared a moment later. "Alex?" There was a hint of alarm in Merlin's voice. "Why do you have the poison?" He was trying to sound casual, but when Alex looked up Merlin's hands were tight in fists. His brown eyes were wide with worry, and the wrinkles on his face were much more pronounced. "Everything alright?"

"Yes," Alex answered smoothly. "Sorry to wake you."

Merlin's eyes were darting between the jar and her. He hadn't moved any closer and seemed braced for something. For a moment, Alex was confused about the behavior. Then, it occurred to her that Merlin was worried she was going to hurt herself with it. She frowned a little at the idea. Death didn't hold a whole lot of importance for her. She was the Iron Soul; she'd just come back eventually in a new body. If the voices in her head were now a permanent thing, then her next life would even know what they were, something that she hadn't started with. The poison however destroyed magic and she was pretty sure that there was a lot of magic in her soul, so maybe it could completely destroy her. Interesting thought.

To put Merlin at ease, Alex set the jar down on the table and leaned back on the sofa to consider it. In the corner of her eye, she saw Merlin's shoulders relax. Holding back a frown, Alex kept herself from grumbling at both Merlin's mothering and his apparent concern that she might be suicidal. That wasn't an option. Her mother would never have forgiven her for that, and while nothing had indicated that ghosts were real except as illusions created by Brekszta, Alex wasn't going to risk being haunted.

"I thought you were at Morgana's?" Merlin said.

"I was thinking about the poison last night," Alex replied. She shrugged a little and tilted her head, making her long blonde braid fall over her shoulder. The magic around her hand was beginning to dissipate in the air, and she briefly thought about gathering it up before dismissing it. "One of those late-night thoughts that keeps you up."

"So you came to my house?"

"I do have a key," Alex reminded him. "Not that it really matters, not now that we have a lockpicking spell."

"You mean now that Nicki lifted a spell from Harry Potter and made it work." Merlin sounded a bit more relaxed now and walked over to sit down in his armchair. Alex properly noticed that he was in a robe with pajamas on underneath it and his curly hair hadn't been tamed at all. "I suppose I shouldn't argue. You children are becoming much better at using your magic in useful ways outside of battle."

"You and Morgana never thought to use your magic that way?"

"Rarely." Merlin shrugged. "We've lived through periods of relatively low magic and probably will again. It's the sort of thing that trains you not to rely on magic for day-to-day things."

"That makes sense I suppose," Alex agreed. Her eyes dropped back to the jar of poison. "We really should secure these better. I had no trouble getting into the chest in the basement."

"Yes, you're right of course," Merlin said. "Maybe I should install another safe in the basement. I don't want to keep them near the artifacts."

"I can't argue with that. I'd be pissed if the Chalice or the Hammer got melted. I'd probably even worry if the remains of the Iron Chain dissolved."

"I would not risk them," Merlin promised. "But we do need to find a better way to keep these safe. More people know about this poison than ever before. Its ability to dissolve..." Merlin trailed off and shivered. Alex had yet to see the poison in action, but Merlin's response told her a lot. "There's a chance of news of it leaking out. We need to protect it."

Nodding automatically, Alex felt a dull pain growing behind her eyes. She almost liked Merlin's old idea of hiding it in tunnels. Sadly, Ravenslake lacked tiny ancient tunnels that no one went inside. It was a problem, one more to add to their growing pile and one that wouldn't go away. The first set of poison jars had been made almost three thousand years ago and were still deadly. Time wouldn't help, and eventually, something would go wrong. Alex's headache was growing worse, and Merlin didn't look much better.

A sound from the kitchen made them both turn. Merlin tensed for a moment before shaking his head and relaxing. "It's just Timothy," he said. "I swear, I will never get used to that! Why can't he stay at Morgana's?"

Alex couldn't help but smile at the grumbling. A moment later, a small figure bounced out of the kitchen and rushed across the floor of the living room. Grabbing the jar off the table on instinct, Alex pulled it into her lap as the small Brownie jumped up onto the coffee table between her and Merlin. Small dark eyes peered up at her and Timothy grinned widely. He'd mended the doll clothing he wore a bit, and they were cleaner than the last time she'd seen him.

"Alex," Timothy greeted happily. "Good morning! Will you be wanting some breakfast?"

"Uh..." Alex looked towards Merlin.

"Yes, Timothy," Merlin said. "I think breakfast is in order since Alex rose so early today. And coffee." Merlin was giving her a stern look as he struggled to hold in a yawn.

"Breakfast coming up!" Timothy cheered. Then he rushed out of the room in a blur.

"Honestly, the sooner you children get your own place and take him with you the better," Merlin muttered. "I have lived alone for decades. Every time I hear him move it makes me tense up and at night...." Merlin shook his head. "How are the arrangements coming? Morgana still buying the house on Overlook Road?"

"Yeah, she's grumbling about it not being on her street, but it's only one street over," Alex said. "Part of me still thinks I should argue about her buying a house for us to live in."

"It will make her happy knowing that you're so close and in a more secure location," Merlin said. "Besides, Morgana has had more luck than me with her investments. While neither of us is doing badly, I assure you that she can afford a house. I suspect all the paperwork will be complete before you return from India."

Alex nodded. She wasn't completely convinced but didn't argue. A tray with two cups of coffee floated out from the kitchen, making Alex smile slightly. There was another aspect of magic that she didn't understand. Most of the Sídhe had lost their powers or had very weak powers, but Brownies seemed to do very well in the telekinesis department. Merlin seemed less impressed and more grateful, picking up one of the cups, and taking a long drink from it.

Setting down the poison jar, Alex took her mug and sipped the hot liquid carefully. Merlin's eyes jumped back to the poison jar, and a severe expression settled over his face. Almost smiling, Alex waited for him to speak and mentally counted down for him to return to the original subject.

"So, what thoughts were keeping you up?" Merlin asked. "Must have been important if you decided to come over so early."

"I was wondering again if there's a safe way to use this stuff?" Alex lifted the jar and watched the liquid shift around. "I mean, you make a potion of highly concentrated magic, but this is the leftovers from using it. Surely it has a purpose or at least that's what my brain keeps trying to tell me."

"That might be the literature studies talking," Merlin said. There was a hint of affection in his voice. "I've often wondered myself if there is a hidden purpose to the poison, but never found it."

"Hence you hiding it for thousands of years. And now we have even more of it."

"Indeed."

They fell silent for a moment, and Alex shifted the jar around again. The dark oily liquid moved slower than water would. It was almost like a lava lamp in a way. Merlin's eyes were still glued to her and Alex did her best to ignore it. He'd been helping incarnations of the Iron Soul for almost three thousand years. She wasn't going to change him at this point.

"I did have another thought," Alex admitted. "We told you about Emrys and his prisoner."

"Ah, yes the red dragon and the white dragon hidden in a cave beneath a hill in Wales," Merlin said. He shook his head and gripped his cup of coffee tighter. "Honestly, I still struggle to believe it. You'd think after so many years that I'd be used to legends carrying a grain of truth."

"Yeah, well, I was thinking that maybe the poison could kill the white dragon. If they're hurt, they both regenerate due to being in our world, but maybe the poison would finally do the trick."

"That's.... possible," Merlin said slowly. "You might be right. It does destroy that which it comes into contact with. It might be the key to ending an otherwise everlasting life."

"That would finally free Emrys of his duty, leaving him free to help us or... I suppose free to have us use it on him as well." The words were bitter in Alex's mouth. "He may just want to be done with all of it."

"That might be for the best." Merlin's face was gentle, but cautious. "I'm sure that you children would love riding a dragon around, but keeping magic a secret would be nearly impossible."

"Nicki will be so disappointed." Alex smiled at the thought of it. Riding Emrys into battle would have been fun and certainly would have made a statement. A brief image of dragon fire filled her mind, but she pushed what was probably one of Gofiben's memories away. "Still, someday we need to deal with the fact that two dragons are living on Earth." Then she sighed, and her smile fell away. "There are so many things."

"Indeed, this era is filled with trouble," Merlin said darkly. "There's no news from the Fae creatures. I worry that our peace won't last, at least for now it is only Redcaps harassing us."

"I have faith that you and Morgana can handle it," Alex said.

"Are you sure that you don't want one of us to go with you. Morgana is very capable of protecting Ravenslake-"

"I'd rather you were both here," Alex replied. She didn't want to give Merlin a chance to talk her into any changes to the plan. "We'll have Avani to guide us, and you've admitted that you haven't been to India in a long time."

"Centuries," Merlin admitted. "With Shiva watching over the area and keeping the Demons in check we didn't need to travel there often. I did consider going during the British Raj, but things always seemed to come up." Merlin hesitated and shook his head. "I still worry, Alex."

"You're always going to worry," Alex replied.

"I don't always worry this much," Merlin protested. He eyed her sharply. "Haven't worried like this since Arto. Most of the other Iron Souls lived in more peaceful times."

Alex wanted to argue or laugh, but it was true. Merlin had raised Arto during troubled times before there were any defenses for the Iron Realm. Some of the voices carried affection for Merlin, but Arto's voice was the strongest. Less than half of the voices had anything to say at all. There were so many lives that Merlin had never been a part of.

"I'm not sure what I'm supposed to say here," Alex said. "I can understand why you're worried."

"You're grieving for your parents, Alex," Merlin reminded her. "Arthur killed them such a short time ago, and you're trying to make decisions-"

"Merlin," Alex cut in quickly. "Yes, I'm grieving, but now... with all the memories I'm aware that there's always going to be people I miss." Looking down into her coffee cup, Alex swirled it slightly and watched the brown tones shimmer. "But I also remember Galath, and I don't want to risk Matt feeling like he has an obligation if I'm killed."

"You're not going to be-"

"Don't," Alex ordered. "Don't say that, Merlin. We both know that it's bullshit. I remember dying. I remember dying a bunch of times. Sometimes fast and sometimes slow. Sometimes with others and sometimes alone. It will happen." She forced a smile. "Though I'm hoping for old age to be the cause. That's happened a few times."

"I'm glad to hear that," Merlin said softly. "But Alex, erasing your brothers' memories of you is... not only complicated, but I doubt we'll be able to undo it. Morgana is looking at basically erasing your memory and setting them up with all new lives and faking another accident to kill them officially."

"I don't need to know," Alex said. Holding back a shiver, she wasn't sure if she should try to smile or grimace. "I just... I need to know that I gave them their best chance at a peaceful life. They still have each other, and they're too young to lose that."

Merlin opened his mouth, but then closed it. There was resignation in his eyes and Alex thought that while he wanted to talk her out of it, he really did understand it was for the best. She wasn't sure; it was hard to tell with him and Morgana. They had too many centuries of practice keeping their masks on.

Tapping her fingers against her knee, Alex tried to think of how she could smoothly wrap up this conversation. Then, as if by some great miracle, a tray of food floated out of the kitchen. There was a pot of coffee, flatware, and two plates with bacon and scrambled eggs. Grinning, Alex grabbed one of the plates before things could get any more awkward. As she took her first bite, Alex decided that Timothy was her favorite Fae creature. True there were no others that she liked at all, but it still counted.

2

Lakeside Departure

Her parents had been natural wanderers, people without any chains or at least that was what Nicki remembered her mother telling her once. When she'd been a little girl, she'd lived mostly in the backseat of a car. There'd been showers at truck stops with her mother and lots of picnics at rest areas using the materials in the trunk cooler. She'd seen the Grand Canyon, the ocean many times, and gone through Yellowstone. Then they'd left her with her grandmother and only returned once she was in college.

Nicki would have thought that she'd hate travel as a result. Life with her grandmother had been the opposite in every way. She had a room, privacy, and her own things. School and friends had become possible when they hadn't been before. Once she stopped missing her parents, she'd come to like the stability of being in one place.

There were issues, still many issues, even though she'd forgiven her parents rather than carry around that anger. Yet, she was rocking excitedly on the balls of her feet by the shore of Ravens Lake. The sun was just coming up, and she was holding back a yawn. It was too early for this, and they'd been up half of the night. That part had been Avani's idea to help them cope with the massive change in time zones they were about to suffer.

She was going to India. In the past year, she'd been to Wales and Paris. Sure it hadn't been for pleasure and Wales had been stressful thanks to being worried about Aiden's life. Now she was going to India. Excited didn't fully describe how she felt. Nicki wondered how it would smell. It was much hotter than she was used to and the humidity was sure to be worse in Mumbai. Some of the articles about traveling in India had made it sound dangerous, and Nicki couldn't help but be a little nervous. Were those dangers from humans or Demons? Probably both, she decided. People could be terrible without anything supernatural being involved. After all, Demons and the Sídhe hadn't had anything to do with the World Wars.

Shaking her head, Nicki told herself to focus. She needed to be alert and aware. It didn't help much, and she smiled as she looked over the lake. There was a flicker of worry for the town as the sun gleamed off the red brick buildings of the campus dorms behind her. A breeze rustled the leaves of the arboretum and Nicki nervously scanned the area for any sign of joggers. The thick covering of leaves and the early hour should protect them from being seen. The campus was deserted except for the graduate students doing full-time research and even they weren't up this early.

The world was calm. Nicki briefly wondered if her car would be okay in the school parking lot while they were gone, but her permit was still on display. Taking a deep breath, Nicki shifted the heavy backpack she was carrying. She wanted to take it off and pull out the book on India that she'd ordered through Aiden's family bookshop. Sadly, guidebooks to India weren't in high demand here. The heaviness of the backpack kept her from taking it off. She wanted to be ready. Biting the inside of her mouth, Nicki looked around again as the impatience built.

"Good morning, Nicole," Avani greeted.

Nicki spun around, blushing at being caught unawares. Avani was standing a few feet away with a bag in one hand. She bowed her head slightly and flashed Nicki a smile of perfect teeth. Something in Nicki's stomach slipped lower at the sight of that smile.

"Good morning, Avani," Nicki said quickly. At least her voice still worked. "And please, call me Nicki. I'm finally getting Merlin out of the habit of calling me Nicole."

"As you wish," Avani said. "Nicki it is then." Then the Indian woman pulled out her phone and checked something.

Avani was beautiful. Nicki didn't think it was just her who thought that. Avani was only a little older than her but seemed very mature. She moved gracefully and smoothly, her features were regal and her long dark hair was styled back in braids. Nicki had always thought that Indian women were beautiful, it was probably part of her thing for dark hair, but Avani was really something else. Maybe it was the fact that she was a magician. Even if she wasn't a mage and couldn't do as much as Nicki could, Avani still knew about magic. She was connected to the same craziness that Nicki was.

Maybe she'd be interested. Nicki had looked up information on Indian culture norms, but there was no guarantee that a family of magicians would follow the same standards. They'd have a different understanding of history and Nicki was a mage; that had to count for something. Nicki bit her lip. She was getting ahead of herself. She had no idea if Avani would be at all interested in her.

Nicki tried not to shift but couldn't help it. Her sudden anxiety mixed with her earlier excitement left her a bundle of nerves. For something to do, she shrugged off the backpack and set it on the ground. A relieved sigh escaped her and Avani looked her way again.

"The others should be here soon." Avani stared out over the lake, and a shadow of doubt appeared on her face. "I just hope that Sif is on time."

"It's nice of Sif to help us," Nicki said. She grimaced at how stupid she sounded. "I mean, she's been helpful thus far, so I'm sure she'll be here."

"I don't mean to sound ungrateful," Avani said. "I don't like airplanes... Sif's offer to bring me here was a welcome relief, even with as... frightening as water travel can be." Avani glanced back at the lake again. "There are stories and records in some of my family's books. Of people vanishing into the waters and never coming out."

"Yeah, I can see that," Nicki said. "It's... impressive when you think about it. More than a little crazy too, but the Old Ones are good at it. At least the ones who stay in the water at least."

"Yes," Avani agreed.

Avani seemed like she was going to say more when voices began to drift down from up the hill. Nicki looked up as Bran and Aiden walked into view, talking cheerfully and each carrying a backpack. Part of her wanted to grumble at being interrupted with Avani, but it did remind her of why they were gathering in the first place.

"Morning," Aiden greeted with a smile. Then he yawned. "Man, I thought summer vacation was for sleeping in."

"Don't you have a summer job at your mom's bookstore?" Nicki teased.

"You know very well that bookstores aren't open at 5 in the morning."

"Did you guys come together?" Nicki asked. "Bran, I thought you were at Morgana's?"

"I am staying there, but we were having a game night at Aiden's," Bran replied. "Had to stay awake somehow."

"Do I want to know how much caffeine was involved?"

"No," Aiden said. His face was almost stoic. "You don't. You'd yell at me."

Nicki raised an eyebrow and tried to keep herself from smiling. She failed. Avani chuckled warmly, and Nicki's smile only widened in pleasure. Then Aiden had the gall to wink at her. It wasn't often that she wanted to hit her best friend and sort of brother, but she did now. Thus far, she was enough of an idiot around Avani without him trying to help.

"So, we're just waiting for Alex," Bran said.

"And Sif to arrive," Avani added. She looked back toward the water. "Hopefully before anyone starts moving around in town."

"So far we've kept everything under wraps." Aiden offered Avani a warm smile. "It can be a bit hard for people to accept that magic is real. You should have seen Alex when all of this started."

"The Iron Soul didn't believe she had magic?" Avani honestly sounded shocked.

"Alex struggled with magic for a while," Bran explained. His tone was much more patient. "Did anyone tell you about when she first was able to use magic?"

"No."

"Oh, she was awesome," Nicki said. Grinning, she looked back at Avani and enjoyed the curiosity on the other woman's face. "She forgot about the whole sunset thing before Beltane and got captured by the Sídhe." Avani's eyes widened, and her smile vanished. "Alex woke up in the tunnels, killed a bunch of Sídhe, and saved the children they'd captured. It was very dramatic and heroic."

"Wow... it's just odd to think about an Iron Soul not believing in their power." Avani shook her head lightly. "Just seems very strange.

According to the stories, Lokpal mastered his magic very quickly to fight the Demons."

"Does your family keep detailed histories of the magic users in your family?" Bran asked.

"Not exactly," Avani admitted. "Lokpal is almost more of a legend, but we know he is real, and at least my line of the family has stayed close to Shiva. Most of what we know comes from stories passed down and Shiva. Lokpal did live a very long time ago."

"Indeed," Alex's voice said behind them. "Over two thousand years. I'm flattered on his behalf that you even remember his legacy."

Spinning around, Nicki found Alex with Morgana standing a few feet up the hill on the path. Her eyes widened. Alex was carrying the Iron Hammer in one hand. Mjǫllnir caught the sunlight and the triskelion symbol on its side gleamed. Suddenly, the air thickened and Nicki wasn't sure if the Hammer was really giving off any magical energy or if it was just her imagination. Either way, Alex certainly had a presence as she held the Hammer tightly in her right hand. There was a duffle bag slung over her shoulder, and she offered them all a smile.

"Good morning." Alex was smiling, but there was a note of hesitation in her voice. Morgana was lingering protectively behind her.

"You're taking the Hammer?" Bran asked. Then he blushed a little and shook his head. "I suppose we are going to deal with Demons. Taking a weapon makes sense."

"Glad you approve," Alex said. She smiled a bit, but then her expression turned serious. "I have the Chalice too, just in case. We don't know what to expect yet."

"I'm sorry about that," Avani said. "Honestly, we're having trouble understanding what is happening. There have always been Demons in India, but most just blend in and live in small little communities peacefully. Lately, though, someone seems to have taken control of the population."

"Through force or magic?" Alex asked.

Nicki could already see the wheels turning in Alex's head. Hopefully this wasn't a repeat of the Iron Chain, but honestly what were the chances of that. Nicki wasn't going to play the odds given that magic was actually a thing that happened when aspects of different universes collided. They were the white blood cells of their universe fighting back things that didn't belong. Unfortunately, a lot of the prior invaders had long since settled and their descendants hadn't committed any wrongs.

"Neither, at least we don't think so," Avani said. "There are still peaceful Demons, but Shiva has gotten a lot more challenges lately and has had to be much more active in putting down hostile groups. He destroyed twenty Demons in Mumbai alone last month before I came here. There seem to be more of them than usual."

"I wonder...." Alex trailed off and frowned. "I hope that the way to their homeworld hasn't opened."

"I wouldn't know how to check for that," Avani admitted. "But you've been building new Iron Gates so I don't know how that would be possible."

"New Iron Gates, but even the Sídhe are still breaking through," Alex said. "As the old ones are breaking down, it makes sense that it would take time for the magical defenses to settle in place."

"That is certainly possible," Morgana said, speaking for the first time. "I dislike the idea that there are new Demons in the Iron Realm. Stay on your guards."

"We will," Alex promised. She gave Morgana a soft smile. "You and Merlin take care of things here."

There was something in Alex's tone. Morgana nodded sharply though her green eyes were dark with discomfort. Nicki frowned. They were missing something. Sure, Alex was the Iron Soul, and there were probably things they didn't need to know. Then Alex moved closer to them and offered everyone a much more real smile that lit up her gray eyes. Jenny and Lance appeared up the hill, and Jenny smiled sheepishly at all of them.

"Sorry," Jenny said. "Are we late?"

"No," Alex replied, a soft expression on her face. Jenny and Lance were walking down the hill hand in hand. "In fact, everyone is early."

"We're going to India!" Aiden grinned widely.

Nicki almost felt Alex's chuckle as the taller blonde moved over next to her. It was comforting, and Alex seemed to really be there for the first time since the death of her parents. Risking a look at her, Nicki found that Alex's eyes were a bit sad, but her determination was clear in how she held herself. That didn't stop Morgana from looking at Alex with worry. They were definitely missing something.

"So," Alex said. "Avani while we're waiting for Sif, is there anything else we need to know."

"It will be late when we arrive," Avani cautioned them. "We won't spend time on introductions tonight. My family knows that we are coming and has rooms waiting. You can get some sleep and start fresh tomorrow morning."

"This is going to be so strange." Jenny tugged at the hem of her shirt nervously before grabbing Lance's hand again. "Are you sure about this? We could fly?"

"I'm not a fan of water travel myself," Alex said. "But we won't get the Hammer through airport security without a lot of questions."

"We could always check it," Aiden suggested. "There are ways to transport weapons."

"I'm not entrusting an artifact to an airline," Alex said. She offered them a slightly nervous smile. "I can go with Avani and Sif. You can follow on a plane if you prefer."

Nicki shook her head. "I'll go with you," she said quickly. "Water travel is weird, but sort of fun."

"And I suppose we wouldn't be able to take our daggers," Jenny conceded. "It wasn't pleasant not having them when we went to Europe."

"Demons don't have a weakness to iron like the Sídhe," Avani said gently. "At least not to the same level."

"Oh," Lance said. He sounded stunned and worried. "That's... unpleasant news."

"Don't worry," Avani said. "They can still be harmed. In truth, they've been in our world for so long that they are a lot like humans, just... when they use any of their innate powers, their faces change." Raising an eyebrow, Nicki waited for more of an explanation, but Avani seemed a bit lost. "It's hard to explain. You'll see soon enough, but if you need to kill a Demon hit it where you would attack a human. The neck is the best place to attack or the ankles."

"Headshots and hobbling." Aiden raised his eyebrows but nodded. "Duly noted."

"Mumbai, probably better known to you as Bombay, is on the western coast of India. It was built on a series of islands and is a major shipping city," Avani continued. "While mythology often puts the Old Ones in other locations, the reality is that a lot of them sleep in the area. Several of them are firmly on the side of protecting humanity from invaders and take turns sleeping in the waters of the Indian Ocean to maintain their sanity."

Nicki had more questions that were all scrambling for her attention. She was sleepy and had forgone coffee in favor of making sure she adjusted to the sudden time zone change. The nervous energy was still bubbling in her chest, and she opened her mouth in an attempt to speak, but nothing came out.

The sound of splashing made them all turn towards the shoreline. Small waves were rippling out from one point in the lake a few feet off the shore. In the corner of her eye, Nicki saw Alex straighten up and smile. Right, Sif had been the wife of Alex's past life Thor. She would have thought it would be awkward, but between Jenny and Sif, Nicki was beginning to think that Alex had a serious weakness for her past spouses. Even the ones who betrayed her. Water swelled out of the lake, rising to form a pillar of liquid that spun apart to create a strange vertical whirlpool. Moments later a beautiful woman with long blonde hair stepped out and smiled at all of them. Nicki scooped up her backpack and pulled it on.

Showtime.

3

Defender of the Village

21 B.C.E. Mazagaon, India

The waters of the sea were calm and reflected the brilliant blue of the clear sky overhead. Numerous fishing boats dotted the scene, and he could make out the movement of nets being pulled in and cast out. A soft breeze rustled the leaves of the nearby trees in the thick forest behind him. Spinning, he swung his blade over his head before bringing it sharply to a stop in front of him. His muscles obeyed, and the world stilled. A slight ache was building in his muscles, and he forced himself to sheathe the blade.

Inhaling slowly, he waited for his heart to slow to its normal rate. It didn't take long. Already, the thin layer of sweat on his skin was evaporating. He didn't move from his spot atop the hill. Instead, he took a slow and deep breath and kept one hand on the hilt of his sword. The weight of the weapon on his hip was comforting, and he counted the ten fishing boats again before looking towards the other islands.

Nothing was amiss, but he was keenly aware of the dangers lurking at the edges of what he could see. A sense of unease weighed down on his shoulders, but he was at a loss to explain it. He looked around one more time, checking the other islands. Across the water, he could just make out the small brown wooden buildings of the fishing village on the next island over. There were such villages on most isles. He cast his eyes down the hill and noted the small curls of smoke rising from his village.

Enough of this, he decided, and he started walking down the path back towards the village. The sun beat down on him, and he wiped a small line of sweat off his brow. He sped up his pace as the smells of the smoke, cooking food, and animals hit his nostrils. For a moment, the view of the village vanished behind some trees, but as he came around the curve, he could once again clearly see his home.

The village was built around the small natural harbor that the ocean had created. There wasn't much order to the layout of the wooden buildings that served as homes, workshops, and storage. The oldest buildings were closest to the water with the newer buildings further up the slope of the hill in recently cleared land. Fences enclosed a few pastures, and well-worn paths wove between the buildings. There were wooden docks built out into the water and people were hard at work. Just a quick glance found people repairing and making nets, gutting fish, and working on repair of the boats. It was busy, and the smell of fish filled his nostrils. People were chatting, laughing, and in a couple of cases, yelling at each other. Normal life.

A few people looked up at him and nodded in quick greeting. He nodded in return and scanned the shadows between the small houses around the harbor. His eyes moved towards his own home up the hill. The odd sense of wrongness remained. It tickled at the back of his neck, and without thinking, he reached back to rub the dark skin. His hair was bound up in a bun, and he considered letting it down to dispel the sensation. He didn't and kept looking around.

"Something wrong, Lokpal?" One of the fishermen unloading baskets of fish from a small boat was looking right at him. The man's sunbaked face was tight with worry. He glanced around nervously. "Are we safe?"

"I'm not sure," he answered honestly. Lokpal let his worry show and looked back at the small spaces between the houses. The shadows wouldn't provide much cover for an attack. "Just a feeling."

The man nodded quickly, but the nervousness remained. Lokpal lingered on the shore while the last of the baskets were handed off. Then the man and his partner jumped back in the boat and began to row out into the bay. Lokpal held back his amusement. There were better things to do with his time than stand here and worry.

"Do you think Demons are coming?" a voice asked next to him. He turned to find one of the older women in the village studying him with concern. Her white hair was tucked beneath a scarf, and she was frowning deeply. "Is that what has you on edge?"

"I'm not sure," Lokpal answered. The odd twisting in his stomach was worse than before, and there was a spark of something hot in his chest. He didn't understand it, but he'd become more and more aware of it in the past few months. "I just have an odd sense of dread."

"Then Demons may indeed be coming," the woman said. "Trust your instincts; you were trained to protect the village for a reason. You had the best instincts, the most talent, and the most courage."

The words were comforting, and he offered her a smile. For a moment, the dread vanished, and he inhaled deeply. His lungs fully expanded and he savored the familiar taste of the salty sea air with a hint of fish. Then there was a crashing sound behind him. Lokpal turned quickly just as a small cart went flying. He dashed forward, ignoring the cries of alarm from the docks. The little wooden cart was in pieces with hay, and some produce laying around it. He looked around for anything unusual, but the village was still.

"Lokpal! Behind you!"

He didn't hesitate. Swinging around, Lokpal drew his sword and brought it up in one smooth movement. Metal clanged as he caught the tip of the spear being thrust at him. Lokpal shifted to avoid the sharp point of the weapon and used his sword to push it further away before he dared look at his attacker. The Demon hissed in frustration and Lokpal's chest tightened.

He'd seen them before, but the sight of them always gave him pause. They were just enough like a human to be familiar, but the reddish skin and huge flaming eyes were wrong. Two long fangs protruded from the top of the creature's mouth and gleamed as it released a bloodthirsty roar. The monster loomed over him, the massive body preparing to move. Lokpal moved before it could, pulling his sword away from the spear and slashing into the creature's belly.

The light fabric it wore didn't stand a chance. It shrieked in pain, and too dark red blood seeped from the long wound. It wasn't like his blood. There was no scent of iron in the air; instead, it carried the sharp tang of sulfur. Demon indeed. He backed up a few steps and brought his sword up in front of his body. The Demon growled, eyes gleaming hungrily and it took a step towards him.

Lokpal shifted into a defensive stance, readying his blade and bracing himself for whatever happened next. He could hear screaming, and there was movement in the corner of his eye. Jumping to the side, he risked a glance as a lighter Demon rushed towards him, swinging a spear in one hand and a sword in the other. More screams filled his ears. Rolling to the side, he ducked under the sweep of the spear and stabbed the Demon's leg with a sharp thrust of his sword. The large one thundered towards him, and he forced his legs to move.

"Out of the way!" Lokpal shouted.

He ran for the docks, hearing the Demons following him on the road between houses. People were grabbing baskets of fish and other goods as they evacuated the area. Some jumped into boats and began to row out into the sea frantically. Others rushed for the hillside, and some shouted encouragements to him. A group of children lingered in the shadows of a building until a woman dragged them off.

Spinning on the ball of his foot, Lokpal brought up his blade once more and eyed the two Demons. They were similar enough, and both stood a good foot taller than him, but the lighter one was watching him with sharper eyes. His gut marked it as the greater threat.

"What do you want here, Demons?"

"Whatever takes our fancy," the thin one hissed. Its voice was too smooth. It rolled over Lokpal's shoulders and down his back, making Lokpal's skin crawl. "Stand aside, warrior, and live."

"Leave my village."

"And leave all these tasty treats?" The Demon licked its lips with a too long tongue, making Lokpal's stomach turn. The meaning was too clear. "I think not. You're one warrior. Hardly a threat."

There was a flutter in his lower chest, too low to be his heart racing and too high to be his stomach. It was distracting but grew as he stared down the Demons. The smaller one took a slow step forward, eyeing him with greedy eyes, and a nasty smile. The larger one grunted and laughed, tapping the bottom of its spear against the ground. All the usual sounds of life in the village were gone. Distantly, he could still hear shouting as people ran for cover.

Then the large Demon lunged forward. His body moved before any thoughts even processed. He swung around the spear as it was thrust towards him. Bringing down his sword, he cracked the wooden shaft and snapped it. The big Demon roared and swung at him with bare fists. Slashing his sword, Lokpal watched the blade slice into the dark skin.

The smaller one leapt up and bounced off the wall of a house, soaring down at him. Lokpal rolled back, his shoulder hitting a stray stone, but it was enough to take him away from the sharp thrust of the small Demon's spear. He jumped to his feet, his fingers tightening around the grip of his sword. Thrusting forward, he caught the Demon in the side, slicing a dark line through its flesh. The Demon pulled away with a snarl. He used the chance to back up, only to hit a cart full of produce with his legs.

Jumping around the cart, he pushed it forward into the smaller Demon. It snarled, but caught the cart, sliding back a few steps at the sudden weight. The large one didn't wait and rushed him. Relief and terror hit him at once. They were separate, but the creatures were bearing down on him. Dropping down, Lokpal ducked a wild blow and slashed at the Demon's ankles. Dark blood spurted forth, and there was a roar of pain. Hobbled, the Demon fell against the side of the nearest building, grabbing onto the roof to stay up.

The small one jumped around its fallen comrade. Lokpal tensed, suddenly unsure which one to attack. A sword lashed out at him, but he leapt for the large Demon. He smashed his sword into the creature's neck. There was a crunch, and the flesh gave way again. Dodging away, he barely avoided another attack from the small one's spear. Bringing his sword forward, he pushed the spear away. To his shock, it caught the large Demon in the chest as it stumbled forward. It was a grazing blow, but it shocked both Lokpal and the Demons.

He took the chance to jump back, but the small Demon slashed with its sword, catching his arm. The large one groaned in pain. Dark blood spilled out across the dirt as it swayed and then collapsed. Everything trembled at the impact. Its blood began to vanish as the body crumbled away into dust, falling into itself, and then scattering into the wind. The small Demon paused to look down with an unreadable expression. Then its eyes dropped to its sword. His own red blood colored the tip, and Lokpal's arm ached in response to the sight.

Then with a nasty little smile, the Demon shifted the sword and dropped its spear. With dark fingers, it gathered up some of the blood and raised its hand to its mouth. Licking at his fingers, the Demon's eyes widened even further and darkened. Lokpal kept still, refusing to allow the show to disturb him. This creature would happily kill and eat him. He wasn't going to give it the chance.

Another heartbeat passed. Just the one Demon now, he reminded himself. Still, there was a tremble in his hands as he brought his sword up. The blade caught the sunlight, and his chest tightened. There was that flutter again, but then the Demon moved. Blocking the blow, he side-stepped and attacked. They traded blows, this Demon's speed a match for his own, but the Demon's control wasn't as precise. The Demon had accidentally wounded his dying comrade, and his sword strikes were too wild.

Lokpal kept moving back. The Demon kept driving forward, but he dodged and blocked the movements. Staying defensive, he watched. There was another flutter deep in his body. It was distracting and yet drove him to finally move. Twisting to the side, he snapped out his right foot to hit the Demon's leg. The creature stumbled, only for a moment, but it was enough. Lokpal snapped his sword down into its neck.

The second Demon fell with a thud against the packed down earth. The jolt of the impact traveled through his body, but he didn't dare move. Then the body began to collapse into itself and turn to dust. An exhale finally escaped him when the wind picked up the remains and began to sweep them out to the sea. Lokpal took a step back and took another slow breath. He needed his muscles to relax, but his brain was still struggling to process. Two Demons. He'd fought two Demons at once and survived.

It was the sound of someone running up to him that pulled him back to reality. Braced for another fight, he swung around and brought his sword up. The other man thankfully stopped and brought up his hands in a gesture of peace. Lokpal lowered his sword and rolled his shoulders. The flutter vanished and the odd sense of wrongness that had plagued him faded. Inhaling slowly, he looked around the village. There were people bravely looking out of their homes, but they were all like him. All human.

Smiles began to appear, and he glanced down as the last of the Demons vanished. It was almost like they'd never been there. His left arm twinged in disagreement, and he looked at the slice in his shoulder. It wasn't deep, and he felt a rush of relief.

Everyone was celebrating. They'd lost a cart, and there was some damage to a single wall. No one had been killed, not even him, and no one else had been injured. They were all alert and celebrating. Lokpal smiled as people rushed over to touch his uninjured shoulder. Someone ran off to alert his family while he lost himself in the circle of faces. Children were drawing in the last of the dust left on the ground from the Demons, people were offering him fish, and others were making plans for a real celebration.

His throat tightened at the ring of people. His teeth ground together, and his stomach turned. His smile was gone. Shaking his head slightly, he ducked away from one well-wisher. He made some excuse but didn't hear it. More people tried to talk to him, but he shied away. There were too many too close. Thankfully, someone caught on to his discomfort and grabbed one of the children trying to race after him.

Ducking behind a house, he took a moment to steady himself against a wall. His fingers were almost white around the grip of his sword. He walked to the edge of the village and used a leaf to clean the blade. It hissed smoothly as he sheathed the sword once more. His stomach slowly eased, and relief crashed over him. Finding a spot off the path, he eased his body down onto the ground to rest.

He looked out over the water. The two Demons were dead. In truth, they didn't see Demons often, so in fairness they shouldn't see another in months if not years. The uneasiness remained. Straightening his spine, Lokpal rested his sword across his lap and breathed in the smell of the ocean deeply. He closed his eyes and willed his limbs to relax, to forget the ache from his training and the battle. Around him, the world muted slightly before all the small sounds washed over him. It was soothing but sent his heart racing as more worry began to take hold in his chest.

4

Welcome to Mumbai

Alex never knew how to act around Sif. When the Old One was near her, there was always a floating sensation accompanied by grief, want, and a sense of distance with a hint of fear. The beautiful blonde, or at least that was the form she'd chosen long ago, had been Thor's wife and, from the fragments that Alex remembered, the pair had been happy. Sif had put up with Thor's too loud mannerisms, respected his power, and supported his steadfast desire to keep the peace between the various magic groups in his homeland. Though, she sort of remembered the Frost Giants becoming an issue to the point that they were wiped out. That had been before all the Dvergrs died out in the tunnels they'd taken over from the Dark Elves.

It was hard to keep it all straight sometimes, and whenever Sif was around, Thor's voice was the loudest and his emotions blended with her own. Still, Alex honestly liked Sif. She was pretty sure that she would have liked her even without Thor's influence. Sif's tight grip on Alex's hand as they surged through the swirling vortex of water was reassuring. All around them were brief flickers of other places including a few famous buildings. It was exciting but frightening, and only Sif and Avani knew where they were going. Alex didn't dare try to speak for fear of distracting Sif.

Then the water opened. It became brighter, and a vision of a cityscape appeared in front of them. Everything slowed down, and Alex nearly laughed as the flow of magic across her skin tickled. Water rippled past them, and Sif gave one good tug on her arm, pulling them all out of the collapsing tunnel. Alex's feet hit a white stone step, and it was only Sif pulling on her arm that kept her moving. She heard water splashing and glanced back as the others came out of the water tunnel.

They weren't outside. Alex looked around in surprise at that. They were next to a large round, but shallow pool with an elegant mosaic design on the bottom that became clearer as the water settled. The building was circular and built around the pool with the walls a few feet from the edge. All the walls were white as was the tile floor, Alex thought it might even be marble. Small lights hung around the space, but there were no windows and only one door. They'd climbed out of the water on a small staircase, which at least explained why Alex's shoes weren't wet.

"You have a water travel room?" Nicki asked in shock.

"I suppose so," Avani answered. "This is also where Shiva usually comes to speak with my grandfather. But it also works for water travel."

Alex didn't know what to say to that. They had a special room to meet with Shiva. She wasn't sure if that was pride, resignation, or amusement from Lokpal. Avani nodded them towards the doorway. "Come on," she called gently. "We don't want your luggage to get wet, hanging around in here."

Nodding slightly in agreement, Alex turned to Sif only to find the Old One stepping back towards the water. "Aren't you staying?"

"No," Sif answered kindly. "There are more Old Ones that I wish to investigate. We still need to know who is awake and their intentions."

"Yeah," Alex agreed. She didn't feel like that was important right now, but she nodded. "Uh, any last-minute advice? We're sort of out of our usual region here."

"The Desai family will help you," Sif promised gently. "They all seem to speak English."

"We do." Avani nodded eagerly. "It's one of the languages that we all have to learn as children."

"I doubt you'll spend much time away from Avani or another Desai, but if you do then trust in your magic to help you."

"How so?" Nicki asked.

"Your magic will automatically help you understand the language of invaders." Sif was smiling gently. "But you might be able to focus your powers to help you with the native languages." Her eyes glistened at the stunned expressions on their faces. "You'll have to work hard at it though, but no time like the present to start trying."

"Merlin and Morgana could have mentioned that," Aiden grumbled.

"I think they did in the past," Bran said. "But they also kind of danced around it." He was a smiling a little. "Anyway, we should be careful about using too much magic."

"Indeed," Sif agreed. She brushed a speck of dust off her long coat and then smiled at Alex. "Please take care of each other."

"Be careful," Alex said.

"You too." Sif gave her a soft smile that made Alex's heart stutter for a moment, but Sif's green eyes were sad. "Try not to worry about me, Alex. I am thousands of years old and competent."

Her chest tightened, and Thor got louder, but Alex didn't say anything. Sif held her gaze, and Alex wondered if she knew that inside her head Thor desperately wanted to hold and kiss her. But Alex didn't. She offered Sif a small smile, not trusting herself to speak without Thor coming out again. This was apparently one of those noisy days in her head.

Sif moved back down the steps and waved her hands. A soft glow surrounded her as water began to splash up and form another whirlpool. Sif didn't look back at them and stepped into the spinning water. It churned around her, swallowing Sif's form up and then the water collapsed back into the pool with a splash. Sif was gone again. Nicki nudged her arm, and Alex forced her attention back to Avani who was watching them curiously.

"Everyone have everything?" Avani asked. She was smiling widely, and a bit forced, like a flight attendant. Alex held back a nervous laugh at the thought. "Alright then, welcome to Mumbai."

Avani walked to the double doors and opened one quickly with a flourish. The door opened outward, but it wasn't to a hallway like Alex was expecting. Instead, she could see a covered walkway with small lights on the lawn around it. A hundred scents hit Alex all at once, some familiar and others very alien. The humidity was a punch in the chest.

The house made Alex stop in her tracks. She wasn't sure what she'd been expecting, but this wasn't it. The covered walkway led straight up to a side door, but while it may have been the side of the house, it was a beautiful slightly beige façade. There were arched windows, small bits of detail work on the borders of the windows and corners. Around them were lit gardens with blossoming plants and large trees that seemed to shut out the rest of the world. Avani was beaming at all of them, but there was a nervous spark in her eyes.

"This is your home?" Nicki asked.

"Yes, we've lived here for centuries," Avani said gently. "The house gets updated every few generations." She scuffed the toe of her shoe on the stone path for a moment before rallying. "This is usually called a haveli around here. It has a lot of traditional elements to it to help it stay cool. You can't see it from here, but there is a courtyard. I'll give you a full tour tomorrow, I promise."

"It's beautiful, Avani," Bran said pleasantly. "I think we're just a bit surprised at the size; I mean knowing how densely populated Mumbai is."

"It's been our family's land for centuries, it used to be a farm, a long time ago, but a lot of the land has been sold off. Now it's a little oasis in the midst of the city." She smiled wider again. "Still, it serves its purpose."

"Why is that room separate?" Nicki gestured over her shoulder to the water pool room. "Is it new or something?"

"No, actually we've always had something of a separate shrine. I'm not sure of the original reason why it was separate from the house, but it has always been that way. Follow me," Avani said after giving them all a moment to process.

They all followed her obediently, and Alex tried not to gawk as she looked around the landscaped yard. There were multiple levels, different sitting areas, lots of statues and art, and rows of plants. Small lights scattered around the area lit the night, though there was a lot of light spilling over into the yard from the city beyond. Avani unlocked the side door and gestured them inside. It was a smaller room but had warm off-white walls, mirrors, and bright paintings.

Avani just kept smiling softly, all but floating through the silent house. They went up a staircase that curved around an open area, and a double door that Alex assumed was the main entrance. It was very nice, and Nicki kept looking around and making small squeaking noises at the artwork. Alex thought that she heard people across the house and wondered if they'd all agreed just to give them the night to adjust. It wasn't that late, and Alex wasn't sure she'd fall asleep quickly, but she supposed the sentiment behind the idea was nice.

Jenny stopped in front of a painting that showed a blue being with multiple arms on some sort of flower. It tugged at Alex's memory, but nothing clear came forward, and she wasn't sure if it was Lokpal, something else, or something random from her own life.

"Isn't it strange, having paintings of the Hindu gods in your house?" Jenny asked. "I mean, given that you know their origins?"

"In a way I suppose, but we do also worship them in our own way." Avani suddenly seemed nervous even as she gave Jenny a small smile. "Please keep in mind that while my family and I are fully aware of Shiva's origins outside our world, we do live in a culture that still worships him as a deity. Hinduism is a living culture and religion."

"Don't you have like a million deities that you worship?" Jenny raised an eyebrow, and Alex tensed.

"Don't you have like 10,000 saints you pray to?" Avani was smiling, and to Alex's surprise, Jenny chuckled.

"Touché," Jenny said. She was smiling a little herself now.

Alex exhaled slowly. The voices quieted, and she smiled to herself. Apparently being torn between descendants and loyalty to Shiva and loyalty to Jenny was a thing. Nicki glanced her way and offered a small smile while Bran grinned in approval at Jenny. It made Alex wonder if she'd missed something.

"Anyway, I know we scheduled this so you could rest right away," Avani said. "Come on, follow me and I'll show you your rooms."

The hallway Avani led them into ran along one side of the house with windows that looked down into the yard. Alex found herself glancing out and trying to see the water travel building, but they were on the wrong side of the house now. She could barely see a tall wall through the line of trees that seemed to surround the house.

"Nicki, here's your room," Avani chirped. She opened a door for Nicki to reveal a room with red walls. "If you need anything just let me know."

"Thank you," Nicki said. "Uh, bathroom?"

"It's attached." Avani smiled again. "This part of the house was updated about fifteen years ago."

"Wow… nice."

Nicki's voice was a little stunned, and the redhead blushed before quickly wishing them good night. Alex couldn't help but smile, if nothing else, Nicki's crush on Avani was going to be amusing. Keeping a tight hold on her bag and focusing on the gentle hum of the Hammer and Chalice, Alex was silent as Avani showed Aiden and Bran their rooms. Then Avani hesitated and folded her hands delicately in front of her.

"Uh… Jenny, Lance do you prefer one room or two?"

"Just one will be fine," Jenny replied.

Blinking, Alex tried not to smile or gawk. She wasn't sure how to respond to that, but there was a pleasant flutter in her chest and something settled. It was like the first time she'd seen them kiss, an odd sense of relief and release. Jenny blushed slightly, a wavy strand of dark hair falling into her face, but she was smiling.

"Goodnight." Lance opened the door for Jenny; his bag still slung over his shoulders. "We'll see you in the morning." He nodded to Alex, and she nodded in return, letting him see her smile.

The door closed with a soft click. "It's fine," Alex said. "You did fine."

Smiling at her, Avani almost glowed at the praise. Alex wasn't sure what to make of it and waited for her host to show her a room. Avani stepped away from Lance and Jenny's room and headed further down the hall.

"Here's your room, Alex." Avani stopped in front of the last doorway. "I hope you'll be comfortable. If you need anything, anything at all, please don't hesitate to let me know."

"Thank you." Alex put a hand on the knob but didn't turn it. "Will I be meeting your family tomorrow?"

"Yes, if you're comfortable with that. You seem…" Avani trailed off, and her smile became nervous.

"I remember some things," Alex offered gently. "There are… emotions and I feel excitement and pride that the family has survived, but I don't remember everything." Alex shook her head and smiled. "Still, I'm looking forward to meeting your family. I hope that we can help with the situation."

Avani rewarded her with a wide grin, and there was another flutter in her chest. It wasn't magic, and it wasn't like the sensation she got with Lance and Jenny. Maybe it was parental, Alex wasn't sure, but it felt nice. Nodding to Avani, she turned the knob and stepped into the room. It was a small room but had beige walls with pretty lotus designs along the top. A large bed with a warm red comforter and pillows filled the middle of the space. There were a few pieces of art hanging around the room, a dark wooden wardrobe that matched the bed's posts, a small desk, and chair. Opposite the bed was a doorway leading out onto a small balcony. Alex dropped her things on the bed and headed outside, inhaling the night air.

She was looking out the front of the house. There was less landscaping, and instead, a long loop driveway led to and from a heavy looking gate. Beyond the wall and trees, tall skyscrapers rose out of the bright city. In the dark of the night, she couldn't see the ocean that she knew was out there.

Looking around, Alex waited for something to be familiar. There was nothing. Everything was new, shining, and metal. There was a sense of awe, shock, and a touch of grief from Lokpal that Alex agreed with. Nothing here was familiar. His world was long gone. Except that, apparently beneath the surface, Demons were preying on humanity. That was familiar, and it wouldn't stand. Gripping the railing, Alex inhaled the night air slowly and fought to steady herself. A nervous twitch jolted through her hands, and she rushed back into the room. She opened her duffle bag and grabbed the smooth handle of Mjǫllnir in her right hand. The pulse of magic steadied her heartbeat and Alex sighed. Then she sat down sideways on the bed and pulled out the Chalice with her left hand.

She collapsed back on the bed, her long blonde hair flying out around her, and her legs still hanging off the bed. Despite their weight, Alex brought the two iron artifacts up to her chest and let herself be soothed by the familiar flow of her magic. In her head, Gofiben and Thor became louder, but their voices were gentle and calming. Alex pulled her feet up onto the bed and kicked off her sneakers. She nudged the bag over with her knee and let her eyes slide closed.

5

The Desai Household

Morning came with a golden ray of light hitting the corner of Alex's eye and giving her no choice but to wake up. Even with the balcony door closed, the sounds of the city were creeping in. It was loud. There was a dull drone of distant voices, cars, and a million other things that even life in Spokane hadn't prepared her for. Groaning, she pushed back the blankets and sat up slowly. More light was pouring in, and she glared at the curtains.

"You had one job, and you failed."

Her feet hit the wood floor, and Alex sighed in relief that it wasn't tile. The room was already getting hot even though there was a vent in the corner and Alex could hear the whirl of the air conditioning. India in summer. Sadly, it was doubtful that they'd be able to hide inside all the time. Alex tensed up at the realization that she'd be meeting more of Lokpal's family today. The voices twittered in her head like birds, suddenly too mixed up for her to make anything out.

"Enough," she grumbled. "It's… different, but it'll be fine." Sitting on the edge of the bed, Alex closed her eyes and breathed in slowly. "These are good people," she told herself. Her voice was a bit too loud in the room. "It'll be fine."

Unable to sit still with her thoughts, Alex jumped up and found the small, attached bathroom. She didn't know if attached bedroom bathrooms were common in India or not, but liked the privacy of the shower as she fought down another panic attack. Images were flashing through her mind as she rinsed shampoo out of her hair, but the nausea didn't come. Instead, the voices had settled. She could tell which one was Lokpal, though it was more muted now, and she didn't have to hear any of Cuthbert's dark running commentary. His racist tendencies had never been easy even on her best days.

A knock on her door while she was getting dressed almost made Alex fall over when she tangled up her feet. Thankfully, she recovered and was able to call back that she'd be right there before things turned embarrassing. Sweeping her hair up into a ponytail, Alex went to the door and opened it, assuming it was Nicki or Jenny.

It was Avani, but she looked a bit different now. Avani wasn't dressed in jeans today; instead, she wore something that reminded Alex of the photos of saris but didn't seem like the same thing. It was a soft orange color that made Avani's brown eyes look almost amber. Her long dark hair was in a long braid over her shoulder, and she had the red dot on her forehead. Nicki had told her it was called something like a bindi. Alex wondered if Nicki had seen Avani yet today. The thought of how the redhead would stutter was enough to make her smile.

"Morning," Alex greeted. "What's on the agenda today?"

"Well, there is some breakfast downstairs for you and your friends, and then grandfather wishes to speak with you."

"Oh... all of us?"

"No, just you," Avani said. "I'll host the others in the library. I suspect that Nicki and Bran will be very interested in some of the volumes that my family has. I also promised to start introducing Lance and Jenny to some of the rituals that we use.”

“Do you-” Alex cut herself off, not trusting her chaotic thoughts. “Do you think that's wise? I mean, won't that make them targets?”

“Mages stand out, but I am just a regular human to most creatures until I actively release any magic. Besides, it sounds like your enemy Arthur already knows that hurting them would hurt you. I doubt his... history with Jenny would move him to spare her.”

“Probably not.” Alex's stomach turned. “How much can you teach them?”

“That will depend on them. I'm hoping that their exposure to all of you will have made it easier for them to visualize magic. I've been trained since I was a child and can only do things that would seem basic to you so they won't be conjuring fireballs anytime soon, but hopefully, they can learn a few spells. Just to give them an edge.”

“Thank you, and don't dismiss your skills. We spend so much time fighting with our magic that honestly, we don't use it for much else. Nicki uses it to move heavy stuff, and we've all used it to repair clothing after fights, but it isn't a daily life thing.”

“Still, you probably call on it far more than you realize,” Avani said. “Even I do, and I'm not a mage.” She gestured towards the stairs at the end of the hall. “But enough of that, you must be hungry. We have some Indian cuisine you may enjoy as well as some more American dishes.”

“Oh, thank you. That's very kind of your family. You don't need to worry about us.”

“You're guests.” Avani started walking towards the stairs, and Alex followed. “Besides, I spent several years of my education in England and did a year in New York City. My brother and several of my cousins did similar studies abroad. As did my father, this is nothing new to us.”

Alex tried to file the information away. Avani had a brother and cousins. She wondered if there was a family tree anywhere in the house that she could take a look at. Pushing that random thought away, Alex followed Avani through the house. In the warm sunlight coming in through the windows, Alex was able to appreciate the vibrant yellows and reds that decorated the house. Nothing about it was familiar. The style was almost alien, the art didn't inspire any particular memories, but that was nice because Alex found herself able to just enjoy it.

Breakfast in the dining room was a loud affair. She heard the others before Avani led her into the large room with a long table. There was an older Indian woman dressed in a sari with glasses perched on her nose talking to Nicki who was leaning forward in her chair. Bran was eating some kind of rice dish with a happy little smile that made her wonder if he'd had similar Korean food in the past. Aiden was eating what looked like an egg and vegetable sandwich while Jenny was eating some fruit and basic eggs. Lance and Nicki were both eating a rice dish with eggs on the side.

"Morning, Alex." Bran offered her a smile. "Sleep well?"

"I did," Alex replied. She looked apologetically at the others. "Sorry I was the last one up."

"Someone was going to be," Aiden pointed out. "That's just how it works, and we only just came down."

"Alex," Avani said. "This is my mother Gita. Mother, this is Alexandra Adams, the current bearer of the Iron Soul."

Alex had no idea what to make of that title. It wasn't too bad she supposed, in a way she almost liked the whole 'current bearer' thing, but Jenny grimaced at the table. Maybe it was too on the nose about the fact that when she died there would be a replacement and she'd just become another voice. Trying to smile, Alex nodded to Gita who studied her for a moment and rose from her seat.

"Welcome to our home," Gita said kindly. "If you need anything please don't hesitate to ask." Her smile softened. "I am sorry for your loss."

"Thank you."

"Now please, sit down and help yourself. I am happy to prepare something else if you wish. I even have pancake batter mix in the kitchen." Gita leaned forward and added in a low voice. "My father-in-law adores waffles."

Unsure of what to even say in response to that, Alex found herself laughing. Gita nodded slightly and glanced at her daughter with a look of triumph. Most of the others gave her encouraging smiles, though Nicki was staring at Avani with very red cheeks. Catching Aiden's eye, Alex shared a look of amusement with him and let herself relax and get something to eat.

Avani joined them for breakfast, but as soon as she was finished, she vanished down one of the hallways. Gita chatted with them, telling Nicki about a few local sights nearby though Alex wasn't sure how much time they'd have to sightsee. She nibbled on pieces of melon and kept glancing towards the hallway until Avani returned.

"Grandfather is ready for you in the study," Avani said. "If you'll come with me, Alex, I'll show you the way."

"Uh, yes, thank you for breakfast, Mrs. Desai." Alex stood up, and Gita smiled at her.

"Just Gita, please."

"We'll see you later," Nicki said. She gave Alex a soft smile, and Jenny nodded in encouragement. "Let us know all the juicy details later."

"Behave yourselves," Alex said. "Bran, you're in charge."

"Awesome!" Bran cheered.

"What?" Nicki protested.

"Bran's in charge." Alex hurried after Avani, leaving the others to argue without her.

Avani led her down another hallway that had several large mirrors in it and a few pieces of art. This hallway didn't have windows, and Alex wondered once again about the layout of the house. Then Avani stopped in front of a doorway and Alex's stomach, and shoulders tightened.

"Relax," Avani said. She sounded amused which only unsettled Alex further. "Grandfather is looking forward to meeting you."

"That isn't helping," Alex grumbled. "I doubt I'm what he's expecting."

"What should he expect? He knows that the Iron Soul is a reborn human, he isn't expecting an Old One or anyone like the Grand Mages."

"The Grand Mages?"

"It is what we call Merlin and Morgana. It recognizes their long service to our world." Avani's smile turned a little sad. "How long they have fought for humanity."

Unsure of what to say, Alex nodded and tugged at the cuff of her shirt. It wasn't a very nice shirt. She was a college student and unlike Jenny wasn't a frequent shopper. The blue button-down shirt was loose enough to fight in should it be necessary, but nice enough that she didn't feel like a waif off the street. Avani reached over after a moment of hesitation and touched her shoulder.

"You're worrying too much. Grandfather is just grateful that you've come at all. India is usually left to the Old Ones to protect alongside our family. It has been a long time since a mage has traveled here when magic was at such a high level."

"Yeah, okay," Alex said. "Uh, what's his name again?"

"Well, I call him grandfather." Avani smiled again, and Alex allowed herself to roll her eyes. "But his name is Lochan Desai. He's a nice man, very kind and knows a great deal about magic. He sent me to meet you, remember, so he values magic and ability over male or female so please stop worrying."

Avani opened the door and gestured Alex inside. She hesitated, but only for a moment before stepping into the room. They were on the east side of the house, and the sun was pouring light into the room through two large windows. Lochan was seated in a wooden framed chair by the window next to a small table and matching chair. There was a desk on the other side of the room and bookshelves lined the walls, but he was looking out at the leaves of a tree. Turning towards them, he smiled broadly at both Alex and Avani. He was a shorter man of advanced age with gleaming white teeth, long wrinkles across his face and dressed in a long blue tunic-like shirt over loose pants with slippers.

"Ah, good morning," he greeted. "I hope that you are well rested and fed."

"Yes, thank you," Alex replied.

"I'll leave you to your conversation," Avani said politely. "If you have need of me, Grandfather, you have but to call."

"Thank you, my dear." Lochan's smile widened, and the lines around his brown eyes crinkled up further. Then he looked at Alex, and his eyes sparkled with curiosity. "Please sit down." He gestured to the chair across from his own. "I have been so looking forward to meeting you."

"Well, I'm probably not what you expected," Alex said. She held back a nervous laugh and ignored Lokpal's whispering as she sat down. "Being a girl and all."

"Does it bother you?" His voice was kind and curious. "Being born a female?"

"Bother, no," Alex said quickly. She already regretted the comment. "I mean, I've never felt like I was born in the wrong body or anything like that, but... well, I hear the others sometimes." Lochan said nothing, giving her a moment to gather her thoughts. "And I've never heard anyone who sounded female. Maybe I'm just not listening enough, but I don't think there has been another female. I guess I wonder about it. I wonder if it means something."

"It might." Lochan patted her hand and gave her a gentle smile. "Sadly, it may also simply reflect the truth that women historically have been largely unable to ascend to leadership roles. The Iron Soul is sometimes called upon to become a leader in warfare and in many cultures that remains a difficult position for a woman to ever obtain. Even with magic and a powerful soul, the magic may have known that it would be impossible."

"That's... I suppose that could be it." Alex's stomach tightened.

"That distresses you."

"I don't know. It still bothers me I guess... the idea that magic might be sentient in some way."

"There are many truths about magic that are still unknown to us. It may be sentient, but not in a way that humans or even human mages could ever understand. It may simply be a complex pattern that is merely reacting to events," Lochan said. "After all, we understand magic in a way that those who read books would not. We understand that it is energy that allows us to bend the rules of physics in small ways. It allows us to influence the world on a deeper level, shaping atoms and jump-starting natural processes."

"A fair point," Alex replied. "I'm still not sure what to make of it."

"You are both young and old in magic," Lochan said. "You can look at it with fresh eyes in this life, but I suspect that your reincarnation merely accepts some things without you even realizing it." He looked over at the teapot waiting on the table. "Some tea?"

"Uh, yes, thank you."

"I'm grateful that you came. I can only imagine what a strange request it is, to have a distant descendent from another life come to ask for your help."

"Avani said that there was trouble and Sif aided her. I trust Sif's judgment."

"Ah, Sif." Lochan poured the amber colored tea and slid the cup towards her. "I was more than a little surprised when Shiva informed me that she had come to see him. While I have studied magic my whole life, it seems that I can still be surprised." He took a sip of his tea and Alex did the same. "There is so much to say and ask, but my curiosity is not the most important thing at stake here."

"The Demons."

"The Demons," he agreed. "I believe they have a new leader, but beyond that, I know little. Historically, they have merely caused some occasional trouble. When they become a problem, Shiva is quick to put them down, but lately, there have been many more of them."

"Do you think they're coming from the Demon homeworld?

"It is possible, even the earliest stories tell of the world of the Demons. Shiva will be able to tell you more of his observations."

Lokpal's voice grew louder at the mention of Shiva. She could feel his curiosity and eagerness growing, but there was also a hint of fear. Worry that he wouldn't like what they found. Wouldn't like what had happened since his death. Alex focused on the voice for a moment, urging it to calm. It slowly faded into the back of her mind, and Alex firmly ordered him to stay there.

"Are you alright?" Lochan asked.

"I'm fine," Alex said. "Lokpal was just-" Alex cut herself off and shook her head, not wanting to explain further. "Reincarnation is a bit weird."

"Reincarnation is complex. Hindus and Buddhists embrace it as truth and worry about it differently. The question of karma encourages us to be good, so we are rewarded in the next life, but it sadly also provides an excuse to be cruel to those born less fortunate than ourselves under the belief that they are being punished. I have never fully accepted that explanation of how reincarnation works, though I know it is real."

"I'm not sure either," Alex admitted. "I mean, Lance and Jenny have been reborn a bunch, and we usually end up in a love triangle. We only dodged that this time and part of that was because Arthur was standing in for me. I'm straight, but maybe if he hadn't been there, I would have become interested in Jenny. She's beautiful, smart, and very kind when you get to know her, so I'm not sure how much my being female helped."

"It may have merely given you a chance to be more objective," Lochan offered. "You're correct in your curiosity. The story of those two souls has long fascinated me. I find myself curious if through their loyalty to you in this life and honesty in their love, they will finally escape their cycle."

"I hope so," Alex said even as part of her mourned that. "Though... I think I'd miss them... in my next life."

"Yes, even those that harm us can be a comfort."

"They never tried to hurt me, any form of me. Jenny usually just met me first and then would meet Lance. They belong together. She and I were usually young or it was political."

"She still makes choices," Lochan countered. His voice was still calm and gentle. "Be assured that I hold no personal grudge against her. She was not a part of Lokpal's life and therefore has no bearing on my own family. It has simply been a point of interest." Lochan folded his hands on the table. "I understand from Sif, that there is another reincarnation of known origin amongst you?"

"Yes, Bran is a reincarnation of, well Bran the Blessed, if that makes sense. We think that due to him and his other life linking up through visions, he accidentally inspired the story of the Fisher King. Or maybe it was another mage with visions. We're still not sure how all the myths surrounding him, and the Iron Chalice formed."

"Ah yes, we've seen things like that here as well. It is fascinating what humans will remember and then invent to fill in the holes. Now, this Bran was connected to the Chalice. Forgive me, but I lack knowledge of many of your lives."

"Okay, Bran was the best friend of Gofiben, the incarnation of me who made the Iron Chalice. Bran... died along with Gofiben battling the Old One Babd and had his head hidden with the Iron Chalice after some visions linked him up with our Bran. That's actually how we found the Iron Chalice." Alex curled her nose a little. "It sounds creepy when I explain it."

"Ah, so your friend returned to your side when you needed him."

"I guess so." Alex bit her bottom lip for a moment. "Again, that makes it sound like something is pulling the strings."

"Or perhaps, whatever magic helped the two Brans link together created a spell that would trigger his reincarnation at the right time. A loop of magic if you will. Strange, but then we deal in the strange."

"You're very calm about all this," Alex observed. "Are things that crazy in India?"

"Demons can appear human for a few hours at a time. They use the lore of India to show their true faces with people merely believing they are actors for tourists. I have been trained in how to channel what magic I can through ritual and spells since I was a child. And I meet with a deity at least twice a month. Lady Alexandra, I am very aware of how crazy life can be."

"When you put it that way, I suppose I'm not that strange."

"No," Lochan replied. He stood up and extended a hand to her. "I will try not to pry, but should you wish to discuss anything with me, I will be happy to listen. I have an interest in Lokpal, but he lived thousands of years ago, so obviously, I cannot claim to have known him."

"It's getting easier." Alex took the offered hand and stood up. "We're gradually... I don't know, getting used to each other."

"It would seem that the life of the Iron Soul is ever more complex than I ever anticipated."

"Merlin and Morgana say I'm the first one with this particular problem. It started when we found Arto's bones and..." Alex shook her head. "There's another bizarre sentence. Anyway, I think that part of the Iron Soul was still with Arto, but I can't be sure."

"Not the soul," Lochan said. "But maybe a spark of magic left behind that you needed. I do not believe that you've been living through time with only part of your soul." Lochan gestured to the door. "Now, if you please, Lady Alexandra, Shiva will be here soon and as fascinating as this conversation is, he is the one you truly need to speak with."

6

Demons in a Storm

6 21 B.C.E. Mazagaon, India

The house was a welcome sight to his aching legs. His muscles were all still protesting the abuse from the fight, but it did nothing to dim his spirits. He had won, and now he was home. The earthen brick house had a warm glow in the light of the sun. A thatched awning spread out across the front of the house providing shade, and the small well had jars waiting next to it. Two smaller buildings constructed of stout wooden posts with woven thatch roofs and walls flanked the main house for storage. Their animals were enclosed in small fenced off areas just to the west of the main structure. Everything looked calm.

Turning around, he eyed the rest of the village just down the slope of the hill. There were a few more small farms around his own to supplement the fishing. A woman stepped outside into the shade of the awning, wearing a simple long dress with her hair covered. The furrow between her dark brown eyes eased at the sight of him, and her whole body relaxed. Smiling, she walked towards him.

"Lokpal!"

"Ananta," he greeted. Smiling slightly, he hoped that she wouldn't say anything about his condition, but as her dark eyes narrowed at the dirty fabric and the sweat lines across his brow, he knew that she would. "I am well."

"What happened?"

"A pair of Demons attacked the village."

Ananta's eyes widened, and she gasped. One hand reached out and caught the sleeve of his shirt to reassure herself. Her other hand touched his chest over his heart before moving to his face. He stilled and allowed her to touch his cheeks and chest as the panic slowly vanished from her eyes. Leaning forward, he kissed her forehead.

"I am well," he repeated. "I defeated them."

"Both of them, on your own?"

"Indeed." He smiled now, pride growing in his chest. "It wasn't an easy battle, but I managed it."

"I..." Ananta shook her head. "I'm glad you're alright then. Maybe it is time to consider an apprentice."

"I'm too young for that!"

"Not if Demons are going to be teaming up!"

"Lokpal? Ananta?" another female voice called. "What has happened?"

His second wife appeared in the doorway, her head cover slipping to reveal a braid of long dark hair across her crown. The small boy on her hip began to cry, drawing her attention back to him. She adjusted him carefully, bringing him into both of her arms.

"Shhh, Ojas," the woman cooed. "It's alright. Your father is safe."

"I am." Lokpal crossed the yard and kissed the woman's forehead. "I'm home, Heema." He gently set a hand on the head of the small boy, his fingers stroking the soft dark hair. "And I am well, little one. No need to cry."

His son calmed at the sound of his voice and looked up at him. The child smiled, and Lokpal couldn't help but return the affectionate gesture. He kept his hand on the boy but didn't move to take him from his mother.

"There were two Demons in the village," Ananta said. Lokpal glanced back at her with a frown. "He defeated them both."

"Two Demons?" Heema looked between him and his first wife. "That's... unusual." Her response was guarded, and he was grateful that she wasn't allowing her worry to show and upset the little one.

"Yes, but..." he hesitated for a moment. Ojas shifted and grabbed his hand, holding one finger in a tight grip. "They were working together. They were rather coordinated in their battle."

"Do you think the Demons are organizing?" Ananta asked.

"That's a serious assumption," Lokpal said. "We don't know much about their family structure. They may have simply been relatives working together. No reason to panic."

"Except if your husband is charged with protecting the area." Heema clutched Ojas tighter and looked towards Ananta with worry. "You are unharmed?"

"I'm tired, but not hurt. I promise, Heema. I am safe."

Both women gave him uneasy looks. He'd need to tell them more, but he wasn't sure where to even begin. Instead, the tension in his muscles and the lingering aches was front and center in his mind. Heema's expression softened, and she shook her head slightly.

"You need rest," she said. She ran a hand over Ojas' head, and the baby cooed happily at his mother. "And to clean up."

"Yes, Ananta agreed. "Please."

Their worry hung in the air. He debated saying more, but both women were tense, and Ojas began to fuss in response. Leaning forward, he quickly kissed the boy's head and hurried into the house. He changed his clothing and rinsed off in a bowl of water with quick motions. His worries and questions swirled through his mind, but no one could help him answer them. Perhaps he could make contact with a trader heading east and inquire if Demon activity had increased in the cities.

His village was insignificant. It was small, and while the fishing was good, he couldn't understand why Demons would be interested in it. The cities to the east had wealth and culture that they couldn't match. Then again, they also had armies that could fight the Demons.

"Father!" A small blur hit him as he pulled on his fresh shirt. The young girl's dark hair was a mess of tangles where it was escaping her braid. There were stray sticks in it, and he laughed out loud. "Father."

"I'm home, Daksha." Kneeling, he scooped up the small girl and gently pulled one of the small sticks from her hair. "I don't know how you always get so messy. Your mother will not be pleased with you."

The three-year-old merely beamed up at him and reached for his damp hair, but thankfully did not tug on it. Taking her to the main room, Lokpal joined the rest of his family for a welcome meal. Now that he was clean and in fresh clothing, Lokpal was aware of his hunger and need for rest.

They had a quiet dinner. Everything was peaceful and calm as Heema fed a squirming Ojas while Ananta carefully removed the sticks from Daksha's hair. Lokpal stayed silent, listening to the sounds of his wives and their children. It was peaceful, and the last of the tension in his shoulders finally began to ease, allowing him to breathe more easily and eat a bit more. Lokpal tried not to smile as his daughter smeared her meal on her chin while Ananta tutted unhappily.

A sudden roar of thunder shook the house. All three adults paused and looked to the doorway in surprise as Ojas began to cry and Daksha flinched. Ananta pulled her daughter onto her lap while Heema rocked Ojas. Frowning, Lokpal became aware of the odd fluttering in his chest once again. His hand crept to his sword, and he rested his fingers on the hilt. He strained his ears and listened, but the thunder and the wind were too much. Heema shook her head and spoke softly to Ojas while Daksha recovered and looked towards the door curiously. It almost made him smile, but his unease at the strange sensations in his gut was crawling over his shoulders like a swarm of insects.

Jumping up, he fought back a shudder and stalked to the doorway. Another rumble of thunder shook the house and made him hiss in alarm. He stepped out onto the porch. There was no rain yet, but dark clouds were churning overhead and blocking out the sun. A strange and thick darkness fell around him. It was wrong. His skin crawled, and his grip on the hilt of his sword tightened. Stepping back inside, he grabbed a cloak and pulled it on with a quick motion. Both of his wives were watching him with wide and worried eyes.

"You're leaving?" Ananta's voice was too soft and thin.

"I need to be sure." Lokpal's hand shook as he picked up his sword, but only for a moment. "Be careful. Stay inside and away from the door."

"It's just a storm," Heema insisted. She touched Ananta's arm gently, but couldn't hide the worry on her face. "Lokpal, what is happening?"

"I... feel something," he explained weakly. "I'm not sure what it is. There was something in the air today before the Demons attacked. It's back now. An unease. Something isn't right. I do not know how to explain it."

"You shouldn't be going out in the storm!" Ananta insisted. "Not just because you're worried. That is madness, Lokpal."

For a moment he hesitated. The looks of fear and doubt on the faces of his wives was more than enough to make him pause. Overhead, there was a soft pattering noise as the rain started. It made his heart sink. In a storm like this, a trail could easily be washed out and leave him injured. There was no real reason to go out. But his chest was thrumming uncomfortably. That same sense of unease that had driven him into the village today was firmly back.

He stepped out into the warm rain. It wasn't heavy yet, but the smell of it surrounded him. In the dark evening, he looked around for any sign of Demons. The lights of fires in the village were muted, but still visible. No sounds of screaming or cries for help could be heard, just the rain and the rumbling of the thunder.

His foot sank into the moist earth. He held back a sigh and drew his sword. It was only going to get worse. He took a few steps forward and looked around. There was still enough light from the summer sun to navigate, but darkness would come soon enough. Glancing back towards his home, he debated going back inside, but the feeling hadn't eased. If there hadn't been Demons this morning, he might have been able to ignore it, but he couldn't now.

Walking forward, he blinked back the raindrops trying to get his eyes and studied the village below. All the boats were in, and the torches alongside the docks were flickering dangerously in the rising storm. They'd be out soon enough. There were shouts from below, but not of fear. He could barely make out a few people running onto the docks to check that the boats were secure. Others were pulling some of the smaller ones up onto the docks. Nothing unusual.

He moved down one of the paths towards the docks. If something was happening then surely it would be near the village. At least he thought that until a dark thought of Demons going to a secluded farm to eat the family there without being noticed hit him. Lokpal shivered, a sudden tight fear gripping him for his own family. A crash behind him made

Lokpal spin. The rain blinded him for a moment as fat droplets hit his face, but a flash of lightning illuminated the towering figure of a Demon as it stumbled out of the trees.

The Demon froze at the sight of him, and Lokpal blinked in surprise. A large gash in the Demon's head was seeping dark blood. Two more Demons came out onto the path, panting heavily and looking back into the trees fearfully. Lokpal stepped back from the Demons. The trees stretched up the hill away from the village. Several had been knocked over by the Demons in their haste, and even now they didn't seem interested in him.

Then one of the Demons sniffed at the air, its flat nose rising slightly. It relaxed, and Lokpal tensed at the sudden change. Its eyes swung over to him, and it smiled. Holding up his sword, Lokpal eyed the three Demons as all three turned their attention to him. The roar of the storm softened, and one of the Demons laughed.

"We've escaped!"

Blinking, Lokpal was at a loss of what that meant, but then one of the Demons licked its lips and lunged. His foot slipped, and his leg went the wrong direction. Hitting the mud, Lokpal tried to catch himself, but the rain smoothed surface pulled him down the slope. He held his sword up in a desperate attempt to hold onto it and not harm himself. Behind him, he could hear the Demons stomping after him. He hit the bottom of the slope and grabbed onto the trunk of a tree. Pulling himself up, he raised his sword and panted for air.

One of the Demons wasn't far behind. It thrust a spear at him. Dodging it, Lokpal heard it crack against the trunk of a tree and swung his sword forward. The Demon twisted and brought the spear shaft up. It snapped at the impact of the sword, and the Demon stumbled back. Lokpal's feet slid, but he kept himself upright before slashing forward with the sword. The other two Demons were coming closer. He threw his weight towards the Demons, thrusting the sword forward. The Demon's large hand moved to grab him, but it was too late, and he sliced into the thick flesh. He spun around and ran.

Demons roared behind him as their fellow collapsed to the ground. Lokpal made himself move. The rain-slicked path was hard to follow, but he kicked his feet into the ground for leverage. There were a few stones that served as steps as the rain pounded down. He heard the Demon's following him and led them further from the village. One of them was arguing to turn back. It made no sense, why were they here? They'd said something about escaping.

He kept moving. They needed to get away from the village. Five Demons in one day. Lokpal couldn't believe it, but it was real. He could hear them, and he could smell them. His heart raced, but he climbed around the hillside, acutely aware of the Demons still following him. Something sailed past him as he slipped in the mud. A spear hit a rocky outcropping, and he spun around, bringing up his sword. Somehow the Demons had closed the distance.

"Stop," one of them snarled at the other. "We should go."

"I'm hungry." Long teeth glinted in a flash of lightning.

"We should run!"

"You run, me eat."

"Fool! We don't know the island! The human could be leading us right back-"

Lokpal didn't know what was happening, but his body reacted when the hungry Demon reached towards him. He slashed his sword and cut into its flesh. The creature grimaced but didn't retreat. It lunged again, and he turned his sword slightly to cut deeper. There was more resistance now, and more dark blood spilled out. It didn't give up, reaching for him frantically. The gleam in its eyes was wild and starved. Lokpal's body tightened as fear tried to take over.

The second Demon grabbed the other's shoulder and pulled it back. Lokpal used the moment of distraction to slice into its belly. The flesh ripped open, and blood spilled out. A too large hand caught his head and sent him falling backward. Shrieks of pain filled the night, and Lokpal hauled himself up. The Demons were shouting now, but his ears were ringing. It was hard to see in the rain, but he turned and began to move up the slope of the hill away from the Demons.

Something crashed behind him. He reached up with his free hand, but in the rain, he couldn't tell if he was bleeding or not. More noise behind him. The storm was getting thicker. The thunder rumbled and shook the world, but he kept forcing his body to move. He missed the warmth of his home. He whispered a prayer to any gods that were listening that there weren't more Demons. The path ended up ahead, and he stumbled forward onto the flat area, panting for air and clutching his sword in a shaking hand.

His head spun. The world seemed too bright and too dark all at once. But he understood where he was after a moment. The cliff of rock had been cut away to create a small shrine that was protected from the rain. Lokpal looked up into the dark churning sky. Lightning flashed across the dark gray clouds, and his stomach tightened. His eyes jumped to the small stone shrine and the rough carving in the rock. A rough figure with eight arms was carved into the stone. He could see it clearly, too clearly and he realized why with a terrified jolt.

"Rudra is coming," he murmured. "What is happening?"

There was no answer except for the rumble of thunder and another flash of lightning. Above him, the storm raged, and the rain pounded down on him. His skin stung as the fat drops struck his cheeks, shoulders, and hands. Another rumble. He stepped closer to the shrine, but the roar of the Demon pulled his attention back to the danger. It was the last Demon, the one that had wanted to leave, but now had followed him. He didn't understand it, but it didn't matter.

He slammed his sword forward. There was a moment of resistance, but then hot liquid spilled over his hands. It burned, but only for a second. The Demon's dark eyes widened and looked past him at the shrine. Blood trickled from the corners of its mouth. Something like amusement took over its features. He pulled the sword back and then thrust it forward, slicing into the Demon's gut. A gurgling sound escaped it, and a clawed hand reached for him. Twisting away, he released his sword and backed up. The Demon collapsed, and the shrine carving glowed a brilliant blue.

His breath caught. The urge to run filled his legs and chest, but his feet didn't move. The sky shook, and lightning illuminated the stone shrine with a brilliant flash of light. A figure appeared, from where, he didn't know, but it was far too large to be human. His knees quivered. There was nothing he could do against a god.

7

With Magic in the Dining Room

Nicki regretted not knowing more about India, but she was more than happy to learn through immersion. Thus far, the Desai house was a wonderful place. They had good food, and Gita was a sweetie that Nicki thought would get on very well with her grandmother. As strange as the situation was, there was a sense of calm in the house. She felt welcome, but not like people were hanging around for no reason. Occasionally, she heard other people moving in the house.

Glancing towards the window, Nicki itched to go outside. There was the whole of Mumbai out there, just waiting for her to explore. She tightened her fingers around the glass of water she'd been drinking with breakfast and fought to keep her feet from tapping. India was such an exotic place in all the media that she'd seen and she just wanted to see what it was really like. How did the people dress day to day? Were bindis common or rare? Just how did Demons hide amongst the population of such a big city? Aiden caught her eye and smiled a little, assuring her that he knew exactly what was on her mind.

"What happens now?" Bran asked Gita politely.

"Lady Alexandra and Lochan will likely speak for a time, and then he will take her to speak with Shiva."

"So, Shiva will be coming here?" Aiden confirmed.

"Usually he does. On occasion, he meets with family representatives on Elephanta Island in one of the old temples, but I suspect the meeting will take place here."

"Is there something we should be doing?" Nicki asked. "Anything we can help with?"

"You are honored guests." Gita smiled at them, but there was a hint of warning in her eyes. "Just sit and enjoy yourselves." Her accent became a touch thicker for a moment. "Do any of you want anything else?"

"No, thank you." Aiden was grinning like a madman. "I'm very full!"

"I think we're good, Gita." Jenny smiled at the woman. "Is there somewhere we should wait for Alex?'

"Avani will be back soon," Gita promised. She looked at all of them in turn. "She'll probably show you the main library."

"You have a library?" Lance asked.

"Oh yes." Gita smiled proudly. "Full of books, many of them on magic and records from magicians. They might contain useful information for you."

"Sounds great," Bran said. "Merlin and Morgana don't have a lot of books or records. Which now that I think about it is a little strange."

"They are the Grand Mages," Gita said. "They remember." She looked thoughtful and gripped the handle of the teapot she was holding tightly. "And I suppose that they come from a different time. It might not occur to them to make such records."

"And they might worry about those records falling into the wrong hands." Bran nodded slightly, and Nicki held back a grumble about him brown nosing.

"We'll have to ask," Nicki said. "They're pretty good about answering questions if we think to ask them."

"We just don't always know what to ask," Aiden said.

Gita gave them all a searching look, but then her eyes brightened slightly, and Nicki thought she understood. "It must still be a shock to all of you," she said kindly. "Finding out about magic."

"Yes," Nicki agreed. Leaning forward slightly, she debated how to phrase her question for a moment. "You married into the family, right? How did you find out about magic?"

"Avani's father and I were an arranged match," Gita explained. "My family are distant relatives who were also magicians. There are a few branches of the family around that intermarry from time to time. I never had much of a talent for magic myself but grew up aware of it."

"That... explains that," Nicki said slowly. "So uh... is that common in the family? Arranged marriages?"

"Still fairly common. Avani's elder brother Ranbir was married through that fashion, though to a friend of the family rather than a distant cousin. She's a nice girl and has adjusted well, but those who come from outside of magician families are usually tested."

"Tested?"

"Nothing dangerous, I assure you," Gita promised. "We have a... potion, I believe is the right word. They are told about magic, and their reaction is judged. The potion wipes their memory when they sleep, and if they reacted well, then they are told again."

"Wow." Aiden was grinning like an idiot. "So, you have potions, actual potions."

"Yes, magicians don't have access to the full force of natural magic so we must pull it out of other natural elements. It takes time and isn't very useful in combat, hence why we rely on the Old Ones to fight the Demons."

"Still, that's incredible!" Aiden shook his head and was almost vibrating out of his seat. "I guess it explains why Merlin and Morgana don't worry about India much."

Gita smiled, apparently thinking it was a compliment, but Nicki had never thought that Morgana seemed impressed with magicians. On the one hand, they weren't taught by Merlin and Morgana and didn't have the full powers or the responsibility. But on the other hand, they had to be creative in ways that Merlin and Morgana didn't have to be.

"Is it hard using magic when there isn't a lot in the world?" Nicki asked.

"Oh yes, India usually has some level of magic due to the presence of the Demons, but using a basic spell takes a great deal of focus and even several hours to several days. It is why, while magic is a part of the fabric of this family, we don't rely on it."

There was a beeping from the kitchen and Gita quickly excused herself. Releasing a deep breath, Nicki became acutely aware of how her legs were shaking a little. Her nerves were becoming embarrassing.

"So, are you going to make a move on Avani?" Aiden asked softly. He was leaning over and smiling a little too widely.

"These things take time," Nicki replied. Her cheeks were beginning to heat up, and she looked towards the doorway where she could see Gita moving around. "And don't whisper about it here. I don't want to horrify her family. I don't know enough about Indian culture. They may not- I mean..."

Aiden's expression softened, and he looked a touch guilty. Apparently, he'd caught on to her worries. She had no idea how India reacted to lesbians and regretted not consulting the internet before they left. Sure she had her tablet, but the idea of using the Desai's internet for that search seemed inappropriate.

A heavy thud made all of them pause. Jenny who had been whispering with Lance jumped out of her chair and looked around with wide eyes. Bran eased himself from his chair and looked around as another thump made some of the plates shudder on the table. Then the wall of the house exploded, showering them with small bits of drywall and brick. Light poured in through the opening, cutting through the cloud of dust. Nicki coughed to clear her lungs and focused on the spark of magic in her lower torso. She pulled it gently, smiling when power pulsed through her veins. Twitching her fingers, she kept the magic caught up in her hands and looked over to see what had happened. Three large figures moved into the hole in the wall, filling the space and blocking out the sunlight.

Stumbling out of her chair, Nicki stared at the Demons. Her lips tried to curl into an awed smile before she caught herself. Yes, they looked like they'd jumped straight out of a mythology book, but they didn't look friendly. Large and dark-skinned, there were strange colored ridges on their heads that almost looked like masks. It was only Nicki's experience as a mage that told her this was all real. Otherwise, she would have thought they were just huge men.

Then one of the Demons with long, vicious looking teeth rumbled forward. It stood at least six and a half feet tall with broad shoulders and a wide girth, but it moved quickly. A blast of yellow magic shot past her and struck the creature in the chest. A grunt from Bran behind her was all the warning they got before the Demon was pulled into the air and its chest began to be compressed.

Any joy of victory was muted when one of the other Demons threw something large and metallic towards Bran. The trapped Demon fell to the ground as Bran dodged out of the way. There was a crash behind them, but Nicki didn't dare look away from them. A sharp scream from the doorway made Nicki tense as she heard Gita shout something.

"Alex!" Aiden shouted. "We're under attack!" Flames erupted in his hands as more Demons began to push into the dining room through the hole in the wall.

Narrowing her eyes, Nicki flung her right hand forward as one of the Demons charged her. Ice shards hit the Demon's flesh, slicing through the thick layer of skin. Dark red blood seeped out, but it was far darker than a human's. Nicki was certain that it wasn't based on iron like her own was. The Demon roared and narrowed its red eyes on her. She raised her hand and pulled on more magic, letting the blue sparks erupt from her fingertips. In the corner of her eye, she saw a beam of tight red fire blast one of the Demons out into the yard. It was almost funny, they could all do different things, but in a pinch, they all reverted to what was most natural.

Focusing on the magic, Nicki sternly ordered it not to take the form of ice. Instead, the stream of blue magic formed a thin ray of light that hit the Demon's chest. Another beam of red and then one of yellow hit alongside her magic. The Demon fell to the floor. Nicki blinked in surprise. Its body didn't dissolve into dust like a Sídhe but instead collapsed in on itself like it was being dried out fast. Then it turned to dust. It was a small difference, but it was another reminder that these were a completely new enemy.

There were still more Demons. Two more had skirted around the room and were further into the house. Lance climbed up onto the table as one thundered past only to jump onto its back. His dagger flashed as he stabbed it into the Demon's neck three times before it threw him off. Lance hit the floor with a thump and a groan. Jenny shouted his name and as the Demon turned, Jenny dropped down and sliced at its ankles with her dagger.

The Demon screamed in pain and a mess of words that Nicki half understood as cries for help. A wave of yellow caught the creature as Jenny threw herself over Lance to protect him. Bran levitated the creature away from them as Lance climbed to his feet.

"They aren't weak to iron!" Bran shouted. "We can't rely on that. Jenny, Lance, fall back!"

Nicki didn't see if they listened. They probably did, but another Demon was coming towards her. She tightened her fists and pulled on the magic. The world hummed softly, and she felt and heard her heart racing. Magic gathered in her fists, and when the Demon got close enough to swing, she threw her arms up and opened her hands. Hundreds of ice shards slammed into its chest. A wave of red magic shot past her towards another Demon, thankfully not setting anything on fire.

Another Demon came towards her, swinging a small club that hit the dining table and sent dishes flying. The sound of the ceramics shattering on the tile made Nicki flinch. There was movement in the corner of her eyes. She wanted to jump away, to look and check but had to trust the guys to be watching out for her. Two ice shards were launched into its chest, but it barely slowed. More Demons were coming, and Nicki dropped to the floor on her knees to avoid another swing of the club. A red beam shot over her head. The Demon howled and dropped to the floor as Nicki stood.

She wished that she hadn't. Another Demon was approaching, this one smaller and shorter than the others, but carrying a gun. Gasping, she threw a ball of magic towards it. The orb spun and sparked, lacking focusing even as it hit the Demon's arm. It flinched back. The gun went off, blasting a small hole in the wall by the doorway. Nicki almost fell over in shock. Magical enemies weren't supposed to use guns. The shot rang in the air and Nicki pushed more magic forth. It formed a tight blue beam that struck the Demon's chest. Sparks of yellow wrenched the gun from its hand. Flames exploded across its chest, and it fell.

Lightning flashed past her and collided with a pair of Demons near the opening. Alex was here at least. Nicki sidestepped a wild swing from the Demon and let her magic swirl together into an orb in her hand. Shoving it forward, she watched it sink into the Demon's skin. Ice began to seep across the dark skin with a soft crackling sound. The Demon clawed at its skin frantically as the ice spread further and further. Jumping forward, Nicki called on more magic and willed it to do the same. This time she caught the Demon on the arm. Its limb turned to ice, and its remaining hand failed to stop the spread in its chest.

"Got it!" Nicki shouted. She grinned, despite the situation. "Managed the turn to ice thing!"

"That's nice, honey," Aiden shouted back. "But we've got more Demons incoming!"

"I got them!" Alex called.

That was all the warning they got before the air in the room charged. Nicki shivered as her skin goose bumped and spared only a glance at the new ice sculpture before moving towards the far wall. Two Demons were pushing their way into the room only to stop with wide eyes as a series of lightning bolts, and dark gray beams blasted them.

Nicki watched the dust from the destroyed wall float through the light pouring into the room. No one moved, all of them still braced for an attack. The last of the Demon bodies were collapsing into themselves leaving Nicki with no idea of how many there had been. Alex's shoes crunched on the floor as she walked past them to the hole in the wall. She stepped outside and looked around.

"Looks clear," Alex said carefully.

"Glad you heard the noise," Aiden said.

"We hadn't made it to the water room yet," Alex replied. "Hard to miss the sound of a wall being blown apart."

Nodding in response, Nicki turned to look around. A cry of alarm from the next room made her muscles tense. There was a collective sharp inhale, and then everyone moved. In the main room, Gita was on the ground with Avani standing a few feet away with a horrified expression. Nicki glanced at the wall and swallowed. The hole from the Demon's gun lined up with Gita's position.

Nicki dropped to her knees, ignoring the crack of her kneecaps against the tile. Gita was struggling to breathe and holding her side as a red pool of blood seeped out around her. There was a collective gasp of alarm all around them. Avani was there in a heartbeat along with two other young men who might have been her brother and cousin. Nicki shifted out of the way to let Avani take her mother's hand. Her chest tightened as Avani started speaking to her mother in an unfamiliar language that rolled off her tongue. One of the men shrugged off his outer vest and pressed it tightly to the wound making Gita hiss.

Looking over at Alex, Nicki tried to form the words, but Alex nodded in understanding. She and Bran took off in a dead run for the staircase.

"Alex is getting the Chalice," Nicki said softly. Avani looked up at her. "It will heal her. Just hold on and stay calm."

"I've never seen a magical creature use a gun before," Aiden muttered. "We need to be ready for that."

"Shush!" Nicki hissed. "I need to focus!"

Gita looked at her with wide, frightened eyes, but the woman managed a small nod. Avani was holding her mother's hand tightly and looked up at Nicki hopefully. Risking a glance back towards the stairs, Nicki calculated how long it would take to grab the Chalice. They could fill it with water from a bathroom sink, but then they had to get back here.

Without thinking, she extended her hand over Gita's side, leaning over the injured woman. Blue magic jumped off her fingertips, and Aiden caught her waist to keep her steady.

"Just a little," Aiden whispered. "Just enough to keep her stable." His presence soothed her. "You got this, Nicki. Just hold on until Alex gets back."

Nodding, Nicki slowed her breathing to a calm rhythm and let her soft blue magic flow around Gita. There was a soft prickle against her magic as the first sparks seeped into the wound. The hole in the fabric shimmered slightly. Nicki didn't dare move or look up until she heard the frantic footfalls returning down the stairs.

8

The Power of the Chalice

After a battle, the world was always too still and silent. It didn't matter that Alex could hear the cars of Mumbai; everything had gone quiet. Her heartbeat slowed down to normal even as she rushed up the stairs to her room. Worry was there of course, but the sharp fear that always came with a battle was gone. She'd survived. She wasn't dead and on course to be reborn again just yet.

Somehow, she found her way back to her bedroom. The Chalice was exactly where she had left it, snuggled up amongst spare socks and t-shirts. She all but clawed it out of the bag and pushed a spark of magic into the metal. It began to warm, and Bran took her arm, guiding her into the small bathroom. He turned on the sink, and Alex automatically moved the Chalice forward to catch the water.

The water filled the Chalice which began to glow a soft gray color. It soothed Alex, and she eased her white-knuckled grip. The wide cup was almost more of a bowl on the narrow base, and beneath her palm, she could make out the triskelion on the neck. Pulling the Chalice away from the spout, Alex began walking quickly for the hallway. She heard the water turn off behind her but didn't wait for Bran. He'd understand her haste.

Hitting the bottom of the staircase, Alex kept the Chalice balanced and watched the water ripple with every jostling step. Gita wasn't far away, and she could see a telltale soft blue glow around Nicki's hands. Avani was staring at her mother fearfully but looked up hopefully as Alex approached. Aiden pulled Nicki back, and Alex knelt. Dropping her eyes, she focused on the Chalice and pushed more magic into it, making the metal glow a soft gray color.

"Lift her up a little."

Avani rushed to obey and one of the unfamiliar young men in the room, helped Avani ease Gita up to a sitting position. The older woman leaned against the young man's chest and grimaced in pain, but her eyes were still sharp. Alex brought the Chalice forward and gently tilted it up. Gita didn't hesitate and took a long sip. She gasped a little, but then took another sip and another.

"How long will it take?" Avani asked nervously.

"Not long," Aiden said. "It brought me out of a coma in under an hour."

"I'm not sure how long it was," Bran replied. He loomed behind Alex. "Just stay calm, everyone."

Gita took another sip and brought a hand up to support the Chalice on her own power. Her eyes were brighter than before, and her breathing was even. Alex noted her leaning forward now without regard for the injury. Avani was stroking her mother's arm and smiled when Gita pulled away from the Chalice.

"I think..." Gita inhaled slowly, looking relieved as her chest expanded. "I'm a bit sore."

A chuckle escaped Alex, and she shifted back a little to give the woman more space. The Chalice was still half full, but Gita carefully lowered a hand to her side. Alex looked down curiously, and after a moment of hesitation, Gita slipped a hand beneath the hem of her shirt. Standing up slowly, she glanced towards Bran who stepped back to give her more room.

"Seems healed," Gita said. "Thank you."

"The Chalice has one job," Bran said. "And it does it well."

"That's the... Holy Grail, then?" the young man asked.

"Well, the inspiration for it." Bran shrugged a little. "It's unclear just how the myth evolved there, but this just proves that it was a good move to bring it with us."

"Yes," Avani agreed. "Thank you!" She looked at her mother. "Are you sure you're alright mother?"

"I'm fine," Gita said. "But we need to deal with the hole. And thanks to that gunshot the police may be on their way." She looked up at Alex as the young man began to help her stand up. "Where is Lochan?"

"We were outside... near the front of the house when we heard the noise," Alex answered. "I took off running inside, and he said that he'd go to the water room."

"Hiran, check on your grandfather," Gita ordered the young man. "I'm alright."

"Yes, Aunt Gita," Hiran replied. He glanced at them all curiously before nodding. "Please excuse me."

Alex watched the young man rush for the door. She twitched, ready to follow him as worry that the old man might have been attacked by the Demons reared up in her head. It was followed by her reassuring herself that the Demons would have stayed together for safety and Shiva might have arrived in the water room. Sucking in a sharp breath, Alex's struggled to stay calm as her stomach twisted. Was she supposed to go out and meet with Shiva now? Should she go now?

"Have the Demons ever attacked your home like this before, Gita?" Bran asked.

"No," Gita said. Her voice was low and sharp with barely restrained anger now that the shock and fear had passed. "We have protections in the portals of the house, all the windows and doors are warded."

"Which is why they knocked down a wall," Nicki muttered. "That was charming."

Bran ignored the remark and kept focusing on Gita. "What about the gun? Is that common?"

"Not common," Gita answered. "But yes, during their skirmishes, it isn't unusual for weaker Demons to turn to human weapons. Thankfully, the firepower they have access to is limited. Knives are far more common."

"But no magic?"

"Not magic they can fully control and manifest," Gita said. Alex glanced her way before walking towards the kitchen doorway. The wall had a massive hole in it, and small pieces were crumbling off. One chunk hit the tile floor with a plink. "But they can make themselves pass as human. There is enough magic in India that they can usually hide, but nothing beyond that."

"At least we have that," Aiden said. "Alex?"

"You're worried about the police," Alex said. She turned back to Gita. "Then we should get the house cleaned up. We can always say that a tv was turned up too loud if someone did call them."

"Yeah, we can work on the walls," Nicki said. Alex looked her way, fighting down a small smile. "We've fixed things using magic before."

"And seen Merlin fix the whole porch of a house," Bran pointed out. "Worth a try."

"You can do it!" Jenny smiled encouragingly at them. "Stop being negative and doubting yourselves."

"She has a point," Aiden said. "And nice moves against that Demon, you two." He grinned at Lance and Jenny. "It was nicely done."

"Them not being weak to iron is a bit... problematic," Lance said. "Not sure what to make of that."

"I'm not sure if they've always been that way." Avani tucked a strand of long black hair back behind her ear. "According to records, they occasionally eat... humans."

Alex stared at Avani, but she wasn't surprised. Nicki paled and made a face with her freckles standing out sharply. Jenny flinched back and grabbed Lance's hand. His disgust was evident. Watching their reactions, Alex pushed down a sigh. Strange as it was, she sort of remembered that and she was able to dismiss it.

"To be fair," she said. "They aren't human, so it isn't cannibalism. Still, I wouldn't want to eat a fully sentient being." Clapping her hands together, she ignored the stunned looks from her friends and gestured towards the wall. "Are we going to fix that or not?"

"Maybe you should hang back," Bran said. "Just in case more are coming."

"I can recharge from your magic," Alex reminded him. There was lingering worry in his eyes that made her ease off the issue. "But if you want the practice, knock yourselves out."

"So, what do you think?" Aiden asked. He looked over at Bran, resting his hands on his hips. "Do we all need to focus on one part or just focus on fixing the wall."

"Our magic should work together for a single purpose," Bran said. "We've channeled it together to make the gates."

"That was a bit different, but I guess it's a good thing to know," Nicki said. She kept looking over at Gita. Avani still had a firm grip on her mother's arm.

"Maybe we should go upstairs, Mother," Avani said softly. "You should rest."

"No," Gita said. She patted her daughter's hand. "I'm fine. I'd like to see this." Gita looked over at Alex and smiled slyly. You know I've never been good at magic, so I take any chance I get to observe it at work."

"Alright," Alex agreed. Her fingers tightened around the neck of the Chalice. "But healing will still tire you out. The magic helps your cells regenerate, but it is still hard on the body. A nap might be a good idea later."

"As you say," Gita agreed. "But we need the wall fixed in case someone comes around to investigate." Looking towards the main door, Gita's eyes narrowed, and her features tightened. "It isn't likely, but we shouldn't risk it."

"Surely someone will investigate the firearm blast." Bran was frowning, causing furrows between his eyebrows. "That wasn't quiet."

"It's a big city," Avani said gently. "Lots of noises." She gestured into a side room. "I'll go and turn a television up loud."

"Find something with guns," Gita added. "Maybe that will help if anyone is listening."

It was surreal. Alex's lips twitched into a smile as Gita rallied to make sure that police weren't crawling over the house. Avani chuckled and gave her mother a knowing look before speed walking into a nearby room. Nicki's jaw was slightly slack, and her eyes were bright and wide. The last thing her crush on Avani needed was Avani's family being awesome. There was a flutter of amusement and pride in her chest. It warmed Alex but also settled uneasily around her heart.

She missed that. Alex's chest tightened as she admitted it. She missed the easy going understanding that could exist between family members. Matt, Ed, and she had been like that on their good days. On their bad days, they'd still understood each other even when they'd snapped too much at each other. She'd miss them. She'd never let herself ask Merlin or Morgana where they were, but Alex suspected that the temptation to know would always be there. Maybe someday in the future, when she was old, she'd find out where they were and check in on whatever nieces and nephews she had.

"Alex?" Bran called softly. "You coming?"

He was in the doorway of the dining room, watching her with too knowing green eyes. Smiling, Alex nodded and moved back into the dining area. Nicki and Aiden were already near the wall, talking in excited tones as the sounds of squealing tires and gunshots echoed in from the sitting room. Avani had found something of the appropriate genre. Alex leaned against the table and said nothing as Bran gave her another worried look. Waving her hand towards the wall, Alex tried to school her features into a calm, neutral expression, but that was usually Bran's thing. In response, he shook his head and little and stepped forward to join the others.

"Oh," Gita's voice said. "Here they go."

Her excitement made Alex smile, really smile and she glanced over to find Gita watching them curiously. The woman seemed to have for-gotten all about the dark blood stain on the side of her sari though Avani was hovering next to it. Flexing her fingers, Alex ignored the others for a moment and pulled on her magic. Dark gray sparks spun around her index and middle finger. She waved them towards Gita, focusing her thoughts on remembering how the sari had looked first thing this morning.

Gita gasped softly as the first gray spark hit the torn and moist fabric. It shimmered and the gray color spread across the layer of blood. Then it faded, bringing the sari back to the warm orange color it had been when Alex first saw her. Gita grinned, and Avani's posture relaxed now that the last evidence of her mother's injury had been cleaned up. Smiling, Alex turned her attention back to the others, crossing her arms over her chest.

Magic filled the air, streams of red, blue, and yellow swirling around the scattered bits of the wall and sweeping it up in a storm. Alex just watched and waited. She could see burning trails left in the air that gleamed to her eyes. Wisps of power lingered even as the first pieces of the wall began to fit themselves into the hole. Like a puzzle, they shifted until they roughly fit together. The layer of dust in the room flew towards the wall like a living cloud. The specks filled the cracks between the fragments.

A giggle escaped Nicki and Aiden elbowed her lightly. Gita had clasped her hands in front of her and Avani was smiling softly. Blinking, Alex watched the wisps of magic begin to fade into the air as the energy dispersed. The wall was almost complete now as the specks of paint lifted off people's clothing and the table. Lazily they floated through the air and seeped into the wall, vanishing into the paint and plaster.

The room's smell was off. There was a faint lingering scent of food, but paint and dust were dominant. It was too clean, almost unnaturally and Alex figured that some normal dust had probably gotten swept up as well. Thankfully, the color of the wall looked right, and there was no sign of any cracks. She smiled as the others congratulated each other and looked down at some of the shattered plates and the impressive dent in the table. Honestly, she was surprised that the table hadn't completely buckled.

Then Nicki spun on her heel and waved her hand, sending blue sparks to the table. The shattered pieces of the plates trembled and began to rise into the air. Shaking her head fondly, Alex stepped away from the table and watched as Nicki fixed up the damage. To her pleasure, she noted that the redhead didn't look very tired. There was a bit of sweat on her brow, but that might have just been the natural heat of India in the summer.

Alex slipped back into the main hall as an excited Gita made a happy noise and came in to inspect everything. Avani's smile was a little fixed until she gave Nicki a grateful look. Lance went inside to help pull the table back into position and righted the chairs without a word. There was no sign of the fight now. Sometimes Alex really did enjoy having magic.

"How did they find us?" Jenny shifted over beside her. "Or you mages at least? Gita said that the Demons don't usually attack here, but there were a bunch of them."

"Did you get a count?" Alex asked curiously. The question got her an odd, irritated look.

"No, there were other concerns. Lance and I headed out of the dining room and were in the hall with Gita. Then the shot went off, and we were trying to look after her."

"Right, uh thank you for that." Alex stumbled through the rush of embarrassment. "But I'm not sure how they knew we were here. Maybe they felt the magic or something. I don't remember much about them to be honest. Things were a bit different then."

"By then, you mean thousands of years ago." Jenny was raising one perfectly groomed eyebrow and looked both worried and amused at the same time.

"Afraid so. Things are... settling a bit more now."

"Are you still hearing the others?"

"Yeah, I expect I will for a long time. But anyway, Demons. Not sure how they knew we were here."

"Do you think Arthur gave them information?"

"We can't assume that everything bad comes from Arthur," Alex said. To her surprise, there was no burst of hurt, rage, and humiliation when she said the name. Just cold anger. "His interest is the Sídhe and the Fae population."

"But he would probably be glad to use Demons to kill us."

"Maybe," Alex said slowly. "It doesn't sound right, but it's possible." Exhaling, Alex glanced towards the dining room again. "Still... they did have very good information on where all the mages were."

"Do you think that someone in the house..." Jenny trailed off and her mouth shut with a click.

Holding back a groan, Alex settled on a shrug and then shook her head. They'd need to think about that to be sure, but she didn't want to consider a traitor. There had to be some kind of magic that the Demons used. Some sort of scrying or maybe just good old-fashioned spying. Jenny was watching her, and Alex shook her head for good measure. The sound of a door closing made her turn. Lochan was walking towards them slowly alongside Hiran. The old man looked just fine as his eyes swept over the scene. Alex exhaled slowly, telling herself to calm down. Everyone was safe, the Demons had been defeated and hopefully sent a message. There were no traitors here. There was a reasonable explanation for how the Demons had known they were here. This was Lokpal's family. There were no traitors here. But she didn't even need the voices of her past lives to remind her that Medraut had been her cousin.

9

The Demon Slayer

21 B.C.E. Mazagaon, India

Lokpal did not have to wait long. But while he was staring at the shrine, trying to catch his breath, and gather his strength something was moving behind him. Fear tickled at his spine. He wondered if running for home wasn't wiser. Perhaps he could go home. Was he supposed to stay or leave? He didn't need to stay; surely his remaining was of no importance to Lord Rudra. Taking a few steps back, Lokpal flinched at a loud crash of thunder overhead. It made him stop and he lowered his face from the rain.

It was hot, and the wind stung on his cheeks as it beat fat raindrops against his skin. Still, he hesitated to move again. Something rumbled in the bushes behind him, and he tensed. Another Demon? There had already been so many today. How was it possible? Where were they coming from? His grip tightened on his sword, and he risked the wrath of Rudra by turning his back on the shrine.

It wasn't a Demon. Instead, a tall being stood only a few feet away, just off the path, and watching him with a displeased frown. Lokpal's knees quivered, but he didn't drop to the ground. He was frozen. His chest was too tight as the being looked at him. Terror gripped his whole body, and all he could do was stare. It had the shape of a man like himself, but it was taller with broader shoulders. Eight strong arms sprang from the bare-chested form, all grasping weapons. Fire danced in too dark eyes, a sharp contrast to the blue skin. A chain of skulls hung around its neck, all of them staring at Lokpal with empty eyes. Small dark lines stained Rudra's exposed skin, forming a dark patch like a bruise.

The roar of the storm quieted, but it did not calm Lokpal. Now the pounding of his own heart filled his ears. He waited for the deity to speak. His knees trembled, and he tried to kneel, but his muscles remained rebellious. Against his will, his eyes tracked the weapons. There was a quiver of arrows on Rudra's back, and one of the left hands held a strong looking bow. There were two axes, two swords, and two spears. All of them carried faint traces of dark blood that glittered in the light of another flash of lightning. Then Rudra took a step towards him. Howling winds swirled around them both, threatening to pull Lokpal off his feet.

He flinched. A raindrop caught the corner of his eye, and he hissed in pain. Rudra moved his hand, and the wind calmed. It became easier to breathe. The rain continued, but the rumble of the thunder ceased. His knees quivered, but he slowly dared to look at Rudra again. A dozen questions of what to say and what to do came all at once.

"Mortal." The voice was rough and deep, almost a growl that quaked in Lokpal's bones. "Where are the Demons?"

"You seek them?" His voice was too soft and high. Swallowing, Lokpal frantically tried again. "Are they your prey, Lord Rudra?"

"They are. Where are they?"

"Forgive me. I have slain several in the last day. They threatened my village, sought to eat my people."

The fire erupted. Jumping from Rudra's eyes, it spread across his skin. The roar of the wind increased. All the air was pulled from Lokpal's lungs. The faces of his wives and children were suddenly too clear in his mind before the burning flames in Rudra's eyes took over his sight. Lokpal met the gaze and stayed still. The urge to run burned in his chest, but he wouldn't get far. Even though the rain had eased, the paths were still hazardous. He had only two hands to fight against a being with eight. Around them, the wind howled, and Lokpal found himself waiting and completely still.

What did the deity want from him? Lokpal fought to stay still. As a boy, he'd learned to hunt and sometimes the animals would stare at you. It was like they knew, but were powerless to do anything that might save them. Caught in the gaze of a predator and too frightened even to fight to survive. He understood that now. Rudra was watching him, a predatory smile on his face. The small dark patches spread further, crawling over Rudra's skin. What were they? He didn't know and tried not to stare. Rudra's eyes kept drawing him back. They were too dark around the iris of fire.

The thick silence was broken when Rudra's lips pulled back, and he grinned while making a low sound of pleasure. Behind them, there came a snap of twigs, and a crash as something substantial moved through the underbrush. Rudra raised his sword and readied himself for battle. A Demon stepped out of the woods, swaying, and grasping onto the trunk of a tree with one hand as it gripped a wound on its side with the other.

The flaming sword swung through the air followed by an axe. A wave of heat swept through the air. They struck the Demon in quick succession. Another pair of arms notched an arrow on a bow and released it with a sharp twang. It hit the Demon in the eye making the creature squeal. It turned to flee. Rudra laughed. It echoed in the air like thunder.

The Demon went down with two more arrows in its back. Lokpal took a step forward before he could think better of it, sword in hand to make sure that the Demon was dead. Then he stopped himself. Stealing another kill from Rudra would surely get him killed. The Demon's body began to collapse into itself like some sort of hollow shell. Lokpal's hands trembled as the glow from Rudra's sword illuminated the ground. The rain was easing, but the rumbling of the thunder was as loud and ominous as ever.

"You seek to take my prey?" The word reverberated in the air.

"No, Lord Rudra. I sought only to protect myself." Lowering his eyes, he managed a deep nod. "Please forgive me. I have trained for years to serve as the protector of these islands. Instinct took over. My hands and weapon move before I have time to consider."

He braced himself for the fire. Or for the storm to swallow him up. For Rudra to swing one of his weapons and take his head. But it didn't. He risked looking up and found the deity watching him with a frown. The delicate features were illuminated by the fire still surrounding Rudra's sword, but at least there was no sign of true anger. Then the deity growled. Overheard the sky rumbled in response, and a sharp burst of wind hit the side of Lokpal's face.

"Your name mortal?" It was a question, but the tone left no illusions that he was free not to answer.

"Lokpal, Lord Rudra."

"You killed that which I was hunting in my storm." Rudra's features twisted into a nasty sneer. "Why is such a fragile creature out in such a storm?"

A lie sprung to his lips, but Lokpal answered with the truth. "I do not know how to explain it, Lord Rudra. I was home, but something seemed wrong with the world. I was driven to come outside. The Demons and I found each other not far from my home."

Rudra leaned forward and sniffed the air. Lokpal's eyes widened at the odd gesture, but he stayed still. The deity breathed in his scent and made a strange sound. Then Rudra withdrew and walked around Lokpal, moving to the shrine. Lokpal spun around, his feet sinking into the mud. Without a word, Rudra sat down on the ground in front of the shrine, folding his legs. The hand with the arrow quickly returned it to the quiver before coming forward and snapping its fingers. Flames sprang up around Rudra in a half circle, hovering just off the ground. They flickered in the wind but managed to stay alight.

The blackness of the night rolled away from the glow of the flames, but it did little for his fear. Rubra lowered his free hand to his knee and drummed the fingers thoughtfully. Lokpal stayed where he was. For good measure, he sheathed his sword with a wet, slick sound. His feet sank into the mud a bit more, and he pulled them free with a grunt, sidestepping onto a rock.

The deity was watching him. Lokpal thought that the fire in his eyes might have dimmed and hoped that was a good sign. Risking a look behind him, he scanned the little he could see of the forest and hoped there were no more Demons. So many in such a short span of time was an event out of the stories. He frantically wished that the tales of Demon Kings with their armies had no truth to it. If there was such a creature then there was little he could do to protect his home.

"A mage," Rudra said. The silence returned as Rudra looked at him. It stretched out between them, and Lokpal wondered if he was supposed to say something. The air between them shimmered, and Lokpal shivered, telling himself it was the raindrops running down his back. "You are a mage, are you not?" Rudra demanded.

"I... I do not know what you mean, Lord Rudra."

"I have heard of your kind." Rudra frowned, almost glaring at him now. "The question now is should I kill you or focus my energies on the Demons."

Something shifted on Rudra's skin. Those strange dark lines were growing. It was not a trick of the light. They moved further on his skin like a living thing. Lokpal remembered nothing about such a sight from the stories. Yet, the deity was unbothered. Lokpal's mouth was dry. A raindrop rolled down his cheek. Rudra closed his eyes for a moment, thinking deeply. The urge to run was back.

"Do not run," Rudra ordered. "I am a lord of the hunt. The Demons are my prey, for now, do not encourage me to change that."

"I am sorry that I intruded on your hunt, Lord Rudra. It was not my intent."

"You were protecting your home," Rudra said. It was more dismissive than understanding. "You humans live everywhere." Rudra stopped drumming his fingers and brought his sword around to study. The flames on the blade were thankfully gone. "Perhaps you do even have cause to worry. There are more Demons now than in years past. I slay many each night, but there are even more when the sun rises."

Lokpal's questions rose to the tip of his tongue, but his mouth was still too dry. Raindrops rolled down his face. The sting of their strikes was less painful now, and the easing wind was allowing the flames to produce more light. Rudra was completely still, just watching him. Licking his lips, Lokpal swallowed and tried again.

"I don't understand, Lord Rudra."

"No, I suppose you don't."

Tensing at the dismissive tone, Lokpal told himself to be careful. "What can I do about the Demons?"

"You will do nothing!" Rudra's eyes flashed, and the flames jumped into the air, forming columns of fire. Stumbling back, Lokpal fell to the ground. His skin tingled, sending a shiver down his spine, and suddenly Rudra was looming over him. "They are my prey! Mage or not, I have chosen this hunting ground!"

"I'm sorry!" The words spilled out. Mud was oozing around his body. A crash of thunder shook the area. "I'm sorry, Lord Rudra. I just... I need to protect my people."

The deity was studying him and the fire in its eyes was dying. There was something like hesitation or perhaps pity. Rudra sniffed at the air again and frowned. The rage died away and was replaced with irritation. A strong hand reached towards him. Lokpal tried to move away, but the mud was holding him in place. The hand gripped his arm and began to pull him out. His shoulder protested, and Rudra made a noise of displeasure.

"You are a mage. I shall respect that, for the time being. Do not cross me or the rising Demons will not be your only problem."

"Will-will you fight them?" Lokpal asked. The question surprised the deity as he was freed from the mud. "Please, Lord Rudra, I barely managed to defeat those I fought today. If more come, I do not know how I will hold them back."

Rudra's mouth shifted into a smile. More hands came forward and lifted Lokpal into the air. He was raised above Rudra's head. Lokpal held back a shriek as his legs dangled uselessly in the air. Tilting his head, Rudra studied him, and the smile widened. It was amused now, the predator receding. For a moment, the black in Rudra's eyes around the ring of fire lightened, and the odd patches of darkness on his skin vanished.

"I will hunt them. I will slay them all."

Then Rudra dropped him into a patch of ferns. Lokpal hit the ground with a heavy thud. His head struck a hard patch of ground, and while there was no mud to swallow him, darkness crept in. Struggling to raise his head, he blinked frantically. Pain spread slowly across the back of his skull. He groaned and took a desperate breath as he tried to climb to his feet. The fire died, and the world went dark. The light rain continued. Raindrops hit his face, and he tried to see the outlines of the trees above him. It was too dark now. He couldn't hear Rudra. Then everything else went dark as the pain swept over him.

10

Lord Shiva

The calm after the battle faded quickly. There was the noise of the television that Avani slowly turned down. No one came to the door, and the others sat down around the table, laughing in relief at another victory. Alex looked at Hiran thoughtfully. He'd called Gita his Aunt which made him Avani's cousin. He was smiling and watching her fellow mages curiously, but suspicion tugged at her.

Jenny's worries were understandable. Alex knew that, but irritation warred with her caution. Why did Jenny have to put such an ugly idea into her head? The Desais had come to them for help. Sif had even brought Avani to Ravenslake. That had to mean something. But the suspicion was there now, and Alex knew she wasn't going to shake it so easily. So she stayed quiet and watched the others until Lochan stepped over to join her at the edge of the room.

"Shiva will be here soon," Lochan said.

"What?" Alex blinked at him in surprise. "But uh, the Demons-"

"Shiva may be able to provide some answers." Lochan was smiling gently, and Alex was certain that he knew how nervous she was. It was horrible, but she'd been a bit relieved when she'd heard the shouting from the house. "It is why you came. Now you have confirmation that the situation is bad."

"Yes," Alex agreed. "I suppose that's true." She brushed a piece of lint off her shirt and straightened her shoulders. "If you're sure it is still a good time."

"The police have not come, and I doubt they will," Lochan said. "Come, please."

The others were looking at them now. Jenny offered her a small nod, Nicki smiled, and Lance nodded encouragingly. Smiling a little, Alex shrugged at the others.

"Meeting an Old One, take two. Try not to get into trouble."

"We'll do our best," Bran promised. "Do you want us to update Merlin and Morgana?"

"Not yet," Alex said. "We don't know enough, and you know how they worry."

She didn't wait for a reply and gestured for Lochan to lead the way. The old man was smiling, his eyes bright and cheerful which was more than Alex would have been if her home was attacked. Still, no one had been hurt permanently, and it had confirmed that the Demons were a problem. He took the lead, and they headed out the side door once again. Alex paused briefly, waiting for the sounds of something else going wrong, but the only thing she heard was the city.

Sunlight poured down around the covered walkway like a curtain. In the bright light, Alex could clearly see the various plants and flowers. Lochan began naming them off for her in his accented English. She listened politely but knew that she would never remember them. Up ahead, the door of the water room or whatever they actually called it, grew closer and closer. Her feet became heavy, and Alex half wished for

Demons to attack. That was probably a bad thing for the Iron Soul to want to happen.

"You shouldn't worry," Lochan said gently. "Shiva and your soul were friends."

"That was a long time ago." Alex's fingers itched, and she glanced back at the house. Maybe she could run back inside and retrieve Mjǫllnir. She was suddenly very aware of how foolish it was to leave it there. "I've died and been reborn dozens of times, and he has lived for thousands of years."

"This is true. A person is never the same as when you last saw them. Every moment has changed them in some way. The question is simply how much they have changed." Lochan stopped in front of the doorway but reached over to inspect the leaves of a nearby fern. "But I suspect, the changes are not insurmountable."

"I guess." Alex swallowed, the words were both calming and distressing. It was true that she wasn't Lokpal anymore, but she also wasn't the Alex Adams who had moved to Ravenslake for college. "Everything changes, doesn't it?"

"That is the way of things." Lochan opened the door of the small building. "It is better than the alternative of a stagnant world." He gestured her to enter.

Stepping into the water pool room, Alex became aware of just how still the room was. Aside from the open door, it was completely cut off from outside light. It existed as something outside the everyday life of Mumbai. What happened in here affected the lives of the Desai family, but it wasn't a part of it.

Strangely, that was comforting. Separation made sense to Alex. She understood the need for that. Alex walked further inside and looked down into the pool of water. Was there something she needed to do to alert Shiva that she was here? Her stomach tightened, and the butterflies were back. Chuckling at herself, Alex shook her head. Silly to be nervous about this. It was hardly the first deity she'd met.

"I'll leave you to your meeting," Lochan said.

"You're not staying?"

"No."

Lochan smiled at her, but he didn't stop his exit. He didn't offer any explanation for departing. Tensing up, Alex debated trying to stop him, but the old magician had evidently made up his mind. He reached the doorway and gave her a deep nod before vanishing back out into the garden. The door closed behind him with a soft, but final click. The sound hung in the air until Alex exhaled.

She looked around the water room. Despite the lack of windows, it seemed different in the light of day. Small lights illuminated the walls. The water was completely still, and there was a slight reflection of the light off it that added an extra glow to the walls. Something about the circular layout of the room, the pool of water, and the way the light filled the space made it seem otherworldly.

It reminded Alex of the Sídhe tunnels. Her stomach tightened, and she shook her head, trying to push out the memory of the white stone walls and the way that light had filled the lower section of the tunnels. Those walls had allowed the crying of the children to echo all the way up to the exit. Breathing slowly, Alex closed her eyes and sternly reminded herself that this wasn't the tunnels. There was a door right behind her. This was just a space meant to keep prying eyes from seeing something they shouldn't.

"You're meeting Shiva," Alex said softly. It was barely a whisper, but the sound filled the room. "Get it together, Alex.

She waited, shoulders back, and her body tense. Part of her wanted to scold herself on Morgana's behalf about her sudden desire to impress Shiva. They weren't really gods, well, that wasn't true either. By Jenny's definition, they weren't, but people worshiped them, drew comfort from them, and Shiva at least protected them. That seemed like a god to Alex. At least a little bit. Sif and her family had been sleeping for years, but Shiva had taken responsibility for keeping the Demons in check. That meant something.

The voice in her head that was Lokpal wasn't helping either. He was excited, not reverent, but excited. There was also a sense of gratitude seeping into her bones. There was at least one family other than Morgana that understood the Iron Soul and respected it. Maybe it was a bit childish, but it had been nice to be recognized, and Shiva was part of that as well. Brief flashes of memory played across her mind, but nothing was clear enough for Alex to grab hold of.

Her eyes moved around the room, properly noticing the molding at the top of the ceiling and the tiled pillars along the walls. Fighting back the urge to fidget, Alex glanced down at herself and held back a snort. Her blue shirt and jeans weren't exactly formalwear.

Then the water began to ripple. Alex's spine straightened in response, and she inhaled slowly, willing herself to relax. There wasn't time to meditate, but she quickly used the techniques that Merlin and Morgana had taught her to loosen her shoulders a little. Water was churning out of the pool and forming into a roughly circular shape.

It was different than the way that Cyrridven had traveled, Alex realized suddenly. The Old One who had guarded the Sword had always formed herself out of the water like she was always a part of it. Maybe it had something to do with the way Old Ones slept in the water. Or maybe Cyrridven had an even stronger connection to water than most other

Old Ones. Alex was pulled from the strange thoughts by a figure stepping out of the tunnel. They didn't move onto the steps but instead allowed the water tunnel to fall away, leaving them standing in the pool.

Her eyes weren't drawn to the figure first, but rather the long trident in his hand. It shimmered in the light, and Alex's eyes caught magic stirring just below the surface, giving the metal a soft glow. The two outer prongs curved gracefully outward while the center had a slight long leaf shape to it that reminded her of Cathanáil. Where the three prongs met was a triskelion symbol. Alex smiled.

Magic brushed across her skin. A small thread of dark gray connected her and the trident, pulsing with power and belonging. Shiva said nothing while she inspected the trident. Lokpal whispered the proper name to her, Trishula. The Iron Trishula. At least one iron artifact was exactly where it had been put.

Then, realizing that she'd been ignoring him completely, Alex forced herself to look at Shiva. He appeared as a tall man with handsome Indian features, but his skin was completely different. His face and throat were a grayish blue, but his hands were white. Not white like hers, but milk white or white like the petals of a daisy. In the center of his forehead were three horizontal white lines drawn around a small dot. His long black hair was half up in a bun with the rest cascading over his shoulders. Unlike the artwork she'd seen in books, he was dressed in the same sort of tunic that modern Indian men wore. It was white like his pants and with his bare feet, he looked like some sort of yoga instructor. Around his neck was a strange metal necklace that looked like a snake. He wasn't trying to look human like Sif and Alex wasn't sure what to make of that.

"Greetings," Alex said. The desire to add Lord Shiva to her simple greeting all but burned on her tongue.

"I greet you, one with the Iron Soul," Shiva said. He lowered his head in a deep nod, and Alex returned the gesture. "Thank you for coming."

"Of course," Alex replied. She was suddenly unsure of what to say. "Uh, Avani was not exaggerating the Demon problem. A group just attacked the house."

Shiva's eyes flashed red. His grip on the Trishula tightened. The temperature in the small building rose a few degrees. It wasn't frightening. In fact, Alex smiled at the reminder about Shiva's loyalty to Lokpal's family. Then the Old One nodded and eased his grip on the Iron Trishula.

"Then you see the problem," Shiva said. "I can fight them of course. I was charged long ago with keeping the Demons in check. Those that live in peace aren't a problem, but lately, they've become more militant. Lochan and I are concerned about keeping their existence hidden."

"Are the Demons at all worried about that?"

"Demons don't have the weakness to iron that the Sídhe have," Shiva reminded her. "They have never been as fragile in this world as other species. They have kept their illusions and masks on in accordance to a treaty made thousands of years ago that I enforce."

"And something has changed."

"There are always some who dislike the treaty and act up. They are dealt with."

Holding back a shiver, Alex reminded herself that this might not be fair, but it was necessary. "I see," she said softly. "But there are more acting up now."

"Yes, and in an age of camera phones, sooner or later something that we can't hide is going to be recorded. I believe that most Demons know that this would be worse for them than the humans, but others seem convinced that they would win any conflicts that began."

"So, if we have to be careful about exposure then what can we do?" Alex asked. "Do you have any suggestions?"

"You are the Iron Soul," Shiva replied. "No other can command the power of the Iron Realm as you can. I hope that you will be able to negotiate a new treaty or find whoever is leading the militant Demons."

"The Sídhe and Fae creatures were recently under a spell," Alex said thoughtfully. "Could that have affected the Demons as well?"

"I didn't notice any unusual behavior." Shiva shook his head, sending a clump of long hair over his shoulder. "This behavior isn't strange, just the sheer number of Demons turning violent is. I wanted you to come here because as a mage you might see or feel something that I cannot. I fear that there is something that I am missing."

"I understand." They stood in silence, and Alex wondered how this conversation was supposed to end. Would Shiva stay here and talk with her about Lokpal? Would he want to battle her to see what she could do? Was he going to leave? She kept her feet planted on the ground and didn't let her hands move. "Thank you for alerting us," Alex said. "We've been very busy in Oregon dealing with the Sídhe, but I'd hate to let that distract us from another problem."

"India has been long kept stable by myself and a few other Old Ones," Shiva answered. "It is a point of pride to us that while our very nature stresses our adoptive world that we can still serve it. I hope that this situation will be dealt with soon and you can return your attention to the Sídhe. Sif told me a bit of the troubles you face... I almost reconsidered asking Avani to seek you out."

"I'm glad you didn't." The words were strange to say, like reading a script, but she wasn't an actress. "I need to at least try and be aware of the various issues around the world. Thank you for being aware of our preference to keep magic a secret. I'm not sure how people would react to that."

"Indeed." Shiva looked at the Trishula and smiled softly. "Lokpal was always very aware of his duty, but also tried to look into the future. He was a good man. I am glad that the Iron Soul remains to protect the Iron Realm. It is a beautiful world, full of so much life and potential. You entrusted this to me long ago." Shiva's voice was warm with fondness that sank into Alex's bones. "I thanked you then, and I thank you now." Shiva's smile turned sad as he lowered the Trishula so he could grip it horizontally. Then he held it out to her. "I return it to you."

Blinking in surprise, Alex was at a loss of what to say. Her right hand came up and reached out towards the Trishula. Sparks of magic were swirling within the metal, giving the ancient iron a pulse all its own. There was a desperate desire in her chest for the Trishula as her first finger touched it. A rush of power hit her, surging up her arm and spinning around her heart. It forced the air from her lungs and made her dizzy.

But a voice protested, and Alex pulled her hand away. Her faintness faded, and she inhaled, a soft, sad smile taking over her face. Looking up to Shiva, she let her hand drop to her side and noted the surprise on his face. For a moment, she couldn't speak, and then Lokpal began to whisper to her.

"Thank you, Shiva," Alex said. She shook her head slightly. "But I think it best that the Trishula stays with you for a bit longer."

"Are you certain?"

"I have a few of the other iron artifacts that I have made in my various lives," Alex replied. She looked back at the Trishula as Shiva gripped it and pointed it towards the sky once more. "I think you'll continue to do more with it than I would."

"If you have need of it-"

"Thank you," Alex said. "But you've held the Demons in check for centuries. It is safe with you and is used to protect the Iron Realm. I can't ask for more than that."

They stared at each other and Alex smiled widely. Her cheeks were beginning to ache when she tucked a strand of blonde hair behind her ear. "As for the Demons, we'll see what we can find out. Hopefully, we can find the root of this new Demon activity soon."

"I appreciate that." Shiva nodded slightly. "I will speak with the others. If I learn anything, I will alert you."

"Thank you," Alex said. "How do we reach you if we have news?"

"Come to the water here and say my name." Shiva smiled softly at her and looked at the Iron Trishula clutched in his hand. "I will hear you."

Then his body began to glow, and the water spun up around him. Folding her hands in front of her, Alex watched silently as a small water portal opened. Shiva gave her one last look before he stepped back through it. Her eyes jumped to the Iron Trishula, and Alex stared at it until it vanished from sight in the water. The small tunnel collapsed with a splash, leaving her alone in the room with only the sound of the rippling water for company.

11

Forming a Plan

While Alex had gone off to talk to Shiva, Nicki and the others had been shown the library. Honestly, Nicki felt that they got the much better deal for the morning activity. The thought of the Desai library alone was enough to make her grin like an idiot. It was two rooms with the first being a proper public library full of classics, reference books, and a few shelves of mass market paperbacks. There was a secret door, an actual secret door, that opened to the second room that had no windows or any other way in, at least none that Avani had shared.

Nicki adored the room. Without any windows and only one door, the scent of old books utterly filled the space. Every breath she took made her heart flutter and her smile widen. On the ceiling and in the corners were strange looking sigils. Something about them screamed magic to her and Nicki believed that she could almost sense a little bit of magic in them. Even if it was just in her mind, this place was safe. Shelves of tightly packed books lined the walls, and there were even two rows of long and short shelves towards the middle. A long table with lamps and chairs finished filling the space. The others were looking around with varying levels of awe. Bran was already inching towards a nearby shelf while Jenny and Lance stayed close together near the doorway.

"Nice room," Aiden said. He sniffed at the air and smiled. "Never thought I'd find a place that smelled more intensely of books than my family's shop."

"Oh." Avani turned to him curiously. "Your family has a bookstore?"

"Yeah, in Ravenslake. If you go back there with us, I'll show it to you. I warn you though that my parents are still a little uneasy about the whole magic thing?"

"Why? I understand that it would be unexpected, but surely, they'd appreciate how it distinguishes you."

"Uh, well, I sort of ended up in a coma for a bit and the doctors thought I might even become brain dead so... they're a bit nervous about what else will happen to me because of magic."

"That's..." Avani's eyes were wide but cautious. "Understandable. In that light, I thank you once again for being willing to come to India to help with the Demons."

"Speaking of the Demons, we need a plan," Lance said. "The mages came here to help fight the Demons, and the Demons know you're here."

"Or at least they've decided to attack the local magicians," Nicki said. "But we should probably assume they know about us."

"Agreed," Aiden said. "Lance is right. We can't just stay here and wait for attacks. That group all attacked at once, so either they coordinated beforehand to meet here or they came together. And if they came together then maybe there is some kind of base."

"That's not a bad assumption. If there is leadership in place, then they'd likely have some physical location for meetings, training, and arming the Demons." Bran tented his fingers together thoughtfully and stared at a nearby shelf. "The fact that they used a gun concerns me."

"Yeah," Aiden said. "Let's hope that the Fae back at home don't figure that one out."

"Thankfully, most firearms are made with steel," Bran said. "Though, the Fae have been here long enough that they have some resistance built up."

"Fae with guns," Jenny groaned. "Thank you so much for putting that into my head. If I have nightmares of Redcaps with semi-automatics tonight, I'll know who to blame."

"If they haven't started using guns by now there is probably a reason." Bran was being too reasonable again, but Jenny calmed down a little. "For all we know, their bodies can't handle the recoil. They are a lot lighter than humans, and maybe they are just too fragile in our world. Or they are nervous about gunpowder or the iron traces in the weapons. That's not the issue right now."

"Right," Nicki said. "Tracking Demons. How do we find them so we can start figuring out what is happening here?"

Avani was looking at all of them like they were crazy. Sadly, her crush wasn't well versed yet in the weird conversations of mages. Still, she wasn't running away in terror, so that was something.

"Any thoughts on tracking the Demons?" Aiden asked. "We need to figure out some way of helping you get to the source of this problem."

"True," Bran agreed. "And in a city as busy as Mumbai, it isn't as simple as following tracks up a hillside."

"Does that work in Ravenslake?" Avani asked.

"With the Sídhe coming out of their tunnels usually," Aiden said. "That and last time we were up there, Alex was able to sense the... hole I guess between worlds that they'd opened."

"Fascinating." Avani was smiling slightly with a quizzical expression. It was adorable. In a sexy sort of way.

"But we haven't seen her do anything like that with the Fae," Aiden explained.

"To be fair, the last time the Fae attacked in full force, they were just coming from nearby cities rather than one point," Bran said.

"Which is what the Demons are doing." Nicki straightened up in her seat, reminding herself to be active in the conversation. "But I'll bet that we can use our magic to follow some sort of trail."

"Or scry," Aiden added.

"Scrying is very visual," Bran said. "And I don't know the area. I doubt I'd recognize enough in Mumbai for scrying to be useful for just tracking them."

"Well, there are some tracking spells in one of the books here." Avani calmly walked over to one of the shelves and pulled down an old western style book. The cover was a bit worn, and it looked like it had been rebound at least once. "I think it would be in this one. I know that there are spells used to trace enemies. Usually you need something of theirs."

"We have the gun," Aiden said. "And we could probably find the... uh, bullet if we had to since it passed through." His voice softened. "I am sorry about what happened to your mother."

"Thank you... I'm trying to focus on the task at hand." Avani bit her lip for a moment, her face dropping. "But... I do not doubt that seeing her like that will haunt me for a while. I'm grateful that you brought the Chalice with you to India."

"We can review the book ourselves if you need to spend time with your mother," Bran told her gently.

"Thank you, but I'll be fine."

Nicki didn't believe her, but Avani's features were set in a stubborn expression. Her chin was even slightly tilted up. There'd be no arguing with her. Worry tickled Nicki, and she debated trying to order Avani as a mage to stay here. But they were a bunch of Americans and stumbling around Mumbai by themselves without a local was asking for trouble.

"Let us know if you need anything," Nicki said. "We understand family."

"Yeah," Aiden said. "Alex has put protective magic in most of our hometowns." He risked a glance towards Jenny. "And hopefully when we're done here, we'll finish that project."

Bran gently took the book from Avani and opened it carefully. His green eyes lit up, and a small smile played at the corners of his lips. Holding the book towards Avani, he pointed at something and Avani grinned in response.

"Yes," Avani said. "That's Lord Shiva."

"I wonder if he really looks like that." Bran was studying the book intently. "They're beings of energy who create matter forms to function in our world so they can look like anything."

"He looked very similar when I met him," Avani said. Her voice was patient even in light of Bran's rambling. "A bit more modern in terms of his clothing. And he was very patient and calm, very respectful with Sif."

"I wonder if they keep track of each other?" Nicki sat down at the long table and peered around at the different books. "I mean, Sif is going around the world to find and talk with Old Ones but did Shiva know that she was the wife of an Iron Soul? Does that sort of thing impact how they talk to each other?"

"Maybe," Aiden said as he dropped into the chair beside her. "Then again, so far the only Old Ones that we know have a strong connection to the Iron Soul are Cyrridven, Shiva, and Sif."

"Avani, do you think you can find and translate the tracking spell for us?" Bran asked.

"You might be able to translate the words yourself if you focus your magic," Avani replied.

"Yeah, well, better save the magic for now. I'm not sure what kind of headache a translation spell would give me."

"As you wish." Avani was smiling in amusement and took the book to the table. There was a discarded pad of paper and pen near one of the lamps that she quickly collected. "I'll need a few minutes."

"Take as much time as you need," Bran said. "We've tracked things before and found things through magic, but I'm interested if your family has any insights that may help us. And thank you for all your help so far."

"Of course." Avani ducked her head slightly, an embarrassed and flattered smile taking over her features. "I'm glad to help."

Trying not to panic, Nicki watched Avani and Bran carefully before she relaxed. She was being silly. Bran was asexual or at least demi-sexual. Of course, that didn't completely mean that he couldn't be interested in Avani.

"Relax," Aiden suddenly whispered beside her. "Your brain is going to overheat if you keep thinking that hard. Bran's just being polite."

"Do you think she likes him?" Nicki kept her voice low and looked at the others. Bran was examining the shelves, Jenny and Lance were talking in low voices by the door.

"Bit early to say, maybe she's just flattered that a mage was thanking her." Aiden nudged her shoulder gently. "Don't make yourself any crazier."

"I'm not crazy. I'm odd; there is a difference."

"You've been saying that for years."

The clever response that Nicki was gathering on her tongue was interrupted as the secret doorway swung open. Lance and Jenny jumped out of the way, and Lance placed himself between his girlfriend and the door. It was both sweet and irritating. Jenny lightly hit his arm indicating her agreement with Nicki's musing as Alex and Lochan stepped inside.

"Welcome to the secret library," Lochan said. "This is where we keep our spell books and records from the heads of the family." He pointed to one of the high shelves. "My personal records fill up a shelf all on their own. I've always been a bit... verbose I believe is the word."

Alex didn't laugh at the remark. Nicki frowned as she studied her friend. Alex's face was thoughtful, but also dark. While she was moving, there was a lack of awareness. She almost ran into a table before Bran jumped up and took her arm. He disguised the move with a quick hug, and Alex's gaze cleared a little.

"Sorry," Alex said. "Uh, everything going okay?"

"Yes," Jenny answered. She stepped forward and touched Alex's hand as Bran released her. "Bran and Avani are working on a spell to track where the Demons came from. What about you? How was the meeting? Are you okay?"

"I'm fine." Alex gave them that annoying forced smile. "My heads just a bit full right now, but Shiva was nice. He even offered me the Trishula back." Avani and Lochan both gasped at the statement and looked at Alex in near horror. "Well, Lokpal did give it to him. I decided that for now at least, it is safer and will do more good with Shiva. As far as I can tell, it doesn't have any special powers or connections that we need to be worried about."

"Let's hope you're right," Aiden said. "It may just be a weapon, more straightforward than the Sword or the Hammer."

"Well, it probably has something." Alex was a bit sheepish now. "Beyond just being a weapon that doesn't wear out, but I'm not sure what that would be."

"I'm not aware of any legends that describe the Trishula as having special powers," Lochan answered. "Though, it would be worthwhile to check the oldest of our records just in case."

"Thank you," Alex said. "That would be helpful."

"Could you tell me what the other Iron Artifacts can do?" Lochan asked. "It may help me know what to look for."

"Well, the Iron Sword Cathanáil is connected to the Iron Gates, at least that's what Arthur and the Sídhe Queen think. Mjǫllnir, the Iron Hammer, generates lightning attacks like in the stories, but can also break magical connections. The Iron Chalice heals the injured. The Iron Chain... well, that one's been destroyed, so it doesn't matter. Those are the ones we know about."

"Interesting, most of those have some connection with famous mythology." Lochan nodded to himself. "The Trishula has always been more of a symbol in our stories, representing the different aspects of Shiva as a creator, protector, and destroyer. Of course, it also represents Shiva's ability to destroy evil. I cannot think of anything else in the stories."

"It's alright." Alex was trying not to squirm, but it was obvious that something had unsettled her. "It isn't urgent. My instinct is that the Trishula is safest and does the most good with Shiva. Lokpal trusted him with it."

"Indeed." Lochan nodded. "We will, of course, trust your judgment."

"Thank you." Alex straightened up and raised her chin, squaring her shoulders, trying to slip into her hero mode. "So, we want to track the Demons. That's a good plan. We need more information on what is going on here in Mumbai. Bran, have you got an idea of what to do?"

"We're working on it," Bran replied. He sat on the edge of the table by Avani who was scribbling frantically on the paper.

"What do you want us to do?" Lance asked carefully.

Lochan smiled at him, tilting his head as he studied Lance and then Jenny. "The pair of you are interested in learning to use some magic, are you not?"

"We are, sir," Lance replied. "We want to help our friends, but we aren't mages."

"A noble choice. Allow Avani to help the others; she knows the city well enough to be of use. You two stay with me here, and I'll start teaching you the basics."

"Of magic?" Jenny asked.

"Meditation to start with," Lochan replied. "You must first learn to sense magic."

"We're already a bit aware of it." There was a careful note to Lance's voice, and he glanced over at Alex, but she was still looking at the tall shelves of books. "Just from exposure, I'm guessing. Since Stonehenge, I've felt it in the air. Makes my hair stand on end."

"Makes me feel like I've drank a triple expresso," Jenny added.

"Then that will make this all much easier." Lochan clapped his hands together gleefully. "I can't promise you fast results, but with some work, we might make magicians out of you."

Avani handed Bran the piece of paper. Bran blinked at it and chuckled. "Well, gang, the actual tracking spell is exactly what we did in Paris since I don't think we need to use the ritual, but Avani's translation was helpful." Returning her focus to Bran, Nicki peaked over his shoulder, but the instructions were pretty short. The longest section read like a chant, and there was a mixture of some kind described. "As it is, we just need to focus our magic together."

"Paris?" Avani repeated. "Why were you in Paris?"

"That was where we found the Iron Hammer."

"I would have thought that Mjǫllnir would be in the Nordic region."

"Long story," Alex said. "So, gather in a group, join hands, and let's make ourselves a ball of light to guide our way."

"I was hoping for something a bit more exact than that," Aiden grumbled. "I don't know if I'm pleased or sad that what we did on the fly is basically the actual spell." Sticking out his bottom lip, Aiden pouted at her. With his brown eyes, he looked a bit too much like that dog she'd wanted to adopt back when she lived in a car with her parents. "Are we that good? Is there nothing more-"

Nicki smacked him lightly on the head. "Oh, stop whining and ease up on the drama. Take it as our years of geeky entertainment have served us well, and at least we won't be underground again."

"You hope, you probably just jinxed us, you know."

Alex grabbed Nicki's hand and gave Aiden a stern look before they could continue arguing. "Let's at least pretend that we take our job seriously," Alex said. "Let's try to focus on finding where the Demons that attacked today came from. If we just try to find the Demons, that may be too broad."

"Agreed," Aiden said. He puffed out his chest a little but winked at Nicki.

Holding back a smile, Nicki glanced towards Avani. The young magician was watching them curiously as she stood next to her grandfather, Lance, and Jenny. Closing her eyes, Nicki exhaled slowly and pulled on the spark of magic that was humming beneath her heart. She let it flow through her hands and towards Alex, all the while focusing on the wish to find the where the Demons had come from and trying to keep any other thoughts out. In the middle of their small circle, a soft orb of light began to form.

12

The Demon Slayer

621 B.C.E. Mazagaon, India

Heema's voice was the first thing that Lokpal heard. It was quickly followed by the sound of something hitting the floor and Heema calling Ojas' name. He groaned softly. There was a dull ache in the back of his head. His limbs were heavy and stiff. His eyelids wouldn't open. Weakness lingered in every muscle, and he struggled to understand it. Trying to open his eyes again, he huffed in frustration as he managed only a flutter.

Panic surged up his chest, but he beat it down. He could hear Ananta now, speaking with Heema. This was his home, and neither of them sounded distressed. Worried yes, but they were safe. Focusing on his ears, he could hear a light rain on the roof, and it nagged at his memory. Something had happened. Small flickers of something crept up on him, but it wasn't enough. Holding in a grumble, he focused on those little flickers.

Something had happened. He remembered flames and the sharp glint of weapons. There was a face scowling at him, but it wasn't human. Similar, but not exactly human. It came back to him in short flashes. Keeping his eyes shut tightly, Lokpal waited as it all fell into place, but the shock of it made him gasp. Rudra and the Demons. He'd been pushed back and hit his head.

"Lokpal?" Heema called. "Can you hear me?"

"Yes," he answered. His voice was gruff but working. "I can hear you."

"Can you open your eyes?" Ananta asked. He heard her move over next to him. "How do you feel?"

"Tired," he said. "My eyelids are heavy."

"You slipped in the mud," Heema explained. "Hit your head."

"Just breathe slowly," Ananta added. "We're here."

Lokpal relaxed as his wives gently touched his shoulders and hands. Their presence was soothing in the face of the returning fear. There had been so many Demons. He'd heard stories of Demons in larger groups in the past, but around here he'd only heard reports of loners seeking food. He didn't know if they were exiles or scouts or how the Demon hierarchy worked, but he'd been unprepared for last night.

"I'm alright." Lokpal slowly opened his eyes. It was difficult. The desire to keep sleeping was intense, but he was aware of the ache at the back of his skull too much. "I'm alright."

"Be careful," Heema said.

Sitting up slowly, Lokpal held back a hiss of pain. Everything was a little blurry, but it slowly cleared as he blinked. The pain faded to an ache, and while he hated it, Lokpal took heart in the fact he was alive to hurt. It was a surprise. He'd been sure that Rudra was going to kill him and yet now he was home. Heema and Ananta thankfully moved back to give him some space.

Despite the fire, the house was a little chilled. Blankets were spread across his lap, and he was on the floor near the hearth. He looked around, minding his neck, but thankfully the ache wasn't centered there. Everything was how he left it.

"How long was I gone?"

"Only the night," Ananta replied. "We were lucky."

Daksha crawled towards him, her dark eyes glowing in the firelight and bright with glee. Smiling, Lokpal watched the little girl. Gratitude sank into his bones, and he reached out for her. She made a happy sound and sped towards him making him grateful that she was crawling rather than walking. He picked up his daughter, getting a relieved smile from his wives at the action.

Holding Daksha close, Lokpal stared into the low flames, trying to gather his thoughts. It was difficult. The memory of Rudra filled him with dread and a strange sense of pity that he couldn't shake. Something about his behavior and the odd black mark on his skin seemed wrong. Rudra was a fierce god, but he'd almost been erratic. His daughter tugged gently on his hair, and he smiled, allowing her to toy with the front section, but mindful not to let her near the back. His scalp still ached, and he didn't want any further aggravation to that part of his head.

"Lokpal?" Heema touched his shoulder gently. "What is it?"

"I'm not sure," he answered. "There were Demons, so many Demons." Both women gasped, and Ananta looked towards the door with fearful eyes. "But Rudra was there hunting them. We... crossed paths."

"You met Rudra?" Ananta's voice was weak with disbelief. "Are you certain?"

"Eight great arms, all carrying weapons. There was fire in his eyes, and he called it forth." Lokpal stared ahead into the flames, rubbing Daksha's back gently. His heart jumped as the memory became impossibly clear. "That storm was his arrival. He was hunting Demons."

"Then there won't be any more," Heema said hopefully.

"No, he said that many more appear each day," Lokpal said darkly. "But he didn't know why? Something is happening. Something dangerous." He set Daksha to the side despite the tiny girl's protest and started to stand. "I need to-"

"You need to rest!" Ananta rushed over and pushed down on his shoulders. "We were lucky that the fishermen found you! With this storm, who knows what could have happened to you!"

"There were so many Demons," Lokpal said. He started to shake his head, but a jolt of pain stopped the action. "I'm the protector of the islands, I need-"

"Rest!" Heema insisted. "You need to rest! You can't fight Demons with a head wound. You're lucky that you're even awake to argue!"

"He wasn't trying to kill me." Lokpal frowned as the idea fully formed. "He... I don't know." Sitting up straighter to stretch his back muscles, Lokpal looked towards the doorway. "He was angry at first that I was killing Demons, but then he said I was a mage. I'm not sure what it all means."

"Stay out of his way," Ananta said. "Please, just give Lord Rudra some distance. If he wants to hunt the Demons, then let him."

"Except he might not protect us," Lokpal said. "I don't want to learn that a Demon ate someone because Rudra was killing others."

"And there is no way to be sure that you won't be killing one Demon while another kills a villager." Ananta shook her head. "You can't be everywhere, Lokpal, but Rudra is a god."

"I know!" The words were sharper than he intended, and his own head protested at the loud sound. "I know, but something about him seemed... off. Like he was ill or-or, I don't know. I'm not sure what it was."

"Is this like the feeling that made you leave last night?" Heema asked.

"I- yes, there's just this certainty that I can't explain."

His wives exchanged worried glances as the silence stretch out around them. Daksha stirred in his arms, but the little girl was drifting off. Ojas was snuggled into a blanket a few feet away. It should have been reassuring, but the peacefulness of the home was an illusion, fraying at the edges, like fabric being unraveled. Lokpal waited for them to say something. He needed them to say something.

"What do you want us to say?" Anata asked. He wondered if he'd voiced that thought out loud.

Holding back a sigh, Lokpal carefully tugged the blanket off his legs and laid Daksha down on it. The little girl scowled in her sleep, but gripped the edge of the blanket and tugged it tighter against her. The knot under his lungs tightened. Images of the Demon's face flashed through his mind. They ate people. They ate other things of course, but they would eat his children if nothing was done.

"I don't know what you can say," Lokpal said. "I don't understand it myself. I don't expect you too, but I...I have to try and find out. Someone has to keep the villages safe and Rudra, I'm not sure he cares. He wants to hunt the Demons, but I don't think he cares about what happens to any of us."

Fear, horror, and resignation filled the features of his wives. The words tasted bitter, but they were true. Yet, Lokpal half regretted speaking to them. The truth was terrifying. He'd gotten in Rudra's way, and only this mage aspect seemed to save his life. Though he'd not left uninjured. The rain had nearly stopped now, but Lokpal still shivered at what might have happened if he hadn't been lucky enough to be found.

A voice from outside called to them. Lokpal looked sharply at the doorway while Heema held back a sigh. He started to stand, and thankfully neither of his wives stopped him. His legs quivered under him but

as he tried not to sound worried. "If I hear anything more, I'll let you know."

"Thank you, Marutta. I'll think on what you have told me."

"Just... focus on getting better," Marutta said. "It sounds like we may need you." Down the hillside, a pair of voices called up to them, and Marutta smiled. "That's my sons, Lokpal. Get some rest."

The man hurried down the hill, and Lokpal watched the flickering torches move away. Lingering by the doorway, Lokpal considered going inside. It was warm inside, his family was inside, but the answers weren't. There were too many questions. Too many thoughts were tugging him in different directions. Like a memory from a dream, Marutta's words hinted at something that he'd forgotten. Something that he was supposed to know. Unease grew and worry rooted in his gut. It would not be so easy to dismiss any of this now.

There were too many Demons in one area, and now a god had taken notice. Rudra's presence was not comforting. Lokpal starred out into the rain, his ears straining for the sound of thunder. The ache at the back of his head was no longer his greatest concern as he heard a distant rumble of thunder. He couldn't help but wonder if Rudra was hunting more Demons and what would happen if those strangers came. Nothing good, that much he was sure of.

13

Tracking Demons

Leaving the Desai house quickly revealed to Alex just how pleasant a home Lokpal's descendants had. It sat high on a hillside, surrounded by other beautiful buildings and trees that helped to block out the noises of the city. It didn't seem to be a true suburb to the extent that Alex was expecting. There were a few other houses, but it was clearly in the midst of businesses and other developments. Skyscrapers rose up just to the north of them with the harbors to the south. They were just on the edge of the densest construction.

"So where are we in terms of Mumbai's location?" Bran asked.

"We're in South Mumbai; it's the busiest section of the city and the main sector of what people think of as Mumbai. Now." Avani adjusted her sunglasses and pulled out her phone. "Let me give you my phone number and the house number in case we get separated."

"Uh... I'm afraid that my phone doesn't work as a phone over here," Alex said. She looked down at the phone. "In fact, I'm not sure how much longer it will work period." With her plan to make her brothers forget her in place, Alex's family plan was probably going to vanish soon. "I should probably get a global plan with the way we travel."

"Still, we can record the information," Nicki said. "Give us the address of the house so we can get back here too."

Avani did as instructed and Alex recorded the information without another word. "Now, Mumbai is huge," Avani said. "I've got money if we need to hire a taxi service so don't exhaust yourselves trying to follow the guide."

"Fair enough," Aiden replied. "Though we will be stuck directing some poor driver where to turn."

"I'll leave it up to you," Avani said. "But South Mumbai alone is 26 square miles."

"Lovely," Alex said. "Well, at least I'm wearing sneakers."

"You always wear sneakers," Nicki said.

"That's true, but with my life, I'm not going to risk having to fight invaders to the Iron Realm in heels."

The soft round of chuckles ended the dialogue for a bit. Walking together, the small group made their way north down a hill. In no time at all, they left the quieter side street and were following an extra wide boulevard. There were cars, trunks, and people all competing for a bit of space. The air was thick with heat and pollution, creating a dense layer of grime right in the air. It was countered by bursts of wind off the ocean that cleared the area between buildings. As they began to pass restaurants and Alex was assaulted with a million strange smells, she wasn't sure if she loved it or hated it here.

They followed the light down the busy streets of Mumbai. It reminded Alex of her family's trip to New York City when she was fifteen and the bright colors of SoHo. There were signs everywhere, people coming and going, and small displays scattered about. The buildings were a mixture of different eras and styles with some leaning towards gothic revival and others very modern. Some were towering over them with sleek lines, and others were much shorter apartment buildings with balconies decorated with bright hangings and laundry.

No one paid them much attention as there were other tourists on the street. Avani stayed close and kept pointing and talking about different places. Most of her words just washed over Alex as her gaze searched the alleys and crowds for any sign of Demons. She caught sight of historical and important looking buildings, but they just kept walking. With the sun constantly vanishing behind buildings, Alex had a hard time keeping track of their direction. At one point, Nicki passed around a water bottle and then Avani ducked into one of the shops and returned with two more before they resumed following the little ball of light.

"I hope we find it soon," Avani said. There was a note of deep worry in her voice. "We're getting awfully close to Dharavi."

"Dharavi?" Nicki repeated. "That sounds familiar."

"The slums." Avani looked around nervously, her gaze focusing on every dark alley. "The largest in Asia sadly. Almost a million people live there."

Alex stopped in her tracks. Turning to look at Avani, she waited for the other woman to correct herself. But she didn't. Avani's expression softened slightly. She downcast her eyes for a moment and sighed.

"Over half of Mumbai's population lives in slums. There are limited areas to expand in Mumbai since it's surrounded by water on three sides. So, we have areas that don't have running water and electricity. The city government doesn't recognize some of the slums, so they aren't entitled to water or sewer services." Avani squirmed at the attention. "People are working on it, but India has a huge population."

"I suppose there are really bad areas in the United States too," Nicki said.

"Not that bad," Aiden muttered. "How is that even possible?"

"There's a lot of factors," Avani said. "Look, it's bad, and those areas are where Demons are most active. If the light leads us there, then we have to be careful. Thankfully we aren't into the monsoon season yet."

"Have you been there before?" Bran asked. "Or is this just what you know from your family?"

"No, I've been there before. One of my cousins works with a medical program that takes vaccinations, medications, and food into the slums. I've volunteered with him several times." Avani forced a smile. "And it isn't all bad. There are development programs in the slums, and they have very dynamic informal economies, though that is why there is resistance to some of the development programs." Avani shook her head. "Anyway, we need to be careful. In general, it is a very peaceful area, but it is easy to get lost, and if there are Demons around then they could cause a lot of damage."

Exchanging a look with Bran, Alex was very aware of the discomfort building in her gut. Alex had never seen a slum. To be fair, she'd never spent much time in large cities. She was aware of homelessness and had seen plenty of that on the streets of Spokane, but the idea of a slum with a million people was difficult to wrap her brain around.

"So, when is the monsoon season?" Nicki asked Avani.

"It starts in June usually. We're lucky you came in May. This is our relief month. With any luck, we'll have things wrapped up before the worst of the wet season starts."

Images of heavy rain flashed through Alex's mind. The sound of constant heavy droplets on a solid roof and the sound of waves crashing against a distant shore. She missed the others talking as she clawed her way back into the present, filing the memory away. The small light was fluttering further down the street. In the shadows cast by the buildings, it became a little easier to see the light and Alex rubbed her sore eyes with a groan.

They came to an odd and sudden division in the city. Tall buildings vanished, and instead, they were looking into what was almost a hole. It was like part of the city had been pulled away to leave scraps behind and yet...

The buildings were made of pale dried mud and clay, planks of wood, and sheets of discarded metal. There was visible brick in places, and small balconies made of twisted metal. Clothing was hung out to dry on strung lines and over the edges of windows giving the otherwise brown and gray landscape vivid flashes of color. Avani was studying the area, but nothing looked too wrong. Alex couldn't help but stare at the people. She'd been expecting people covered in dirt and filth, but many of them were washed and wore tidy clothing. The streets were packed down dirt in most places, but there were slabs of concrete as well. Small huts and even a few tents were lined up in rows forming streets. There were hundreds of people moving down these unofficial, but clear roads in bright colors, talking, working, and laughing.

"This isn't what I was expecting," Bran said beside her. "Not at all."

"Well... they are still in a city," Aiden said. He sounded just as confused as them.

"Some places have illegal links to water and electricity," Avani explained. "Try not to stare. We need to find the Demons."

Looking down the street, Alex grimaced at the foul smell wafting down on the hot air. Piles of trash were mounded up against the buildings, half covering a massive pipe as children sorted through it. Around another corner, a pile of dead animals was sitting stacked up outside the door of a butcher's shop with a man guarding it and talking to a woman. There was a group of women sitting in a patch of shade weaving baskets out of folded up strips of plastic. All around them, the densely packed place was filled with people moving and working.

The light just kept moving through the small streets. A few people looked their way, but Avani smiled at some and continued speaking with Nicki in a calm voice. Alex wondered if they were used to people coming down here. She hoped not, it didn't seem right, but then again people were making things all over the place. Maybe it was a good thing.

"Easy, Alex," Aiden said. "I can hear the wheels grinding."

"I'm... not sure how to feel about this place," Alex said. "I hate the poverty, but there's also a community here."

"It is its own little city," Aiden said. "I see it too." He smiled a little and shrugged. "Still, they should have water and electricity. I know you've had plenty of lives without them, but in modern times they are pretty much necessary."

"Don't worry. I'm not going to start with the 'in my day' speeches."

"Yeah, that's probably good." Aiden's eyes were searching as they looked at her. Alex wondered what or rather who he saw but didn't dare ask the question. "That's not what we're here for," he added gently. "If there are Demons here who are turning militant than this is a horrible place for them to be. Too many people in one place. If something goes wrong..."

Aiden didn't finish the thought, but Alex's mind was all too helpful in providing some ideas. That was half of the problem with anything happening in a major city. Could they contain the collateral damage? They'd been lucky that the holes in Earth's defenses against the Sídhe opened near a smaller town, but now it seemed that Demons may also be pushing through near one of the world's largest cities.

The light led them to a small building at the far corner of one of the long streets. There was a massive pipe behind it and piles of plastic debris, but there were bright garments hung up to dry and a small worktable in the shade of an awning by the front door. Alex caught herself thinking it didn't look like the home of a Demon before she pushed that ridiculous thought away. Aiden and Nicki exchanged a look before marching to the doorway. Nicki all but pounded on the door which opened with a metallic squeak a moment later.

A woman was looking at Nicki in surprise as her eyes took in their little group. She started to speak but then sniffed at the air. Eyes widening, the woman jumped back and began to shut the door. Leaning forward, Aiden braced himself to keep the door open as Nicki shoved her foot forward. The woman's brown eyes flickered and darkened. Her dark skin shimmered just before she stumbled out of sight. The orb of light zipped inside and Nicki pushed her way forward before Alex could say anything. Avani made a worried sound and looked around, but no one was paying them any attention.

Rushing inside, Alex was expecting something more than what she found. The woman or rather the Demon was backed up against a wall. She looked a touch larger now, and her skin had darkened with a hint of blue, but otherwise, she looked mostly the same. Nicki and Aiden's hands were glowing, but everyone was still and just waiting.

It was a one-room hut with a bed in one corner, a shelf with cooking supplies, and a chamber pot. Depressing and small, but there were bits of art on the walls and another shelf with books and personal items. The Demon was glaring at them, but making no move for a weapon. Behind Alex, the door closed as the others stepped inside and out of sight.

The Demon scrambled for a window. A wave of yellow magic knocked it back onto the floor. Surprise at how easy this was warred with Alex's suspicions, but she jumped over to the prone Demon. Placing a foot on its neck, Alex raised her hands and pulled on her magic. Dark gray sparks spun from her fingertips, and the Demon's eyes widened further. It didn't move.

The Demon glared up at her. Its dark eyes were sharp with intelligence, anger, and resignation. It was enough to stay Alex's hand. She inhaled slowly and kept watching the Demon's expression. The Demon snarled a few words that Alex didn't understand. Her magic quivered, and a slight pressure in Alex's head alerted her that something was happening. Avani started to say something, but Bran shushed her. Narrowing her eyes, Alex pulled on more magic as the Demon started to speak.

"What?" the Demon snarled. "Just do it!"

"How long have you been here?" Alex asked. "In the Iron Realm, I mean."

She heard Avani gasp behind her, but the magician thankfully stayed quiet. Not taking her eyes off the Demon, Alex put a bit more pressure on her foot. The flutter of her magic was familiar, and Alex almost smiled as the translation spell kicked in to help her.

"Iron Realm?" The Demon chortled. "Is that what you mages call it?" It sneered up at her even as the fear lingered in its eyes. "I just call it Earth. Or rather Mumbai. I was born here. Right in this slum in fact!"

"Then what's happened?" Alex asked. "Our spell led us to where a group of Demons that attacked us this morning came from. If you were born here, why attack and start trouble?"

"I didn't want to!" The Demon lurched under Alex's foot but stilled after realizing what it had done. The air was thick with their fear now, but Alex didn't move to hurt it. The Demon settled back on the packed down dirt floor. "I didn't want to. I live here. I work in one of the small leather factories. I never wanted any trouble. But the new arrivals- they're different."

"New arrivals?" Alex repeated. "There are new Demons coming into this world?"

"Yes, from the homeworld, so they say. It doesn't matter to me, but they're trouble. They threaten and bully. They demand that any Demons in the area help them whenever they call."

"Why help them?"

"I'm afraid!" The Demon cried. "They'll kill us. They consider us 'tainted' by this world and disloyal. Of course, I'm disloyal! My family has lived amongst humans wearing our guises for centuries!"

Alex shifted her foot off the Demon's chest and stepped back. Lowering her hands, she allowed the sparks of magic to dissipate into the air as the Demon shuttled back across the floor and slammed its back into the far wall. It watched them carefully, not trusting the sudden change.

"Where is this new opening?" Alex asked. "And what do these Demons want?"

"I don't know where the opening is," the Demon said quickly. "I don't. They come to me and others for information on the human world or supplies. As for what they want... they said that the homeworld is dying."

A vision of a dark world covered in ash with a low light sun flashed in Alex's mind. For a split second, she could taste the ash and smell the years of decay. It was all too familiar. While the others were exchanging doubtful looks, Alex was aware of a chill crawling up her spine and a suspicion settling in the back of her mind. The image of the crumbling buildings and dead trees from the Sídhe homeworld was all too vivid in her memory.

"Alex?" Bran called. "What do you want to do?"

"Let her go," Alex said. She took another step away from the Demon. "I don't approve of you helping them, but I can sympathize with fear."

Avani was looking at her with assessing eyes. Alex wasn't sure if she was living up to her title or disappointing her. "If something is happening then I can understand their panic. Do you know anything else? Any details of what is happening?"

"No," the Demon whispered. "I don't know anything. They don't trust me."

"Do you expect to see them again?" Alex asked.

"Maybe... but probably not," the Demon admitted. "There are a lot of us and if they smell mages then they won't come close to my home."

"You can smell us?" Nicki wrinkled her nose. "Really?"

"Yes, you smell like iron, but different." The Demon shrugged helplessly. "I don't know anything. I swear."

"Any idea how many Demons have come through?"

"No, sorry no. At least a hundred. Their leader is some kind of military commander from the homeworld."

"So, it's a full invasion," Aiden said.

"Maybe, I don't know!" The Demon shook their head. "I don't know what's happening in the homeworld. I'm just a tool for them here. They'll kill me and the other Demons who were born here."

"Avani? Can you write down your phone number for her?" Avani blinked but dug through her purse until she found a bit of paper and a pen. She handed the torn off scrap to Alex who gave it to the Demon. "Please, call us if you hear anything more. If there is an invasion starting, then a lot of people stand to get hurt and not just humans."

Alex had no idea if the Demon would call. Judging from the baskets that were packed with personal items, she expected that this Demon was going to start running. The memory of the dead Sídhe world pushed its way forward again. Alex gestured to the doorway and led the others outside, all the while silently wishing the Demon luck.

14

Questioning the Way

Avani led them away from the slum quickly. No one was paying them much attention, but there was an urgency in Avani's stride that made them all move quickly. People were still working at their stations, people were moving products in and out, and children were carrying supplies to the small houses. A soft breeze made the hanging laundry flutter in the wind and the colorful decorations twist and swing. Their little group wasn't important, and thankfully the Demon they'd left behind them wasn't raising a fuss.

At first, all of them stayed silent, even though Alex could all but hear the wheels turning in their minds. She wished that Jenny and Lance had come. Alex's own brain was spinning in confusion and worry. Different pieces of the dreams and the Demon's statement tried to fit together, but it didn't seem right yet. The idea of a world dying was too big. Alex remembered reading something once that the human brain just wasn't built to handle large numbers. Empathy shut down because a person just couldn't comprehend millions dying. And for a world to die, Alex didn't want a number.

Sure, she knew it was possible. She'd watched more than a few disaster and world ending films. There was a weird thrill in watching it happen and then settling back into the comfortable reality of relative safety. Yet, if the vision of the dead Sídhe world was right and what the Demon said was true, then worlds did die. Thinking back to the Tree of Reality, Alex bit her lower lip. Those two branches didn't connect.

Earth, the Iron Realm, was the trunk of the tree. It was where the different branches linked together. The Demon and Sídhe branches didn't meet otherwise so how were both worlds dying? Was it the same thing or something entirely different? She needed more information. While she wasn't a science major like Bran or Aiden, even Alex knew when there just wasn't enough data. Of course, it could all be a red herring too.

"It might not be true," Bran said. Looking at him, Alex blinked, struggling for a moment to understand what he was saying. "The Demons might have lied to her to get her help. Or it might be a metaphor. A regime change that exiled them, their world ending, something like that."

"Do you really think that?" Alex almost smiled, it was like Bran could read her mind sometimes. And right now, it was comforting. "Does that seem right to you?"

Bran exhaled slowly, his eyes dancing around the street to take in the shops and decorations. "I don't know. I can't really wrap my head around the idea of a world dying, even though it is very possible. I guess it would make sense for the species to become refugees."

"But what could cause something like that?" Nicki asked. "I mean, Demons have some kind of magic, at least when they're in our world and they look pretty strong."

"Maybe some sort of plague," Aiden suggested. Then he suddenly stopped. "Shit! I've never thought about that! If living things can come through, then so can bacteria from other worlds. What if their diseases can spread to us?"

"Don't panic," Bran said. "We don't know enough about the transfer between worlds to be sure about what can survive. It's possible that most of the bacteria they carry are destroyed." Alex glanced over at him. His brow was slightly furrowed, and he didn't look convinced. "But then again, maybe their crossing over does bring new diseases over."

"I've always been unclear about the crossing," Avani said. "It always seemed like it shouldn't be possible... I mean matter cannot be created or destroyed, right?"

"Yes and no," Bran said. He rubbed the back of his neck. "That's the law of the conversation of matter, but there are exceptions. Again, it comes back to the fact that we don't really know how the travel between worlds works. We know that they come from places that have slightly different physical laws to our own and the collision of those laws is part of what generates the energy we know as magic."

"Right," Aiden agreed. "But we don't know what else might happen. That fact alone might mean that the whole thing is an exception to the laws of physics."

"Or, there might be a sort of transfer from our universe to where the being originated to balance everything out. A release of energy or something like that since we know that energy and mass can be converted into each other." Bran glanced at Alex and offered her a slight smile. "And again, the magic of the Iron Realm may very well have some defenses in place. For all we know, magic burns away anything living that isn't sentient so that diseases from other universes aren't spread here. Then again, different universes, so they might not even have diseases as we know them."

"My brain hurts," Nicki grumbled. "Sorry about the boys, Avani, they really can't help themselves."

"No, it was fascinating," Avani assured Nicki. "Though not my field of study."

"As interesting as it was, it is all just speculation right now." Bran sighed lightly. "I'd love to try and test some things, but with the danger of the various beings crossing over that's never an option. I'm sitting on a Noble Prize discovery and can't do anything with it."

"Poor baby," Nicki teased. "But seriously, let's not invite our world to start making holes in the fabric of the multiverse in some search for energy or resources. The Tree of Reality already has the Sídhe; it doesn't need the human race."

Alex shivered at the reminder of the Sídhe. "Do you ever wonder what started that expansion for them?" Alex asked. The others all turned to look at her. "I mean... think about it. We at least know that it is possible to survive crossing between worlds, but did they? What would drive a being to leave their homeworld and start expanding."

"Maybe something happened," Aiden suggested. "That's what you're hinting at right? Maybe climate change, some horrible asteroid impact, or maybe it was a scientist who went through and found new worlds to take over. The Sídhe's culture is different from our own."

"Exactly," Nicki said. "We can't assume that the attitudes grew out of something unlike our own. Besides, colonialism drove European powers to conquer and slice up huge chunks of Asia, Africa, and the Americas for centuries. What inspired the Sídhe might not be so different."

Avani nodded in agreement, her eyebrow rising a little as she almost laughed. Of course, she'd be more familiar with the history of colonialism than any of them. Holding in a sigh or maybe a groan of frustration, Alex toyed with the belt loops of her jeans and tried to find something to maintain her focus. With the guiding light gone, its job done, they were relying on Avani to navigate their way.

"There's a lot to consider." Bran sounded far too calm. It grated on Alex's nerves even as she was grateful for it. A brief flickering memory of another young man with the same name tugged at her. "But we need to keep it in mind. Truth or not, the Demons are using this story in an attempt to control the native Demons."

"Native Demons?" Avani repeated. She was frowning back at Bran, pouting a little.

"They were born here," Bran replied. "I'm not sure what else to call them. They aren't a natural species, but the Iron Realm is the only world they've ever lived in."

"Classifications aren't the issue right now," Nicki said smoothly. She was smiling at Avani, walking alongside her crush at the front of the group.

None of it was reassuring, but Alex let the voices of her friends wash over her. It was comforting and helped dull the voices at the back of her mind. Some soft suggestions and questions that weren't fully formed came forth, but Alex filed them with her own growing list. Her fingers twitched for a pencil and paper to start taking notes. A salesman on the street tried to draw them into his shop, and Avani quickly waved him off.

"Alex?" Bran called. "You alright?"

"Just trying to process." Alex shrugged. "Not sure what to think."

"Yeah... you're not wrong you know. There is something to the question about why someone would risk traveling to another world. Even if you don't know that the physics of the world are different... it's still a terrifying idea. And if you do know that the physics are different, well then it's insane. Gravity being different, a different amount of matter or energy, there's so much that could go wrong. It's scary when you think about it."

"I've never thought about it that way," Nicki said. The redhead was frowning thoughtfully, causing a furrow between her eyebrows. "I've always thought of the Sídhe as having a manifest destiny ideology. Like culturally, after they united their own world, they started conquering other worlds. Colonialism for slaves and resources."

"Except that they aren't always politically united," Alex said. "Back in the tunnel, I overheard mentions of princes and Morgana said once that they aren't always so united."

"Then maybe the conquests of other worlds for slaves was a way of gaining power," Nicki suggested. "Europe had several wars as part of the process of carving up the continents so that wouldn't mean it was impossible."

"Maybe," Aiden said. "Or maybe there is more than we know going on here."

"Not to dismiss all this," Avani said. "But it doesn't change the fact that them being in our world can have some bad repercussions. I know that nowadays our world has Sídhe and Demons living in it full time, but that's why there is always a little magic. Massive numbers coming through, for whatever reason, is dangerous."

"You're not wrong." Bran nodded in agreement. "Especially since the Queen and Arthur are rallying the Sídhe and trying to open the Iron Gates at the same time that apparently more Demons are coming through."

"Let's just hope that no Dragons start showing up," Nicki said. "I like Emrys and all, but that is the last thing we need."

"Wait, Dragons?" Avani asked. She leaned closer to Nicki and Alex could barely hear her. "There really are Dragons? I thought that was just mythology inspired by dinosaur fossils."

"Well, I can't say no to that for sure," Nicki said. "But, there is a Dragon in Wales. He lives in a magical cavern beneath a mountain as the guard of another nasty Dragon."

"They can't die in our world," Bran said. "So, they're just stuck underground hiding. But apparently, Emrys has used the bit of magic surrounding him to watch the outside world. It is probably the only reason he isn't crazy at this point."

Alex made a small noise of agreement. Her mouth had dried out painfully, and she kept rubbing her tongue against the roof of her mouth. Drumming her fingers against her belt, Alex scanned the crowd again. She didn't see any Demons, but they might be there. Watching them and following them to the Desai house. More questions were occurring to her that she should have asked the Demon. But she was also afraid to go back.

"Alex?" Bran said. "You okay?"

"I don't know." Alex told herself to breathe, but her muscles fought against the command. Lightheaded and confused, Alex swayed for a moment before Bran took her arm and kept her upright. "It's a lot to think about. I need time to process."

"Have you seen anything in your dreams?" Bran asked. His voice was lower, and he looked carefully forward where Aiden and Nicki were arguing lightly while Avani chuckled.

The words dried up in her mouth. They burned the back of the throat. Her eyes shifted to look around them at the living city. "I'm not sure," Alex said. "I've seen some things, but nothing that I understand yet."

Bran nodded in understanding, but guilt welled up in her chest. That wasn't honest; it was deflecting too much of what she'd seen. While on some level, Alex was very afraid that she knew.

"I'll try scrying when we get back," Bran said. "I'm not sure what I'm looking for, but maybe it will help. We don't know enough yet. To fight or to be worried."

"Right," Alex agreed. "More information. Scrying is a good idea." She exhaled slowly and her muscles relaxed. "Thanks."

"We'll get through it," Bran said.

"Don't make that promise," Alex said. "You can't keep it."

"We'll stay together and work through the problems. No matter what comes."

"Bran... you've already died once."

"At least once," Bran said. "But I'm Buddhist. Reincarnation is part of my understanding of the universe." He was smiling gently, but Alex could see the worry in his eyes. "We're with you, Alex, and we'll help you with whatever is happening."

"First things first, we need to find out what is happening," Alex said. "And that won't be easy. Not unless you're interested in traveling to other worlds."

"No, I'd rather not." Bran shuddered. "The effects coming into our world are bad enough to observe, I'd rather not see what happens in reverse." Then he paused and blinked rapidly. "Then again, our world is the trunk of the Tree of Reality. Maybe it would actually be easier for us to go into other worlds. I do wonder if there is a reason that the connected worlds form the shape of a tree, given that the branches have some commonality, maybe there is significance to the trunk."

"What are you thinking?" Alex asked.

"Now I'm not sure," Bran said. There was a soft frown on his face, and his green eyes were glinting with... something. "Just an odd little idea. I'll have to think about it more."

"Anything useful?"

"Maybe or maybe just something to help us better understand what is happening." Then he shook his head. "Anyway, do you want to call Merlin and Morgana when we get back?"

"I probably should. We've been attacked and had to use the Iron Chalice. I would have liked more information, but... that doesn't seem like it is going to happen."

"Hey!" Nicki's voice suddenly called. "You two hungry?" They looked forward, and Nicki was pointing into a building. "Come on, Avani's buying lunch. I don't know about you, but I'm starving."

Bran laughed lightly and gestured Alex forward. Nicki was shifting eagerly from one foot to the other, and Alex let her friend's urging amuse her. She wondered just what was going through Bran's head, but could barely handle what was going on in her own right now. The sense of being swallowed by a rising tide and unable to move crept up on her. There was just so much that she didn't know and it was finally sinking in. Even the soft whispers of her past lives couldn't offer anything useful.

15

Strangers in His Midst

621 B.C.E. Mazagaon, India

Two more Demons dead and still no idea of where they were coming from. Lokpal bit back a hiss as Heema gently applied fresh wrapping to the long scrap across his back. He was seated next to the fire, letting the warmth soothe his sore muscles even as his wife's small breaths of displeasure made him nervous. Across the room, Ananta was grinding some grain while the children napped in their beds.

"It's healing nicely," Heema said. "Still, you need to be careful, Lokpal." Soft lips brushed over the skin between his shoulder blades, grounding and comforting. "Please don't come home with injuries that can't heal."

"I promise that I will always do my best to come home safely."

"That's not the promise I really want, but I suppose it will have to do."

"You knew that you were marrying the village guard."

"Yes." Heema's hands vanished, and she sighed. "Yes, but at the time we weren't expecting a horde of Demons to come into the area. You were only supposed to fight off bandits and maybe one or two Demons throughout your whole life."

"I know," Lokpal said. On his back, the injury stretched with a slight burn, but it was healing well. "I wish things were different, but I have to keep the village safe." Turning around, he caught Heema's hand and met her worried gaze. "I have to do all I can to keep my family safe." Looking over at Ananta, he caught her eyes and saw love and resignation there. "But, with the growing danger, I've decided to ask for volunteers to train. I'm hopeful that I can get one or two recruits to help."

"Let's hope so." Heema didn't sound convinced. Her hand trembled in his and Lokpal gave it what he hoped was a reassuring squeeze. "Given the number of Demons in the area, you may have trouble finding allies."

"I might," he agreed. "But one man against all these Demons is likely to-" He cut himself off. "A group of trained men stands a better chance of stopping Demons before they do any harm. We've been lucky so far that I've been able to stop them all before they ate someone."

"Shhh," Ananta said. "Don't wake the children to such talk."

Sheepishly, Lokpal nodded. He kept his breathing even and shallow, letting himself adjust to the tightness of the bandages wrapped around his chest. They were already itchy, the fabric confining and rough against his skin, but it would keep the wound covered. Still, that fact wasn't enough to keep his fingers from twitching with the desire to scratch the skin beneath the bandage. He shifted and earned a knowing look from Heema. Her eyes were brighter now, amusement pulling at the corners of the lips, and Lokpal smiled in return.

"Lokpal!" The call came from outside. Both Heema and Anata frowned towards the doorway, but Heema picked up his shirt. With gentle motions, she helped him pull it over his head and adjusted it. "Lokpal!"

"A moment," he called back. In the corner Ojas made a soft sound and Lokpal grimaced. Heema just shook her head. "Thank you." Leaning forward, he kissed her forehead quickly before moving to the doorway. He paused to grab his sword and secured it on his belt.

The sunlight made him blink a few times, but his gaze settled on the pair of men in front of his hut. Both looked stunned and nervous. Lokpal's hand went to his sword, already bracing for a Demon attack.

"Yes, Uttara?" he asked, addressing the older of the pair. "What brings you here? Is there a problem?"

"I saw Rudra today." His voice was still stunned, and his eyes were frozen wide open. "It was..."

"What did you see?" Lokpal kept his voice calm and even. He stepped away from the house and looked at the second man who seemed stuck in a haze. "Please, tell me, Uttara."

"He was fighting Demons. There were so many of them. At least a dozen." Uttara shook his head. "It was terrifying, we turned around and came back to the village as quickly as we could!"

"Where was this?"

"The small island to the south. The one with all those caves!" Uttara turned and pointed out into the sea, his finger and his gaze settling on one of the smaller islands. "There was smoke and lightning, and-" He shivered again and spun back to Lokpal. "Where are all these Demons coming from? My father never heard of so many!"

"We've had years without Demons!" The other fishermen added. "What is happening?"

"I don't know," Lokpal admitted. They all fell silent and shared worried looks. "I understand your fears. I do."

"Then do something!" Uttara begged.

"Now stop that!" Ananta snapped. Lokpal turned to find his first wife marching out onto their porch. "My husband is injured from killing two Demons yesterday! How dare you suggest that he isn't fighting to protect you!" Her voice rang down the hillside before vanishing into a heavy second of deafening silence.

"We support him for that reason," Uttara muttered.

Ananta gave him a dark look, and the man shrank into himself. Lokpal brought a hand up to his mouth, rubbing his chin thoughtfully and covering his smile. Pleasure filled his chest and the ache in his back dulled. The dull headache that he'd been dealing with since the first Demons appeared even retreated, giving him a moment of bliss.

"And he is fighting to keep you safe," she said firmly. "Now, I believe a delivery of fish was due yesterday."

Uttara backed away and nodded, his eyes darting around the area. "Yes," Uttara said. "Of course. I'll make sure that it is here tonight."

"Thank you." Ananta's tone was pleasant now. "That would be appreciated. And you can start spreading the news that Lokpal is willing to train young men to help defend against this Demon incursion."

"I will." Uttara actually looked a little relieved at the news. Not that Lokpal expected him or any of his sons to volunteer. "Thank you."

"Thank you for the information."

Lokpal watched the pair walk away. Uttara was talking to his partner who seemed to be finally coming out of his daze. Wondering just what they had seen, he turned towards the south on instinct, but of course, the island wasn't in view. Lokpal couldn't remember the last time he'd been out to that island. There wasn't a village there. If memory served, there was a small dock and a shelter building for fisherman who were caught out in that area in a storm. Rumors said that there'd been a village there long ago, but Lokpal wasn't certain of it.

"Please don't go out to the island," Heema said. "Last time you crossed paths with Rudra..."

"I won't," he promised. "I just want to get a clear view of it."

"You won't be able to see much," Ananta said. Her frown was slightly suspicious.

"I know, I just want to make sure that everything isn't on fire." Lokpal managed a small smile. "That's all, I promise. If Rudra is killing most of the Demons, then I am happy to let him, especially if they stay on the cavern island."

They weren't sure if they could believe him. Grimacing at their expressions, Lokpal reminded himself that they'd had a difficult last few weeks. The rainy season had helped keep the Demons at bay, but there was an awareness that the next fight was coming. It hadn't been this way when he'd married each of them. He hoped that they didn't regret marrying him, but wouldn't blame them. They hadn't been prepared for this.

"I promise," he repeated. "I'm trying to be careful."

Ananta sighed. Her eyes were shining with tears that she didn't allow to fall. Instead, she nodded and leaned forward to kiss his cheek. Then, without a word, she went into the house. Heema was silent for a moment before she looked towards the south herself.

"If you decide that you need to go, please come home and tell us." Her voice was entirely too soft.

"I will, I swear, I am just checking. I have no desire to fight a Demon today. I was lucky in the last fight, and I'm not at my best. I know that, but I need to check."

"One of us could-"

"Please, don't, Ananta. You know that I couldn't run the risk. I'll be back soon. I'm just stretching my legs."

The look she gave him was doubtful, but a soft sigh of resignation escaped her. Watching her return to the house, Lokpal was acutely aware that he needed to hurry. Worry was written in every muscle of her body, and it was too much to hope that it would improve in his absence. He scanned the house and the yard quickly for any threats lurking in the shadows before he began making his way south.

The walk did little to clear his head. That odd need to be somewhere was back and worse than ever. Now it was like something was jumping around in his chest. His skin was too tight beneath the bandage, and despite the warm humidity hanging in the air, he felt dried out and cold. A few people were on the path and nodded to him before hurrying off. Another annoying side effect of the number of Demons appearing in the area; no one wanted to be around the village warrior very long. He understood. There were nights that he considered sleeping somewhere else so as not to draw danger to his family.

Up ahead there was a sudden splash of water. Lokpal blinked as he tried to understand the source of the noise. Then voices came down the path, one of them loud and speaking an unfamiliar language. His stomach tightened, and Lokpal hurried over to a nearby fig tree. It was difficult to reach the lowest branch, but he pulled himself up onto the narrow branches. For a moment, he doubted that it would hold him and scrambled toward the trunk. The branch held and he kept himself hidden behind the veil of leaves. His hand went to his sword hilt, and he waited for the Demons to appear.

It wasn't Demons. Instead, the strange sounds were coming from a pair of humans. They were definitely human. Leaning out of the tree, Lokpal watched the pair as they walked up the path. They hadn't noticed him yet, and he carefully took them in. There was a man and woman, but their body language didn't suggest they were a couple. The woman had long brown hair that was braided up into a bun and green eyes. The man had curly gray hair and brown eyes. Their skin, however, was paler than that of any being save Rudra that he had ever seen.

His heart jumped against his ribcage. A laugh of relief bubbled up in his chest but was quickly followed by worry. Rudra hunted Demons just as the rumors said this pair did and Rudra was dangerous. This pair might also be dangerous. He watched them follow the path past him before carefully starting to climb down from the tree. They were talking in low voices, but he didn't recognize the words. The woman's tone was tense and frustrated while the man seemed much calmer. The man reached over and squeezed the woman's shoulder. She sighed and said something in a calmer voice before pushing his hand away.

Easing himself out of the tree, Lokpal flinched when one of the branches snapped in his hand, finally giving out under the weight. The woman spun around, her sharp green eyes meeting his own and Lokpal's stomach dropped. There was a tingle across his skin, and the world fell away.

He was on some sort of hill. Ahead of him, the seas sparkled in the light of the sun. A cool breeze ruffled his hair and carried the thick scent of the ocean and salt into his nose. Distantly, he heard strange, unfamiliar voices and music. They echoed around him, sending a strange, familiar shiver up his spine.

Then he was back on the path. The woman was still in the same place, but the man had moved closer even as he kept his eyes down. Lokpal had just enough time to steady himself before the man raised his eyes to look at him. It happened again. There was a strange sensation spreading over his skin, and something pulled him down.

He was in a forest, but the trees were unfamiliar. Large branches reached towards the sky, covered with small bright green leaves. Birds were chirping around him, their song filling the forest, but none of the sounds were known to him. He turned around quickly, searching for any signs of buildings or other people. There was nothing, just the forest.

The vision ended as quickly as it had started. Panting softly, Lokpal shook his head and braced himself. His senses were still hazy. The real world returned too slowly for him and left him exposed. Yet, as he found himself looking at the pair, they were watching him patiently. The man even had a slight smile on his face. Lokpal wasn't sure he trusted it but didn't draw his sword.

"What was that?" he heard himself ask.

"That was a Connection," the man replied. "It is a pleasure to meet a fellow mage. I am Merlin, and this is Morgana. We understand that you are having trouble with some unusual creatures."

Staring at them, Lokpal opened his mouth, but no sounds came out. The woman raised an eyebrow and Lokpal had the sudden desire to draw back. He didn't. Instead, he swallowed and licked his lips.

"You understand me?"

"Yes," Merlin said. "We can understand you."

"But earlier you were speaking- never mind." Lokpal shook his head. "Are you mages?"

"Indeed, we are," Morgana said. She was smiling a little now. "Why don't you tell us about your problem."

"Uh... yes, I was just on my way to check the southern island." He gestured down the path. "A fisherman reported seeing Rudra fighting Demons there."

"Rudra?" Morgana repeated.

"The god," Lokpal explained. "He's the Lord of-"

"An Old One then," Morgana dismissed.

"But fighting Demons," Merlin said. "That's a good sign."

"Maybe." Morgana took a few steps towards Lokpal. "But a mage here amongst Demons and an active Old One. I'd say that we got here just in time."

"Can you help me fight the Demons?" Lokpal asked. "I don't understand who or what you are, but there are too many Demons here now, and they have to be stopped."

Merlin smiled at him with warm brown eyes and nodded. "Yes, that is why we came here. Magic guided us to you." He took a step forward and studied Lokpal for a moment. "What is your name, lad?"

"Lokpal."

"Well then, Lokpal. Let's check on this island, and you can tell us what you know. And we will tell you about mages."

16

Looking In and Out

Alex was used to the dreams now. She was almost used to needing a moment when she woke to remember where she was and who she was. The movement and sensation of her own body were odd now after a night of the dreams which she attributed to having been male in all her other lives. Lochan's words while kind and soothing were not enough to counter the confusion.

Her hand would reach for a sword that wasn't there. The smooth and soft modern fabrics were too light and strange, leaving her exposed. Even the taste of the air was unfamiliar now. Dreams would linger, and Alex would sort them out the best she could. Sometimes it was someone she was familiar with. Sif and other blonde beings along with a Hammer were easily recognized as memories of Thor. The damn ship was Cuthbert's, and flashes of a younger Morgana were from Arto. Sometimes there were lines of Nazi soldiers or children parading while their heart ached, but others were unfamiliar.

There was smoke in a forge, but then there was a forest aflame. They remembered faces, but the places were all wrong. Alex didn't always know where she was or who she was. She still didn't know how many lives she'd had. Bran was right, in real life, sometimes there were questions that were never answered. Making it all worse now were flashes of a dying world that kept pushing its way forward, turning the already confusing dreams into nightmares. Book burning blurred into an ash-covered landscape. Hillsides wavered and the trees crumbled. It made the confusion of waking even worse.

Catching her breath, Alex focused intently on the ceiling. The fear of what she'd see if she closed her eyes slowly ebbed away. Focusing on the events of yesterday, Alex sighed in disappointment. Thus far, they'd learned next to nothing. Merlin and Morgana had no information to offer and scrying hadn't gotten them anything either. Alex groaned and focused her thoughts on the room.

For now, the room was beginning to brighten. Alex shifted just enough to stretch her back before relaxing into the mattress. It was high quality, far better than anything she'd slept on in her other lives. Her fingers brushed over the sheets, and she exhaled slowly, grounding herself in the present. She couldn't remember the actual date but repeated the month and year to herself for good measure.

Staring at the ceiling like it had answers, Alex began to review what she could remember from the most recent dream. She smiled at the vague flashes of a younger Morgana chasing her- them over a hillside. It was strange, Alex knew that even then Morgana had already been part Changeling and loyal to the Queen of the Sídhe. Despite that and their age difference, she and Arto had loved each other very much. So much that Morgana chose Arto and the Iron Realm. She'd kept choosing them for the last three thousand years.

The dreams were fading, but Alex still tried to identify the different lifetimes. She wondered if she'd ever have normal dreams again. The odd and random sort that other people had, and she hadn't had for... she wasn't even sure now. Alex knew that she'd used to have dreams like that. When she'd gotten her first retail job, she'd dreamt about the cash register and cleaning the store for days as it lodged itself into her mind. Yet now, her brain was too full of different lifetimes. There was no room for anything else.

"That's a cheerful thought." Alex kept her voice low. It was early still, and the others were hopefully resting. "Keep it together, Alex. This life is yours for now."

The words weren't that comforting, but she knew what she meant and sat up. Rolling her shoulders, Alex inhaled slowly and folded her legs under her. The muffled sounds of the city were actually a bit soothing in the quiet house. Alex focused on her meditation exercises. She'd neglected them lately, but today it calmed her. Small snippets of her dreams were still clear in her mind. The old Bran, not her Bran, laughing with Gofiben and Galath made her sad and happy at once.

Blue light shimmered at the edge of her vision, illuminating the blackness behind her eyelids. Alex tried to let herself drift off, but the soft whispers of her other lives were weighing her down like small anchors. They wrapped around her like chains. Shivering, Alex pushed away the stray thought of the Iron Chain, firmly reminding herself that it was destroyed. Her mother's face flashed in front of her, but it was already becoming hazy. Alex was aware of tears gathering at the edges of her eyes. Her lips pressed together tightly, and it was difficult to breathe. The moment passed slowly, but it did pass.

Swallowing, Alex brushed away the tears. A sob caught in her throat and Alex shivered. She looked to the side at her phone. For a moment, Alex didn't move. Then she snapped up the phone and accessed the gallery within seconds. Photos of her family looked up at her. Awkward shots from Christmas of her and her brothers in front of the Christmas tree stood out. One of her parents in the kitchen working on Christmas cookies. One photo had the family golden retriever, Anne, jumping up onto her lap while she nearly fell over in surprise. Alex hoped that whatever Morgana had planned would include Anne. The idea of the dog being left behind was too sad, and she didn't want to risk a dog to the teeth of the Sídhe hounds.

Alex tried to meditate for a few minutes, but the ache in her chest wasn't easing. Tears were still prickling at her eyes, but a few sniffs were keeping them at bay. She considered pulling on her magic and binding the pain again. However, as she looked out the window and watched more light spread through the room, she couldn't muster the desire. Something about the tears dripping down her cheeks was right. Her fingers tightened in the blankets. Alex allowed herself a few quiet moments. She flicked through more of the photos. They were mostly recent, but she had a few older ones as well. Suddenly a longing for her mother's photo albums struck her and Alex flinched at the realization that they'd have to be edited by magic or completely taken from her brothers.

"Shit."

Unwilling to stew, Alex swung her feet off the bed and put her phone back on the side table. She dressed quickly and unbraided her hair only to tie it up into a ponytail. Her feet were quiet against the thick carpet running down the center of the hallway. Alex moved through the house quietly, looking at the different paintings, trinkets, and photos scattered about. Perhaps it was rude, but she was content to blame the burning curiosity on Lokpal. It was distracting. Alex embraced it, studying the faces in the different photographs and smiling every time she was able to identify the people. There were many she didn't know, especially from the large family photographs, but Gita, Lochan, and Avani were welcome sights.

She found a set of double doors that led out onto a large balcony. A table and sun chair were in one corner, and a large flowering plant of some sort was on the other side of the doorway. Despite the hustle and bustle of Mumbai, the balcony had a view out over the water. There was a small green island front and center in her view. An odd flutter in her chest surprised Alex, and she heard Lokpal whisper something about Shiva, but it wasn't clear. Staring at the island, Alex tried to make sense of her emotions even as she glanced at some of the ships coming and going in the harbor despite the early hour.

"Good morning, Alex." The voice was unexpected but familiar enough that Alex just turned to find Lochan stepping out onto the balcony. "Lovely morning."

"Yes, it is," Alex agreed. "And good morning to you."

"I confess that it is rare I have company so early." Lochan was carrying a mug of tea which he set down on the small table in the corner by the chair. "Not that it is unwelcome."

"I hope I'm not intruding."

"I said that the company wasn't unwelcome." Lochan studied her and frowned slightly. "Are you not sleeping well?" Lochan asked before taking a sip of his tea.

"I've just got a lot in my head," Alex replied. She kept looking out towards the small hill of green. "I sleep, but I always dream."

"Ah, the body rests, but the mind does not." Lochan hummed in understanding. "I see."

"I'm fine. It's just... memories that I'm still sorting."

"I would be honored to listen if you wished to talk."

"It's getting easier," Alex assured him. "Really, it is. There are moments when the weirdness of it hits me, but... I don't feel like I'm going to be washed away."

"You lost your parents recently, did you not?"

"Did Sif tell you that?"

"She mentioned that she was concerned for you."

"That's not at all weird." Alex forced a laugh and looked back towards the harbor. "My Old One ex-wife being worried about me. That's sweet of her, but it is getting easier. Sometimes it hits me. This morning I looked at some photos of them. It hurt, but it wasn't as bad as I thought it would be."

"Pain heals, but you have to let it. That can't be forced."

"No, I suppose not," Alex said. "But after so many lifetimes, it just seems like it should be easier."

"Loss and the fear of death are deeply human traits. No matter how many times you are born, you are always a human."

"Which is a poor way to have things work." Looking back at Lochan, Alex smiled a bit. "Having some memories and knowledge would be useful. Might have kept some bad things from happening."

"Or the sense of power and the knowledge of the scale of your existence might have made things worse."

"Fair point."

It was strange being made to feel like a little kid again. Sure she had the memories of men who had lived over the course of three thousand years in her head. She could remember the way the sun caught the water of the fjord near Thor's home. She could remember when Arto had first presented the idea of the Iron Gates. There were so many little moments in her head from so long ago and yet Lochan just cut through all of it.

"How has your family remembered all this?" Alex asked. "How have you held onto Lokpal? It was such a long time ago. Civilizations have risen and fallen in the span of time since his death."

"Well obviously we are not Lokpal's only descendants," Lochan said. He was smiling at her with glittering dark eyes. "I would not dare even attempt the math to estimate how many descendants a man who lived so long ago would have." Lochan hummed slightly. "To be honest, we are not sure which wife we descend from. Possibly both if there were cousin marriages in the early years."

"Wait, uh... which wife?" Alex frowned, something rebelling at the idea even as she intellectually acknowledged it. Two faces briefly played across her memory, but they vanished too quickly. "You don't mean that he remarried, do you. He had multiple wives."

"It was not uncommon at the time. Our stories record two wives though there may have been others. While there are things we remember, there is much about Lokpal we do not know."

"You could ask Shiva."

"In my youth, I considered it, but deemed it too rude." Lochan made an odd thoughtful sound. "We try not to presume, and we rarely see him outside of times of concern. My father only met with Lord Shiva twice during his tenure as the head of the family."

"Still, I don't think Shiva would mind."

"Well, should you decide to ask him for details to help you sort all those memories, I would be happy to sit in. But please, Alex, remember that our magic is but a flicker to you. Shiva may not be of this world, but he has helped defend it for centuries. He is known as a god to many around the world and respect is natural to us."

"That makes sense; Shiva is part of your culture." Alex smiled and tapped her fingers on the railing of the balcony. "When I first learned that Professor Cornwall and Professor Yates were Morgana le Fey and Merlin I had trouble dealing with it. In fact, I tried to reject magic. Obviously, that didn't work well."

"You were born with a great burden."

"Yeah, but at least I know that I occasionally have peaceful lives." Alex was very aware of her throat tightening. "It's strange to know that when I die, I'll come back."

"I suppose to a western mind that is a strange thing."

Alex smiled and looked at Lochan with a raised eyebrow. "Do you think that people really, completely believe in reincarnation?"

"Do you think that people really, completely believe in an afterlife?"

"I don't know," Alex admitted. "My family wasn't religious. I saw depictions of Heaven in movies, and it seemed nice. I suppose on some levels I believe in it or at least want it to be real."

"I would say that the belief in reincarnation has the same variations. Some will deeply believe in it while others will embrace it as something they hope is real." Lochan joined her at the railing. "At least, you understand now the reason for your reincarnation. It may be a harsh path, but at least you have the Grand Mages to watch over you and allies that seek to aid you no matter the lifetime."

"Yes." Alex inhaled slowly and let the words sink into her mind. "You have a talent for saying things in such a way that they make sense."

"Well, I am an old man who has been trained in magic since I was a child, I suppose that leaves some impressions. While I wasn't born with a natural gift of magic, I access it by opening myself to the flow of energy in the world. That is the way of the magician."

"Thank you, though, for talking to me. That's been one of the harder things since... well, since the beginning almost, but especially since I found out that I was the Iron Soul."

"I'm sure the recent deaths of your parents didn't help."

"No," Alex agreed. "I'm trying, but sometimes... it's hard to keep things straight. The different lives are getting easier, and the grief is... well not fading."

"Livable," Lochan said. "I remember. It becomes livable. You stop being surprised by the absence of a person or people."

"That's a good way to put it." Alex's mouth tingled and her stomach twisted. The urge to wrap magic around the painful flutter in her chest was overwhelming. She suppressed it. Pushed the desire away and let it hurt for a long silent moment. It wasn't just the absence that hurt, the knowledge that she couldn't see them again, it was also the guilt. "I'm getting used to it. At least I think I am."

"You spoke with Merlin and Morgana yesterday, did you not?"

"I did, but not about that."

"Ah, did they have anything to say about the Demons?"

"Merlin wasn't sure. I don't think he's worried about it beyond the invasion. Morgana... I'm not sure. She was happy to hear that we're safe, but didn't have any insight." Her fingers tightened around the balcony railing. "It feels like we aren't getting anywhere. Yesterday created more questions than it resolved. Those Demons found us and more will too. Yet we still don't know what is going on."

"You have plans," Lochan reminded her. His tone was soothing once again, sinking over her shoulders. "We discussed all this last night, Alex. I agree that scrying is the way forward."

"But right now, I'm not sure that I trust what I see." Looking out into the water, she let her eyes settle on the island once again. Lochan hadn't countered her remark and Alex didn't want him to. "What can you tell me about that island?" Alex pointed out towards the small green hill rising out of the water. "It seems familiar. Nothing else does, but it does."

"That is Elephanta Island." Lochan was smiling again. Alex was beginning to dislike that smile. "Also called the Place of Caves though its ancient name was Gharapuri." None of the names were familiar to Alex. "While I do not know the details, I do know that Lokpal spent a great deal of time there with Shiva." He gestured around them. "Mumbai sits on an area that was once all islands and water, but that island has remained much the same."

"Place of Caves." Alex blinked as flickers of walls with carvings in them flashed before her. "There are decorated caves."

"Indeed, though the caves are more sophisticated now than they would have been in Lokpal's time, but I suppose he would have lived to see some of the earliest artwork." Lochan looked over at her. "You remember?"

"Maybe, but it might not be from Lokpal." Alex tried to smile but didn't manage it. "I might have had another life that saw it. Sorting it all out is difficult."

"I would imagine. You can't see yourself; you see what they saw."

"Exactly." Alex leaned forward on the railing, her eyes still locked on the island. "How far is it?"

"Ten kilometers from Mumbai by ferry, a little farther from here, but as you can see we have a view of the island."

"Is that why you live here?"

"Well, old stories say that Lokpal lived on this very hill." Lochan chuckled again. "I rather doubt that, but yes, being able to see the island is comforting. I believe that Shiva slumbers in the nearby waters. It was a site of worship for him."

"Do Demons go there?"

"No, not in any records we have. While it may not look like much, it is a stronghold of Shiva and his allies." Lochan's tone turned harder. "Shiva would not tolerate them going there. One thing to remember Alex is that while Shiva is good and a benefactor of society, he carries an aspect of death."

"The Destroyer."

"Yes, natural and necessary, but also dangerous."

"I understand."

And she did. Alex exhaled slowly and smiled. Death wasn't so bad. She understood it, and surprisingly, it was comforting. Someday, she would die, and the pain of Arthur's betrayal, her parents' death, and leaving behind her brothers would be gone. Lochan made a soft sigh behind her, and she heard him sit down in the chair. Staying silent, she looked out towards the island and enjoyed the weak sense of peace it gave her. In an ever-changing world, some places remained safe and whole. It was a comfort.

"It will work out," Lochan said. "The world is still spinning despite everything that has happened. I have faith that it will continue to do so. In the meantime, would you like to visit the island?"

"I... yes," Alex said. "Yes, I think I would. If it isn't too much trouble."

"Oh, no trouble at all. You came all this way, and I'm inclined to say that the island is the jewel of Mumbai. Of course, I am a little biased in that belief. I'm certain that Avani would be happy to serve as your guide."

17

A Library Without Answers

The leather was soft beneath her fingertips, ready to cut and shape. A thing of beauty and just the sense of possibility took Nicki back to simpler times. Things had gotten lost in the land of magic. As much as the little girl in her had longed for magical powers, it had come with a lot of strings. Training, fighting, and lately research had all taken away her art time. She flipped over the piece of leather and pulled out her iron dagger, experimentally wrapping up the blade.

Nicki had a stack of promising books piled up next to her. Thus far the Desai library was a treasure trove, but the language was proving to be an issue with only a few volumes written in English. The room was still. There was no breeze, and the only sound was her own breathing. Once upon a time, Nicki might have enjoyed being in a secret library all by herself, but not now. She found herself looking up hopefully at the doorway every few minutes even as her fingers traced the leather. There was hesitation, unease in her fingers that made them too heavy to work. Something was bothering her, but Nicki didn't know how to articulate the feelings.

Dreams had never been her thing. She had weird dreams with pirate birds or mecha suits used by people who had been taken to another planet. But she'd never really had a dream that she wondered if magic had a hand in. That had always been Bran and Alex's domain. Occasionally, she felt a hint of jealousy over that. Seeing the future had always seemed like an exciting ability and one that would empower a person. But after yesterday, she was grateful that the strange visions of a barren landscape and screaming Demons that had plagued her dreams could just be written off as nightmares. It had been a strange mixture of post-apocalypse desert and the fires of hell. Probably not related to what, if anything, was actually happening at all.

The sound of the door opening made Nicki look up. Bran stumbled in with a mug of something in hand and glassy eyes. She half expected him to walk into the wall with how unsteady he was on his feet. His gaze focused a bit when he looked at her, and there was the ghost of a smile at the corner of his mouth.

"What happened to you?" Nicki set the leather and dagger down with a soft thump. "Please tell me that you didn't stay up all night trying to scry."

"Then I won't," Bran said. He sat down at the table, nursing what Nicki could now smell was coffee.

"Did you have any luck?" Nicki asked. She raised an expectant eyebrow. "Or was it all fuzzy like it was when we came back yesterday and after dinner."

"It was, but I have to keep trying."

"You need rest too." Bran nodded without looking at her and took another sip of his coffee. "Have you seen Alex?" Nicki asked.

"Not since last night. She was... frustrated. Merlin and Morgana didn't have any information. Morgana was going to try scrying too, but unless she had a lot more luck than me, I doubt she got anything."

"So, you didn't see anything?"

"Vague flashes." Bran waved his free hand. "It's images, not text scrolling over the mirror. I was hoping to trigger a vision, but no such luck. I'll have to try combining my magic with Alex's."

"Hopefully Alex will be up to it." Nicki ran her finger over a line in the wooden table. "I'm not sure what's up with her lately."

"I don't know." Bran leaned back in his chair, causing the wood to groan. "Sometimes I think she's okay and then sometimes I think she's anything but. I'm not sure Alex even knows anymore."

"And she's not really talking to us anymore," Nicki said. "Yeah, right there with you." She glanced towards the door. "Have you seen Aiden this morning."

"He was still talking with Gita in the dining room. I think they were talking about the Iron Chalice."

"Please tell me they were bonding over if it felt weird."

"I'm not sure, possibly, but she was asking questions about where we found it. Aiden only knows it secondhand so she might have more questions later." Bran took another drink of his coffee. "What about Alex, have you seen her this morning."

"Not yet, but Gita mentioned that she saw her with Lochan earlier."

"That's good. He's a calming presence. Maybe that will help Alex. I don't know what to do anymore."

"Plus side, she doesn't seem as... uh... traumatized as before."

"I know, but that's the part that worries me."

Raising an eyebrow, Nicki was about to ask, but her brain quickly connected the dots. "You're worried about the memories overwhelming her."

"I'm a reincarnation, but I don't have the memories," Bran said. "At worst I have vague dreams that I mostly forget when I wake up, and that's just one life. It worries me a little."

"I'm sure that Morgana is worried too." Nicki picked up the knife and studied the way the light played off it. "But Alex is more likely to talk with her than us."

"Yeah, you're not wrong there. Honestly, it seems silly that we ever believed Arthur was the Iron Soul given how Alex and Morgana connected." Bran's eyes dropped to the leather. Smiling softly, his eyes glinted with amusement. "Where did you get the leather? I don't remember you ducking into a shop yesterday."

"I might have brought it with me," Nicki said. She was aware of a rush of heat on her cheeks but didn't lower her eyes. "I've always figured given the Iron Artifacts that a mage can create objects with at least a little bit of magic and Avani's family were magicians and might know something. I'm curious if something other than iron can be infused with magic."

"You could ask Merlin."

"Something always comes up." Nicki shook her head. "And I have some great ideas!"

"Like what?"

She looked back at Bran, but he was smiling encouragingly. Smiling back, Nicki wrapped the blade up in the leather again. "Like sheaths that hide our daggers so we can keep them in easy reach without having issues on campus." She tapped the pile of books and gave Bran a sharp look. "Like a reading glass that translates written languages into something I could understand. I managed to read a little, but it drained a lot of magic trying to change it to something I could read. Not to mention it was almost impossible to focus on using a translation spell and the material at the same time."

"So, you actually managed a translation spell?"

"Yeah, but I couldn't keep it up, hence wanting a magical item that would do it. That could probably even be tied to an iron object. Just a small ring or something that you could look through."

"I'm not sure if you're really that creative or you just read that much fantasy."

"We're officially global now. This time we aren't even doing a fetch quest. This time, we've deployed troops against some kind of threat." Bran flinched lightly at her wording and Nicki inwardly smacked herself for using a military term. Bran usually didn't seem to let his father's death in Afghanistan bother him, but she knew he worried about dying on his mother. "So we need to think of ways to make the process easier. Using our magic usually requires visualization and focus which can be hard sometimes."

"I'm not arguing with you on that," Bran said. "Not at all. You've got a good point, but you might want to talk to Avani. Merlin and Morgana don't use much in the way of enchanted items, probably because using their magic is second nature at this point, but Avani's family might already have things like you're talking about." Bran grinned at her. "Besides, it gives you a reason to talk more with her."

"Aren't you asexual or something close to that?" Nicki fought back a smile and a blush.

"Asexual, but not aromantic. I appreciate the cuteness of your crush just fine."

"It's official. You are spending too much time with Aiden! You boys aren't allowed to live together anymore!"

"That's going to throw a wrench into next semester's housing plan." Fighting back a smile, Nicki took a deep breath and noted that it wasn't as hard now. Bran's sharp gaze noticed and he offered her a soft look. "You okay?"

"Just still trying to understand what the hell happened yesterday. It was one of my stranger days. And that's saying something." Nicki shook her head. "Do you believe it?"

Bran looked surprised at the question. "I don't know. Scrying didn't show me anything, no matter how many times I tried. I got the impression that Alex didn't have any luck with Merlin and Morgana, but it isn't impossible to think that a world could be in trouble. Our planet has had several extinction events."

"Maybe." Nicki looked down at the leather again. "It's just in my head, you know? I feel off today, sluggish maybe. I've been playing with this leather forever now. I need to cut it and sew it, but I haven't."

"In your defense, there's probably more than that."

"Maybe. I'm wondering if I need to come up with some symbol to help hold the magic together."

"Like a seal or sigil? Well, that would make some sense. I've always been curious about whatever magic is on that staff Merlin sometimes uses."

"I'm amazed he doesn't always have it with him." Nicki shook her head. "Bran, what are we doing here? I mean, really, what do we do now?"

"We hurry up and wait."

Snorting, Nicki rolled her shoulders and tapped her fingers against the table. "I hate waiting. I hate being helpless. We need to figure out what the Demons are doing!"

"How?" Bran gestured a little with his mug. "If you have an answer then please speak up, Nicki. I'm not sure what to do or where to go now. My only thought is to try scrying with Alex, but-" Nicki noted a slight quiver in Bran's hand and narrowed her eyes.

"I'm a little worried about how that will work now, with her memories," Nicki finished. "She's been a bit different lately."

Bran nodded slowly, clearly agreeing, but judging from his lowered eyes he didn't want to talk about it. Fair enough, Nicki decided. Them talking about it once again wasn't going to fix anything. Not until someone managed a real conversation with Alex. Bran reached over and picked up one of the books, narrowing his eyes at it. Nicki thought she caught a glimmer of yellow in his eyes and gave herself a moment to study him. It was hard to say, and she thought about asking, but didn't want to disrupt his concentration. She didn't even say anything about him taking the book she'd been looking at.

Bran sat down in a corner chair with the book, and Nicki turned her attention back to the leather. Still, she did nothing with it. Her fingertips explored the rough, yet almost silky texture that shifted slightly beneath the tiny ridges of her fingerprints. It was almost soothing, but also underlined her own uncertainty. There was probably something she should learn from that, but Nicki lacked the motivation to do so. Bran's coffee was beginning to smell really tempting.

The door opened, and Nicki looked up, hoping for Aiden, but it was Avani instead. To Nicki's great pleasure, the pretty young woman was carrying an extra mug. She set it down in front of Nicki, causing a braid of long black hair to fall over her shoulder. Nicki's fingers itched to touch it, but she kept still.

"Mother said that you didn't take any coffee in here with you," Avani said. She smiled nervously. "I'm not sure how you take it exactly, but I remembered you adding milk yesterday."

"I'm not picky actually," Nicki said. She reached for the mug and grinned. "Thank you. I was starting to have coffee envy thanks to Bran."

"What are you trying to make?" Avani asked. There was real interest in her voice, and the other woman leaned closer. Nicki caught a hint of her cherry blossom body wash. "Something magical?"

"I'm curious about putting magic into something other than metal," Nicki said. "I know that we can put magic into iron, and it will hold for a bit and make the metal stronger. If you're the Iron Soul, then it can last a long time, but I've been meaning to try something for a while."

"Oh?"

"Yeah, enchanting was one of the first things I asked about, but we had to learn magic and then it seemed like we were going from one disaster to another."

"I see." Avani moved around the table and sat down, folding her hands in front of her. "What are you trying to make?"

"I'm... maybe a sheath. We all carry daggers, but we have to keep them hidden." Nicki looked down at the leather. She could feel her cheeks heating up and cursed her sudden lack of control. It had been a while since she turned into this much of a fool around a crush. "I'd like to make something that repeals people who don't know it's there... not exactly invisible, but unnoticed."

"To everyone except mages?"

"No, not that either. I want Jenny and Lance to be able to use them. They need the daggers more than the rest of us." Nicki licked her dry lips. "It's more dangerous for them. Honestly, after Arthur killed Alex's parents, I'm surprised that they stuck around."

"They're loyal." Avani's tone was measured, and Nicki suddenly couldn't remember if anyone had briefed her about what happened to Alex's parents. "Besides... leaving might not protect them. After all, this Arthur used Jenny as a tool in fooling Morgana and Merlin that he was the Iron Soul, did he not."

"Yeah, he did," Nicki conceded. "But I think she is just too worried about Alex to leave. Their friendship is hard to explain..."

"Some things transcend." Avani was smiling sadly when Nicki looked up. "She may carry some awareness of her past wrongs and seek to do better. That's honorable."

"I'm not sure Jenny really remembers anything, she knows, of course in general terms, but Alex is the only one who really has any memories."

"Speaking of Jenny, she was finishing up breakfast when I came over," Avani said. She leaned over to look at the books. "Do you need help finding something? Grandfather asked me to work with them on meditation."

"Uh..." Nicki looked at the books, suddenly very lost. "Well, are there any books on enchanting here?"

"A few, but to my knowledge, it is always done with metal," Avani said.

"Okay then, do sigils have any set power?"

Avani's smiled, almost in amusement, but it was pleasant. "Come on, Nicki. There isn't an inherently magical language. It's just about how you tie the magic to your purpose." Avani pressed her lips together thoughtfully. "Maybe think of an image or a word that you could burn into the leather. Something that could be the focal point of your wish."

Nicki nodded slowly. "That's what I was thinking. I was hoping there was something more powerful. More permanent."

"I'm afraid not. The only objects I know that have always held power are the Iron Artifacts made by the Iron Soul. All others eventually lose power unless more magic is bound into them."

Avani got up to find her another book, that was sadly not in English. The others came in from breakfast, Alex walking alongside Jenny with Lance right behind them. Jenny was smiling warmly up at Alex, and some of the tension in Alex's shoulders was gone. Lance caught Nicki's eyes over Jenny's head, and Nicki exhaled slowly as Avani moved over to greet them.

Everyone fell silent. Lance and Jenny went off into a corner with Avani, sitting down in a space between the short shelves where they could still be seen. Aiden stumbled in a few minutes later, still chewing and carrying a cup of tea. He swallowed and offered her a sheepish smile before tilting his head to look at the books she had stacked next to her. Aiden shuddered and sat down, slapping down a notebook. Looking over her shoulder, Nicki found Alex running a finger along the wood of one of the shelves, her gray eyes moving across the row of books.

There was the soft turning of pages, whispered instructions from Avani to Lance and Jenny, and the scratch of Aiden's pencil. Behind Nicki, she could hear Alex moving with soft steps along the shelves. Fighting back a shiver, Nicki tried to focus on the leather in front of her. She'd have to cut it into the proper shape then sew the pieces together. Maybe if she focused the magic into the seams that would give her stable focal point. The theory was the same as pushing magic into iron except it wasn't just about summoning raw magic, this had to be programmed, given instructions like a computer program. Her eyes jumped up to Aiden thoughtfully. Maybe he'd have some thoughts on how to organize her process.

Jenny's phone beeped, the sound unnaturally loud in the library. The woman grimaced, long wavy strands of dark hair falling into her face as she dug out her phone. Nicki rested her chin on her hand and watched as a look of confusion took over Jenny's face.

"Uh, Alex, it's Morgana." She waved the phone in the air. "Just a text message."

"What's it say?"

"They are safe." Alex tensed, her fingers tightening around the spine of the book in her hands. "Is everything okay?"

"Fine." Alex didn't even try to smile. "Morgana was just taking care of something for me."

Nicki glanced towards Bran and Aiden. Neither of them seemed to know what was going on. Jenny caught her eyes when she looked back towards the phone, but she could only shrug in response. Nicki had no idea what it might be referring to. Besides, the message said they, not it, so Morgana couldn't be talking about an object.

"Do you need to call her again?" Jenny held the phone out towards Alex. "I don't mind, though if the world travel is going to stay a thing, we should get you a phone that works internationally."

"No," Alex said. She smiled a little now and waved her hand towards the phone. "I don't need to call her." Alex closed her book and slid it back on the shelf. "Translation spell is giving me a headache. I need some air."

No one moved to stop Alex as she strode towards the doorway. Avani looked towards her with pleading eyes, but there was nothing Nicki could do. She didn't have any idea of what to say and a strange suspicion about who they might be was beginning to take hold. Staying in her seat, Nicki watched Alex disappear out of the library and the door close behind her. Everyone let out a collective breath, and it was Lance who took the first step towards the door. Then he stopped and sighed, rubbing the back of his neck.

"So," Aiden said. "Who wants to go and ask?"

"I'll go," Nicki said. She stood up from the table and stretched her arms. "If I'm not back in an hour, send the cavalry."

18

Lokpal and the Grand Mages

21 B.C.E. Mazagaon, India

The mages Merlin and Morgana were unlike anyone he had ever met before. Each of them moved with a confidence that he'd only seen elders possess, but their ages were difficult to tell. Their eyes were old and while each of them had some lines, they did not look nearly old enough to possess the shadows carried in their gazes. Though he was uncertain, Lokpal listened. They found a spot off the main path with a few smoother rocks to sit on where they wouldn't be disturbed by curious fishermen.

They explained magic to him, promising that he possessed this strange power himself and its purpose in protecting their world. Something tugged at the back of his mind. This was somehow familiar, but it was like a dream. He couldn't grasp the sense of déjà vu and make sense of it. He was only aware that it was there. Frustration and confusion crept up his spine, but he focused on the mages.

Morgana was jaded. She walked confidently, but her posture was defensive. Her long hair was piled up on her head and there was a sheen of sweat on her brow. Lokpal wasn't sure where they came from, but the climate here was apparently alien to them. Merlin seemed to be handling it better than his companion. His body language was more open than Morgana's and his smile reached his brown eyes. He might have thought they were a couple, but they didn't gravitate towards each other. Each one was distinct and separate even as their words and explanations wove around each other's.

Sitting down helped. His heart finally slowed back to normal, though the strange smell of the forest he'd seen lingered in Lokpal's mind. At least the ocean from the vision Morgana caused had been something familiar. The notion that trees and birds could be so different was hard to believe.

"Are you alright?" Merlin asked. He offered Lokpal a kind smile. "It is a lot to take in, I know. I'm sorry that we ambushed you."

"He was spying on us." Morgana's lips curved into an amused smile and her green eyes sparkled for a moment, reassuring Lokpal that she wasn't truly angry. "I hardly think you need to apologize, Merlin."

"You know the Connection can be difficult, Morgana." Merlin looked over at her and shook his head. "We've been traveling this way for some time. Morgana's scrying and our magic helped us determine that the rising magic is a result of events happening here."

"Rising magic," Lokpal repeated. He shook his head. "It's all a bit much. Why me?"

"We don't know why one person is born with magical talent and another is not," Merlin said.

"Does it run in families?"

Merlin again glanced towards Morgana, but she didn't react to the look. "In some ways. Being a mage does not, but a person can learn to harness a little magic with focus and the proper mental state. My own mother was not a mage, but when necessary, she could command magic." Merlin stroked his short beard for a moment. "My grandfather might have been a mage, but I'm unsure. I'm inclined to think that like my mother he just understood how to move magic." Focusing his eyes on Lokpal again, Merlin chuckled. "But to answer your question, no, being a mage is not a question of your bloodline."

That was a relief. Lokpal felt his back muscles relax. Hopefully, that would keep his children a little bit safer. The two mages were silent, giving him time to gather his thoughts. But Lokpal had barely begun to form his next question when a thud from the trees made all three of them straighten up. Morgana moved first, jumping off her rock and placing herself between Lokpal and the noise. He was stunned.

Morgana tightened her right hand into a fist, and silver sparks appeared out of her skin. Gasping, he almost forgot about the loud noise in favor of staring. A moment later three Demons came crashing through the trees. His eyes widened in shock just before a wave of silver light washed forward as Morgana shouted. The Demons stopped short and screamed as the waves of light hit them. Lokpal blinked, clearing his vision. Only one Demon remained as charred bodies collapsed on the ground. Then more Demons came out of the trees. All in armor and armed with spears. A pair in the back were notching arrows in huge bows. Morgana took a step back, and the Demons charged.

Drawing his sword, Lokpal leapt off the rock and ducked beneath a Demon's arm. Morgana shouted something, but it was difficult to understand her. He slashed the sword forward. It sliced into the upper leg of the mountainous Demon. The dark skin split, and dark blood spilled out on the ground. Twisting away, the Demon swung its spear, but it was too slow. Lokpal dodged back and jumped around the back of the Demon. It was turning when he stabbed his sword into the back of its ankle. There was a hideous cry and the Demon's leg gave out. He didn't wait for it to try anything. Pulling his sword loose, Lokpal lifted his arms and using both hands drove the sword down into the Demon's neck.

An arrow sailed past him. He gasped, turning his attention away from the body. One of the Demons was notching another arrow. A bright green bolt of light hit its chest, sailing through the body. The Demon fell and the bow snapped beneath the weight of the body before it started to collapse. Silver light flashed in the corner of his eye. Lokpal turned and gasped. Two streams of silver light were lashing through the air like whips leading back to Morgana's hands. There was a cold expression on her face and her eyes were locked on the nearest Demon. It was backing away, but she didn't hesitate. With a shout, she shifted her arms, and the streams of light rose sharply into the air before crashing around the Demon.

Moving back, Lokpal resisted the urge to fight. Both mages were right in front of the Demons and showing no signs of fatigue. Morgana was scowling at the Demons while Merlin had a serene expression. With each flick of their hands, the magic in the air shifted. He watched in stunned silence. These were acts of gods and yet here were two beings that said he was capable of such things. His left hand flexed nervously. How could that be him?

The question was put aside as a Demon roared and jumped over the fallen Demons towards Merlin. It hit the ground with a heavy thud and reached for Merlin, snarling, and swinging a long wooden club. The ground trembled and began to bubble up. It was like boiling water, but a thick swirl of mud rose from the earth and around the Demon's feet. As suddenly as it had become so fluid, it solidified and the Demon crashed to the ground with a howl of pain as its ankles snapped. Flinching in sympathy, Lokpal tightened his grip on his sword and stayed still. The Demons were focused on the mages entirely now.

Green sparks rolled through the air like tiny leaves caught in the wind. But they turned and twisted unnaturally, gathering into small orbs and crashing down on the heads of the Demons. Another one screamed in pain as a beam of green light broke through its chest, leaving a hole. Its body convulsed and fell, twisting in pain before it began to collapse inward.

Morgana raised her right hand and more silver sparks sprung forth, flooding the air around her. Demons drew back, but she didn't give them a chance to run. The sparks swirled together into a tight, glowing orb. As the Demons began to shift away, beams of brilliant light shot forth and stabbed them like blades. It was terrifying. And beautiful. There was no blood. It happened too quickly, and Lokpal's jaw went slack.

It was only the roar that alerted him to danger. One last Demon was running at him. A spear launched towards him from one hand. He jumped out of the way just in time to avoid the attack and the Demon rushing past. He slashed at the Demon. It was looming over him. He cursed himself for being so distracted. The sword slipped through the outer layer of flesh, sending dark droplets flying through the air. Swinging the sword back, Lokpal brought it up to strike again. The Demon was moving its spear and snarling. Lines of drool escaped its mouth from between sharp teeth. Its wild eyes met his. Terror gripped his heart. The sword was moving too slow. His body was too tired. A beam of silver light struck the Demon's head. The scent of burning flesh hit him. The spear dropped to the ground and the body followed a moment later as Lokpal twisted out of the way.

All the Demons were gone. Defeated as quickly as they'd emerged. Lokpal still didn't understand why, but as he scanned the trees, Lokpal was assured that they were gone. Lowering his sword, Lokpal inhaled slowly and urged his heart to slow. The two mages glanced over each other, checking for injuries before looking to him. Merlin brushed some dirt off the front of his robe. Morgana kicked at one of the lingering piles of dust that the wind hadn't swept away yet.

"Are you alright?" Merlin asked.

"I'm not injured." The sting of his injuries lingered, but he said nothing about it. "Do you always fight like that?"

Merlin chuckled and nodded. "I'm afraid that Morgana and I are very familiar in fighting with our magic. And we've battled our fair share of Demons on the way here." He glanced down at where one of the Demons had been before moving to sit down on his rock once again. "What can you tell us of these Demons?" Merlin asked. He had tented his fingers in front of his face and was staring at Lokpal intensely. "We've fought several on our way here, but they are new to us. Even now, I still feel as though I know nothing about them."

"Iron doesn't seem to bother them," Morgana observed. She was pacing behind Merlin, her hands on her hips. "Unless you stab them with it."

"Why would you have thought iron would bother them?" Lokpal asked.

"Other creatures from certain worlds are weak to iron," Merlin explained. He offered Lokpal a patient smile. "But these creatures come from a completely different branch of the Tree of Reality."

Nodding slowly, Lokpal considered the earlier explanation of the Tree of Reality. Why and how such a thing existed was still a mystery, but it was enough to know it was there for now. The pair of mages gave him a moment to gather his thoughts. Glancing up, he checked the position of the sun and hissed in surprise.

"I was on my way to check on the southern island!" Leaping off the rock, he rushed for the path. He heard the mages following him within seconds. "My wives were expecting me home! The way things have been lately, I don't want to worry them."

"What is this southern island?" Merlin asked.

"Lord Rudra was seen there earlier fighting a large group of Demons."

"And Rudra is?" Morgana asked.

He still didn't turn around. The urge to go and check on the southern island clawed at him, but he was too aware of his promise not to take too long. As he moved, the bandages beneath his shirt holding his wound tightened. At least he wasn't returning home with even more injuries.

"He is the god of thunder." Morgana scoffed behind him, but he still didn't turn around. "And a great hunter. He's been hunting down Demons in the area. I crossed his path not long ago." Lokpal's stomach twisted and his head ached for a moment at the memory. "He told me I was a mage, but I didn't understand at the time. I've been keeping my distance, but we're lucky he's here. I've barely been keeping the Demons away from the village."

"With a sword?" Merlin asked. Lokpal nodded vaguely. They were at the first of the houses now and he earned a strange look from a woman out in her yard. "I'm impressed, we've had the benefit of using our magic."

"So, I saw," Lokpal said. His voice was weak, but the comment made Merlin laugh. "I do need to get home though."

"Of course," Merlin said.

He kept walking and the pair of mages followed behind him. Refusing to look nervously back at them, Lokpal licked his lips and focused his eyes up ahead. His arms and back hurt, but the sword in his hand was reassuring. They were halfway to his home before he finally sheathed the blade. The air tasted like a storm, warm with energy and tension. The hairs on the back of his neck were on end and he tried to say something.

"How far did you come to be here?"

"A very long way," Merlin replied. He suddenly sounded tired. "We come from far to the north and west."

"Past the mountains then."

"Yes, past the mountains," Merlin said.

"And you came because of the Demons. Is that what you two do? Travel to stop dangerous creatures."

Morgana chuckled. "Yes, in a way that is exactly what we do."

They lapsed into silence again. What was he supposed to say now? How did he explain this to his family? It was a good thing, at least he hoped so. They could fight the Demons. If he'd been up against that large a group by himself, then he would have died. The thought made him sweat. But what now? They didn't seem to like Rudra, and if they crossed paths with him, it might make things worse. His stomach tightened and he gripped his belt to keep his hands steady. They followed the bend of the road and his home came into view.

"This is me." He turned around to face them. "What will you do now?" Lokpal asked. He kept his spine straight and mustered an apologetic look. "I'd invite you to stay with us, but since the birth of my son I'm afraid the space has become a bit small."

"You have children?" Morgana asked. Her sharp green eyes softened, with guilt, worry, or fondness he wasn't sure.

"Yes, two. A daughter and a son." Lokpal couldn't help but smile a little. "I'm sorry, but the situation with the Demons already has my family-"

"We understand," Merlin said kindly. He held up a hand in a gesture to stop him from speaking. "We will be alright. With this incursion of Demons, our magic is strong. We will make ourselves a shelter nearby where we met you. I hope if we set up there we will not disturb anyone."

"No, that area should be fine." Turning and looking at his door, Lokpal released an uneasy sigh. Worries and doubts flickered through his mind, overwhelming the strange sense of safety these two gave him. "What then?"

"You are a mage, but have yet to access your power," Merlin said. "We will teach you. It will be a great asset in fighting the Demons. While you learn, Morgana and I will investigate the influx of Demons and see if we can't find out what is happening."

"Rudra might be able to help," Lokpal said. "But be careful if you approach him. He is a violent one and..." he trailed off, his tongue turning heavy as he thought of that strange dark mark on Rudra's head. "I'm not sure, but something about him seemed wrong like he somehow was sick."

"Old Ones aren't supposed to be in our world," Morgana said. She had a thoughtful frown on her face. "But some learn to live in peace with the nature of our world."

"Was there something about him specifically?" Merlin asked. "Something he said or something you saw?"

"Well, there was this dark patch on his skin. I'm not sure what to make of it, but it didn't seem right."

Merlin and Morgana exchanged a worried look. "He's losing to corruption," Morgana said. "We'll need to sort out a way to deal with him before he becomes a greater danger than the Demons."

"But he's helping," Lokpal said. "Surely you don't mean to-"

"Did he attack you?" Merlin asked, his voice was low and serious now.

"Sort of," Lokpal said. "But he didn't kill me even though I interfered with his hunt. Because I was a mage."

"Then he's not fully corrupted," Merlin said. "Old Ones know better than to strike down mages. At least so long as they are not corrupted."

He and Morgana shared a glance and she nodded slightly. "We will leave you to speak with your family. Please, seek us out tomorrow. There is much to do."

Nodding slowly, Lokpal stood at the end of his own yard and watched the pair turn around. Merlin rubbed his eyes and his steps faltered for a moment. Morgana grabbed his arm, helping him keep his balance. She glanced back at him before speaking to Merlin. Once again, their words were strange but rolled off their tongues quickly as they walked down the path. Lokpal stayed still and watched them until they were past the trees and out of sight.

19

Long Overdue

Seeing Alex standing on the balcony with the landscape of the city and the ocean behind her made Nicki pause. Alex was dressed as she'd been before, in a simple t-shirt and jeans. Her long blonde hair was piled up in a messy bun and yet there was something regal about her. In her hands was a cup of tea and she hadn't seemed to have noticed Nicki yet. Moments like this made it easy to forget what Alex could do and how much magic she could call on. She appeared calm and the cup in her hand indicated that she'd at least stopped in the kitchen. There was no rage, no tears, or sighs.

Yet, something was off. Something had been off for a while and Nicki silently cursed her own unwillingness to push. The death of Alex's parents, their murder at the hands of Arthur by magical proxy, had shifted the dynamic of the group and changed Alex herself. Watching Alex, Nicki struggled to connect the calm young woman here with the warrior she saw on occasion, the person who killed deities, broke global spells, and could control energy.

Alex didn't understand. Nicki was sure of that. When they'd first met, Nicki had found Alex almost timid. She flinched back from magic and hesitated to believe until it was stuffed down her throat. Alex had been the one amongst them to refuse the call. Rejecting the visions, she'd done her best to stay away from them until the Sídhe hounds finally proved that magic was real. She'd been the last to gain control of her powers, but her magic had been frightening. It scared Nicki, the knowledge that Alex could take Nicki's own magic and throw it back at her.

Merlin and Morgana never seemed to realize what that could mean or if they did, they hid it well. It was Alex's lack of imagination that held her back. Magic was just another form of energy and Alex could pull it to her, draw it into her grasp. Nicki wasn't a physics major like Bran, but even she knew that Alex's control over energy could evolve. Energy and matter were interconnected and in theory, Alex could use her power over energy to do almost anything.

Despite her potential, Alex stuck rather strictly to just pulling on wisps of magic. Nicki wondered if Alex understood what she could do and was afraid of it or if she genuinely didn't understand. Nicki blamed the lack of comic books. It was almost tragic, the one of them with the most power had the least history of reading books of magic and playing games. A lack of imagination, but maybe it was for the best. Absolute power and all that jazz.

Then again, Alex had turned around when the Sídhe had captured her. She'd been a prisoner and frightened, but she'd gone back for those kids despite not having control over her magic. Alex had connected with her magic as a hero while Nicki had connected to hers through the trauma of her parents coming back where they weren't welcome.

Alex really was that good. Nicki leaned against the doorframe and stayed quiet, just observing Alex. It was one thing to imagine that if the moment came, you'd be brave and do the right thing, but it was another thing to have it confirmed. She'd always had the benefit of the others in her battles. Alex was brave, Aiden was fearless, and given his past life,

Nicki knew in her gut that Bran was brave. It was herself that she was unsure of.

"What is it, Nicki?" Alex asked. She didn't turn around. "You're staring."

"Yeah, sorry about that. Woolgathering," Nicki said.

Alex turned her head slightly and Nicki saw a wistful smile on her face. "My mom used that expression sometimes."

"Sorry."

"Don't be. That's not a bad thing."

"So... are you okay?" Nicki asked. "I mean, after your parents' death you never wanted to talk about it. You seem to be a bit better now, but are you really?" Nicki took a few steps forward, wringing her hands. "We're here for you, Alex."

"I know and thank you for that. I am doing better now. And just knowing that all of you were here helped."

That didn't seem like enough to Nicki. "So, what did Morgana's message mean?"

"Morgana has completed their preparations for changing my brothers' memories," Alex answered. Her voice was a matter of fact, though she didn't look at Nicki.

"What?" Straightening up, Nicki stared at Alex in shock. "What are you talking about? You're joking right?" But Alex just looked at her calmly for a moment. Then Alex picked up her tea again and took a sip, looking out over the city. "Wow, that's... I'm sorry, I suppose." Nicki shook her head. "I wouldn't have thought that Morgana would do something like that." Her stomach turned, and she wondered if the rest of them were going to be told something like that regarding their own families. "That's horrible! Are you sure-"

"I told her to," Alex explained. "Arthur killed my parents despite the blood protection. I didn't want Matt and Ed in his sights. Morgana was going to erase their memories of having a sister and arrange some things to get them out of Spokane. She promised to keep me updated, though no details in case Arthur hacks the phone."

"I didn't know our magic could do that." Nicki shook her head, trying to imagine all the little things that Merlin and Morgana must be working on. To keep Arthur from tracking them, they'd basically have to create new identities for the Adams brothers. "That's…"

"Are you going to tell me that it's a bad idea?" Alex asked. Her voice was soft, almost amused and the blonde just kept looking out into the water. "Morgana already tried to talk me out of it."

"No," Nicki said. "I think you had the right idea."

Then Alex looked at her, blinking in surprise and Nicki smiled. Finally, a real emotional reaction. She reached over and put her hand over Alex's, squeezing it for a moment. The idea was scary but realistic. Pragmatic and maybe that was what Alex needed right now. Not heroic idealism.

"You're trying to protect them." Nicki didn't try to smile and focused on keeping her voice steady. The flicker of grief and relief in Alex's eyes spoke volumes. There was still fear there. "No matter what happens, you've been brave enough to let them go to give them a chance to live a life without being afraid of Arthur."

"Morgana thought it was a bad idea." Alex looked away from her and tucked a strand of blonde hair behind her ear. There was a slight quiver in her voice, and Nicki moved even closer to her.

"She was the sibling of an Iron Soul," Nicki said. "She's motivated by a whole lot of loyalty. Which is odd, because I've never gotten the sense that she cared that much about the other incarnations." She frowned a bit at the thought but didn't recall Morgana ever speaking of another

Iron Soul incarnation other than Arto with true fondness. "You seem to be the exception there."

"I'm not sure that's right," Alex replied. "When... when I remember her or see her, other voices are happy to see her besides Arto."

Nicki's eyes jumped to Alex's face. Desperately, she searched for any sign of a joke. There wasn't any. Her face was serene though there was a distant sadness in her eyes. It was a bit terrifying. Swallowing, Nicki looked out over the city. Her fingers tightened around the railing as she held onto reality.

"I'm sorry about your brothers."

"Thank you, but I'm certain it is for the best," Alex said. Strangely her voice was strong with just a hint of wistfulness. "I just wish we'd had a better parting. Things were tense between us, but given the reason, I doubt it would have improved."

Her mouth was hanging open a bit. Nicki blinked and tried to find some words to say that wouldn't come off completely rude. She failed. "Did Matt blame you?"

"I think he did, he didn't want to, but I think deep down he was angry about how things turned out." Alex shook her head and a few strands of hair fell out of her bun. "I don't blame him for that. My parents' death... it still hurts, probably always well, but at least I can try to make sure that they aren't victims too." Turning towards the house, Alex peered inside with a sad frown. "I should have made Lance and Jenny stay in Ravenslake." Her gray eyes were dark now, almost stormy.

"They wouldn't want that," Nicki said gently. She took a step forward and touched Alex's hand again. "They want to help, and they do bring a useful outside viewpoint to things."

"I suppose, but someday it is going to get them killed."

The words were calm, not fearful and Nicki's heart jumped. She swallowed and tightened her hand around Alex's. The other woman looked down at their hands with a hint of confusion. Then she looked back at Nicki's face.

"They've asked Avani to teach them some magic." Smiling, Nicki tilted her head. "We are in a good place for that. And you know how determined Jenny is. Plus, Lance has outright tackled Sídhe warriors to the ground. If they can call on a bit of magic to help them, then they'll be even tougher in combat."

"Yes, but that will only encourage them to endanger themselves more." Alex shook her head and pulled her hand away. Stepping back, Nicki gave her some space. Alex huffed softly and ran a finger around the rim of her teacup. Then she chuckled. "It's odd. I expected some of the lives to be angry with them, to resent them, but none of them seem to be. When I'm around them, there is just always... relief that they are still together, like that makes it all okay and there's also guilt. I don't know if it was their own grief that trapped them or something else, but those lives caught repeating the cycle were unfair. At least even my other lives seem to understand that."

"So, you really can hear them?" Nicki held back a shiver. How could a person live with that? "What's it like?" She didn't mean to ask that question and tensed up, bracing herself for Alex to react badly.

"Noisy." Alex snorted a little, her lips curling into a smile. "But it's not so bad now. They can be distracting. I'm getting more used to it. Trying to organize what I remember and what they say. I'll never remember all of it, but at least I can sometimes recognize the speaker."

"Are they noisy now?"

"Not so much," Alex said. "Nothing is happening to rouse them."

"Not even being in Mumbai, I would have thought that Lokpal would have been interested in that."

"Everything is changed from what he knew," Alex replied. "He lived over 2,000 years ago. This city... it isn't home to him. He's been quiet for the most part. Sometimes I feel something from him, but he's not really active." Alex looked over at her and gave Nicki a reassuring smile. "Don't worry. I'm in control. Even my slave trader life Cuthbert can't change that. This is my body, even if my soul is a bit more complicated."

"So, you hear all of them?"

"There are many that I don't know. Maybe someday I'll know them all. But part of me doesn't want to."

Her hands were shaking. Alex's voice was calm, but Nicki's eyes found the slight tremor in her fingers. The teacup shivered as she set it down, a soft clinking noise reaching Nicki. She debated saying anything. Alex pulled her hands back and flexed her fingers slowly, looking down at them. What she was seeing, Nicki didn't know. Maybe just having female hands in contrast to all her male lives was enough.

Crossing her arms over her chest, Nicki struggled not to fidget. Dozens of words gathered in her mouth, dancing on her tongue, and tempting her to say them. She rolled her lips together and just watched as Alex turned back towards the sunset. The calm was terrifying, unnatural, and worrying.

"You could have talked with us, with me, about your brothers," Nicki finally said. "We want to be here to help, Alex. We may all be friends as the result of circumstances, but we are still friends."

"It was a decision I needed to make and not second guess. Besides, I thought you agreed with it."

"You don't need to carry choices like that alone." Nicki softened her voice. "Even if you just need a hug after it, we're here for that."

Alex looked at her with a hint of surprise. Then Alex opened her arms for a hug. Laughing, Nicki stepped forward and wrapped her arms around the taller girl. Alex lowered her chin to Nicki's shoulder. A shiver from Alex went into Nicki as she held her friend close. The sounds of the city rolled over them, but neither moved. Bringing up her hand, Nicki rubbed Alex's back as Alex relaxed. She wasn't shaking or crying to Nicki's relief. Closing her eyes, Nicki tightened her grip just a little and was rewarded by Alex doing the same.

"Mauerbauertraurigkeit," Nicki said softly.

"What?" Alex's voice was a bit muffled.

"The inexplicable urge to push people away, even close friends who you really like," Nicki said. "One of those strange emotions that make no sense."

"It's not that," Alex protested.

"We'll give you time, Alex," Nicki promised. "Just please don't give up talking to us."

"I have been."

"No, you've been chatting with us," Nicki corrected. She swallowed back the sudden tightness in her throat. "You haven't talked to us since your parents died."

"I don't know how to."

"Okay. If you can't talk, then hold open your arms for a hug. I can do that," Nicki promised.

"I'm okay," Alex said. "I know that's hard to believe, but the death of my parents... it is passing. I was keeping it bound up for a bit."

"Bound up?" Nicki tensed, and Alex pulled away from the hug. Her friend was blushing a bit.

"Magic," Alex said. She shrugged weakly and didn't look at Nicki.

"Alex!"

"Yes, I know, bad idea, but when I used the Hammer to break the spell… a lot activated in my head. There are memories that I don't know how to deal with that are only starting to settle." Alex rubbed the back of her neck. Her jaw tightened and she rolled back onto her heels. "I didn't want the anger. It was too much. And I love you guys, but how could you begin to understand. I just don't know. I can't articulate what's going on in me."

"Occhiolism," Nicki said.

"What does that one mean?" Alex huffed and looked over at her teacup.

"The awareness of the smallness of your perspective."

"That's not my problem." Alex chuckled darkly.

"No, it's mine," Nicki said. "I'm sorry, Alex. I wish I could understand what you're feeling." Nicki shook her head sadly. "You're this… massive great thing. Old and powerful and yet also human, but I don't know what to make of it." Alex flinched. "But just because I'm aware of how out of depth I am, doesn't mean that I won't try to understand. Words are hard, cultures rise and evolve as they create new ones to articulate their thoughts. It isn't easy, but please try. Now or later. Whenever you want. I will listen."

"Sometimes it's like I don't feel anything," Alex whispered. Nicki stepped closer and took her hand again, squeezing it tightly. Alex's fingers turned and gripped back with white knuckles. "Anger comes through sometimes when I think of Arthur. There's embarrassment and guilt and yet also relief that I'm alive to experience all of it. When I think of my parents-" Alex stopped for a moment, rolling her lips together. "It hurts, but there's also this sense of a foregone conclusion. And the voices don't help so much. I'm not holding it back anymore, but now I'm not sure that there is anything there. My parents died and maybe I don't care."

"Grief is messy," Nicki said softly. "And it isn't easy. It isn't always big emotions, Alex. Sometimes it's the small moments that catch you off guard. That doesn't mean that you don't care. Not at all."

"That's what you've got?" Alex raised her eyebrow again.

"You look like Morgana when you do that," Nicki huffed. Then she sighed and put her free hand over Alex's. "What can we do, Alex?"

"Just... remind me that I'm Alex." She turned her head up and looked into the sky. "Remind me of who I am right now. That's the part that keeps trying to flicker away. Maybe I should have held onto my grief more. Maybe it would have grounded me. But... every time I sleep, more pieces of the puzzle fall into place. Only if they all fall into place, I'm not sure what will be left of Alex. Sometimes it scares me and sometimes I think it's a good thing."

"Why?"

"Because it will mean that I never die." Alex shook her head and pulled her hand away, curling her fingers into fists. "When I was little, I was terrified at the idea of death. It didn't make sense. How could the world keep going without me? I had nightmares that I died, and now I wonder if that was just the others bleeding through. Weird that I can't be sure of things that far back, but anyway I'd wake up my parents and they'd try to reassure me. It just didn't make sense."

"And now?"

"Now, I'm not afraid of death. It's like a switch has been flipped. Even though I miss my parents, there is also this strange sense of acceptance that I was always going to lose them. I'll lose my brothers one way or another and just want to make sure that it isn't because of the Sídhe or Demons."

"I'm glad you're grieving properly, but you have to hold on to them as well."

"I know, as I said, you all remind me. You keep me chained to Alex Adams. I need that."

"Okay," Nicki said. "We will. I promise." Then for good measure, she stepped forward and hugged Alex again.

20

First Steps on Elephanta Island

Alex had never spent much time on boats. Her family had gone to a camping area by Coeur d'Alene lake almost every year where they rented a boat, but the annual trip hadn't exactly made her at ease on the water. She had been just enough along with her swimming lessons to make sure that she didn't fear the water, but the sharp, salty scent and the rough waves kept reminding her that she was on an ocean, not a lake. Sure, the harbors of Mumbai were still in sight, and they weren't going far, but her stomach churned uneasily. Even worse were the memories of Cuthbert Allard's slave ship trying to poke through with every dip and rise of the boat.

"I might get sick," Jenny whispered to her. "I don't like boats." Jenny gripped her arm with her right hand while keeping the left hand tight on the railing.

"Really?" Alex asked. She was grateful for the distraction. It was surprising that Jenny was with her rather than Lance but ever since her conversation with Nicki, all the others were staying closer. She didn't want to know what Nicki had told them, but while she wouldn't say it out loud, she was grateful. "You grew up in San Francisco."

"I'm good with beaches, but we never really went out on the water. Bonfires on the beach, sand castles and maybe the occasional surf lesson, but no real boating. Besides, the water in San Francisco isn't exactly warm. The actual spend time in the water season is pretty short."

"Fair point."

Lance came up behind them and wrapped an arm around Jenny. She turned her face into his chest with a grateful sigh. He offered Alex a small nod and she smiled in return before turning her eyes to the island. The mass of green rose out of the water, a strange sight after the busy city of Mumbai. Alex's fingers drummed nervously on the rail of the ferry and she mentally reviewed what they knew about Demons.

It wasn't much. Not compared to the Sídhe and they didn't have easy weaknesses. The only real advantage they had was that they were a better-organized unit. They all knew what each other was likely to do in combat. Of course, if someone was organizing the Demons, then that wouldn't last for long. She looked over at Lance and Jenny again and found herself wishing that they had just stayed in Ravenslake. It was selfish to keep letting them come along.

And it made her wonder about her brothers. If they'd had the chance maybe after a period of mourning they would have wanted to join the fight. No, she decided quickly enough, Matt wouldn't have. Eddy, maybe, but not Matt. He'd never been at ease with even the idea of magic. Ed had been so excited by all of it until the real cost had shown itself. Maybe in another life, her brothers would have taken up arms against the Sídhe, but then they would have been like Galath or worse Morgana.

"Better this way," Alex said to herself.

"What?" Lance asked.

"Nothing."

"Thinking about your brothers?" Jenny asked. Her voice was too gentle, and Alex took a hand off the railing to push her sunglasses further up her nose. At least her eyes were hidden.

"Nicki's got a big mouth."

"A bit," Jenny agreed.

The island came closer. Aiden and Bran were near the front of the ferry, talking loudly and getting a few disapproving looks from locals with bags of groceries and other tourists. Nicki was with Avani, sitting on a pair of bright red seats bolted to the green deck. Judging from the expression on Nicki's face, she was definitely flirting with Avani. Alex started to smile fondly before another roll of the ferry over a wave made her grip the railing.

It didn't take long for the ferry to come up to the small dock. A red sign in English welcomed them to the island. The dock linked up with a long stretch of road. A long line of booths waited for the tourists and beyond the brightly colored roofs of the booths, Alex could see the collection of buildings that made up the village. They let the other people off the boat first except for Avani. There was some kind of tour group, all armed with cameras and excitedly following their guide over to where a bright, red small train was waiting. It was on a set of small tracks with an actual platform built around it with a reddish tile roof. Alex held back a laugh as the tourists climbed into the small compartments.

Avani helped an older woman with a heavy box over to a man who was waiting with a handcart. The woman seemed to know her and gave her a smile and them a curious look before heading towards the village. Their paces were quick as if they were seeking to escape the tourists. Once the tourists were off and the woman was safely away, Avani turned back to them and gestured them off the ferry.

As she set her foot on the island, Alex was assaulted by a rush of magic through her legs and up her spine. Shivering in response, she inhaled slowly to control the surge of power that was rippling down to her fingertips. It wasn't often that she sensed magic so strongly, but this place clearly was significant. She wasn't sure if it was the result of old spells like the Tor in Glastonbury or Stonehenge, but there was an underlying well of power here.

"Alex?" Avani called. "Are you alright?"

"I'm fine," Alex forced out. "Just…"

"Yeah," Nicki agreed. "I felt that too. There's a lot of magic here."

"Really?" Avani blinked in surprise, and then curiosity and excitement filled her eyes. "You can feel that?"

"We are constantly absorbing magic from the world around us," Bran said. "We tap into that energy, but I guess if an area is saturated by it then our bodies instinctively pull in more."

"Hope it isn't to prepare for a fight," Aiden said.

"I doubt that." Avani shook her head and adjusted the strap of her backpack. "This island is a stronghold of Shiva and a few other Old Ones. They are here a lot. I can't imagine any Demons coming here."

"That's probably it then," Nicki said. "Allies or not, their presence would trigger magic as they aren't actually supposed to be in our world."

"Do they sleep here?" Alex asked. Her eyes scanned along the shoreline.

"Just offshore," Avani answered. "In the water and there might be some caves below. I'm not sure and Shiva doesn't share information like that."

"No." Bran nodded as he looked around the docks. "I suppose he wouldn't. I do wonder what they are like when they are sleeping. I mean no subs have ever detected them so are they hidden by magic? Do they disperse into the water?" He blinked at Alex as she and the others looked at him. "Am I the only one to wonder that?"

"Don't worry," Aiden laughed. "I've wondered too. It's one of those weird thoughts I've had." He gave his friend a one-armed hug. "Can I just say, how happy I am to have someone else who thinks about these things?"

Bran held back a sigh and shook his head. "Well, that probably means that I'm not crazy."

"You're not crazy," Alex said. She was smiling so wide that her cheeks ached. "Unless all of us are and I think that ship has sailed."

Nicki beamed at her, and Alex was very aware of the fond looks the others were sending her way. Feeling her cheeks starting to heat up and a strong burst of affection growing in her chest, Alex looked around. The island was a stark contrast to the world of skyscrapers and metal across the water. Instead of buildings, they were surrounded by trees with a road leading around the curve of the island. There were a few small houses here and there, but it was green and full of life. The smells of Mumbai were distant with a sharp tang of ferns and moist earth filling the air here.

"It's like another world," Jenny said softly. "So different."

"The island has never seen serious construction," Avani said. "Part of it is the sacred nature of the area and preservation efforts. In fact, tourists to the island aren't allowed to stay overnight."

"So, we'd better hurry," Bran said. "We've already lost a lot of the day."

"My family has a home here." Avani smiled and gestured down the road. "So, I have residency status here and you'll be staying with me. Which is ideal for us as the island is a major tourist spot."

"If you have a home here, why does Shiva come to your house in Mumbai?" Aiden asked.

"Grandfather is a bit old now," Avani replied. "He came to see Shiva here when he was younger, but after he turned seventy, Shiva said that he'd come to us."

Alex smiled. She couldn't help the warm sensation that the statement invoked. Lochan had told her as much, but it still... just felt good. Part of her was horrified at the idea of a deity making changes to its routine for a mortal, but it was a kindness she valued. Lochan was strong for his age, but looking at the rolling hills, Alex could understand why Shiva might have decided to spare the current head of the family the trip.

They followed Avani up a small side road. The village was small, but all the houses were different colors giving it vibrancy. People were out on the small road, and a few waved in greeting to Avani while giving them curious looks. Alex glanced around but didn't see any large homes that looked like they belonged to the Desai family. Then again, if they only had a house on the island so they could be close to the caverns, then she supposed it made sense.

"We'll go down to the caverns soon," Avani promised. "I'm afraid that it sees a steady stream of tourists through the day."

"So, we're heading down at night?" Nicki asked, lowering her voice.

"That's the plan."

"We aren't residents," Aiden said. "Will that be a problem?"

"You're guests, so it'll be okay for one night. More than that and it'll attract attention. Thankfully there isn't much security around the cave. The fact that this is an island with no hotels means that things are fairly calm."

"Glad to hear that," Bran said.

Alex nodded in agreement. The steady hum of magic around her was blending with the crashing of the waves on the shore below and the faint sounds echoing up from the dock. Anticipation brewed in her stomach.

"So," Aiden said. "Do we have a plan, Alex?"

"I- well, I wanted to see the island," Alex replied. A flush crept over her cheeks. "It was... pulling me. I was hoping that it might trigger a vision for Bran or I, something to help us figure out what is going on."

Everyone looked over at Bran who just shrugged. "Nothing yet," he said. "But I'm more than happy to try meditating later." He nodded towards Alex, a flicker of hesitation in his eyes. "If you have an idea of what you're looking for, then we can try to combine our magic later."

"So, this is mostly a sightseeing trip?" Jenny was smiling and gave Alex a teasing look. "That's a nice change."

"Do you feel anything?" Avani asked, looking to Jenny.

"Uh... no, should I?"

"I was wondering if you or Lance would be able to sense the magic surrounding the island." Avani looked thoughtfully at the pair of them. "Perhaps we will try meditating later with the pair of you."

"Can you feel it?" Lance asked.

"Yes," Avani said. "But only if I look for it. I lack the instinct that mages have."

"I don't know about that." Nicki gave Avani a warm smile. "You know more than I do most of the time."

"That is my education, not innate talent."

"Still, don't sell yourself short."

Aiden was holding back a grin, and Bran elbowed him lightly, probably to keep him from teasing Nicki. Alex looked over at Lance and Jenny. They were walking hand in hand and seemed more relaxed than she'd seen them for some time. Lance caught her gaze and gave her a soft smile. Alex contented herself with looking around. The afternoon sun had a ways to go, but the evening wasn't too far off.

The Desai house on the island was modest but comfortable. According to Avani, the kitchen pantry was stocked with food, and there were containers of water. There were spare blankets and pillows in one of the closets. It wouldn't be a comfortable night, but they'd be fine. There was a bit of guilt for dragging the others out here without any discussion, but Alex was just happy that Lochan had made good so quickly on his promise.

While Bran put some water on to boil for making rice for a simple dinner, Avani took Lance and Jenny into the back bedroom for meditation. Alex lingered by the front window which looked out onto some trees and a few others houses. In the distance, she thought she saw the toy train running along the shore, but couldn't be sure.

Evening came slowly. After a simple curry that lacked any kick for dinner, Alex sat down and meditated. It was difficult. Nervous energy thrummed through her body. The urge to pace was almost unbearable. When Avani finally announced that they could head for the caverns, Alex jumped up eagerly.

"Now," Avani said. "The caverns are ancient. They were a site of worship so be respectful."

"We will be," Bran promised.

Avani knew the way; she led them to a dirt path that went from the village down the hill and towards a wider road. Out in the ocean, Alex could see a ferry heading back towards Mumbai and smiled nervously. The hills of the island were gentle slopes and the rough heat of the day was finally beginning to ease a bit.

"This is more like it," Jenny said. "See mages, it doesn't always have to be frantic quests for magical artifacts."

"We've only done two of those!" Nicki protested, but she was smiling broadly. "Not so bad and normal life can be boring."

"I miss normal life," Aiden admitted. "I miss being able to sell my soul to video games."

"Hey, at least you get out in the sun now more." Nicki's voice was almost sing-song, and she was smiling. "I remember losing you for days on end during the summer months."

"And now the sun is my problem," Aiden groaned. "Evil day star. Avani, how do you handle it?"

"Well, my ethnicity adapted to live in the sun." Avani gave him a teasing smile. "As opposed to those who turn red in the sun. Seriously, changing colors is ridiculous."

"I can't argue with that," Aiden grumbled. "But I didn't design the system."

A hot breeze hit Alex's face, cooling some of the sweat sticking to her skin. She looked towards the setting sun and urged it to hurry up. Avani was calm and smiling, seemingly unconcerned about any lingering tourists or locals spotting them. The tracks of the toy train were in view, half hidden behind the trees. Voices and the sounds of people moving below were softening, but still distinct.

"Here," Avani said. She gestured to them. "There is a side entrance here."

They followed her down a rocky slope. "We're not going in the main entrance?" Bran asked. "You said there wasn't any security."

"Not compared to other places," Avani said. "But there is the ticket counter. And some of the vendors who set up by the entrance take their time leaving."

"And this back way?"

"There are several caves on the island," Avani explained. "The one most people are familiar with is the Great Cave, but there are seven in total: five Hindu and two Buddhist caves."

"And they link up?" Bran asked.

"Not like you think, there aren't any fully developed passages, but there is a way in that my family knows. Even after the caves became a World Heritage Site, they never sealed it up. Probably because it can serve as an emergency way in." Avani pushed away some thick brush between two large rocks to reveal a small hole in the side of the hill. "It's fine, I promise."

"Maybe we should have just paid to get in and then hidden," Jenny muttered.

"This is less likely to go wrong," Avani said. "If something magical does happen we don't want the tourists around."

"Look, Avani, if someone catches us, you hide," Alex said. "I don't want your family getting into trouble."

Avani's expression was soft and grateful, but also a touch surprised. Lokpal stirred in approval and Alex pointedly ignored him.

"We managed the Paris catacombs without getting caught," Lance said. "Let's stay positive."

"Just don't hurt anything," Avani said. "The caves have survived centuries and the Portuguese."

They stepped into the darkness. It was a now familiar thing to go into tunnels and caves, but Alex was beginning to hate it. The temperature dropped a few degrees, and the world tightened. She took a slow breath, refusing to allow the dark stone walls to frighten her.

"It's not far," Avani said. "We'll be in the main cavern in no time. I'm sure you'll love it. The facades are very beautiful. Come on." Avani took Alex's hand in hers and tugged her forward gently. "Hopefully, you'll find what you were looking for here."

Alex was beginning to doubt that, but she followed Avani through the first of the small chambers.

21

The Southern Island

21 B.C.E. Mazagaon, India

Lokpal was beginning to hate Morgana. Merlin wasn't so bad, but Morgana had managed to get his wives on her side in a matter of days. While they worried about his training sessions, Morgana had convinced them that it would help keep him safer in the future.

"Try again," Morgana ordered. "Remember to breathe. You must keep your focus while using magic. If your intention becomes unclear, then you will lose control over your magic."

Nodding, Lokpal closed his eyes and inhaled slowly. Morgana's words echoed in his mind. He'd heard them before. Over and over again. Focusing on the slight flicker of warmth in his chest, Lokpal tried to pull it forth. The way Morgana and Merlin had explained it wasn't very helpful. It kept slipping through his fingers, but he was aware of it. If only he could tighten his fist around it... but that wasn't how it worked. A sigh of frustration gathered on his tongue, but he kept it in check. Morgana's irritation wasn't what he needed.

The chirping of a bird soothed him. A soft breeze swept through the yard, and Lokpal strained his ears to hear Ananta moving a pot inside the house. The sounds were comforting and familiar. They reminded him that while his eyes were closed and he was sitting on the ground, that he was safe. His family was safe and for the moment so was the village.

But the Demons would come back soon. Three nights ago, Morgana and Merlin had killed a group of five that were raiding one of the farms. Thankfully, no humans had been murdered and eaten, but it proved that even Rudra and the mages hadn't frightened off the Demons.

"Don't think so much," Morgana said. "Try to relax. The magic is a part of you. It runs through your body like your blood. You must become aware of it. Once you do, everything will become easier."

"So, it will get easier?" He was whining a little and hated it. But Lokpal couldn't understand how something so hard to grasp could be held onto and directed in battle. "You're certain."

"I'm certain," Morgana said. "Magic is a part of you, Lokpal. You were born a mage." Her voice rang with finality.

Closing his eyes, Lokpal focused on trying to feel the magic and not Morgana's words. They made his chest tighten. They were too large for him to make sense of. As a young man, he'd been fast and strong and thus chosen to learn how to fight. His master had been a good man, but not very patient. Years of practice had taught him what he needed to know. It wasn't a glorious life, but it was fulfilling. The Demons had changed everything.

There was a flutter in his chest that spread to his arms. Lokpal tried to mentally grab for it, imagining his hands catching hairs flying on the wind. It helped, and he held it longer this time before it slipped away. Tightening his fingers into a fist, Lokpal held his breath in as he counted slowly to four and then let it out while counting to four again. It helped curb the frustration.

"What am I doing wrong?"

"Nothing." Morgana moved closer and offered him a smile as he looked up at her. "You aren't doing anything wrong, Lokpal. You are trying to use an aspect of yourself that is completely new. You didn't learn to walk or run right away." Morgana moved back and sat down on a small bench. "Just keep practicing."

"Are you sure I'm a mage?"

"Of course, the Connection you experienced proved that. It forms as a reaction to the magic in two people. If you didn't have magic of your own, it wouldn't work."

She sounded sure, and Lokpal nodded vaguely. "Where are you and Merlin from?"

"We told you, far to the north and west."

"How did you get all the way here?"

"We used a magical tunnel made of water to get most of the way here." Morgana tilted her head and examined him. "Why so curious?"

"I've heard you speaking strangely, your own language I suppose."

"Yes, language varies around the world. We use magic to help us."

"You're using magic to talk to me?"

"Indeed," Morgana said. "There wasn't time to learn your language."

"Aren't you at risk of fatigue then?"

Her lips curved into an amused smile. "Merlin and I are very robust, and you are the only person on this island we interact with. When we aren't with you, we return to using our own language." Lokpal observed her lips. It was strange; they moved as if she were speaking his language naturally and yet she said she wasn't. Morgana must have noticed. "It takes focus. I must keep telling my magic that I need you to understand me. That you must understand me."

"But you said that I had to visualize what I wanted. How do I visualize that?"

"That isn't visualization, that's commanding. You'll learn the difference someday, but for now, your magic needs you to guide it. Explain what you need to it."

It sounded a lot like a child. Needing guidance to do what was required. Lokpal wasn't sure he liked the comparison. Glancing back towards his home, he was relieved to find that nothing had changed. Everything was as it should be.

"Do you have children?" he asked.

"No," Morgana replied. "I can't have children."

"Are you married?"

"I was. He passed away many years ago." Morgana's eyes turned distant, and Lokpal studied her face. There were faint lines, but she looked young. A few years older than him, but there had been too many things telling him that she wasn't. "Stop staring and focus on your magic."

Sounds of someone coming up behind him distracted Lokpal before he could even start meditating again. He twisted around and found Merlin jogging up towards his home.

"Morgana!" Merlin panted slightly and adjusted his cloak, glaring up towards the sun. "News just came."

"What happened?" Lokpal climbed to his feet. "Was there an attack?"

"This southern island of yours where the Demons keep being spotted, I think we should take a look," Merlin said. "Another fisherman reported seeing pillars of fire."

"There won't be much left there at this rate," Morgana said. Looking back to Lokpal, she raised an eyebrow. "Have you a way to go to the island?"

He held back a sarcastic question about them flying over the water and nodded. "There are fishing boats we can use. It'll be a bit of rowing, and it's a ways out."

"We'll manage," Merlin said. "Better tell your family that we're stealing you away." His smile was teasing, but there was an underlying worry in his eyes.

Lokpal's mouth was too dry to speak, so he nodded. Stepping into his house just made it worse. Heema walked over to him and brought her hands up to frame his face. Her hands were cool, and he allowed himself a moment to be with her. Ananta joined them a moment later, rocking Oja gently in her arms.

"We're going to the southern island," Lokpal said. "I'm not sure when we'll be back. More Demons were reported there."

"Then let Rudra-"

"The mages want to take a look."

Heema's hands dropped, and her eyes flashed. "Then let them go!"

"I can't just have them running about," Lokpal said. "There is so much that we don't know."

"What I know is that those two are dangerous."

Ananta nodded in agreement. "Lokpal, we're worried."

"I am too, but they've been a great help since they arrived. No one else wants to learn to fight Demons, but they can help me defend the village. And they are trying to explain things to me and teach me. It will just take time."

"But the island-" Ananta started to say.

"We need to know what is going on," Lokpal said. He leaned forward and kissed both their foreheads. "I'll be home as soon as I can."

Heema nodded and shared a look with Ananta before turning away and grabbing a pack. Before he could protest, his wife began to collect some food and supplies for him. When she was done, she kissed him quickly and handed him the pack. He slung it over his back and checked his sword. Morgana called for him, and Lokpal held back a sigh. It was bad enough without letting his family see his frustration.

Morgana and Merlin spoke in their own language as they walked down to the docks, giving him some distance. Their little group attracted a lot of looks from other locals, but no one stopped to greet the strangers. Lokpal didn't blame them for giving the two mages some distance. There were still moments when he worried about letting them into his life and near his family. But it was too late for that now.

Lokpal didn't have a boat of his own, but there were a few spares that had just been repaired that were kept on the shore. Merlin and Morgana hung back while he spoke with Marutta. He offered no objections to them using a boat though he was quick to move away from them once the conversation was done.

They climbed into the boat, but before Lokpal could grab the oars, Merlin tapped each one with his hand. The two oars sprang to life, dipping themselves into the water and pushing them away from the shore. Around them, a bright green aura pulsed with each movement and Lokpal could only stare at them. Merlin chuckled at his reaction.

"Magic can do many things," he said. "It is a tool to protect this world, but it can also make a mages life much easier."

"But you can also use too much," Morgana added. She gave Merlin a weighty look. "So, it is important to be careful with your magic. You want to be sure that you can make it through a fight."

"So, it's like being fatigued?"

"Exactly." Morgana gave him a genuine smile. "It creates a... burn in your chest, not unlike after running too long, but you feel it through your limbs as well. It can cause you to faint which is dangerous when faced with Demons."

Looking down at the oars, Lokpal considered the words and then glanced towards the island. He wasn't sure if Merlin should be using his magic like this or not based on Morgana's words, but he supposed that Merlin knew how much he could do.

"I'm an old man," Merlin said. "And I don't want to row."

"You're a stubborn old man," Morgana corrected. "But you do know your limits. If you go too far, I'm not saving you."

"Yes, you will."

The boat rocked with the rise and fall of each wave, but they slowly drew closer to the island. Morgana gave Merlin a look that was almost concerned, and he nodded to her in silent reassurance that he was fine. She raised an eyebrow at him, informing Lokpal silently that she didn't believe Merlin. It was almost amusing, but it wasn't enough to break through the unease in his chest.

"Hopefully we can find this Rudra when we reach the island," Merlin said.

"What are you going to do?" Lokpal asked.

"The plan is just to talk," Merlin said. He was calm and watching the island curiously. "Is there anything special about this island?"

"Not really," Lokpal said. "There's a hut on it for fishermen who need shelter in a storm."

"Why isn't there a village here?"

"I don't know." Lokpal frowned at the question. "I've never thought about it... I suppose it would make sense for there to be another fishing village here. I suppose that we don't need it. Our islands are comfortable, and there is plenty of fish."

"I wonder if there is something on the island repelling them." Morgana and Merlin shared another significant look and Lokpal turned his eyes towards the island. "Perhaps the location has meaning to the Old Ones," Morgana said.

"Careful, Morgana. It's dangerous to theorize without information."

"I suppose so."

Morgana made him try meditating again. The rock of the boat made it more difficult to stay calm with his eyes closed. Every time a wave hit the side of the boat, he instinctively shifted his weight and opened his eyes to check.

"Focus," Morgana said. "In battle, there will be many distractions. You have to be able to focus on your magic as well as the dangers around you."

Holding back a response, Lokpal exhaled slowly and decided to focus on the rhythm of the boat rather than try to ignore it. The soft lapping of the water against the wooden sides of the boat slowly turned soothing. In his chest, something fluttered like a bird in a trap. It was there, he was aware of it. A soft pulse filled his ears. His fingers twitched. He could almost see it. Then the boat jostled, and his eyes snapped open.

Before him was the thickly forested hill of the island. Merlin was climbing out of the boat and pulling them onto the shore. Twisting around, he looked back towards his own home across the water. It was just a hill on the water now. He gripped the side of the boat to keep his hands from trembling. Morgana climbed out of the boat and looked at him expectantly. Slowly, Lokpal climbed out of the boat and helped Merlin pull it further onto the shore.

"Which way?" Merlin asked.

"I don't know." Lokpal glanced through the trees, noting that several had burned branches. "I haven't been here in years. Mostly its fishermen who come here and I'm the village guard. My job is to stay in the village."

"It isn't that large an island," Morgana said. "It shouldn't be too hard to find either Demons or an Old One."

As if summoned by their words, a loud bang rang through the trees. Merlin grabbed Lokpal's arm as he began to draw his sword and shoved Lokpal behind him. Blinking in surprise, Lokpal focused on the trees. There was another crash right before a Demon came stumbling out onto the beach. It spotted them with wild eyes. Before it could move, a beam of silver light shot through its chest and the body collapsed onto the ground.

"Really, Morgana?"

"What?" Morgana smiled, shrugging one shoulder. "From Lokpal's story about Rudra, that Old One should show up in no time to complain about his prey being stolen."

"You-you're-" Lokpal stuttered and stared at them both. "You're crazy." He shook his head. "I have a family and a village to worry about, could you please try not to aggravate Lord Rudra!"

"It will be alright, Lokpal," Merlin promised. He smiled and put a hand on Lokpal's shoulder, his grip surprisingly strong. "I swear that we will not allow harm to come to them. Protecting this world is our reason for being and yours as well." His smile widened. "It is no wonder that you were drawn to the role of protector."

There was a rumble from the trees. Morgana chuckled and strode forward to Lokpal's dismay. Merlin squeezed his shoulder once more before letting it go and following Morgana. For a moment, Lokpal couldn't breathe. His knees quivered, and the sand beneath his feet quaked. Somehow, he took a step forward and began to follow.

They didn't have to go far. There was a small clearing that was smoldering. The burned down stumps of trees were still flickering with embers and waves of heat rolled over them. Thankfully, Merlin and Morgana stopped at the edge of the burned-out area. Rudra turned towards them slowly, eyes bright with anger. The dark mark on his head was more extensive now, shimmering in the low light like the sun against a polished stone. Morgana and Merlin's presence was just enough to keep Lokpal from stepping back, but he still flinched in fear as the deity's eyes landed on him.

"Mages," Rudra said. His voice was rougher than it had been before. "Why have you come here?"

"To this land or this island?" Merlin asked. "Morgana scrys frequently and saw visions of strange dark-skinned creatures not of our world. We used our magic to lead us to this land so that we could protect our realm. As for why we came to this island, we wished to speak with you and see if you know why there are so many of these Demon creatures."

"No," Rudra said. "I don't know what they want. They have a new leader and a pathway to their world somewhere nearby. That is all I know. I'm just killing them."

"You're struggling," Morgana said. Her eyes were narrowed on Rudra, and Lokpal stepped back instinctively. The air thickened like setting porridge. It smelled like a storm. "Struggling to keep your mind," Morgana said. "You're slipping."

"I'm fine!"

"How long have you been in this world?" Morgana pressed. "You weren't born here, were you? No, I don't think so. You were one of the ones banished here."

"What was your crime?" Merlin asked.

Lokpal's eyes widened and he looked between the two mages frantically. The fire in Rudra's eyes was bright against the blackness of his pupil, like burning coals in the night, and just as dangerous. Thunder rolled in the distance, but neither Merlin nor Morgana moved. Their cloaks fluttered in the growing wind, but they stayed in front of Rudra.

"I questioned," Rudra growled. "When I shouldn't have."

"Ah yes, your world is rather harsh," Merlin said. Sympathy filled his expression. "I'm sorry for that, I know only a little of your homeworld, but it puts ours in danger by using the Iron Realm as a prison."

"They don't care." Rudra's voice was almost sad. "As long as it doesn't disturb their perfect order."

Merlin nodded. "Order has value, but it is not inherently good." Then his expression hardened. "You're becoming corrupt, Rudra."

"No!"

"Yes, you are. Your body is showing signs of it. Being in our world is taking its toll on you."

"I am fine."

"No," Morgana said. "You are not."

"Then leave me be," Rudra growled. "I will remain on this island and slay the Demons. Stay away from me and I will stay away from you!" Rudra's teeth flashed as he snarled. The skulls hung around his body clinked together far too loudly. "Be gone."

"We will be mindful of you." Merlin's tone was stern. Green sparks of magic circled the mage. "When you become a threat, we will end you."

"That is not a fight you want," Rudra growled. "I can see it in your eyes. Begone!"

Merlin nodded, and the veil of green sparks vanished. Morgana turned first and grabbed Lokpal's arm, pulling him back towards the shore. His mind spun. He didn't understand what had just happened, what they had been talking about. Underneath him, his feet almost tangled up, but Merlin caught his elbow to keep him upright.

"Wait? We're leaving?"

"For now," Morgana said. She glared back into the trees as they quickly walked towards the shore. "I don't like this, Merlin."

"I don't believe we can fight against him and the Demons at the same time, not until we know more at least." Merlin's voice was calm but rang with finality. "It's time to go."

"But we need his help!" Lokpal gestured back towards the burned out clearing. "We can't fight all those Demons-"

"Yes, we can," Merlin said. "Lokpal, you are a mage. I know that you don't think of yourself that way yet, but you are. You have power and a connection to this world beyond that which mundane humans will ever understand." He smiled softly at Lokpal, reaching out and putting a hand on his shoulder. "I believe you are even special amongst mages."

"Why?"

"There is a special soul. A champion of the world, if you will, who is reborn as a mage to protect the world. You are here at the center of this new danger. You were fighting Demons before Morgana, and I ever arrived."

Merlin all but pushed him into the boat. His sword sheath scraped against the side of the boat, and he blinked at the mages in confusion. The words didn't form properly in his mouth, and he looked towards the trees. For a moment, Lokpal thought he caught a glimpse of Rudra watching them. Morgana climbed into the boat as it hit the water and Merlin jumped in a moment later. He waved his hand, and the green sparks surrounded the oars, propelling them back towards his home island.

"I don't understand," Lokpal said softly. "What will happen now?"

"Hopefully, he will allow himself to disperse through our world." Merlin's gaze was stern as he looked towards Lokpal's island. "If not, he will continue to be corrupted. His kind does not belong here, not unless they fully embrace our world. If the corruption erodes him away, he will become violent towards humans. We fought an Old One a hundred years ago named Badb, she was insane and vicious."

"A hundred years ago…" Lokpal's chest tightened. "Will I live that long?"

"Unlikely," Merlin said. "Morgana and I are different, even for mages. The point is that Rudra is not your friend. He isn't part of our world, and he will become dangerous."

"Try not to worry about it," Morgana said. "The Demons are a far greater danger. If we're lucky, perhaps they will destroy each other."

"Is there nothing we can do for Rudra?" Lokpal asked. They both looked at him. "I know that… that he isn't good exactly. I understand that he isn't from this world." He swallowed back the word god, knowing that Morgana would hate it. "But he isn't evil. He can help us."

"Lokpal," Merlin said gently. "Very few Old Ones survive in our world. Cyrridven is a rare Old One who has been embraced by the Iron Realm and acts as one of its protectors."

"What makes her different then?" Lokpal asked. "Rudra is trying. He's struggling against that corruption. Surely you can see that."

"Cyrridven… stays in the water," Merlin answered slowly. "I do not know if that helps her or not, but Rudra is not your responsibility. These Demon creatures are dangerous and organized. They are our priority."

Frowning at them, Lokpal turned and looked back at the island. He didn't understand Merlin and Morgana. The name Cyrridven seemed familiar, but he had no idea who they were. If one Old One could stay sane and gain the approval of the mages then surely something could be done. He looked down at his hands, uncertainty bubbling in his gut. Why did he even care? Rudra had saved him, but he'd also injured him. So why did he care?

22

Reaching Out and Collapsing In

She wasn't sure who cast the spell, but small orbs of light illuminated the narrow pathway of stone as they followed it. Suddenly everything began to open, and the small lights spun together to form a more massive orb. The light orb floated up into the air and Alex gasped as the stone was lit. An elegant building façade had been carved into the rock beside them. The rock had been worn down with age, but the image was still clear enough to inspire awe. Alex's eyes jumped to the right as Aiden conjured another orb and lit up another façade with dancing figures. Beside her, Avani chuckled and released Alex's hand.

"We're in the main cave now. Just be careful not to go too close to the doorway. It's dark enough outside that we'd draw attention."

"Oh wow!" Nicki squeaked. The redhead clapped her hands together in excitement and bounced around on her feet. "Look at these!"

"Yeah," Jenny said. She pulled out her phone and snapped a photo even as her mouth hung open a little.

"Don't share that," Avani cautioned. "No one is supposed to be here after dark."

"I won't."

"This is impressive," Aiden said. He was nodding with a grin. "Sort of like Petra. That city carved into stone mountains in the middle east."

"This is the largest collection of stone art in India." Avani smiled proudly. "And it remains in its original location."

"So, this was a temple to Shiva?" Bran looked at Avani curiously.

"Yes, its history is tied to the worship of Shiva. It isn't a very active site now, but centuries ago this complex would have been crowded and busy with people coming to pay their respects and priests overseeing ceremonies."

"I can believe it," Bran said. "There's an energy here. Almost like I could pull back a curtain and see all of that."

"It might not be a good idea to scry here then." Nicki's smile was both teasing and a little worried. "Sounds like it could be overwhelming."

Alex was still near the small opening in the rock wall, tucked back in the shadowy corner. She didn't move. She inhaled deeply, taking in the musky, earthy scent that mixed with the hint of ocean breeze that made its way inside the cavern. Nicki was tossing up more light orbs with a gleeful smile while Avani was chanting a soft spell with her hands outstretched. Bran had moved over to one of the reliefs and Aiden was hanging nearby her, watching either the entrance or her.

Alex's eyes finally moved. She braced herself for familiarity, but there wasn't any. It had changed. Like going back to an old school. There was a ghost of what she knew, but something that was past. Her flashes of memory were too old. Everything had changed. The once curved and rough walls that a few carvings had decorated had been transformed by years of work. Elegant statues rose out of the stone itself. The multiple faces of the Hindu Gods looked out at them. Or at least, Alex assumed that's who they were. Even the representations were alien to her.

She took a step forward. Beneath her feet, a surge of magic made its way up into her chest. It circled her heart, warming and comforting her. The voices were soft and low, leaving her to her own thoughts. Walking across the cavern, Alex focused on the largest of the carvings. It wasn't familiar, but the image of the one it showed was.

It was a detailed relief, carved from the cavern wall and depicted a figure from the torso up. The statue towered over them, rising almost twenty feet into the air, and protected by the tight embrace of the rock. There were three heads, all of them with closed eyes. While it didn't look like the Shiva Alex had met, she knew at once that it was supposed to be him. Elegant headdresses were carved into the stone, and the figure was adorned with carved necklaces. It was beautiful and Alex's lips curved into a smile. On either side of the grand figure, stood a duo of statues, one taller and another kneeling to serve as attendants.

"This is Sadhashiva," Avani said. The sudden sound in the cavern made Alex's heart jump. "He, Shiva, is the destroyer, the creator, and the preserver of the universe."

"I didn't think that was how it worked," Jenny said. "Isn't Shiva the Destroyer?"

"Yes, but even as the destroyer he is part of a trinity of gods who represent creation, destruction, and rebirth. It's an important cycle in both Hindu and Buddhist traditions. And just as Christianity has its variation, so does the worship of the Hindu gods. There are many traditions, and an ancient one around here is Shiva as the protector of all aspects of the world."

"I wonder if that links to Lokpal," Bran said.

"Most certainly," Avani replied. "While I don't know the details of Lokpal and Shiva's time together, Lokpal did entrust Shiva with his Trishula."

"Yeah," Alex agreed. "I'm surprised that it isn't here." Her hand almost reached out to touch the carving where Shiva's hand would have been holding the Trishula.

"Yes, I suppose so," Avani agreed. "But Shiva has always been very protective of it. Maybe back in the early days, he didn't allow mortals to see it at all."

"Maybe."

"Or perhaps, they didn't understand its importance."

The words were an attempt to comfort her, but Alex's skin tingled. Somehow it just made things worse. She didn't understand the sudden onslaught and moved away from Avani. Glancing at another façade, Alex moved closer to the doorway. It wasn't the air, she wasn't claustrophobic, and thanks to the light orbs it wasn't very dark. Nicki was bouncing between facades, talking to an amused looking Aiden. Jenny was hanging on Lance's arm and taking photos of a female figure while her boyfriend smiled indulgently down at her. Bran was wandering towards Aiden, looking at the façades with a soft appreciative smile.

Her chest tightened. Stepping off to the side, Alex reached out a hand and caught herself on the wall. She focused on Nicki's voice as the redhead tried to keep from making too much noise even as she rattled off questions for Avani. Aiden and Bran were talking across the room, and she could hear Jenny and Lance speaking in low voices. They all sounded calm and relaxed. It was safe; they were safe here.

Repeating that didn't help. Her fingernail scraped against the wall. It was a struggle to keep her frantic breathing under control. A desire to cry out for help and a need to stay silent warred in her throat. Indecision kept her frozen. The others were fine. So, there must be something else, Alex decided. Her magic fluttered in her chest, and Alex eagerly reached for it. Her eyes slipped closed in relief as the energy flowed into her lungs and eased the ache.

She let the magic reach out. Dark silver threads spread through the cave, outlining the walls and facades in a pale gray glow before stretching out for the surface. Alex let them. Magic pulsed up through her feet, giving her more energy and power even as she sent it outward. The strands began to twist and turn around each other, weaving into a web of awareness. She watched a small woman finish packing up her fruit stand outside and head home with a handcart. She was the last one there. Now there was just a line of empty stalls that had been covered for the night. Waves were lapping at the shore gently. It was a calm night. She pulled the strands back before they headed across the ocean to Mumbai.

Lines of magic made the facades around her glow. It was so different. She'd been expecting a simple cave. The image of a shrine with a small carved statue pushed to the front of her mind. Waves of emotions flooded over her defenses, leaving her floating in unfamiliar grief, confusion, and anger. She urged them back with a soft whimper.

Most of it retreated, but the pulsing core of the emotional storm remained. Her hand was shaking. Lokpal's confusion, his grief at everything changing was pounding at the back of her skull. She didn't understand it. His island home was long gone, swallowed up by human progress and centuries of construction. Why did the cave matter so much? Why was this what caused such a reaction.

Other memories pressed forward. The room swayed, and sea salt filled her nose. Alex frantically pushed away Cuthbert's ship. She could still hear the chains rattling below, binding the slaves to his will, and keeping them compliant for the voyage, draining all fight out of them. Bile filled her mouth, and Alex shivered. She tried to focus on something, anything else. There was a glimpse of a young smiling Morgana laying on a green hillside and looking up at the clouds as a dog barked out of sight.

Then the truck appeared right beside her. She was in the back of the car, and her parents were in the front. They made a cry of alarm, and the connection was cut. Arthur was laughing. There were two coffins on twin tables at the front of the hall. People were crying softly, but she couldn't. Matt and Ed were silent beside her in somber suits that they were too young to be wearing. Matt was angry. The constant threat of magic and Arthur was taking its toll. She didn't know what to do anymore. So she let them go. Please let it be enough. Let them be safe without a sister. Let Matt be a good parent to Ed and let them be happy as they heal from the loss of their parents. She can never see them again. She can't talk to people she used to know. It hangs by a thread. A Sword of Damocles and her chest hurts.

Inhale and exhale. Her chest resisted, but ultimately, she started to win the fight. Her fingers tried to dig into the stone wall, and the long-lost scents began to fade. She could smell the rock surrounding them, the musky scent of the underground. The voices of her friends became clearer. All around her, the strands of magic were still spread out and waiting for her. There was a soft hum of energy around her. It sank into her muscles and bones, easing the aches of the day. Reassuring. Even when everything else changed, she had this.

"Alex?" Someone was holding her free hand. Their voice was soft and hesitant. "Alex? Are you alright?"

She tried to claw her way out. She really did. Alex had thought herself beyond this. Strange what could count as the final straw. Something being unfamiliar to Alex that she should never have been familiar with in the first place. Silly. It made no sense at all. This shouldn't matter to Alex Adams, and yet somehow it did. It almost made her laugh. Air built up inside of her chest sending a dull ache through her limbs. She let it out, suddenly lightheaded as the magic kept flowing out. Dizzy and confused, she ignored the voices trying to reach her and focused on the magic. Her breathing evened out, and relief flooded her.

The strands of magic knotted together before pulling back sharply. There was something there. Something not of Earth. Alex pushed the strands forward. Around her, the world shifted, and she wasn't in the cave anymore, but now looking at a hillside. Magic outlined the trees in a faint gray glow, but there were towering dark figures huddled together and talking. She caught a few words, her magic gathering in her chest to translate. Then someone called her in a louder voice.

Gasping, Alex opened her eyes. She was in the cavern again. Bran was beside her, holding her free hand with wide, nearly frantic eyes. As she focused on him, he visibly relaxed. Alex's magic fluttered across her skin. The strands still spread out.

"Alex? Are you okay?"

"I was just... Demons," Alex said. Her thoughts came back to her. "There are Demons nearby."

"Surely not," Avani said. She shook her head, anger, and disbelief warring on her face. "They wouldn't come here."

"If Alex says there're here then they are here," Jenny said. She was staring at Alex, but everyone except Bran was keeping their distance.

"Inhale, Alex," Nicki said. "Hold it for four seconds and then let it out."

She obeyed, but the Demons were still rubbing against her magic. Like sandpaper on skin. Harsh and unnatural at the edge of the senses. Straightening up, she avoided looking at the facades. The ache was fading, and her mind was buzzing.

"There are Demons," Alex repeated. She tugged at the bottom of her t-shirt. The material was too thin, and the chill was sinking in. It shouldn't have been. It was summer in India. She should have been hot. "Let's go and see what they're getting up to?"

"Alex, let us-"

"I'm fine, Aiden." Alex allowed herself to shudder. "Just lost control of my magic for a second there. I should have been more careful about using it at a place like this."

Nicki's eyes bored into her, but then finally the redhead nodded. Before Alex could move away, Nicki ran past Bran and caught her chin, making Alex look right at her.

"You sure you're okay?" Nicki asked.

"Fine, just a bit... overwhelmed."

Nicki hugged her, caging Alex's arms against her sides and resting her chin on Alex's shoulder. Her surprise cut through the rest of the emotions and Alex sighed in relief. Pulling back from Nicki, she gave a little nod and looked to Avani.

"I'm serious, Avani, I sensed them. There are Demons on the island."

"That's not good," Avani looked towards the entrance of the cave. "This is a peaceful island! The people here aren't-"

'Come on," Alex ordered. She gestured towards the entrance. "They aren't near the village yet, but we need to go and find them before they cause trouble."

"Do we know if they're new or locally born?" Aiden asked.

"No idea so let's try to say hello first," Alex answered.

She walked quickly out of the cavern. The warm night air hit her face, and she promptly descended the short staircase that led up to the entrance. They were in a small courtyard flanked by small cliffs to the left and right. In front of them were a small ticket building and a low fence.

Low security indeed, but for now that was a good thing. Alex closed her eyes and tugged gently at the strands of magic still holding around her. They twisted and tangled around one of the Demons, darkening in response to the being from another world.

"This way!"

Breaking into a run, Alex jumped over the low fence. The wash of the air over her skin made her smile. Running was familiar. Her long legs easily found the right rhythm. She hadn't run in weeks. Thanks to the threat of the Sídhe and Arthur, her early morning runs had become a thing of the past. Her racing heart slowed, and Alex lost herself in the thud of her own feet against the road. The magic drew her towards the Demons, the moon and a few streetlights gave enough light to let her navigate. Her body finally gave her grounding.

23

Demons on Elephanta

Air rushed over Alex's skin. Her legs stretched out, and her muscles sang. She regretted surrendering this habit out of fear and promised herself to start running again when they returned to Ravenslake. Behind her, she could hear the others scrambling. It was too dark for them. Alex knew that intellectually, but it didn't slow her down. Around her, the magic outlined every tree and rock, giving the world a ghostly outline.

The magic tangled a few feet in front of her, but she didn't see the Demons. Alex stopped. Something tingled against her skin. A cold puff of air that made her hairs stand on end. The oppressive heat was gone for a moment, but only a moment. Everything started moving again a second later, but she looked around suspiciously.

"Alex?" Bran called. "You okay?" He was panting and leaned against a nearby tree. "I don't see anything."

"They're coming."

The others didn't ask any more questions. There was no doubt or confusion in their eyes. Lance and Jenny pulled out their daggers. Magic flashed around the hands of Nicki, Aiden, and Bran in their respective blue, red, and yellow. Avani moved back to join Lance and Jenny, putting her palms tightly together in front of her chest.

A low snarl came from the trees. The strings of magic tugged at Alex's skin, poking her like an eager toddler. Then something came out of the trees. It looked around with surprised eyes that landed on them. The Demon wasn't as large as the others, it was even shorter than Jenny, and at first glance, Alex almost dismissed it as human. But the dark skin was accented with red marks around the eyes and the lips twisted up at the corners to reveal too long canines. A long metal chain was wrapped around its shoulder, and with a pig-like squeal, it pulled the chain loose and swung it towards them.

Alex sidestepped the chain attack as three more Demons came rushing out of the trees to their right, attempting to flank them. Fire flashed in the night as Aiden released a wave of red magic towards them. The creatures jumped back and drew weapons that Alex could barely see in the low light.

"Gun!" Bran shouted. Yellow magic surrounded one of the Demons and swung up into the air. "Got it!"

Hoping that was the only one, Alex called forth her magic. Beneath her feet, the ground thrummed in response and the spark in her chest expanded, sending power rushing down to her fingertips. The Demon swung the chain at her again, but Alex brought up her hand and released a bolt of lightning. It screamed, dropping the chain, and stumbling back. Without catching its breath, it snarled and sprang forward. Alex released another bolt of lightning, this time keeping the energy flowing. The Demons screamed and clawed at the empty air, fighting against the pressure to reach her. Then it stopped and slumped to the ground, its body beginning to collapse inward.

Spinning on her heel, Alex checked on the others. Aiden was standing over another pile of flesh that was turning to ash and gathering a fireball over his head. Only one Demon remained, and it was facing a calm looking Bran with a field of yellow energy between them. Avani was nearby, clutching a small handgun in her hands with Lance standing protectively next to her with his dagger in hand. Heat rushed across Alex's face as the fireball pulsed and Aiden moved to release it.

"Just capture it!" Alex shouted. "We need information!"

The fireball stayed in place, the surface of it shimmering with red for a moment before it began to dim. Flames vanished and were replaced by a smoother glowing surface. Smiling, Alex noted that Aiden had turned it into a light orb and focused her attention on the Demon. A beam of yellow hit one of its legs and pulled it up into the air as it shrieked. Alex barely noticed Aiden moving over to where she'd been fighting and scooping up the fallen chain.

A sigh of relief escaped Alex, but she kept her focus on the Demon. It was trying to sit up and reach its ankle, but a yellow shackle kept it hung in the air. In the glow of Aiden's new light orb, Alex could see that this Demon had strange black scars on its left cheek. There were red marks around its eyes, and she wondered if they were naturally occurring or some kind of tattoo.

Aiden walked over with the chain in hand, startling Alex. He nodded to Bran as he released the Demon who hit the ground with a thud. Without a word, Aiden wrapped the Demon up in the chain with Nicki coming forward to grab the other end. The pair held it tight, and the Demon fell silent. Alex hesitated, her eyes scanning the trees. Her magic rippled out along the strands of energy still hanging in the air. She didn't feel anything more. This was the last Demon, for the moment, at least.

"Why are you here?" Alex asked.

The Demon said nothing. Aiden pulled on his end of the chain, tightening the metal prison around the Demon. The dark metal dug into the Demon's flesh. Holding back a hiss, Alex tensed and froze in place. It wasn't the same. She knew that. Her mind told her that it wasn't the same, but it was still a creature wrapped up in a chain. Nicki looked at her with concern and confusion.

"Let it out of the chain," Lance ordered.

"What?" Aiden blinked at him and then looked down at the Demon. "Oh shit." He released his end of the chain and took an aborted step towards Alex before remembering the Demon. It shook off the chain and started to move. Aiden raised his free hand, forming a fireball. "Don't try it."

The creature squirmed on the ground, trying to move away, but also eying the fireball. Dark blood seeped into the ground and slowly disappeared in low flickers of light. A bitter smell hit Alex's nose. She stepped forward, keeping her hand up and the magical sparks spinning through the air. Electricity arced between her fingertips and the Demon stilled. Bringing her left foot forward, Alex stepped down on the creature's throat, pinning it in place.

"What are you doing here?" Alex demanded.

"Scouting party," the Demon groaned. Its breath was thin and weak. Alex eased the pressure. "Local Demons said there is something powerful on the island. Said it belonged to someone who could destroy us. King sent us to scout it out."

Avani made a sound of anger behind her, but Alex didn't look away from the Demon. "What is your plan?" The Demon chuckled, and she let more of her weight roll forward onto its throat. It wheezed but didn't say anything. "Your plan! Now!"

"You couldn't even keep me chained," the Demon gasped. It turned its eyes to glare up at her. "You'll kill me fast at least."

"Maybe we won't," Nicki said. "You're invading our world!"

"The Darkness is taking the homeworld. Better to die fighting than die cowering in the dark."

"Darkness?" Alex repeated.

The Demon said nothing more, glaring up at her. Suddenly, he lashed a hand up and scratched her leg with long talons. Flinching, Alex gasped in surprise and pain but pressed her weight down onto the Demon's throat. Nicki darted forward and released her magic in a flash of blue light. The Demon screamed as a long blue icicle shot into its right shoulder and pinned it to the ground. Flinching, Alex saw Nicki grimace in the corner of her eye, but the redhead swallowed and rallied.

"Tell us what you know," Nicki ordered. "How are the Demons getting here?"

"Found a portal," the Demon gasped. It started bringing its free hand up, but Nicki raised her hand and let it see the flash of blue light. Dropping its hand back to its side, it sneered up at them. "It doesn't matter. Gargen will never stop. He's brought us this far. He'll kill all of you, your whole race if he must." Smiling and revealing rows of sharp needle-like teeth, the Demon started to sit up, but the icicle stopped the movement. "We'll eat as many of you as it takes! There's nothing left to lose!"

"Where is this Gargen?" Alex asked.

The Demon didn't answer. It stayed still and waited, just watching them. Ideas ran through Alex's head, but she dismissed them all. Her stomach turned at the mere thought. In the corner of her eye, she saw Nicki shift uneasily. She was still watching the icicle with a hint of regret in her eyes.

"You can't do it," the Demon laughed. "You mages are weak. You have power, but no strength." It pulled against the icicle, a rough groan of pain escaping it as the flesh stretched and ripped. "You can't stop us. We will take this world. We need it! We'll fight for it in ways that you won't!"

There was a gunshot. Everyone jumped and then froze. The Demon clutched at its chest. Alex's ears were ringing, but the sound quickly faded away. Turning around, she found Avani pointing the gun at the Demon. Her face was utterly blank. Her hands weren't shaking, and a strand of her dark hair was hanging over her face. For a moment, Alex was frightened of her. Then Avani inhaled slowly and lowered the firearm. Looking down at the gun, she shivered.

"That was easier than I thought," Avani said. Bran moved over next to her and held out a hand. She handed him the gun with an almost grateful smile. "Sorry... I just-"

"He wasn't going to tell us anything more," Aiden said. "Creepy, but he'd already decided he was dead. Not sure if he was afraid of this Gargen or the Darkness more?"

"Darkness," Nicki said. Alex could hear the dubiousness in her voice. "Really? That's where this is going? The Darkness is coming. What next, the Nothing?"

"If they don't know what it is then they have to call it something," Bran said. His hands were on his hips as he watched what remained of the Demon collapse. "This confirms what that other Demon said."

"Yeah, but what does it actually mean?" Jenny asked.

Her mouth was too dry to answer. Ash hung on her tongue. The memory of the dead world filled her mind. For a moment, she couldn't see any of the trees or her friends; just a desolate wasteland spotted with ruins. Then she inhaled the cooling night air and was back with the others. No one had moved. No one seemed to know what to do.

"Merlin and Morgana don't know anything?" Lance asked. "How is that possible?"

"If it hasn't come up before then there's no reason for them to know," Bran answered. He was the calmest as Avani nervously toyed with her necklace and looked around into the trees. "They aren't all-knowing, despite what Morgana might want you to think."

"Do you think the Darkness could be something like the poison made by removing magic?" Nicki asked. She was looking at Alex. "Something like that in another world?"

"I don't know." Alex swallowed and rubbed her tongue on the roof of her mouth to generate some moisture. "That doesn't sound right."

"What poison?" Avani asked. "What are you talking about?"

"Don't worry about it," Lance said. He shook his head. "I'm with Alex, that doesn't seem right. This sounds more like a catastrophe."

"So now what do we do?"

They were looking at her for an answer. Her fingers tightened into fists. Holding back a growl of frustration, Alex told herself to stay calm. An itch at the back of her brain was pulsing and taunting her. A shudder traveled down her spine. Her magic hummed, but the frequency was off. Sour and out of synch. But she didn't understand why. Another shiver went down her back, and she dug her nails into her palms. The others were waiting. She chewed on her lip.

"I don't sense any more Demons," she finally said.

"I can't believe they were here," Avani said. "To come here-"

"They don't understand this place," Jenny said. "You heard the Demon. They were sent to scout because of the stories the Demons who live here tell."

"We need to treat your leg." Nicki was kneeling next to Alex with a small light orb in her hand. "It went through your jeans and tore the skin.

Who knows what those things might be carrying." Nicki stood up and looked at the others. "Who's got the-"

"I've got it." Bran was already swinging his backpack off and tugging at a zipper. "One second. I've still got some water in my bottle too."

The hushed conversation was mostly lost on Alex. She watched Bran pour water in the Iron Chalice, and he held it towards her. Alex's eyes checked the metal, but she didn't see any glow in the iron.

"You try to charge it," Alex said.

"It didn't work before."

"Maybe it needed a jump start from the Iron Soul first." Alex shrugged. "Just try it."

Bran nodded slowly, sharing a look with Nicki before closing his eyes. A soft yellow glow seeped from his hands into the metal as Avani crept closer. Her brown eyes were wide with curiosity, and Alex almost smiled. The magic flowed into the Chalice, and Alex noted a fresh gleam in the iron.

"Uh... maybe it worked," Bran said. He held it out to her. "Only one way to know for sure."

"I doubt that it only works for me," Alex said. "At least I hope not. That's not as useful." She took a sip of the water. It tingled against her tongue and slid down her throat towards her heart. "Oh... that's interesting," she said. "It's doing something." Alex took another drink.

Nicki knelt again. "The skin is healing," she announced. "Good to know that others can charge the Iron Chalice."

"Still, hardly the Holy Grail of legend," Aiden said.

"You shouldn't complain!" Nicki spun around to face him.

"I'm not complaining! Just... remarking."

Alex ignored them and looked down into the Chalice. A faint shimmer of magic was still humming in the metal, and the water at the bottom was rippling slightly. The magic dissipated around her. Alex almost released more, but there was a soft ache growing in her chest that warned her against it. The flood of emotions from earlier had eased and yet there was still a nagging feeling. Like something, she'd forgotten. The water in the Chalice shimmered, and Alex's eyes widened.

There was a large Demon, taller than any she'd seen thus far, dressed in studded hide armor standing before lines of Demons. His mouth moved though Alex couldn't hear him. It changed, the water rippling too much as she moved in surprise. There was a hole in the dark, shimmering edges lined with white and gray. This time, she heard something, the crashing of waves. It was muted, but there.

"Alex?" It was Bran's voice. "What's wrong?"

She looked up for a moment but quickly dropped her eyes back into the water. There was nothing, just the iron bottom of the Chalice.

"I saw something in the water. I'm not sure what it was."

"That's- that makes sense. It could be an excellent scrying surface since the Chalice is magical." Bran stepped close to her and peered into the Chalice. "I don't see anything." He took the Chalice carefully from her hands and studied it.

"No... it ended. I wasn't looking for anything." The itch was worse than ever. She shivered, trying to shake it off and stepped back from Bran. "Shiva!" Alex shouted. Her voice cut through the dark hillside. Birds took off from the trees, and the flutter of the wings echoed too loudly around them. "I need to speak with you!"

"What are you doing?" Avani asked. "He won't hear you, and you shouldn't seek to summon-"

Something pulled at the strands of magic. Turning her head, Alex looked down the hill for a moment before closing her eyes. The glowing strands showed her the way down and there at the shoreline was a churning wave of magic. Not her own magic, not magic of the Iron Realm, but familiar magic. Friendly magic. She smiled, opened her eyes, and began to move. Running down the hill, Alex pushed some hair from her face and inhaled the scent of the sea.

Shiva was standing on the shore. Behind her, Avani gasped, but Alex just smiled and walked forward. The Iron Trishula was clasped in Shiva's hand, and he raised his chin as she approached. He didn't look angry, more surprised.

"You called?" He raised an eyebrow, and the corner of his mouth turned up. He put his arms on his hips. Then he seemed to notice her torn jeans. "Are you alright?"

"There was a Demon, well a group. We're fine," Alex said.

"Demons, here?" Frowning, Shiva's eyes flashed red for a moment. "There haven't been any Demons here since the ancient war. They all learned better."

"Shiva, before was there ever any mention of a plague or darkness?" Alex asked.

"I do not believe so," Shiva said. He shifted slightly, tugging his foot through the sand, and tightening his grip on the Iron Trishula. Hesitation filled his face. "But, Alex, I was different then." His body was tense, almost pained. "Corruption and madness from being in your world had begun to take its toll on me. There are many things that I struggle to remember about that period. And this invasion seems different. Back then, Demons came into this world and caused chaos, but often returned to their own. Why things are different now, I have no certain answer for you."

"Oh." Questions burned on her tongue, but images began to play out in her mind's eye. Fragments of Lokpal's memories that she knew held the answer, but this wasn't the time. "Alright, so if this is a new problem then the Demons are different. If they really are running from a plague, then they're more like refugees then an invading army."

"Some of them at least," Aiden said. He grimaced slightly. "Cause some of them are organized and hostile. Remember that group that came looking for us and almost killed Gita. And that one talked about a leader named Gargen. We may be dealing with a fanatical army that wants Earth as a new home and others are coming through with them that aren't violent and break off from the main group."

"We can't let them just take Earth," Nicki said. Then she frowned. "But we also can't have the entire population of another world move into ours. We've got human overpopulation as it is."

"And depending on what this Darkness is, letting too many Demons through may spread it here," Bran said softly. "This isn't a good situation no matter how you look at it."

"Things are worse than I feared it seems," Shiva said. "I will remain near the island and guard it." He looked towards the lights of Mumbai. "There are far more Demons in the area then there should be. I killed seven yesterday, but they keep coming. Yet, I am struggling to track them. Their movements are strange."

"The Demon said they'd been sent as scouts. Probably to try to attack you," Alex said. "The local Demons gave them information about you."

Shiva's expression turned harsh. The worry melted away into confidence and he smirked. His eyes flashed once again and this time, Alex could see tiny flames dancing in his irises. "They will find that defeating me is not a simple task."

"You're the Destroyer." Nicki was smiling again, looking almost giddy. "Of course, not!"

Smiling a little at her, Shiva nodded, but turned his attention to Alex. He said nothing, just watching her. The smile fell away, and his fingers drummed on the shaft of the Trishula.

"I will return you back to the mainland," Shiva finally said. "You need rest, though I'm sure you won't seek it. Always be ready for a fight." Reaching out with one of his free hands, he put his heavy palm on Alex's shoulder. "We will get to the root of this threat, my old friend. I promise you that."

Turning towards the water, Shiva held out the Iron Trishula. Alex's heart jumped and she watched magic spin off the edge of the weapon. In her chest, her own magic sparked in recognition and the urge to reach out and touch it returned even stronger than before. Alex kept her hands still at her sides and breathed slowly as a water tunnel opened for them. Given that a gun had just been fired on the island it was probably for the best that they left, and an idea was beginning to form in her mind.

24

March of Demons

620 B.C.E. Mazagaon, India

Frustration was not a new emotion to Lokpal. He'd been training in the art of fighting since he could run and while he'd had an excellent master, there'd been many moments of frustration. At least then, he had understood his goals. There had been a future planned out for him, and he'd known that he improved a little each day.

Now, he had no such reassurance. The meditation was soothing, but thoughts of the continued Demon attacks always crept in and distracted him. He needed control of his magic, and he needed it now. Even the calm clearing at the edge of town where Merlin and Morgana had built a small hut for themselves wasn't enough. Every sound of the village he heard just reminded him of what was at stake. Maybe his time would have been better spent training more warriors, if he'd ever gotten volunteers at least. He opened his eyes and looked out toward the ocean. From here, he could just see over the treetops down the hill and into the bay where the local fisherman had a small dock.

"Try to stay calm, Lokpal," Merlin said. "I know that it is difficult for you, but your magic is there, just waiting for you."

"I think you're wrong about me," Lokpal said. He didn't look at Merlin, keeping his eyes fixed on the waters below. "I'm not this Iron Soul of yours."

"I know that it is a great deal to understand." Merlin's voice was calm and soothing, but Lokpal resisted listening to the old mage. "In truth... I do not completely understand it myself. You are the third incarnation of the Iron Soul that Morgana and I have found."

"What makes you so certain that I'm not just another mage, like you?"

"Little things," Merlin said. Lokpal gave him a doubtful look. "And Morgana was scrying for the Iron Soul. It led us here where we found you and the world in need of its protector. I have no doubts that you are the Iron Soul."

"And yet, I still can't use magic. The seasons are changing, another wet time is coming, and I still can't conjure forth these powers that you say I have."

"It can take time." Merlin touched his shoulder. Despite the urge to, Lokpal did not pull away. "There is magic inside of you Lokpal. You've felt it; you're close to it. Something will help you cross that final threshold."

"What?"

"I don't know. That is also part of you."

Groaning, Lokpal began to pace. The frustration weighed down his shoulders. His back was painfully tight now, no matter how much he stretched, and his sword seemed heavier each day. There was an itch to run; to take his family, some possessions and go east. Surely there were safe places. But he had responsibilities to the village. They relied on him.

Merlin didn't try to stop him. In fact, the old mage just watched him with a soft, almost sad expression. His eyes were dark and distant. He looked so very old. Lokpal stopped his pacing and took a long look at Merlin.

"How old are you?"

"Centuries at this point," Merlin answered. He didn't seem surprised at the question. "Morgana and I both are, we are kept alive by the magic of the Iron Realm. Our purpose is to guide and protect mages. That includes you. When I tell you that you can do this, Lokpal, it is not an empty promise. There is magic in you. Power is pouring into your body from the world around you, and despite your worries and doubts, you will find it."

It was an odd sensation that rose in his chest. Warm and yet heavy. Lokpal was saved from having to try and understand it by a scream. His hand jumped to his sword, and he rushed towards the road. A loud roar filled the air followed by a tremendous crash. Large feet pounded on the ground, their speed increasing, and shaking the earth. A woman came running up the path, carrying a child with terror filling her face. Lokpal drew his sword. Two fishermen followed, dropping baskets of fish across the road. One of them dropping a fishing trident in his haste.

A line of Demons appeared, five forming the first line with another line behind them and another beyond that. There were dozens of them. All different sizes and slightly different shapes, but all of them glaring at him with dark eyes. All were armed with spears, clubs, or swords and marching with purpose towards him and the village beyond.

Green magic rushed past him, swirling into the air, and then exploding into a rain of green fire. Demons shrieked, and their lines broke as the Demons tried to dodge. Lokpal didn't move. His hands trembled, but he brought his sword up in front of him, bracing himself for the first Demon to come close. Two Demons dropped as the fire struck them.

There was another burst of magic. Heat flashed past Lokpal, and a fireball flew by horizontally. It struck a Demon who screamed and burst into flames. It dropped a flaming club and grabbed a nearby Demon, setting its arm on fire. Another Demon hit it in the face, sending it crashing to the ground before it could spread the fire.

"Merlin!" Morgana called. Lokpal didn't turn around, thankful that Morgana had returned from the village. "Lokpal, fall back!"

"There's too many," Merlin snapped. "Your sword won't help you here, Lokpal. Focus on your magic and retreat."

He ignored them. One of the Demons charged forward. Dropping down, Lokpal managed a slower swing of his sword but sliced into the Demon's ankle. It fell to the ground, dark blood spilling across the dirt as it howled. One of the Demons shouted at the others, and they reformed their line, marching forward. Morgana released another wave of silver sparks. The Demons charged forward in a massive wall of dark flesh, weapons, and violence.

Magic showered down on them. Many fell but more made it far too close. Lokpal stabbed one and had to dodge the blow of a club instantly. Thankfully, the swinging Demon hit the first Demon which crumbled to the ground due to the wounds. Lokpal ducked between two Demons trying to pin him down and sliced at the back tendon of another one. It was harsh, but it worked, and the creature fell. There were too many. His eyes couldn't track them all. Backing up, he fought to keep them all in front of him, but they pressed and pressed.

In the corner of his eye, he saw Merlin sending magic spinning towards him, knocking down more of the Demons. But another Demon was coming up behind him. He opened his mouth to shout, but it was too late. Merlin grunted as the Demon struck him. Lokpal's eyes widened as the old man dropped to the ground unmoving. Morgana screamed something. Silver power exploded around them, the wave of magic hitting the first line of Demons and sending them flying. Lokpal took a step towards Merlin, but Morgana shouted for him to keep fighting.

Keep fighting he did. Morgana's blast did not slow them down for long. The line reformed and marched forward. Morgana shifted just enough to stand between the fallen Merlin and them but made no move to help him. The Demons gave neither of them a chance to do anything. Lokpal swung his sword and stepped back. Swing and step. Dodging the different Demons as they attacked him. He was out of room to retreat without leaving Morgana and Merlin.

One of the Demons swung a spear at Morgana, catching in her side. Lokpal's heart stopped, and he was almost hit himself before instinct made him drop. Morgana fell to her knees, a cry of pain escaping her. She tried to stand, but her legs gave out. A silver field appeared in front of her just in time to block the Demon's second blow. She was panting in pain and Lokpal was too far away. More Demons were pressing forward. Silver bolts were released from Morgana's magical field and struck down the closest three Demons, but there were still more.

He could hear the screaming behind him. Everyone was running. He hoped they'd make it. He wanted to turn and look, to try to find his family in the people evacuating, but he didn't dare. Shoving his sword forward, he slashed the side of the nearest Demon. He jumped back to avoid being stabbed with a spear by the next one. There were too many. They were too close. Another Demon reached for him with a grin. He swung. It jumped back, and another circled behind him. A sharp push to his back made him stumble, and a Demon snapped its foot forward. He tried to stand, tried to bring his sword up. He couldn't.

Lokpal's heart stopped. His blade was stuck, caught under the Demon's foot. He couldn't move it. Grinning, the Demon put all his weight down, and Lokpal finally released the hilt, watching as it hit the ground. The metal looked wrong, already twisted, and ready to snap. Backing up, he looked around for a weapon he could use. There was a massive club a few feet away, but he'd never be able to fight with it properly.

Dodging a swing, he dashed to the right and scanned the ground. There was an abandoned spear. He grabbed it, picking up a fistful of mud in the process and lashed it forward at the nearest Demon. The skin of the creature was tough, and the sharp point barely drew blood. It was something. Demons were scattered around him now. There were too many to count, but the lines had broken down. He shoved the spear forward, getting a Demon in the arm. Another grabbed the shaft of the spear and pulled. Releasing it, Lokpal darted away, closer to Morgana. There was a snap of wood behind him.

"Where did that all come from?" Lokpal asked Morgana. The words were hard to manage.

Morgana was on her knees, holding her side with one hand and breathing slowly. Her hair was a matted, sweaty mess and lines of exhaustion furrowed her brow. "I don't know," she managed. "Lokpal, you need to run."

"Run where?"

"Anywhere? Find your magic and stop them."

"You can't mean for me to leave you?"

"There's too many!"

He ignored her. Unmoving, Lokpal braced himself. The Demons were closing in. The spear was gone, his sword was gone, and Merlin and Morgana were both prone and struggling to defend themselves. In his chest, his heart was pounding like a frightened animal's. That's what he was now. He almost laughed and took another step back. Strange. The knowledge that he was about to be killed and possibly eaten was almost calming. He didn't understand it, but the panic was fading into cold anger. Rage, but contained. Then he felt it. Beneath his heart, beyond the frantic beating, there was a flutter. Exhaling slowly, he reached for it.

The Demons were right in front of him. There was no more time. Desperation, hope, and determination blended, and he threw up his hands as a spear was hurtled towards him. Bright blue magic surrounded him, catching the spear and holding it. Everything shimmered. There were small sparks, and the magic began to fade. Merlin's words about focus and controlling magic echoed in his head. Without much of an idea what he was doing, Lokpal pushed the image of the magic turning into bolts like Morgana's to the front of his mind. The field shimmered for less than a second before a wave of small blue bolts like arrows shot forward. Two Demons were hit and fell to the ground with dying cries of pain.

"Yes!" He hadn't meant to cheer, but the flutter bloomed into a sharp heat that flowed down his arms and legs. His blood was pumping faster and better than ever before. "Stay back!"

The Demons didn't listen. Another charged him, and Lokpal threw his arm forward. A disk of blue sprang forth and rushed through the air. It wobbled, sparks flying off it, but it swung through the nearest Demon, slicing it in two. Dark blood splattered across the ground and the other Demons. The body began to vanish, but the stunned looks on the faces of the remaining Demons did not. There was still a dozen left, and their hesitation did not last long.

An orb of silver killed another Demon. He risked a glance towards Morgana who was struggling to stand up. Merlin was finally stirring, but the wound on his head did not give Lokpal hope. They were still outnumbered. He envisioned the disk slicing through more Demons, tried to picture it killing them all. It exploded forth from his hands, and all the air was pulled from his lungs. The disk sliced through three Demons before flickering away.

"Don't overdo it!" Morgana called over. "You don't have enough control yet!"

He tried to heed the advice. But the magic slipped away, rushing out of him with every attack. More disks of magic sliced through the Demons. Envisioning fire, he created a shower of blue flames that killed two more Demons. The end was in sight. Their numbers were finally dropping without more marching up the path. Another disk killed two more. Morgana killed another pair, and a flash of green shifted the ground and caught the legs of two Demons that howled in frustration. The old mage's hands were shaking, but the faint green glow around them gave Lokpal hope.

His chest began to ache. His lungs were too tight like bands had been fastened around his chest. Through his feet, more magic raced up to fill him, but the ache was spreading. Fatigue blurred his vision, but he released another wave of magic. It caught more of the Demons and forced them back. Magical sparks spun off the sides of the wave uselessly, and he tried to think of a better way. He needed to stop this fight. Morgana was still fighting but couldn't stand and move. Demons were trying to get closer to her. There was only so much she could do.

Trying to summon more magic, Lokpal's body convulsed. There was a burn spreading through his chest. An ache settled into his bones, but they weren't done yet. He waved his hand, but no sparks came forth. A Demon grinned and ran forward. Lokpal's eyes landed on the nearest discarded weapon, an iron trident dropped by the running fishermen. Scooping up the trident, Lokpal held it out in front of him. There was a soft hum in the metal as magic jumped from his fingertips. The ache eased a little.

"Rudra!" Lokpal shouted. "Please, Rudra. We need your help!"

His words hung in the air but didn't stop the Demons. Another one swung a massive club at him. Lokpal dodged it and thrust the trident forward. Blue sparks licked around the tips, forming an arch of lightning between the prongs. The sharp burn in his chest grew worse, but Lokpal stabbed the Demon. Lightning jolted off the metal prongs, and the Demon collapsed to the ground.

"Rudra! Please!"

The pain in his side was distracting. The world was starting to shake and blur, but he locked his knees. Blinking, he tried to count the remaining Demons. Six. Only six left in the small army. He swayed, trying to bring the trident up. Fire sprang forth in front of him forming a wall. The Demons drew back in shock. He looked towards Morgana, but surprise was written on her face. Then she looked towards him slowly, but Lokpal shook his head. The trident sparked in his hands, and he inhaled slowly, the burning ache cooling.

More fire exploded amongst the Demons, encircling their bodies. Stumbling back, Lokpal flinched at the rush of heat. But the fire didn't spread and when it faded all the Demons were gone. Ashes wafted into the air before they too vanished. Rudra was standing at the far side of the path where the Demons had stood, his eyes glowing bright red and orbs of flame circling him. The dark patch on his skin had spread, covering almost half of his face.

"I heard you." Rudra's voice was soft, almost impossible to hear. "I heard you call me."

The deity was panting; its dark eyes fixed on Lokpal. Lowering the trident, Lokpal swallowed and tried to form words. Rudra took a step towards them. Then he stopped. His hands were shaking. He looked down at them, his expression turning confused. Lokpal stepped forward, but the deity turned sharply and dashed into the forest, disappearing from view.

25

Breathing After Battle

Shiva's water tunnel collapsed behind them, splashing through the small pool in the Desai's side building. Nicki looked over her shoulder but noted that Shiva had not come with them. She wondered if that was due to him wanting to check the island or some other reason. What those other reasons might be, she didn't really want to know.

Everyone was accounted for. They didn't seem any worse for the wear, but Alex's jeans were torn, and she hadn't bothered mending it with magic yet. Aiden and Bran were fine. Avani was shaking. It was subtle. Her expression was blank, but her eyes were distant, and the quiver of her hands was unmistakable. Nicki was ashamed to realize that she'd been confused about the source of the distress for a moment. Avani had taken the discarded gun from the Demon. She'd been the one to shoot it, and it was probably the first real act of violence in Avani's life.

Somewhere along the line, Nicki had almost become used to it. For a moment, she turned that over in her head. It didn't make her ill or angry or even sad. It just was. She swallowed and glanced towards Avani again. Lance was right next to her, a large solid hand on her shoulder and Jenny was on her other side. They were both silent, but they were there. Whatever lingering resentment towards the pair that Nicki had been carrying melted away.

She took a step towards Avani, starting to reach out to her before thinking better of it. Lance was holding the firearm stiffly in his left hand, keeping it tight to his side. Nicki stared at it. Firearms had never really been a part of her life. Her father had kept a gun in the glove box if she remembered right. She had vague memories of him pulling it out and shooting at empty cans against hillsides when they were in deserted areas. He'd never let her touch it though, and her grandmother had no interest in firearms. Lance seemed familiar with how to hold it, his finger was well off the trigger, but he didn't look easy about it.

Movement in the corner of her eye drew Nicki's attention towards the water once more. Alex was kneeling by the side of the pool and looking down into the water carefully. Bran was right next to her. Torn between Avani and Alex, Nicki couldn't move for a moment. Then Alex looked up from the water at Bran. The look in her eyes was sharp, intense, and thoughtful, but not frantic or frightened. Releasing a soft sigh of relief, Nicki stepped back to join Avani, Lance, and Jenny.

"Alex?" Nicki called. "You okay?"

It was a poor question. None of them were completely okay anymore, but it was all she had. With a sinking feeling in her gut, Nicki forced herself to meet Alex's eyes as her friend turned to look at her. The gray orbs were cloudy and distant. Yet Alex nodded. Then she turned back to the pool and reached down to touch the water. It was still churning from the collapse of the tunnel, but the rhythm of the waves was slowing down.

"I want to try scrying with this water and the Chalice," Alex announced.

"What are you looking for?" Bran asked.

"I'm not sure, but I wasn't even trying to scry with the Chalice. It was like... maybe the water was so magical that it tried reaching out for something. This water has been infused with magic over and over by Shiva and magicians. Maybe adding some of it to the Chalice will strengthen the effect."

"It's worth a try," Bran said carefully. "But knowing what you're looking for would be safer. There's a lot of world out there." His tone was light, but Nicki could hear the underlying worry.

"Arthur and the Queen then, or this Demon King. The sooner we figure out where this portal is, close it, and stop the Demons, the sooner we can get back to worrying about the Sídhe."

It was like being dunked in cold water. Nicki knew they were still out there of course. She hadn't forgotten. It was impossible to forget Arthur who had seemed to be their ally even if he'd never fully transitioned to friend for her. He'd tried to kill Alex and had left Aiden in a coma after the idiot used too much magic saving Alex. Yet, he'd slipped to the back of her mind. Angry at herself for the slip, Nicki tightened her hands into fists. Aiden caught her eye. He looked calm and gave her a small nod. Great, he was being reasonable again.

Avani shifting beside her pulled Nicki from the rage building in her stomach. The woman seemed to be trying to make herself smaller and was creeping towards the doorway. Rage washed away. Then the cold returned for a moment as worry took over. She hesitated for a second, a little voice whispering that she'd only make things worse. But that seemed to be holding the others back too.

"Are you okay?" Nicki took Avani's shaking hands. They were cold. In the corner of her eye, she saw Lance and Jenny back off though they stayed close. "You're shaking."

"I- I know it wasn't human. But it was sentient. It was alive and..." Avani chuckled, but it turned into a soft sob. "Maybe it's silly."

"It isn't," Nicki said firmly. "Don't apologize for not needing something to be just like you to feel compassion for it. Death isn't supposed to be easy."

"Is it hard for you?" Avani asked. She turned over their hands and examined Nicki's steady palms. "You aren't shaking."

"No." Nicki licked her lips and shook her head. "It isn't so hard anymore. I... I sort of wish it was, to be honest. The first fights were all about survival. The Sídhe were coming into Earth, capturing people, and sending their Hounds to kill us. It made things easier. Kill or be killed. Then there was the Iron Chain and the spell."

"Why did that chain bother Alex so much?" Avani all but whispered the question, looking past Nicki at Alex. Judging from how Alex tensed, she heard the question, but didn't say anything.

"There- one of the incarnations of the Iron Soul wasn't a good person. We don't think he knew what he was doing, but over the years he created an object, a chain, that bound people to his will. He was a slave trader. The Sídhe Queen got ahold of it and used it to bind all the Sídhe descendants to her will. She made them attack us, and for a while, we didn't know that they weren't acting under their own free will." Swallowing, Nicki kept her eyes down. She didn't want to see the look on Avani's face, and her own heart clenched. "We were killing beings that were victims of magic. We killed a bunch of them before we knew what was happening. Alex found the Chain through magic and broke it and the spell, but... I don't think she's going to forgive the part of herself that made that Chain anytime soon."

"Of their own free will or not, they would have killed you." Avani's voice was soft. "And I suppose that's true of that Demon. It might have been afraid of something, but it came to the island with dark intentions."

"It's messy," Nicki said softly. "I wish it wasn't, but it is. They're desperate and going about saving themselves the wrong way. When I first learned I was a mage, I thought that it was straightforward good versus evil, but the shades of gray creep up on you." Shivering, Nicki closed her eyes and inhaled slowly. "So slowly that you don't even really notice that things have changed until you make yourself stop and look back."

Avani's grip changed. She squeezed Nicki's hand, and when Nicki opened her eyes, she found Avani smiling sadly at her. Lowering her eyes again, Nicki knew that she was blushing. "I came over here to comfort you. Apparently, I'm bad at that."

"You did comfort me," Avani said. "Maybe I should be bothered by the reality that mages aren't perfect, but it makes it a bit easier. Maybe I shouldn't have- well I shot that Demon. I was angry, it was scaring me, and all of you seemed stuck."

"Torture... that isn't something we've done before." Nicki closed her eyes again and fought back a shiver. "I hope that's a line we never cross. The Demon seemed to know that. It wasn't frightened of us. Still, that wasn't something you should have had to do. I'm sorry you were put in that position."

"I'm the one who took the gun and... well, I won't pretend that I wasn't still angry about my mother. Seeing her on the ground like that-" Avani cut herself off and shook her head. "I'm okay, Nicki. I really am. I'll be fine."

"Yes, well maybe I'm not."

It was a poor excuse, but it made Avani's expression soften. Something like understanding flickered in her brown eyes. There was a lovely rush of warmth in her chest, excitement tempered by a bit of fear, and a stern reminder to herself that friendship was different from someone returning her crush.

"Alex, do you need us for anything?" Nicki asked. She stayed close to Avani but looked over at the pool. "I'm not much of a scryer. Or you know, at all."

"I'll stay with Alex," Bran said. Sometimes she wondered if that boy could read minds. He already had the telekinesis down. "Too many of us here is likely to be distracting, and I'm the other scryer."

"Alright," Nicki said. She nodded and glanced over at Aiden.

"We'll hold off on contacting Merlin and Morgana for a bit longer." Aiden fixed Bran with a surprisingly stern look. "Don't exhaust yourselves. I'll check on you in a bit."

"That's fair," Bran agreed. In fact, he looked relieved. "Thanks."

"Yeah, come on," Aiden said. "Let's get Avani inside."

"I'm sorry today didn't go as planned," Avani whispered.

Nicki took her arm and gently guided her towards the doorway. Thankfully, Avani didn't fight her. The tremor in her limbs was still there, but it was easing. "Come on, let's leave Alex and Bran to their scrying."

"I've never seen scrying."

"There isn't much to see." Nicki patted Avani's arm and smiled. Jenny opened the door outside, and the fresh air washed over them. "Sadly, it doesn't play out like a tv show or anything so useful."

"At least not that they've managed yet," Lance said. His tone was warm and calm. Nicki was unbearably grateful for that. "Give them some time and who knows."

"True," Nicki said. They walked down the lit pathway towards the side door. "That's something that we're learning; you've got to be creative with magic. Merlin and Morgana are powerful and very skilled, but I don't think they've tried anything new in centuries."

Avani laughed. It was strained but real, and the tight bands around Nicki's lungs loosened. "That's odd to think. Growing up… well, we hear so much about the Grand Mages and their power and knowledge."

"Well, that part is true," Nicki agreed. "I mean, they have got thousands of years of experience and knowledge. I'll admit, sometimes I wish I could lock them up and make them tell me everything about day-to-day life through the ages. I wonder what they'd say if they were drunk."

"Don't," Jenny said. Nicki could hear her smile. "Don't get those two drunk. I imagine it would go very badly."

"Yeah," Nicki sighed. "That is one downside of magic, no drinking."

"We have that rule too," Avani said. "It is for the best."

The inside of the great house was warm. There was a hint of something sweet in the air. It wasn't familiar to Nicki, but Avani instantly sighed in relief. Avani's grip on Nicki's hand tightened, and she pulled her gently towards the kitchen. It wasn't the best way to cope with the situation, but Nicki had to admit that there were worse reactions to your first real battle than seeking out baked goods. Many worse reactions.

Nicki wasn't sure how late it was. The dark sky made her think it was late, but the thrum in her veins meant she wasn't at all tired. Avani must have felt the same way because she led them into the kitchen. There was a plate of something that smelled good but was completely unfamiliar to Nicki on the counter.

"Will they be alright?" Avani asked. She opened a cabinet and pulled out some glasses. "Alex and Bran?"

"They'll be fine," Aiden said. He gave her a soft smile. "They work well together. Bran is actually the reincarnation of a mage that worked with the Iron Soul in another life." He grinned and nudged Nicki's shoulder.

"I guess you could say that he's the most loyal of us all given he came back to help once again."

"Hey," Nicki protested. "In our defense, we don't know if we've had prior lives. Maybe we've helped before too. We don't know a lot about Alex's other lives."

Jenny chuckled and shook her head at them. To Nicki's surprise, the reincarnation of Guinevere or whatever her original name had been was very calm. Lance took a seat at the counter, relaxing, and watching his girlfriend with a smile as she helped Avani pour some glasses of water. Nicki accepted her water from Avani and gulped down half of the glass in one go.

"So, how long does it usually take for the adrenaline to wear off?" Avani asked.

"Varies," Aiden said. "Sometimes we crash after the fights, and sometimes it takes hours. Bran and I play video games a lot after big fights to cool off."

"It's always different with Alex," Nicki said. "Though back home, Merlin and Morgana almost always want to talk with her after a fight, so she's frequently their captive for a few hours."

Avani chuckled, the tension in her shoulders easing a little. Here in the warm and brightly colored kitchen, it was a little easier to leave the fight behind. Nicki didn't understand that. How a change of location could help so much, but it did. Avani didn't make a move towards the plate on the table, focusing on drinking her water. It was a start.

26

Memory and Vision

The others had gone, and the water in the pool had cleared. Without any wind or filtration system, the water was almost mirror like. Alex's eyes traced the decorative mosaic on the bottom of the pool. It was a swirl of colors and geometric shapes that almost made her smile, but did nothing to relax her. Bran was sitting on the edge of the pool, one leg bent, and his right arm was resting on that knee. He was calm, a steady point in the storm of thoughts and emotions welling up in her head.

The voices were getting louder. The threat of this Darkness shaking them all. Closing her eyes, Alex inhaled slowly. She turned her focus inward, reaching for the flicker of power in her gut. It pulsed in response. Through her limbs, more magic crept up through her body, reinforcing and empowering the spark until it burst to life. Alex flexed her fingers, and dark gray sparks spun forth from her skin, sending the magical energy into the air. She considered the sparks for a moment.

Color varied between mages. She didn't understand what determined the color. Was it a question of personality, resonance with the magical energy, or something odd like an aura? Arthur's real magic had been black which she associated with evil. Arto's had been white, Thor's a bright electric blue like lightning, and her own was dark gray. Maybe it was to match the color of iron or maybe it was something else. Energy rippled across her hands, making her skin tingle and goosebumps form on her arms.

Staring into the water, Alex didn't move. The pool was perfectly still. Then it began to shimmer as her magic settled across the surface. Every spark flashed brightly as it touched the water before vanishing into the liquid. She wasn't sure if she was thinking about this correctly. Picking up the Chalice, Alex closed her eyes and exhaled slowly. Her thoughts were a jumbled mess, but the wish behind all of it was for this to work. There was no visual she could grasp onto this time, only a solid push of will. Alex hoped that it was enough, that her magic could translate that wish into manifestation. She lowered the Chalice into the water, holding tightly to the short neck, and pushed more magic into it.

"What are you looking for?" Bran asked. His voice was barely above a whisper.

"Something... anything that can help." Alex didn't look at him but smiled. "I want to see if there is anything that the Iron Realm wants to show me."

"Do you think it works like that?"

"I don't know, but something made my soul. Something showed Merlin a vision of my soul. I'm not sure what it is, but I'm going to try." Alex swallowed and fought back a tremble. "There was a lot that I saw when I took the potion. Not all of it made sense. Maybe this can help."

"Okay. I'm here if you need me."

Nodding, Alex kept her eyes on the surface of the water. There was nothing. It was clear and slowly stilled as the last of the ripples slowed. She waited. Still nothing. There was no rush of information into her mind like when she'd taken the potion. Maybe that was for the best, but Alex couldn't contain the sigh that escaped her. That was a wound that hadn't healed as much as she'd hoped. She'd been shown so much. Many lives that she had yet to sort through and all of it ending with her witnessing the murder of her parents. Maybe reaching out once more was a mistake.

Her mind turned to Arthur. She couldn't help it. Despite the hazard this Demon King posed, Alex thought of Arthur when there was danger. She thought of his blue eyes turning cold. Her stomach ached with the phantom pains of being stabbed. Even her heart which no longer had a place for him twisted when he entered her thoughts. She'd loved him, and he'd done all he could to destroy her. Bitterness filled her mouth, and the water shimmered.

It was foggy, like looking through a mist, but vague shapes began to appear on the water's surface. The Chalice glowed softly, still submerged, and tiny gray ripples moved across the surface of the pool, slowly bringing things into focus. Slowly the image of two figures appeared, one of them tall with bright blue eyes. His blond hair was long now and pulled out of his face in a ponytail.

"But where have they gone?" Arthur's voice asked. Alex tensed at the sound of it, fighting back a shudder. "Merlin and Morgana are still in Ravenslake, but the others are gone."

"Rumor has it that the Demons in India are becoming more active." That voice belonged to Scáthbás, and the water cleared enough that Alex could see the middle-aged woman. Her blonde hair was elegantly coifed, and she was seated at a vanity table, applying dark red lipstick. Arthur was a few feet behind her, leaning against a white doorframe. Alex didn't recognize the location, but it was elegant and nondescript. Potentially a hotel room somewhere. "There are other branches, Arthur dear. You must remember that."

"I've never seen one of these Demons."

"Well, they do tend to stay in Asia." Scáthbás blotted her lipstick and smiled at her reflection. Arthur kept sulking in the doorway. "Which is just as well for us. We still have a ways to go in securing control of the Sídhe. I have faith that once we do, it won't be an issue to take back my throne."

"We don't have the Sword."

"The Sword can help open the way, but I'm certain we can speed up the decay of the Iron Gates. Even those shining new ones that your girlfriend put up." Turning around, Scáthbás reached her hand out for Arthur. He stepped closer and took it, letting his mother draw him closer. "Patience, my dear. Our souls, our essences waited thousands of years to regain physical forms and have this opportunity. We must be careful and precise." Arthur drew Scáthbás up onto her feet, and she ran a finger down his chest, outlining his muscles beneath his plain white t-shirt. "These Demons may be useful to us. They are distracting the mages and splitting them into two groups."

"But there's no good way to gather information in India," Arthur protested. "Sídhe descendants don't live there. We have no network there."

"Arthur, stop trying to control everything and know everything all at once." Scáthbás tapped his cheek sharply and pointed the finger at his face. "You'll never manage it. I was a queen, and I couldn't. The trick is to be flexible and ready to take advantage of opportunities. Just like when you killed your poor girlfriend's parents. That knocked her to her knees."

"Except Morgana made her brothers disappear!" Arthur's features contorted in anger. "I can't find them. I lost that leverage."

"Yes, but that means that the girl is giving them up. That's emotional vulnerability. That pain can be far deeper than anything other. And I know my traitorous daughter, she's not maternal enough to help the Iron Soul through this. Obsessed with her late brother's soul or not, Morgana isn't capable of real human connection."

"I think you may be wrong about that," Arthur said.

Scáthbás gave him a withering look, and he grimaced. Reaching up, Scáthbás grabbed his chin and pulled his face closer to hers. Then she smiled slowly.

"I suppose we'll find out, won't we, my darling." She brushed her lips against Arthur's. Alex's stomach turned, but she didn't dare break the magical connection yet. "Even if she is, that will still distract Morgana and Merlin. The Sword is out there in the world, and we will find it."

"It's at the bottom of the ocean! It's all Aiden's fault-"

Scáthbás kissed Arthur again, harder this time, silencing him. They rubbed against each other until Scáthbás pulled away, making Arthur whimper. She smiled triumphantly and sat back down at her vanity. Picking up a brush, she delicately tended to the soft curls of her hair.

"It doesn't matter. While I would prefer to bring through the Sídhe armies under my control, the poor little descendants of my warriors in this world are useful. They're tired of hiding in the shadows, and more of them are joining us every day."

"But not all."

"No, not all. They'll never all join us. Too many resent my little binding for that, but I'm not the one who made the Iron Chain, and they know it. As much as Alex Adams and that soul of hers play hero, they are still human. Still as flawed and vulgar as the rest."

"Alex is determined," Arthur said. He leaned forward and looked at Scáthbás through the mirror. "She's dangerous. You need to let me deal with her."

"Oh, I'm well aware that you want to deal with her," Scáthbás teased. Her tone was dark, and her eyes hardened. Bringing up a hand, she traced Arthur's jawline, looking at their reflection in the mirror. "You're not happy with this aging form, are you?

"No! It's not that. I'm concerned about the danger she poses. Alex is clever, and there are more mages now than normal."

"Yes, I'm sure that's your only concern when it comes to the pretty female Iron Soul." Scáthbás scoffed even as Arthur laid his chin on her shoulder. "You enjoy the company of your mother, my darling Arthur. I suspect that you enjoyed the company of your former cousin more than you care to admit."

"Really, Mother? It was the plan. Just the plan. I did kill her if you recall. She would have died there if Aiden hadn't saved her."

Scáthbás made a thoughtful hum before reaching out to touch the mirror. There was a small flicker across the surface. Then Scáthbás frowned, her eyes widening. Alex's heart jumped as Scáthbás whirled around and jumped from her seat, pushing Arthur back and tripping over her chair.

"Someone is watching us," Scáthbás hissed. "Oh... very clever, Iron Soul. You found something pure enough and powerful enough to push through. It won't happen again; I promise you that." Scáthbás laughed and looked around as if searching for their viewpoint. "Next time, you might see something that you don't want to see." Scáthbás' eyes began to glow a dull gold color. It was off and slightly green, but the fog began to roll back in.

A shock charged up Alex's arms and a strange fog rolled back over the water. Shaking her head, Alex tried to focus her thoughts, but the realization that Scáthbás had sensed her and had enough power to cut the connection was alarming. Morgana would need to know, but that was a conversation that Alex wasn't looking forward to.

"Alex?"

"Did you see that?" Alex asked Bran.

"No, there was some sort of shimmer over the water, but the vision was yours alone."

"I suppose that would have been too useful, huh?"

"Next time we can join our powers," Bran offered. "That will probably let me see too."

"Yeah... you didn't need to see this."

"Did you find the Demon King?"

"No, I guess I was thinking about Arthur. I found him and Scáthbás."

"You did?"

"Well, not found exactly. I don't know where they are. It wasn't familiar, just a room somewhere." Alex exhaled slowly. At least it had confirmed that Arthur didn't know where her brothers were. She shook her head again. "Somehow Scáthbás knew I was watching and was able to cut the connection. I'm not sure how she did that, but I overheard a few things. They know we're in India, but don't have the details. They're still trying to rally the Fae to their cause. Scáthbás wants to be queen again, and Arthur still wants the Sword."

"Of course, he does," Bran said. He rubbed her back lightly. "Are you okay, after seeing him I mean?"

"I- god I hate seeing him. I feel..." She shuddered and swallowed down bile trying to rise in her mouth. "Dirty whenever I see him. I just want- I want to claw his eyes out, punch him, and I don't know, run him through with Cathanáil."

"I'm both dreading and looking forward to the day we catch up with him," Bran said gently. "It will be amusing to see if you, Nicki, or Jenny do the most damage to him."

Laughing, Alex leaned back from the water though she kept a firm grip on the Chalice. It was nice to laugh, and she indulged in a quick daydream of Jenny and Nicki kicking Arthur as he curled up. As unlikely as it was to happen, it was a satisfying image.

"Do you want to try again?" Bran's voice was almost too gentle like he was afraid of the mere suggestion hurting her. Both anger and affection warred briefly in her chest before Alex just sighed. She didn't have the energy for detangling emotions. She didn't even have the energy for detangling her hair. "It's late; maybe we should get some food and sleep," Bran suggested.

"I'm alright a bit longer," Alex promised. "I want- I need to try and get a handle on this." Frowning, she looked at the pool again. "Maybe it's too big. Maybe I should just use the water from the pool in the Chalice. I was hoping that you'd be able to see the larger surface."

"Maybe." Bran shrugged a little. "It would be useful to know that we could use the Chalice as scrying tool in addition to healing." Smiling at her, he tilted his head. "I wonder if the Trishula has any special powers."

"Purification," Alex said. The word slipped out before she even thought about it. Blinking, she looked at Bran who had raised his eyebrows. "Sorry... that wasn't me."

"Lokpal?"

"I'd guess so since it was his iron item."

"Any idea why he crafted it?"

"I-I don't..." Alex paused. There was a whisper at the back of her mind along with a small, strange flutter. A memory toyed at the edge of her awareness, but Alex wasn't sure if it was really Lokpal's or the creation of her own uncertain memory. "I think that it was an accident."

"Like the Iron Chain?"

"No! No, it's not like the Iron Chain. That was made slowly... the Hammer was made over months of Thor pouring magic into it; the Sword was intentional as was the Chalice. The Trishula was something else. I can't quite...."

"It's okay," Bran said. He reached over and touched her shoulder. "It's okay. If you need that information, then I'm sure it will come to you, but don't worry about it otherwise. I don't remember anything from the first Bran. You don't have to remember all your other lives."

Alex couldn't agree. She nodded, but she wasn't convinced. Inhaling slowly, Alex turned her attention to the flutter in her chest. More magic was slowly spreading up her limbs through her feet, and she could have sworn that she could feel sparks jumping from the water below her into her palms. Closing her eyes, Alex focused on the Demon's words. The Darkness. A chill crept over her, but she clung to the need to see the Demon King.

Opening her eyes, Alex dropped her gaze into the Chalice as she crossed her legs to be more comfortable. The water shimmered. The sides of the Chalice took on a soft gray glow. Suddenly aware that her lips were dry, Alex licked them nervously and focused her attention on the water. It was cloudy. Even with the Chalice's large bowl, the surface she could use for scrying was fairly small. Magic hummed across her fingers, comforting in some moments and painful at others.

In the center of the Chalice, shapes began to appear. Large hulking dark shapes that Alex easily identified as Demons. It was dark wherever they were. Squinting, Alex tried to see more of the details. Maybe it was too small when they used the Chalice; maybe she needed to use the pool of water. Her hands trembled. Licking her dry lips again, Alex swallowed and softened her breathing.

She couldn't hear anything, but a soft glow had appeared. It was a line of white in murky surroundings. There was a strange shimmering distortion that Alex felt she should recognize. It cleared and drew closer to her sight. Gasping, Alex blinked and then smiled. It was Cathanáil. The distortion was underwater, and the Sword was buried in the bottom. A faint light was reaching down from the surface, so it wasn't deep.

"It's Cathanáil!"

"Great, but what does Cathanáil have to do with the Demons?" Bran asked.

"I-" Alex cut herself off and focused on the vision. The shimmer of light twisted, and a dark figure sprang out of it. The form shuddered in the water before pushing itself off the bottom and vanishing from her sight. "There's something...." Another figure appeared, scrambling in the water for a moment before pushing itself off the bottom as well. "A portal."

"Shit!" Bran shook his head. "The Sword opened a portal?" Then he paused. "That... sounds familiar somehow."

"Yeah," Alex agreed weakly. Gofiben's voice whispered to her that it had happened before. "That's how the new Demons are getting here. When Arthur lost Cathanáil, it ended up underwater and opened a portal."

"It must be close then," Bran said. "We need to find it and close the opening. But if it can do that then no wonder Arthur wants it. The Sword bypasses the Iron Gates. I wonder why Arto did that."

"He might not have meant to," Alex said. "But where is Cathanáil? And where is the king?"

"Breathe," Bran said. Reaching out, he gently touched her shoulder. "Breathe, Alex. Don't try to force it. We've already learned a lot just from that." He smiled a little at her. "Besides... would you recognize the area if it showed it to you."

The words made sense, but Alex lowered her gaze back to the Chalice. Pushing more magic into the warm metal, she watched the vision of Cathanáil reform. Arto's voice yelled for his Sword, regret sinking into her bones that it had been so misused. Arthur had once said it was a key. She hadn't understood then; she did now.

Water rippled across her vision. Clouds formed over the vision before it took on a new shape. A massive Demon in armor stood in a cavernous empty building. Perhaps some kind of warehouse. Alex could see the gleaming of his metal and hide armor and hints of the Demons he was looking out at.

"We are here," the Demon said. His voice echoed through Alex's knees, too deep and gruff for the realm of humans. "This world is a sanctuary from the Darkness but is abused by the humans who call it home." There was a cheer from the Demons. Alex's heart jumped at the roar of noise that told her that there were a lot of them. "We will take this world and fill it with light to keep the Darkness at bay." Another cheer and the clang of metal against metal. The Demon King roared, opening his mouth to reveal sharp teeth. "Their flesh shall feed us for centuries! The time of the Demons has come!"

The Chalice fell from her hands. With a clunk, it hit the tiled floor before falling into the pool of water with a soft plop. Alex ignored Bran as he reached into the water to recover the Chalice. It would seem that the Demons would make fighting them easy emotionally after all, but it didn't answer the question of what they were running from.

27

The Purification of Rudra

6 20 B.C.E. Elephanta Island, India

The trident was an awkward weapon. With his sword broken and the village in disarray, it was what he could manage. Still, the fishing spear was made of durable iron and had been well made. Perhaps it was the right weapon against the Demons who had such long arms and frequently used spears. Lokpal knew that he also had his magic, but he couldn't imagine an entire battle with it as his weapon. The burn of exhaustion from his first use was an unpleasant memory.

Lokpal inhaled the sea air as the boat rocked on the waves. It wasn't much further to the island, but his arms were beginning to hurt. The trident across his lap was a comforting weight. It reassured him that he was armed as he headed towards the island that Rudra seemed to have made his home. The sky was clear above the island so at least there weren't any large fires. The hot midday sun beat down on his shoulders and sweat gathered on his neck.

The small boat thumped against the golden shore, and Lokpal pulled the oars in. Standing up, he took up the trident in his right hand and jumped out of the boat. He quickly pulled the boat further onto the shore. Nervousness crept up his chest and second thoughts and doubt prodded at him, whispering all the things that could go wrong.

Walking into the trees, Lokpal searched for any trails that he could use, but the island was mostly overgrown. The small hut that provided shelter in case of storms for fishermen was deserted. He had no idea of where to even look for Rudra. Drumming his fingers against the shaft of the trident, Lokpal fought the desire to look back towards his home. Merlin and Morgana would be angry when he returned. He had a feeling that they'd know where he'd been without him saying a word. Tightening his grip on the trident, Lokpal gave it an experimental swing, but the weapon did nothing against the underbrush. No cutting edge, he reminded himself uneasily.

He wandered further inland, looking around for any signs of Rudra. Everything was still, and there was only the occasional call of a bird. Something hung over the island. It was heavy against his skin, sending a strange tingle up his arms. Lokpal thought it might be magic, but it was all still so new. The strange little flicker under his heart pulsed and the odd sensation grew. Magic it was then.

Had it really only been two days since the attack? Time didn't seem constant anymore. Once the Demons had been dead, he'd just collapsed and slept. His wives had fussed over him, even tending to Merlin and Morgana's wounds. The raw ache in his chest had only faded a few hours ago, but the worry for Rudra and what was wrong hadn't disappeared. This was foolish. He knew that and told himself that as he kept walking forward.

It didn't take long for the smell of smoky wood to draw his attention. Walking slowly, Lokpal moved between the bushes and trees until he came to the edge of a large, blackened area. Everything had been burned out. There were charred logs, and all the grasses had been reduced to a layer of ash on the ground.

Rudra was sitting cross-legged in the small burned out clearing. Charcoal cracked beneath Lokpal's feet as he walked forward. The lingering smell of burnt leaves and trees surrounded him. He could also hear birds and the wind. Rudra was unmoving, and he slowly circled in front of him.

The deity's body was tense. His skin was darker than it should be, taking on a too dark blue shade rather than the pale white of his hands. It was a stark contrast that made Lokpal's stomach turn. Stopping in his tracks, Lokpal set the end of the trident against the ground and swallowed. He'd come this far but didn't know what to say now.

"You- shouldn't- be- here." Rudra's words were strained. His whole body was trembling, and his arms were folded tightly across his chest and stomach. "Go."

"I came to check on you," Lokpal said. "You left before I could thank you."

"Don't need to thank me." Rudra shook his head. The dark lines were spreading across his skin. "I heard you."

"Yes, I called you during the battle. I just- I didn't know what else to do. I had my magic, but it wasn't enough."

"I heard you," Rudra repeated. He finally looked at Lokpal. His eyes were dull and glazed over. "I've never heard anyone before, not at a distance like that."

"Well... I am a mage," Lokpal said. "And I was calling you. Maybe that helped."

"Maybe. You should go. I'm not... not safe anymore." Rudra shook his head. "I can feel it. The magic is creeping over me, trying to expel me, but it can't. The way is shut to me. I can't go back and can't stay."

"Merlin and Morgana said... well, I don't understand."

"The world I was born in is different." Rudra's voice softened; his features were melancholy. "Very different. My form was... free and ever-changing. When I was sent here, all that I was curled together painfully. I do not understand why it is so different, but it is like a bird trying to live in the water. It is not the natural state of things. It is not the place that I am supposed to live. Your magic, the magic of this realm knows that I do not belong here. It attacks. Not in grand ways, but it chips away. Erodes me and my mind slowly like a river carves a canyon." Rudra shivered and shook his head. "My awareness is slipping into something... I don't like. The violence has grown. I've never been kind, but I've avoided cruelty."

"You helped me," Lokpal said. "You didn't have to."

"I nearly killed you the first time we met. Had you been just another mortal human I might have."

"But you didn't," Lokpal said. "You didn't, and you're here now. On this island, trying to stay away from humans, trying to stop Demons."

"It is an outlet, nothing more."

"No, I don't believe that." Lokpal shook his head. "You're trying to do good before you...."

"Before I what? Turn rabid. Merlin and Morgana will kill me or at least they will try." Rudra shook his head. "You should do the deed now while you are here. Yesterday, I would have fought you, but now I dislike the images of what I will become. You humans already thought me vicious and violent, already feared me, but you have no understanding of what I could do."

"You have power."

"Yes, my body is power. It is energy like that of fire and lightning, held together by my will alone."

He didn't understand. The heat radiating off the ground around him already seemed impossible. Lokpal couldn't make sense of the words. They were describing something outside of his world, outside his focus. Closing his eyes, he fought back the ache forming behind his eyes. When he opened them, Rudra had closed his eyes and was bracing himself.

"Go into the water," Lokpal said.

Rudra looked up at him in confusion. Then he almost looked amused. "The water?" Rudra repeated. "Do you mean to drown me? I don't require air. My kind does not breathe in your world."

"Merlin and Morgana spoke of another Old One, something like you. I don't remember her name, but she stays in the water for long periods of time. Maybe it can help you."

"I touch water from time to time," Rudra said. "It doesn't help."

"There must be something!"

"Why do you care?" Rudra tilted his head and peered at Lokpal. "You are a mage. You are here to defend the Iron Realm."

"I suppose." Keeping his back straight, Lokpal met Rudra's unsure gaze. "But you helped me, helped us. There has to be some way to help you." Shaking his head, he examined Rudra. "You look ill."

"The erosion is seeping in. I've told you. There isn't much time. This isn't an illness. This is a corruption."

"The water might help. I want to try."

"It will do nothing."

"They said that the other Old One stays in the water."

Rudra sighed, the sound strange and unnatural from the being. Then he shook his head and slowly rose to his feet. "You are struggling for a way to save me. You cannot."

"I need to try."

Peering at him, Rudra slowly nodded. "You are brave. You try so hard. Most humans hide and only try to protect their own families."

"In a way that is true of me," Lokpal said. "I'm trying to protect my family. I also want the islands safe."

"I will enter the water," Rudra said. "But if this doesn't work, mage, then you need to destroy me." The words hung in the air between them.

"You said you're held together by your will... can't you just let go?"

"I want to live." Rudra's hands curled into fists with a tiny tremor shaking his body. "I want to live. I make no promises that I won't fight you, but I can't- I won't-"

"Very well," Lokpal said. Stepping back from Rudra, he swallowed down a lump of fear. "Very well, but let's try this first."

Rudra led the way. Despite being barefoot, the still hot ground didn't seem to bother him. With almost no sound, Rudra navigated the way towards a large pond while Lokpal just tried not to stomp around too much. His eyes kept moving back to the darkening skin, and he wondered. That other Old One that Merlin knew, had it been like this for her? Did it manifest the same way for them all or was it different for each one? He wanted to ask but thought better of it.

Trees surrounded the pond which was fed by small streams of water flowing out of the hills. A small waterfall churned the water, clouding it so he couldn't see the bottom. Rudra calmly stepped down onto a stone and then into the water. His legs vanished in the water, and if it was cold, Rudra gave no sign of discomfort. He bent his legs and moved further in, the water rising to his shoulder. Lokpal's eyes darted back to the waterfall, realizing that it must have dug a deep hole. Rudra closed his eyes and went below the surface.

There was nothing. Only the thrum of the small waterfall. A moment later, Rudra's head rose out of the water. There was no change. The dark tone of his face was still too much, and small black lines were visible like veins across the skin. Knowing what it was, what it meant made Lokpal's stomach turn. How was this supposed to work? He regretted not asking Merlin and Morgana more about how water worked.

Rudra was rising out of the water, steam hissing off his skin. A pained expression took over his face. Gritting his teeth, Rudra shook his head, bringing up two hands to his head. Groaning, Rudra climbed out of the water.

"Rudra?" Lokpal called softly. "Rudra?"

A long growl filled the air. Rudra shuddered, his fingers digging into his flesh. One hand tore at the darkest patch of skin. A raw scream escaped Rudra. His eyes opened, revealing glowing orbs filled with fire. Lokpal froze in place, unable to speak or move. The Old One struggled, blinking and stumbling. His hands gripped at his chest and stomach, searching for something to hold onto to.

"It's okay," Lokpal said. The words were soft and weak. "It's okay. We'll try again."

"It hurt," Rudra growled. "I tried, magic tried, but too much. Not enough."

"I don't understand, maybe if we-"

"Be quiet!" Rudra's eyes locked on him. "Be silent!" He raised a hand and fire erupted over his palm. "I'll silence you!"

Wild rage filled his eyes. Lokpal believed the words. Jumping to the right, Lokpal tripped over the trident as the tip caught in the ground. Behind him, Rudra was groaning. He looked over his shoulder, eyes widening in alarm. The Old One took a shaky step towards him, but fire was crawling up both of his arms.

Water, he needed water. His hand touched the ground, and he felt a small jolt. Magic flowed into his body, trying to support him. The ache remained. Exhaustion persisted, but raw fear was taking over. He needed help. He needed water. The pond behind Rudra caught his eyes. Desperately, Lokpal reached out a hand towards the water, calling it, begging it. Sparks surrounded his hand but didn't move. His heart sank. He didn't understand but kept trying to see what he wanted, what he needed as Merlin had said.

Suddenly water lashed up from the pond, grabbing Rudra. There was a loud hiss as some turned to steam, but the water coiled around Rudra. Shouting and snarling, the Old One tore at the water, but it did no good. Lokpal's head pounded, it ached, but he kept whispering for the water to pull Rudra down once more. He could barely understand anything Rudra shouted, but inch by inch he was pulled into the pond. Rudra fought back, trying to grab onto the shore. A fireball was sent flying at Lokpal that he barely dodged. A tree behind him burst into flames, but he kept his hand extended. Rudra's legs were pulled out from under him, and he vanished beneath the surface.

Slowly climbing to her feet, Lokpal stared at the surface of the pond. It was still churning from the fight. His heart was racing to the point of pain. Rubbing the back of his head in frustration, Lokpal tried to think. Had there been something else? Had he forgotten something that Merlin or Morgana said? He didn't understand, but this wasn't fair. Rudra was... well rough, but he had saved them. He, Merlin, and Morgana would have died to those Demons. They'd been exhausted, and there was no one else to defend them. If he hadn't called for Rudra and he hadn't come, then they'd be dead. Didn't that mean anything?

In his hand, the trident thrummed. Lokpal blinked in surprise only to realize that magic was flowing from his hand into the metal. It warmed in his grasp. Rudra was still under the water. Bubbles were rising to the surface as the water started to boil. He didn't have time. Rudra was turning rabid. He was going to die! The trident hummed, the sound high pitched and yet pleasant to his ears. His chest ached; the strange burning from using too much magic was spreading across his upper torso.

Hot water splashed across his leg. His hair was standing on end. It was impossible to breathe as steam filled his nose and mouth. What was he supposed to do? A hand began reaching out of the water, causing a sharp pull on his magic. The trident started to glow. Panic. Whatever magic was holding Rudra was failing. Closing his eyes, he focused on his wish. He pleaded with the magic to help him however it could. Pain radiated through his body, but he lowered the trident into the water.

Something changed. The horrible painful tug ended. Gasping for air, he sucked in the steam, and the boiling stopped. Light poured from the three trident prongs, spreading across the surface of the water. Unmoving, Lokpal kept pushing the magic into the metal. It warmed in his grip, turning hot, but he didn't let go. Closing his eyes, he let it wash over him. Magic reached up through the ground, rising into his chest. With every beat of his heart, it spread. The trident pulled, reaching for more magic, pulling it out of him and spurred on by its purpose.

It hurt. It ached, but he didn't stop. Darkness took over the edges of his vision. Blinking he tried to clear it, but he just... needed... to... His knees collapsed. But before he hit the ground, strong hands caught him. Looking up, Lokpal had only a moment to catch sight of a gently smiling blue face before the world vanished.

28

Darkness and Dragons

Hugging the Chalice to her chest, Alex ignored Bran's worried looks. Her mind couldn't settle on a single thought. There were Demons; they were going to cross a line no matter how much sympathy she had for their plight. Maybe she should be grateful for that, but there was no room for that emotion right now. The Darkness. What was it, what was she supposed to do about it? Memories of the dead Sídhe world came to mind, but it might not be connected.

"Alex?" Bran reached over and touched her shoulder. For a moment, she thought he was going to take the Chalice back, but he didn't touch it. "Let's go inside. That's enough for tonight. We all need sleep."

"No," Alex said. She shook her head. "No... I need some answers."

"There isn't anyone to get them from," Bran said. "If Shiva or Sif knew about a Darkness, I'm sure they would have said something."

"But maybe that was part of the reason they were exiled."

"You're grasping at straws." Bran sounded far too calm. "We aren't going to get an answer right now."

"Then how do we get it?" Alex asked. "Bran... I've had visions of the Sídhe homeworld. It's dead, and I can't help but think that it's connected. That worry is in my head now. I can't just ignore it and sleep." Trembling, she tightened her grip on the Iron Chalice. A flicker of magic warmed the metal beneath her skin, but it wasn't comforting. "I'm missing information. Information that I need to decide what happens next. I'm like three-thousand-years-old, this shouldn't be an issue."

"Okay, okay." Bran shifted forward and wrapped an arm around her. "It'll be okay, Alex." There was a pause, and he chuckled softly, even as he rubbed circles on her back. "And you aren't three-thousand-years-old, not even close."

"Am too." Alex pulled away and pouted, making Bran smile.

"No, you're really not. Sure, your soul is, but we don't understand what that is, and you can't count the periods that you aren't alive in some form." Bran blinked and outright laughed. "And that's not a sentence I ever thought I'd have to say." He looked down at the water pool. "So, what do you want to do now? Call Merlin and Morgana?"

"I don't know. I didn't really learn anything."

"Except that Cathanáil is what opened the way for the Demons."

"Morgana won't react well to that news," Alex said.

"No." Bran grimaced at the thought. "No, she won't." There was a pause as he noted her staring into the water. "So, what do you want to do?"

"I want...." Alex trailed off; it was hard to think. Difficult to string the thoughts together and the voices wouldn't shut up. "Be quiet!" She barked out loud. Bran didn't move though he made a small sound of worry. The voices softened. Licking her lips, Alex drummed her fingers on the warm metal of the Chalice. Then it hit her, and she almost laughed. "I want to talk with Emrys!"

"Emrys? The dragon in Wales?"

"Exactly! He came through centuries ago, via a portal made by Cathanáil. Maybe he'll know something about the Darkness or if the portal will affect the Demons."

"Let's hope not on the second," Bran said. "The Dragons are immortal remember? Emrys spends his time killing the White Dragon over and over again." Bran paused. "Alex, scrying is usually just looking. He probably won't be able to hear you."

"There's no harm in trying," Alex said. "If we focus on it and try."

He looked doubtful, but he nodded. Maybe he was humoring her, but Alex was willing to take it.

"I suppose that it's worth a try," Bran finally said. "Who knows, maybe that's where the idea of talking magic mirrors came from. Though if Merlin and Morgana have held that back, I'm going to be irritated with them."

Alex didn't say anything in response to that. She was off her witty banter game. Instead, she lowered the Iron Chalice into the water, shifting onto her stomach next to the edge of the pool. Bran laid down next to her, shooting curious looks at her. Keeping a tight grip on the Chalice, Alex pushed her magic into the warming metal. Fatigue tugged at her arms and legs, but she ignored it.

"Want some help?" Bran asked.

"Yeah," Alex agreed.

Bran reached down with his left hand to touch the Chalice. A soft yellow glow surrounded his hand, and Alex wondered if this would work or not. Maybe she was overthinking it using the Chalice. Opening her mouth, she was about to say as much when the water began to glow a strange off-white color as her and Bran's magic mixed together. The surface of the water was completely still. Then it began to shimmer and ripple. Colors appeared slowly.

"I see something," Bran said. "I see this time."

"Good," Alex said. That was a good sign at least. Group scrying could be very useful in the future.

She narrowed her eyes on the water in confusion, waiting for something solid to take form. It was dark, Alex couldn't see anything in the water except blackness. Then she heard something large moving and inhaled sharply. A fierily red light appeared, and then the head of a giant dragon came into view. Emrys' long red horns glistened in the light, and his eyes glowed red as he peered into the water.

"Mages?" the Dragon asked. His deep voice rolled over Alex, and a jolt of victory flooded her system.

"Yes, Emrys," Alex replied. "Can you hear us? We're trying something new-"

"I hear you!" The Dragon's body shook in surprise, and he crawled even closer to the water. "Remarkable. What magic is this?"

"Uh- I'm not sure," Alex said. "I wanted to talk to you rather than just see you, and I guess the magic gave me what I wanted." She shrugged as best she could from the odd position of lying on her stomach. "It was worth a try."

"It could also be because of this water," Bran offered softly. "It's been used to form water tunnels for transportation many times. Perhaps it carries a bit more magic than usual and is a better conduit."

"Fascinating," Emrys agreed. "Two conversations with living things that are not my enemy in the same century. Most pleasing." His happiness was apparent. Alex exchanged a guilty glance with Bran. It was easy to forget that Emrys couldn't leave his cavern due to his prisoner and even if he could it would cause panic. "What is it that you wanted to ask me?"

"Have you ever heard of anything called the Darkness?" Alex paused and licked her lips, leaning closer to the pool. "It might not have been called that in your world, but did other creatures come into your world and speak of dying worlds or something horrible happening? Anything like that?"

Emrys was silent. He tilted his large head slightly, looking up toward the top of the cavern in thought and exposing the lighter scales of his belly to them. Alex was aware of Bran watching her carefully but said nothing.

"Yes," Emrys finally said. "Yes, that is familiar. I had no personal knowledge of it, but I recall other law enforcement speaking of new arrivals from another world. You would call them griffins, I believe. There were claims of some horrible crisis on their world that was making everything sick." He shook his head. "I know little about it."

"Do you have any idea how long ago this was?" Bran asked.

"No, I fear not. Converting between your calendar and that of my homeworld remains a challenge for me. Maybe two thousand years before my time on the force, things were much less regulated, and creatures passed through our world into yours from time to time. I believe that it is where your human myths of them come from, though I don't know what happened to them beyond that. As they are no longer around, I can only suppose that your world did not affect them as it did me." Emrys sighed, the sound echoing off the cavern walls and through the pool. "As to when exactly this crisis spurred immigration into my world, I'm sorry, I can't say for sure when that was. I was much younger then. Time... it has gotten away from me here."

"Thank you all the same," Alex said.

"You have tensed up," Emrys observed. "I had never given much thought to this. Worlds are born, and surely, they die."

"Yes, but..." Alex trailed off for a moment, suddenly aware of her trembling body. Bran's hand covered one of hers and squeezed. It wasn't much, but it reassured her that she wasn't alone. "It seems that the Sídhe homeworld is long dead and that's what started their conquest-based culture. And now Demons are invading Earth for a new home because of something they call 'The Darkness.' If that happened to the Griffin world on your branch, then that's three worlds on three different branches."

"I see your concern," Emrys went still. Then he ran his long claws across the rocks. "I have no answer for you, I fear. These were concerns that were never a part of my position back home and that I only heard of in passing. I would say that perhaps worlds die and that others are being born without your knowledge. The Tree of Reality may not be a physical tree like you are used to, but perhaps old branches must fall off and die for new ones to be born."

His tone had softened, and the bands around Alex's chest loosened. She wasn't sure if she believed Emrys' idea, but it made a certain degree of sense. Next, to her, Bran made a thoughtful noise but said nothing. Smiling at Emrys, Alex let her shoulders relax.

"You make a good point," she agreed. "Even Merlin and Morgana have never left Earth."

"You are still worried."

"These Demons... they're frightened and fanatical. They talk about killing all humans if they have to. And eating us."

"Then you must defend your world."

"But if they don't come through and their world is dying then that's genocide."

"And if they do come through and kill all humans, is that any better?" Emrys' tone softened, and his eyes met hers. "Are there peaceful Demons already in your world?"

"There are, from an invasion a long time ago. Descendants, like the Sídhe."

"Then they will not go extinct," Emrys said. "It is a difficult choice, Alex. But there is really only one choice that you can make. You have a good heart, and your compassion is a virtue, but you are a mage. More than that, you are the Iron Soul, and the Iron Realm is your responsibility above any other world."

Those were not the words she wanted to hear. Yet, she wasn't surprised. The part of her that echoed with Gofiben all but sighed in resignation. Swallowing, Alex merely nodded. Emrys' glowing eyes were sympathetic as he gazed into the pool of water that served as his window to the outside world.

"Thank you for the information," Bran said. "I'm afraid that it has been a long night already for us and we don't have the magic to keep the connection open. We'll work on setting up regular communication with you."

"I am uncertain of how much help I can be. I've been locked up down here with little ability to track the magical goings-on of the world above, but I would appreciate the contact."

Bran eased his magic back. Alex felt it pulling away from her like a loose thread being tugged from cloth. It wasn't unpleasant, but a void was left in its place. Her magic rolled in to replace it, but it was slow like syrup, leaving her off center for a long moment. The image in the water vanished as Bran's part of the connection was broken.

"Well," Bran said with forced cheer. "Good news, we can contact Emrys and speak with him. Not as nice as a, but workable. I wonder if Merlin and Morgana have ever used it?"

"Maybe," Alex said. She lifted the Chalice out of the water and used her left hand to leverage herself up onto her knees. "Not that they separate all that often. At least I don't think so."

"Might have been nice to know about it."

"We live in the age of cellphones," Alex said. She shrugged and shifted back to sit cross-legged on the floor. "Bad news, Emrys has heard of something that might be the Darkness."

"It might not be the same thing, Alex." Bran put his hand over hers. "And as Emrys said, it might be a natural process and not dangerous to us."

"Maybe." Alex inhaled slowly. The nagging worry wasn't so easy to dismiss, but she tried. There was too much that she didn't understand. Maybe she wasn't supposed to. As Emrys said, the Iron Realm alone was her responsibility. "Do you agree with him?" Alex asked. She didn't look at Bran. "I know that Merlin and Morgana would. About the Demons survival not being our problem."

"I think... he has a good point. Some Demons have been living here peacefully for centuries. This is home to them. This Demon King isn't looking for peace."

"But he's frightened."

"So frightened that he's using the peaceful Demons, hurting them, and trying to take control of them?" Bran shook his head. "If that is only based on fear, I'm not sure that it's going to go away."

"I- I don't know, I guess I thought you'd say something else." Alex tried to chuckle but didn't manage it.

"My father was a soldier. He told me once that sometimes, there isn't time to look for a third option. You have to do what you think is best and deal with it afterward."

"And if what you do is too much?"

"We're all going to have PTSD by the time this is over," Bran said. His voice was sad, but matter of fact. "Sometimes it's easier. The Sídhe or Demons attack us, and we're just defending ourselves, but sometimes it's ugly. Knowing that we all killed things under the Queen's control is one of those. And if we fight this army and seal whatever portal they are using, we'll have to wonder if they'll survive or not. Probably every day for the rest of our lives, but that doesn't mean that we don't still have to do it."

"I hate it." Alex pulled her knees up to her chest. "There are moments when I almost feel like I've got it figured out and then the world pulls the rug out from under me. I don't want the invaders to be in trouble and desperate! I just... when I saved those kids, it was easy. I was a hero, and now I don't believe I am." Bran scooted over next to her, putting an arm around her shoulder. Alex collapsed against him, leaning her head on his shoulder. "You're right. I know you're right. I just... I don't want to think of the third option after the fact and carry that regret. I'm not sure I can cope with that."

"I think that you are stronger than you give yourself credit for. What you've been through thanks to Arthur and the burden of your memories, I couldn't deal with that."

"Yes, you could have."

"No, I couldn't have. You all would have had to sedate me; I would have been freaking out so much. I can't even imagine." He sighed loudly, the exhaled air brushing past Alex's face. "I haven't even managed to tell my mother the real truth about being a mage. You were honest with your parents, but I can't bear to see the look on her face when she learns that I'm a soldier as much as my dad was. She's never completely gotten over his death and should something happen to me-"

"Don't say that!"

"If something does happen to me, then I'm sorry that you and the others will have to face her and the consequences of my cowardice."

"You're not a coward," Alex said. "You're not." She tilted her head to look up at him. "After all, this is the second life that you've stood by me as a mage. Most people wouldn't suffer this once, much less twice."

"Yeah, well, I don't recall anyone asking or signing any forms so I can't take credit for that." Bran was smiling gently now. "But if I could, Alex, I would come back to help you. As whoever you become next."

"Become next," Alex said. Looking down into the water, she shook her head and sighed. "I'm not sure I want to think about that, Bran. Demons, Sídhe, Arthur, Fae, and Old Ones. I seem to have gotten stuck dealing with all of it. I don't want to even imagine what my next self will have to deal with."

"I think we should be grateful that the fantasy trope of different species being able to breed is very wrong," Bran said. "I don't want to consider what fighting a half Demon half Síd would look like."

"I hate you." Alex groaned and collapsed back on the cool tile.

"You want to go inside?"

"No, if I go inside, I have to talk with the others and call Merlin and Morgana."

Closing her eyes, Alex inhaled and exhaled slowly. Bran seemed content to leave her alone. Magic was seeping into her tired limbs, but it was slow. She was sharply aware of the dull ache in her chest, that slight burn from using too much magic. It was easing with each breath and heartbeat. Reaching out for the lingering magic in the air, Alex was surprised to find that there were glistening strands of magic still connecting her to the island. They were stretched and faint, but still there. She smiled, that was a pleasant surprise. She beckoned the magic closer.

But then, something brushed against one of the strands. Something large and alien. Sitting up sharply, Alex tightened her eyes and tried to follow the thread. It was fading, but something was there. Another wave of cold brushed over her spine. More than one. There was another, and she opened her eyes to find Bran watching her cautiously. He was on one knee, ready to lean forward and jump up.

"Something is on the island." Alex turned all her attention to the odd shiver at the edge of her sense. "Something... I think it's the Demon King." She closed her eyes. Small fragments of the magic threads were still lingering in the air, still fading back into the world. There was a snarl, a big one off in the distance. "Yeah, he's on the island."

"Why? I mean he just sent scouts."

"Maybe they weren't really scouts, but a group to wear Shiva down." Alex scrambled to her feet. "Doesn't matter. We need to go. We need to warn him." She backed away from the pool. "Shiva!"

Nothing happened. There wasn't even a ripple in the water. "Shiva! Can you hear me?" Nothing. Bran made a sound and began to reach for her. "No, Shiva is in trouble," Alex said. Her fingers itched, but not for Mjǫllnir or Cathanáil. It was a phantom memory just out of her grasp. "I know it; we have to go."

"We're exhausted," Bran said. He wasn't arguing, and she was grateful for that.

"I know, that may have been the point," Alex said. "But we have to call. Have Jenny call Merlin and Morgana."

"There's no ferry at this time of night."

"Then we'll have to open a water tunnel." Alex looked down at the water and almost smiled. "Nicki's been wanting to try."

Bran shook his head but moved towards the door. "I'll get the others."

Alex nodded but didn't pay attention as he rushed out the door. She quickly went to her backpack that was waiting at the wall. Without much thought, she unzipped it and pulled out Mjǫllnir. The Hammer hummed in response to her touch and Alex smiled as she slipped the Iron Chalice back into the bag. Keeping a tight grip on Mjǫllnir, Alex pulled on her backpack and impatiently waited for the others.

29

Once More Into Battle

At this point, Nicki knew that she should always be ready for the worst. She wasn't. There was a failure between the should, and the was. Well, she'd never been a Girl Scout or anything with a useful motto like be prepared. Was that Girl Scouts or Boy Scouts? Rushing out to the water room with Avani leading the way and Jenny already on the phone trying to reach Merlin and Morgana, her heart was racing with worry.

Alex wasn't hurt. She was standing at the edge of the pool with Mjǫll-nir in her hands. In the low light of the space, she seemed otherworldly, staring off at something that Nicki couldn't see. Her lips were moving the tiniest bit in a soft conversation. That gave her pause. They didn't need the Iron Soul going crazy. Then Alex stopped and turned back to them. Her face was neutral though her gray eyes were stormy with worry.

"Demons have swarmed the island," Alex said. Her voice was too calm, too certain. "I'm not sure how many, but I think they mean to destroy Shiva."

"They can't." Avani shook her head, looking both amused and worried. "He can just go back into the water."

"There are humans on the island," Alex said. "He won't leave them to the Demons." Avani didn't argue with her on that. "Nicki, can you open a water tunnel? We need to get to the island quickly."

"What?" Nicki blinked at Alex. "I'm sorry?"

"I need you to make a water tunnel." Alex sidestepped and gestured at the water. "There does seem to be extra magic in the water."

"I've never done this before," Nicki said. She ignored the quiver in her voice. They didn't have time for it. "Maybe we should wait for Merlin or Morgana."

"I haven't gotten them on the phone," Jenny said. She held up her cellphone and shrugged helplessly. "Just their answering machines. I have no idea what time it is back home. I'll text them too, but I don't know how long it will take for them to check."

Alex made a sound of anger and Mjǫllnir sparked in her hand. "Keep trying, Jenny." Then those sharp gray eyes, now all but glowing with anger turned to Nicki. "We need to get to Shiva. The Demons know that he is the primary protector of this area. We're just visitors."

"Alex, I'm not sure that I can. Don't you remember Merlin saying that some people vanish in the water tunnels?" Looking at their little team, she swallowed. "I'm not sure that I can do this."

The glow of Mjǫllnir dimmed as Alex's expression softened. Stepping forward, Alex grabbed Nicki's hand and squeezed. There was a flutter in Nicki's chest as a jolt of magic shot up her arm. It went from comforting to insistent.

"We'll help," Alex said.

"Will you still be able to fight?" Avani asked. "I mean, it's already been a very long day."

"We have to fight," Alex said. "That's all that matters. Nicki, I know you can do this. Let us help. You know how it's done."

"In theory," Nicki said. "Just in theory."

"It's not far," Lance said. He was trying to be helpful, but Nicki really wanted to yell at him.

"I don't think that matters."

They were all looking at her. It was her own damn fault for ever expressing interest in how the water tunnels worked. Sure, water was her thing, but this was different. They were all still looking at her. Aiden at least appeared worried. Jenny was leaving another rushed message on Morgana's voice mail, and Lance seemed unsure.

Alex's hand shifted, and the flow of magic into her chest increased. Looking at Alex in surprise, it finally clicked that Alex was doing it on purpose. Trying to make her stronger. Swallowing, Nicki pulled her hand away and stepped closer to the water pool. She stretched out her hands but realized that she had no idea of what she was doing. Fear tugged at her, whispering that she couldn't do it. Nicki hated that whisper. Hated it when it told her that her parents leaving and not coming back was her fault. Hated it when she'd been unwilling to tell her grandmother that she liked girls and not boys.

It was hard to ignore. She'd never been very good at Morgana's meditation techniques, but she called on everything she remembered now. Flexing her fingers, she inhaled and held the breath for several seconds while counting slowly. The magic pooled in her fingertips, waiting for a command. For a moment, Nicki hesitated. The nagging worry was quieter now, but what did she say to her magic. What was the right command?

Water tunnel. She settled on that, focusing on the memory of how the tunnel had formed by Stonehenge and in Ravens Lake. It always looked the same, no matter who created it, so she didn't have to worry on that front. Someone shifted behind her, and Nicki suppressed the urge to growl.

"Shhh!" Nicki snapped. "I'm working here. Unless someone has a manual for this?"

"No," Avani answered. "This is beyond what magicians can do."

Nicki was a little proud of that but was still at a loss. Mentally rolling her eyes, she shoved the magic gathered in her palms into the water. All the while, she mentally chanted 'water tunnel, water tunnel, water tunnel.' Her light blue magic flowed into the water, changing it from clear to a rich blue as if she'd dumped a big bottle of food coloring in.

Water began to rise from the pool, twisting into the air in graceful arches. Nicki fought back a smile and the urge to shape something. This wasn't the time. She focused on the memory of the island dock. It was the clearest memory of the area with water. It was difficult, and with one awkward hand, she dug out her cellphone.

"Nicki?" Alex asked.

"Took a photo," Nicki said. "Might help."

Aiden took the phone from her hand, quickly unlocking it with her historical date password. He muttered a few things as he messed with her icons, but a moment later he turned the phone to show her the photo she'd taken. It didn't include the actual water itself but had the long dock walks, various stands, and the welcome building. Good enough.

"Should have taken more pictures," Nicki muttered.

But she studied the picture and tried to visualize the docks more clearly, tried to remember the smells, and sounds. It wasn't perfect, that was day, and this was night, but there was a change in the thrum of her magic. It went higher, and the water in the pool splashed up into the air with a slosh. Streams of pure, clear water took on a faint blue glow, sparks of magic glittering as they turned and began to rush together.

A whirlpool formed in the air, but it was turned on its side. Water splashed and sloshed around the edges, but an opening a few feet tall and wide formed. At the end, Nicki could see the faint lights of the Elephanta Island Docks. There was a loud cheer in her ear from Aiden that made her flinch.

"Sorry," he said quickly.

"Grab hands," Nicki ordered. "I don't…. I don't think I can keep this open long."

"I'll go first," Alex said. She shifted in front of Nicki and grabbed her left hand as Aiden took her right one. "Keep hold of each other and be ready for a fight on the other end."

"I'll wake my family," Avani said. Her dark eyes were calm and commanding. The butterflies in Nicki's stomach were back. "We may not be mages, but we can muster up some defenses in case the Demons are planning a second strike here." Turning to Lance and Jenny, Avani extended a hand to Jenny. "I suggest staying here with us. We may need the extra hands."

"Right," Lance agreed. His hand was already moving to the iron dagger sheathed at his back. "We'll help how we can."

"I'll keep trying to get ahold of Morgana," Jenny said. "I don't like this."

Nicki was going to say more, but Alex tugged her forward. Nicki didn't have any time to process before the pull on her hand turned painful as the water tunnel swept Alex away. Everything became impossible to see as blues, greens, and dark browns spun around her at the edges of her vision. Slamming her eyes shut, Nicki pulled up the image of the docks again, suddenly unsure if she had to keep thinking about it or if the tunnel was locked. Fear came raging back, whispering that they were all going to die in the middle of the Indian Ocean or worse at the edge of Antarctica.

They hit water. Nicki's feet kicked out beneath her frantically, before hitting solid ground. She splashed above the water and grabbed for the edge of the dock. Water clung to her, and she grimaced. Of course, they were in the water. Of course, they were soaking wet. Coughing, she blinked and turned to look at the others. Alex was already climbing up onto the dock while Bran and Aiden were going up to the beach. Nicki quickly followed them, wading up onto the shore and trying not to think about her cellphone.

Everything was still. Night wrapped around them like a fresh sheet and if she hadn't been soaking wet, Nicki would have found it pleasant. Her limbs were shaking, and her knees gave out. Hitting the sand of the beach, Nicki gulped in air greedily and prayed that her magic would recover soon. Aiden was at her side in an instant, kneeling next to her.

"Are you okay?"

"Tired," Nicki said. Then she laughed. "I did it, though."

"Yes." Aiden smiled at her, brushing a wet strand of red hair out of her face. "You did, well done. Do you need the Chalice?"

"No, I'm not hurt." Nicki closed her eyes and shook herself gently. "I'm just exhausted. I'll be fine."

"Okay, stay here on the beach then," Aiden said. "You're in no shape to fight if you're out of energy."

"But-" Nicki shook her head, trying to clear her thoughts as she opened her eyes.

"Hopefully, Merlin and Morgana will be here soon," Aiden added. "This is the docks; it's the most likely place for them to come." Nicki opened her mouth to protest. "Please," Aiden said. He swallowed. "It's possible for a person to hurt themselves overdoing it. I don't want you falling into a coma like I did. Please, stay here and be careful."

Her arguments dried up. Licking her lips, Nicki nodded. "Look after Alex," Nicki said.

"I will." Aiden kissed her forehead quickly. "Bran and I will stay with her," Aiden promised. "Just be careful."

She watched them run off into the tree line, Alex at the lead and not bothering at all with waiting for the others. Heavy silence surrounded Nicki, wrapping her in an illusion of peace. Standing up, she staggered up the rocky hillside. There was only the crashing of the waves as she scanned the road to the village and the path towards the caves. No one was out. There was just nothing, and part of her wondered if Alex had gotten it wrong. But then a low rumble echoed out of the trees, making her straighten up. Nervous energy gathered at the base of her spine.

Nicki brought her left hand up to her chest and laid it over her heart. The rapid beat of the organ beneath her skin only added to her nervousness. There was a painful flutter, like an adverse reaction to medication and she was alone. Was this what had happened to Aiden before he collapsed? Was she going to collapse? Nicki's brain latched onto the thought, and she slowly walked up the beach. Maybe it would be safer if she was near a building.

Behind her, the sound of the waves changed. Nicki stopped. The steady noise shifted, and Nicki turned around to look only to sigh in relief. Water was rising from the ocean and weaving in midair only a few feet away, right at the edge of the shore and the water. Standing up, Nicki shifted into a defensive stance even as she smiled. It had to be Merlin and Morgana, maybe Sif too if they were lucky.

A whirlpool formed in the air, churning far faster than her own had. Relief helped her breathe, and a few stray droplets of water hit her face.

The sudden chill helped wake her up, and Nicki blinked. A moment later, Morgana stepped out of the tunnel with Merlin right behind her. The water tunnel collapsed with a loud splash as Morgana's eyes landed on her.

"Nicki, you're alright," Morgana said.

Nicki was touched by the relief in the woman's voice. "I guess you got Jenny's message," Nicki said. She tried to smile before giving up. She didn't have the energy for it.

"Yes," Merlin said. "Are you alright?"

"I'm fine." Then she did smile. "I made my first water tunnel."

"Well done," Merlin said. "What is happening? Jenny just said that you'd gone to the island."

"Alex felt Demons here. She thinks they're attacking Shiva." Shaking her head, a nervous giggle escaped Nicki. "And there's a strange thing to have to say."

"Where is she?" Morgana demanded. Her green eyes scanned the beach. "Nicki, where is Alex?"

"She just went off running into the trees," Nicki said. She pointed up the hillside. "Off the road."

"This isn't good," Merlin said. He reached over and took Nicki's arm. "I doubt you're safe alone, Nicole."

"Nicki," she grumbled. But she nodded her agreement and allowed Merlin to start leading her up the road. "Village is quiet."

"Yes," Morgana said. She closed her fist and hummed softly. A warm glow surrounded her hand. Morgana stopped moving and opened her palm. Silver sparks danced across her palm like tiny ballerinas until Morgana blew them towards the village.

"Sleeping spell?" Merlin asked.

"Seemed the best course of action," Morgana said. "We'll just have to keep Demons away from the humans. I'd hate for any of them to wake up to a Demon attack."

"Uh…" Nicki trailed off; she wasn't sure what to say to that. Merlin shook his head; apparently, he didn't either.

"Come on!" Morgana snapped.

She marched up the hill, and Merlin offered Nicki his arm. Smiling gratefully, Nicki allowed herself to lean a little on Merlin. With every breath, she grew a little stronger, and the raw sensation in her chest eased. She wasn't sure if it was the lingering magic on the island, Merlin, or something else, but she was grateful for it.

The smell of ozone beckoned. Light flashed through the trees, a bolt of lightning that vanished as quickly as it appeared. There was a rumbling from the sky, and Nicki's heart jumped. Mjǫllnir was in play. Morgana paused for a moment, and silver light burst from her fingers. A shout made them all look to the right. A Demon crashed into a tree, breaking off a lower branch before it collapsed on the ground. Morgana flicked her fingers towards it, and a silver bolt blasted through the back of the Demon's head. As its body decayed away, Merlin led her through the trees and up the gentle slope of the hill.

Another burst of lightning illuminated the area, allowing Nicki a chance to see the chaos that had erupted. Shiva was in the center of a swarm of Demons. They were armed with everything from spears to guns, and all their attention was focused on Shiva. Nicki couldn't see any injuries on the deity, but then again, he was all physically bound energy. She didn't even think that he could bleed.

All of Shiva's hands held weapons. Arrows were being launched from a bow at the Demons carrying firearms. A flaming sword was slicing through the Demons closest to him, and the Trishula was knocking down Demon after Demon. But they kept coming. For an instant, Nicki was frozen in a combination of shock, awe, and fear with the others. For a moment, she was grateful the Demons had come here after Shiva first rather than them.

There was a flash of red in the corner of her eye. She turned along with Merlin and Morgana. Aiden and Bran were back-to-back with a circle of Demons around them. The scent of burning flesh filled the air as two Demons withered on the ground in pain. Yellow bolts shot through another Demon who stumbled back. Alex was alone, Mjǫllnir held up towards the sky and dead Demons falling apart around her. More Demons were moving out of the trees, and Nicki could hear more marching up the hill ahead of them.

Giving her magic a soft tug, Nicki tentatively beckoned the flicker to her fingertips. It was weak, but there. All around her, the world hummed. Demons were coming closer. Shifting back, she stayed near Morgana, trusting the older mage to help her if she needed it, but ready to defend herself with what magic she still had. Her knees trembled, threatening to give out again, but Nicki refused. Staying on her feet, she grit her teeth and braced herself.

30

Burning Island

620 B.C.E. Elephanta Island, India

His dreams were so strange that Lokpal knew he was awake in the real world the moment he opened his eyes. Even waking under the canopy of the forest trees wasn't enough to surprise him. Sitting up slowly, the memory of what had happened returned quickly, and Lokpal reminded himself to stay calm. He wasn't dead and wasn't right next to the pond, so Rudra hadn't been inclined to kill him.

"Good, you're awake," a deep voice said. It was similar to Rudra's, but gone was the pained undertone.

Twisting around, he blinked in surprise. Rudra was seated on the ground nearby, his legs folded, and his arms relaxed, gently resting on his thighs, knees, and the ground. Between them lay the iron trident that he'd been relying on as a weapon after the destruction of his sword. Rudra looked better than before. The pain in his eyes was gone, and the small dark lines beneath his skin had been washed away. Yet, the skin of his head remained darker than the snow-white tone of his arms and hands. It was blue, strange, and otherworldly, but the sight of it no longer made Lokpal's chest tighten with fear. Whatever corruption, whatever poison had been gripping Rudra had been cleared away.

"You look better," he said. Then he flinched. "Sorry, that was a bit blunt... wasn't it?" He climbed to his feet, noting with relief that the burn in his chest was gone. Holding back a shiver, he tried not to think about the weakness that had overtaken him. "What happened?"

"You fainted." Rudra smiled in amusement. Then he unfolded himself and rose to his feet, gently picking up the trident. "After you helped me. The effort must have exhausted you."

"You caught me." Lokpal frowned slightly. It was blurry, all of it.

"Yes. I was concerned that you had done too much, but your breathing quickly evened out. It seemed best to let you rest. I've been keeping guard." Then Rudra held the trident towards him reverently and whatever Lokpal was going to say vanished from his lips. "There is magic in this weapon now," he said. "I do not understand what you did, Lokpal, but it reshaped the very metal. You infused it with great power through your wish to aide me. I am humbled and honored."

With uncertain hands, Lokpal took back the trident. There was something different about it. He knew that it was still iron like before, but the small tool markings, the little imperfections had been smoothed away as if the metal had been heated and worked once more. The two outer prongs curved out slightly, making the shape much more elegant. A soft hum beneath his fingertips made his heart jump. It was soothing and strange, and he almost dropped the trident. Yet, some instinct made his fingers tighten around the metal shaft and hold tight.

"Tridents are often metal and wood," Rudra said gently. His tone was curious and soft, as if afraid of spooking Lokpal. "Sometimes hollow. Perhaps it was fate that this one was made whole."

He didn't know what to say to that. "I don't understand what happened."

"You... cleansed me," Rudra said. "I was sure that I was done for, but now the world is clear." A small smile spread across Rudra's face, and the Old One stepped back to give him room to breathe. "I can feel the pulse of the Iron Realm's magic, but... it does not sting as it once did. I think that I will return to the waters from time to time to ensure that the corruption never retakes me, but something has changed. You changed me."

"I didn't!" Lokpal shook his head, suddenly fearful of Rudra's reaction. "I just-"

"Something in your wish, something in your power has changed me. Perhaps I am now blessed to remain in this realm; perhaps I am marked, I do not know. But it has been a long time since my mind was so clear." Rudra touched a nearby tree, running his hands gently over the trunk with a soft smile. "I know not, but I do not fear it."

"Rudra, I'm glad you're feeling better." Lokpal swallowed and turned the trident, so the tip rested on the ground. The hum against his skin increased. "I just couldn't let you die, not like that. Not after you helped us."

"I fear that I did not help you out of any true kindness, Lokpal. I sought the battle." Rudra shook his head and reached up to touch a leaf, the green sharply contrasting with his white skin. "Rudra," he repeated. Then the Old One shivered. "Somehow... that name now seems wrong."

"Wasn't it your name from your homeland?"

"No, I left that name behind. Rudra is the name I was given here. The roarer for my screams." The Old One looked down at his hands and then lifted a hand to his face. "I should ask, is the corruption all gone."

"Not exactly... I'm afraid that your face is blue. But not dark blue like before," Lokpal explained in a rush. "It's just blue. Like the sky at dusk."

"It would seem that evidence of my poisoning will remain with me." The Old One looked around and took a step up the hill before shaking his head. "It matters not."

"No, I suppose not in the grand scheme." Lokpal finally sighed in relief, but it quickly turned into an odd laugh. "I'm glad you're alright. Merlin and Morgana warned me to leave it alone. They didn't think you could be helped. They would have been... very angry if I-" He cut himself off, trying to stop the nervous flow of words and thoughts. "Anyway, it worked out. Despite their fears. That's good."

"I know little of the Grand Mages," the Old One said. "I've never had much contact with the other Old Ones. I now realize that was a mistake on my part. Perhaps they would have known ways I could have protected myself. But I was angry when I came here. I didn't want to speak with anyone."

"And now?"

"Now I see that I can have a place here." The Old One smiled warmly at him, white teeth all but gleaming against his blue skin. "It is not as simple as I once thought if mages can bend the magic of this world to saving those like myself."

The Old One suddenly froze in place, his muscular body tensing. Two hands moved to the weapons still hanging on his belt. He sniffed at the air with a hint of confusion on his face. It melted away in moments to be replaced with determination and anger. Lokpal tightened his grip on the Trident and brought it up to grasp with both hands. It felt right in his hands; more than it had been before. It would need a more fitting name.

"What is it?" Lokpal asked.

"Demons," the Old One said. He suddenly turned and looked towards the other islands. "Many of them... perhaps even the leader."

"Are you sure?"

"They saw my condition this morning before you came. I killed most, but a few escaped, and no doubt told their king of my condition. They expect me to be dead." The Old One touched two of his hands to his chest. "Maybe the one they sensed as Rudra is gone and something else has risen in his place." He shook his head, and Lokpal turned to study the island, his eyes straining for some sign of Demons. "It matters not. We must get there quickly to defeat the Demons."

"Yes, please!" Lokpal nodded eagerly and began moving down the hillside. "Merlin and Morgana are still there at least, but they weren't able to stop the Demons the last time."

"No," the Old One agreed. "Let us hope that this is the last of the Demons in the area. Your village has lived in fear too long already."

Lokpal kept moving, worry for his family and a hint of anger at himself for coming so far from there filled his chest. He couldn't regret it. He didn't understand what had happened, but Rudra or whoever he was now, still lived and was willing to help them. All the way down to the beach, he felt a strong presence behind him. It tingled at his senses but seemed safe. Like having a dog nearby, you knew it was there, but it wouldn't harm you.

He moved quickly, the distance between him and his home suddenly too much. It was suffocating, and he hoped that Merlin and Morgana were in the village or nearby. What if they were out looking for him? Regret over his secrecy tangled up around his lungs and stomach, squeezing tightly. Catching his foot on a rock, Lokpal became unbalanced and started to fall, but the Old One grabbed his arm. He recovered quickly, and they hurried down to the beach without a word.

The Old One frowned as they reached the shore. Lokpal looked at him and then towards the islands. "You got there when I called last time, can you do that again?"

"No," the Old One said. "I pulled my form apart and flashed across the sky like lightning." He shook his head and studied his hands once more. "What has changed... that changed. Get in the boat. I will speed us along with my power. That is what I can do now."

"Are you weaker now?" Lokpal pushed the boat further into the water and jumped inside.

"No," the Old One answered. He gave the boat another strong shove before leaping in with the grace of a cat. "Stronger, but different."

Lokpal still didn't understand what that meant, but the Old One turned towards the back of the boat. His hands began to glow, and he lowered them towards the water. Suddenly, the boat lurched forward and began speeding across the surface of the sea far faster than Lokpal had ever moved in his life. His heart jumped, and his stomach tightened as the wind stung his face. A laugh escaped him. He didn't know what the Old One was doing, but already the island was beginning to draw near.

Smoke was rising in thin wisps from the village. With each passing moment, Lokpal could see more clearly what was happening. A few buildings were on fire, and the smoke was thickening. Already, Lokpal could see some of the trees catching fire. If they didn't stop it soon, the whole island would go up in flames. People should be fighting to put out the fires, but they were running from the Demons. It was all going wrong.

He jumped from the boat as soon as the bow touched the sand. Columns of smoke rose from the village and screams echoed down towards him. More boats were being launched from the docks, and Lokpal briefly caught the eye of a frightened fisherman. Searching the faces, he desperately hoped for some sign of his family. There was none. They lived too far from the center of the village. He hoped that right now that was a good thing. Maybe they'd heard the screams and were going away from the village, down to the far shore.

Demons were tearing into the buildings with their massive clubs. A large one plucked up a running child, laughing while the child screamed. Flashes of silver and green flew through the air, striking down the Demon and giving the child a chance to run. Demon after Demon fell to the ground. Pushing his way forward, Lokpal dodged the blow from a Demon and the Old One slew it with a flick of his sword. Bringing up the Trident, he speared the side of the next Demon that came too close. In a rush of anger, he turned the heavy shaft and twisted the prongs viciously. The Demons screamed and fell to the ground. He tugged on the Trident, but it was difficult to free. Thankfully, the Demon's body began to crumble away, and he retrieved the weapon.

Acting more cautiously with the next opponent, Lokpal focused on working his way towards the center of the village. Flashes of silver and green filled the air, and most of the Demons had their attention there. To his right, the Old One was slicing down Demon after Demon, using his various hands and weapons to grab them and slay them in quick, efficient motions. They pressed forward. Demon after Demon fell. Lokpal's body ached, but he kept moving with the Old One dancing around him in a devastating whirlwind to clear Demons. His magic flickered weakly in his chest, drawing more energy from the world around him, but still exhausted and spent.

Merlin and Morgana were back-to-back in the thick of the Demons. Magic surrounded them, knocking back Demon after Demon, but it wasn't enough to kill any of them. Lokpal inhaled sharply and pulled on his magic. It fought back for a moment, flowing away from him, but he caught the weak stream of energy. His right hand started to glow and then to his surprise, so did the Trident in his hand. Magic shimmered across the surface of the metal, and he finally understood what the Old One had been saying. This wasn't a mere weapon or fishing tool anymore. It was something else, something more. Excitement warred with fear before solid determination won out.

Demons were closing in on him. The Old One was nearby, but dealing with over a dozen Demons that had identified him as the greatest threat. A whip of silver light struck one of the Demons, dragging it away from him, but another took its place. Fire was spreading through the village, but the screaming had ceased. Lokpal hoped that meant that everyone had fled.

He wasn't sure what to do. Purification. How was that supposed to help him? Then again, the Demons weren't supposed to be here. Swinging the Trident, Lokpal grunted as the sharp ache in his chest returned, but he didn't release the pull for magic. He needed it, no matter what it meant for him. If he was this special mage, then this was why he was alive. Light rolled out from the three prongs of the Trident, rippling through the air like it was water, and when it reached the Demons, their flesh began to crumble.

It spread all around him in a glowing circle. Demons shrieked and retreated. Looking towards the Old One, Lokpal panicked as the light reached his ally. But nothing happened. The Demons screamed in pain and retreated, but the Old One showed no sign of pain. A flicker of surprise covered the Old One's face before satisfaction took its place. Swinging his sword, the Old One slashed through the nearest Demon as two more hands once again nocked his bow.

The light did not last long. Already it was fading. Darkness crept into the corners of his eyes. The burning ache in his chest was worse than ever. Worn raw from channeling too much magic. A sharp pain in his side knocked the air out of him. His knees quivered. Stumbling forward,

Lokpal shifted the trident, so the tip was against the ground. It was enough to keep him on his feet. Blinking, he shook his head. Things were foggy, and his left hand went to his side. It was warm and wet. He looked down. Blood covered his palm as he pulled it away. His legs gave out, but he kept a tight grip on the Trident.

His eyes rose. He could see the ocean. Boats were scattered about on the blue water, no doubt filled with frightened people who could do nothing but wait and see what happened. Panting for air, Lokpal wanted to stand back up. He couldn't. It was just too much. There was shouting. He turned enough to see silver and green magic zipping through the air. It seemed like there were fewer Demons now. The Trident hummed weakly in his hand.

Then something came close to him. In his chest, his magic flared, and he coughed. It burned and froze all at once, pulling his flesh apart. He looked over at the dark shape. A Demon in finely wrought metal was glaring at him. Smaller than the others, it had lines of paint across the dark skin of its face. A spear in its right hand had a sharp tip covered in blood. Lokpal's mind managed to connect the two, and he tried to stand. Leaning on the Trident, he struggled to rise, but the Demon laughed. Lashing forward, it used the spear to slice into his other side. A sharp gasp of pain escaped Lokpal; it was all he could manage.

"Today the mages die at the hand of the King of Demons!" The Demon raised the spear, aiming it at his face and gave Lokpal a vicious grin.

31

Fight for the Island

Alex felt the arrival of Merlin and Morgana at the edge of her senses. Magic was flickering all around the island, combining and pulling apart in strange, unpredictable ways. Waves of green and silver shimmered at the edge of her eyes. There wasn't time to analyze. They'd reached Shiva just as a dozen Demons jumped him and more and more had appeared.

Shoving Mjǫllnir forward, Alex released a large bolt of lightning. It struck the nearest Demon, all but vaporizing the creature. What remained collapsed to the ground. Another Demon moved away from Shiva, rushing towards her. Swinging the Hammer, Alex slammed it into the Demon's chest. The hide like armor didn't protect it. Arcs of lightning flashed off the metal. A burning smell filled her nose, but Alex didn't care. High above her, the sky rumbled, and Mjǫllnir hummed in her hand. Dark gray magic flickered off the Hammer as she swung at another Demon.

In the corner of her eye, she saw a flash of silver light. She'd known Morgana was here, but the confirmation helped. That was good, but she didn't look towards them. More Demons were closing in around her. She'd already lost count. Swinging Mjǫllnir in an arc, Alex smiled as lightning arched off the metal. It wasn't even necessary to hit them. A Demon came up behind her, she spun around and smacked Mjǫllnir against its gut. The Demon screamed and was blasted back by a bolt of pure plasma.

The air was thick with ozone. Aiden had explained once what lightning was. She hadn't been paying attention, but now it made sense. Superheated gas. The warmth of Mjǫllnir spread through her whole body. To her it was comforting, but to the air, it was sharp and overwhelming. More lightning flashed off the Iron Hammer, illuminating the battlefield. Someone had tossed up a light orb, probably Morgana. Alex didn't need them. The steady glow of Mjǫllnir made it easy for her to see her opponents.

More Demons came marching out of the trees. She saw Shiva toss away two more Demons who were quickly pinned to the ground by arrows. Two Demons inched out of the trees, carrying some kind of firearms. There was a cry of warning, maybe from Aiden, then two green bolts shot through the air. They struck the Demons in the head, and both collapsed. Another Demon dashed for the firearms, but a silver whip lashed through the night and struck it. Yellow sparks surrounded the weapons, and Alex turned her attention away.

A group of Demons rushed her, filling in the holes she'd created around herself. Lightning flashed across the sky. Alex's heart jumped as a rain drop hit the side of her face and rolled down. Thunder rumbled, shaking the trees all around them. A pair of Demons looked up in alarm at the sudden onset of the storm. Alex smiled and raised Mjǫllnir towards the sky. A bolt of lightning crashed down and leapt into the Hammer.

Slamming it down against a Demon's chest, Alex smiled as bolts of lightning radiated out. They struck Demon after Demon, jumping between the enemies in a circle all around her. As they collapsed, Alex ran closer to Shiva. His arms were a blur of swords as he cut down Demon after Demon, but his appearance was ragged. His eyes betrayed his exhaustion. Lokpal's voice grew louder, urging her to hurry, to help. Yet Shiva didn't seem worried. Tired yes, but calm. His eyes caught hers just before three Demons rushed out of the trees to flank her.

Shiva's eyes glowed, and light shone from the Trishula. The Old One swung the Trishula in an arc and light radiated forth, illuminating the area. Three Demons charged Shiva, but another of his hands drew a sword and slashed the first one before it finished closing. Another pair of hands pulled a bow off of his back and prepared an arrow. It was strange and familiar at the same time to see the dance of the different arms.

The Trishula released a wave of light as the end was slammed into the ground. Air filled Alex's lungs, and the sounds softened. Magic twisted. She froze. Her ears started ringing. Ice flowed down her spine. Something was off, but what. Alex turned away and looked around. Her eyes scanned the long shadows in the trees. More Demons were moving. Shiva leapt forward and slew the Demons trying to flank her.

"Alex?" Shiva called. "Alex?"

Magic shuddered around her. The dark air beyond the light orbs shimmered. Familiar and wrong. Narrowing her eyes, Alex shook her head and turned towards Morgana and Merlin. Nicki was with Morgana, thankfully being shielded by the older mage as waves of silver bolts flew through the air into lines of Demons. Beneath her feet, the ground shuddered. A Demon rushed her, lashing forward with a spear. Twisting to the side, Alex dodged the attack and swung the Hammer. It sparked as it hit the Demon and sent the creature flying back.

"I'm fine!" Alex didn't look at Shiva. Focusing her attention on the lines of Demons, she flexed her fingers around the handle of Mjǫllnir and pushed more magic into the Hammer. It thrummed in response, and small sparks of bright blue plasma escaped the metal. "Sorry, we left the island."

"That's alright," Shiva said. He almost sounded amused. "You didn't know."

Step, smash, and dodge. It was hard to keep the Demons back. They kept trying to swarm, and every instinct warned Alex not to let herself get surrounded again. Shiva was at her back, his steady presence reassuring. Morgana and Merlin were raining magic down through the ranks of Demons. Trees were cracking and being snapped as more Demons marched on them. Nicki wasn't doing much, small flickers of blue magic escaping her from time to time, but she was safe with Merlin and Morgana.

Aiden shouted a warning just before a wall of fire encircled them. The fallen trees burst into flame, solidifying the line. They were surrounded by a yellow glow and pulled further in from the forest. Bathed in the fiery glow, Alex tried to count the Demons. She couldn't. There were too many. Their faces blurred together with the shadows. A flash of fire-light on metal made her tense. Shiva waved the Iron Trishula, and light exploded forth, vaporizing a Demon that had been holding a firearm.

Bran threw his hand forward. Yellow magic swirled around the gun before it hit the ground and pulled it towards him. Alex looked his way and watched as he plucked the firearm from the air. There was a flicker of hesitation on his face before he shifted to the right and handed it to Nicki. The Demons drew back, low snarls echoing around the line of fire. Bran spoke softly to Nicki and the redhead adjusted the firearm against her shoulder. It was a long and heavy looking one. The sort that Alex had never seen up close, much less fired.

The ring of flames gave them a chance to catch their breath, but not for long. Beyond the fire, the Demon horde thickened. Aiden waved his hands, and the fire exploded up to catch several Demons beginning to step over the logs. Morgana laughed in approval and Shiva shouted a warning. Alex barely heard any of it. Her heartbeat was pounding in her veins and magic was shimmering at the edge of her vision, drawing her attention into the darkness.

On instinct, she fought as the Demons pushed through. The first ones roared in pain and were pushed down to create bridges over the flames. Aiden kept sending forth bursts of sparks to ignite the flames, but it didn't slow them down much. Alex swung Mjǫllnir, striking Demon after Demon. She called down more lightning, frying several more, and kept shifting back. The Demons were coming closer. Yellow magic streamed past Alex's face and swept up several of the burning logs and threw them into the lines of Demons.

"Nice try, Aiden," Bran shouted. "But I don't think that's going to do it."

The ground trembled, and spikes of earth blasted up around them, catching Demons on sharp spikes and helping to block the way. Alex looked towards the others. They had whittled down the Demons some, but a thick semi-circle was still trying to close in. A Demon climbed onto the impaled bodies that were slowly collapsing. It was small and agile, almost tiny, and leapt at her. Shiva grabbed her arm before she could move, pulling her back sharply and swinging a sword. He took off the Demon's head and released another arrow into the crowd.

A blood spell would do nothing. These Demons had no special weakness to iron. More just kept coming. Alex couldn't imagine that they'd brought this many boats over. They couldn't have been hiding. Was the portal nearby? Magic thrummed around her, tightening and twisting as more Demons clamored closer.

Panic crept up her chest. Backing away, she turned to look towards Merlin and Morgana. Both of them were blasting magic into the crowd, trying to thin it out with limited success. There was a sharp tug at the edges of Alex's senses. If the portal was nearby, then that meant that Cathanáil was nearby. Maybe if she broke free from the Demons, she could find it. A Demon lashed forth, hitting Aiden in the leg, and sending him to the ground. Gunfire erupted, ringing in Alex's ears and three Demons fell to the ground. Bran helped Aiden up, letting the groaning man lean on him.

"Mages," Shiva said. "Move for the water."

"Agreed," Merlin said. The ground beneath them shook, almost knocking Alex over. "Hurry!"

The Demons snarled and moved to follow. More spikes sprang from the earth, blocking their path. Nicki shifted over to Bran and helped him with Aiden who thankfully seemed to be recovering. His jeans had been slashed, and there was some blood, but it wasn't too bad. Shiva swung the Iron Trishula, and more light spilled forth, driving the Demons back. Alex raised Mjǫllnir to the sky. Lightning crashed down into the metal, and she pointed it towards the Demons, unleashing a chain of electricity to slow them down.

Running down the hill wasn't easy. Alex cursed herself for dashing in to help Shiva. They should have signaled him, so he fell back. They should have created a perimeter. There were a dozen things they should have done. She knew it wasn't helpful to worry about it now, but she couldn't help it. Looking over at Aiden, Alex noted Nicki releasing him. Nicki swung around and fired into the crowd of Demons again. Then the weapon was apparently empty as Nicki hurled it at the closest Demon.

A line of Demons came running up from the shoreline, cutting them off and enclosing them. The opening they'd fought to keep was suddenly gone. Merlin's hands flashed bright green, and he grunted, sending a wave of magic around them. Earth spikes rose again, threatening the Demons. A silver dome spread out around them, shimmering in the air, and illuminating the hillside. But it wouldn't last long, Morgana was already panting behind Alex.

"Now what?" Aiden asked.

"Let's heal you," Nicki said. "Maybe the Chalice will give you some more magical energy."

"I doubt it works that way," Aiden said.

No one except Nicki moved. She was silent as she pulled out the Chalice and used one of the water bottles to fill it. Alex's eyes searched the landscape beyond the silver dome. There wasn't much to see and nothing that could help them. The Demons held the line, but none moved to attack.

"Shiva, any ideas?"

"There are too many," Shiva said. His voice was low and angry. "They're swarming with no regard for finesse or strategy. These are suicide soldiers." There was a long pause, and Alex stared at one of the nearby Demons. "Except now, they seem to have us where they want us."

The world was humming, a sharp tang in the air made her hair stand up, and the flow of magic from the ground into her limbs was too slow. None of the Demons were moving, all of them keeping their weapons at the ready. Their expressions were hard to read, but they looked exhausted and frightened. Just like the mages. Sparks arced off Mjǫllnir and she eyed the lines of Demons. Her mind whirled, trying to sort out what was happening and what they were waiting for. Lightning flashed far above, and Alex eyed the tops of the metal spears many Demons were carrying.

Aiden brought up a hand, and red sparks ignited into a fireball. Despite the rain, it blazed hot, creating waves of heat that rolled over Alex's back. Demons drew back, a few looking at each other. Inhaling slowly, Alex brought up Mjǫllnir as the air thickened. Just down the hill, water began to churn, and Alex turned just enough to catch sparks of green around Merlin's hand. He was opening a water tunnel. Her stomach tightened. Running would save them, but not the village. Shiva made a low sound of pained anger.

The air shifted. Alex picked the Demon to attack first. The Demons moved uneasily, their weapons quivering. Then there was a heavy sound from in the shadows. Something was moving closer.

"Hold," a deep voice commanded. "Hold."

Some of the Demons in the back shifted. Lowering their heads, they drew apart to create a pathway. Another Demon strode forward. The Demon was huge, larger than the others. It towered over both her and Shiva. Dressed in the same heavy armor she'd seen in the water, the Demon turned dark eyes towards her. The Demons still alive rushed to its side, reforming their lines, and positioning their weapons at the ready. A rumble of thunder filled the tense silence. Taking a deep breath, she raised her chin and studied the Demon. It was the same one, the Demon King.

The Demon King loomed over them. Its massive girth blocked the light, and a foul stink hit Alex's nostrils. Her body tensed and magic flashed around her hands. Muscle bunched in preparation and her fingers tightened on the handle of Mjǫllnir. The iron began to glow, illuminating the shore. Dark rocks sheltered them from the world, but the sounds of the city across the water were ever present. The Demon King wore armor, dark red and thick, that protected its black chest and arms. Gauntlets with vicious spikes covered its lower arms and hands. A strange looking mace with sharp metal and leather strips was in its right hand.

"I want to talk," Alex called. "Please, I just want to talk!"

"Speak." The Demon horde stopped, the front line shifting uneasily like spooked horses. "Speak, little mage."

"Alex," Morgana hissed. Her voice was soft, but Alex heard the plea for caution.

"I am Alex Adams, the Iron Soul, and Guardian of the Iron Realm." Alex almost laughed at the words, but the huge form of the Demon King chased away her amusement. She'd never envisioned herself the hero of any story, much less a fantasy, but here she was. "How did you come to be in this world? And why did you come here?"

"The Sword gave us the way here," the Demon King said. His voice was rough and gritty, hanging moments too long in the air. "We were dying, and a portal opened. We marched through and found ourselves in the waters nearby. Close enough to swim to shore."

"Sword..." Alex's chest tightened. Her mouth went dry. She'd suspected this, but here was confirmation. Alex didn't know the full powers possessed by Cathanáil. Arthur had called it a key. "Where is the Sword?"

"Still at the bottom of the sea, holding the way open for more of my forces." The Demon King's mouth opened in a nasty smile, revealing sparkling rows of sharp teeth. "They know where we fight, and they come to join the battle."

The Sword. Alex's body quivered. Cathanáil. How? Why? She didn't understand. The voices were loud, drowning out her thoughts, but someone, maybe Lokpal called out in warning. It was enough to force Alex back into the present. Magic churned around the island, the ground humming beneath her, feeding her more and more power. It was fighting back against the sudden surge of Demons. Invaders aided by its own power through the Sword.

"We don't need to fight," Alex said. Her grip on Mjǫllnir tightened. "We've been told that you're running from something. You're refugees. We're willing to help." She almost regretted the words, remembering the talk of eating flesh. But maybe it was just posturing for his troops. "You don't need to hurt anyone." Alex's eyes jumped towards Bran and Aiden who were holding off a line of Demons. "Just... stop this. Please. You don't need to be afraid."

"Mages protect this world from others," the Demon King growled. "That much I know. That much we recorded from our first invasion so long ago."

"This... journey doesn't have to be like that invasion," Alex said. "There are descendants of those Demons living here peacefully. You and yours could do the same. Please, I'm trying to give you a chance."

"Not enough room." The Demon King drew himself up and raised the battle-axe. "Only enough room and enough resources for one species! And it will be mine! I have over a hundred Demons, still climbing onto this island."

The number made Alex's heart twist. Her skin crawled and the odd distortion in the magic around her suddenly, horribly, made sense. Words sprang to and then faded from her lips. This was an invasion. No wishing or negotiation would change that. Digging her feet into the dirt, Alex brought Mjǫllnir up to her shoulder level and met the Demon King's gaze. It was the Demons or them.

32

Through the Water

Mjǫllnir collided with the side of the battle-axe. With a thunderous crack, the metal of the axe shattered and scattered through the air, falling to the ground with soft clinks. Lightning arced off her hands and the Demon King stumbled back. The remnants of his axe fell from his hands. Satisfaction surged through Alex. Then the Demon King roared, and the line of Demons rushed forward. In seconds she was surrounded by the creatures. There was a flicker of regret and a rush of anger at herself. Mjǫllnir flashed with magic and lightning exploded down from the sky, striking just in front of her feet. Unsure if it was the Hammer or her subconscious, Alex was grateful as some of the Demons retreated.

A steady hand touched her shoulder, but she didn't flinch. In the corner of her eye, she saw light flare off the prongs of the Iron Trishula as it was waved through the air. The light lingered in the air, forming a blazing trail that forced the Demons back. Shiva was beside her, fighting to protect her and the Iron Realm.

Inhaling sharply, Alex screamed and swung Mjǫllnir as hard as she could to the right. She caught another Demon in the chest and lightning exploded around her. Grunting in pain, Alex pushed through the discomfort in her shoulders and arms. Mjolnir's weight was beginning to take a toll, but there was no time to stop. No time to think or consider other options. It was all a rush and crush of Demons trying to destroy them. The moments to catch their breath hadn't been much, but it was all they had.

A rough perimeter was holding between Morgana's silver dome and Merlin's line of spikes. The silver magic was fading fast, no longer holding the Demons back, but it was slowing them. Not much, but enough that they were falling rapidly as the mages and Old One cut them down. Bodies were piling up faster than they could decay in front of Shiva as his swords sliced through Demon after Demon. Light kept rushing from the Trishula, forcing back Demons and killing some of them.

Swinging the Hammer, Alex felt it collide with another Demon. Lightning flashed off the metal, burning the flesh of the creature. It hit the ground a few feet away with a dull thump. The air was thick with electricity. She could taste the ozone. Far above their heads, thunder crashed, and satisfaction curled in Alex's gut.

Three more Demons rushed her. Alex shoved the Hammer towards them and pushed the magic through the weapon. It surged from her own body and exploded from the triskelion symbol in a rush of lightning. Waving her left hand, Alex pushed another bolt of dark gray magic towards another group of Demons moving too close to Aiden and Bran.

Merlin and Morgana must have been having success behind her because one of Shiva's hands touched her shoulder. He drew her back towards the shore. The sound of the churning water tunnel could still be heard, but Alex wanted to fight. They couldn't leave. There were people on this island. Who knew what the Demons would do to them once the mages were gone?

Swing, release magic, sidestep, and repeat. The rhythm settled into her bones and took over. Even the ache in her muscles wasn't enough to make her stop. Desperation, anger, and even fear drove her body. Mjǫllnir hummed in her hand, and the rumbling thunder overhead reassured her. A hot rain poured down, but she didn't stop. Wet hair stuck to the back of her neck and her eyelashes caught raindrops. She still didn't stop. Alex pushed out more magic and closed her eyes. There were softly glowing forms around her as magic stretched out.

The threads reconnected. At some point, the world had darkened. Or was it lightened? Every tree and rock were outlined in a softly glowing gray line. Next to her, the mages were glowing with the colors their magic manifested in. Shiva was a bright ball of energy with a strange outline marking out his humanoid shape. More Demons were in the trees, but the King was marching forward in a black and twisted mass that swallowed the light.

Ignoring the aches in her body, Alex pushed Mjǫllnir forward. Plasma appeared across the surface of the metal, building slower than before, but it did finally lash out in a massive bolt of lightning. It wasn't enough. The Demon King grabbed another Demon in his gauntlet covered hand and dragged the creature in front of him. It took most of the blast, screaming and convulsing before being dropped on the ground. Electricity traveled over the gauntlet, but it wasn't enough.

She heard the others fighting. Merlin was calling for retreat while Shiva was tearing through Demons as quickly as he could. Aiden and Bran were with Nicki, all three launching weak attacks into the horde. Morgana was ripping through Demons behind her, trying to clear a path to the shore. It wasn't enough.

The Demon King backhanded her. The blow snapped through Alex's body, inflaming every muscle. There was a crack in her chest. She couldn't breathe. Her feet left the ground, and the world spun. A scream filled her ears, but she didn't know if it was her or someone else. Her back hit the sand. There was some give, but all the air rushed from her lungs and pain radiated out. Alex didn't move. Her heart raced, she heard more Demons running towards her, heard the roar of victory from the Demon King, but she didn't move. Blinking frantically, she tried to take stock of where she was, but the lights of the dock were too far away. It was dark save for the occasional flash of lighting above and the faint gray glow from Mjǫllnir. Her fingers tightened around the Hammer's handle. At least she hadn't let go.

Water washed over her side. She was on the beach; that thought pushed its way through. Her already wet jeans clung tighter to her skin where the salt water was rushing over her right leg. A dull crash filled her ears, echoing and repeating over and over. Sitting up slowly, Alex gasped as another sharp pain filled her torso. Shouts and screams were dull, but she was vaguely aware of them. Something large hit the ground in front of her and Alex blinked, trying to clear her vision.

More screaming. Alex looked up at the Demon King stomping towards her. Behind him, still up on the slope, Morgana was shouting and trying to run. The Demons closed in tighter around the others leaving Alex and the Demon King alone. Looking over her shoulder, Alex saw the water tunnel. It was still open, swirling in midair with a hint of Merlin's green magic at the edges. A thought, a plan half-formed, but then the Demon King reached out and grabbed her throat. Dragging her to her feet, the Demon King laughed and tightened his grip. The pressure made her dizzy. Mjǫllnir fell from her hand as her fingers lost their strength. Then, she was pushed. Her feet tried to catch her, but she fell. Water splashed around her feet and then swallowed her up.

Something was wrong. The water was moving. It was wrong. The Demon King roared to the others, but the ringing in her ears was too much. She couldn't hear. Couldn't understand. There was a pained scream that cut through everything and pulled her back. Her eyes snapped open in time to see Merlin collapse to the ground. The Demon King smiled, and water swirled in around her, dragging her out to sea.

Sparks of green in the corner of her eyes faded. Water crashed over her, blinding her and everything had gone dark. There was a shock. Magic rippled viciously over her skin leaving a burn in its wake. It flooded into her chest, tightening around her heart, and pumping too fast in her veins. Alex wanted to stop. Human instinct screamed for her to stop. Survival clawed against her mind, begging, and urging, but she didn't stop. The mage won out, the ancient soul that had lived and died too often to fear it stood firm. Water splashed around her, striking her feet, and freezing the skin. Pressure built and pressed down on her forcing the air out of her lungs.

The tunnel had collapsed. She was inside of it. Alex's senses cleared at the sudden surge of horror. She could only hear the crashing of water. Somehow, she was moving. No longer on the beach and not in a full tunnel. There was nothing but water. No light and no destination in sight. Her chest burned, but she held what air she had tightly.

Fighting back her terror, Alex focused. She did her best to conjurer the memory of the skyline of Mumbai, tried to capture the noises and the smells that had been both alien and familiar. The memory of the island and the caves came more easily. Around her, the water vibrated, and the magic thickened. She pushed back against it. She wasn't going to be swept out into the ocean to die as others had.

Her soul was forged of iron and made for and by the world. She wasn't dying like this, not when there was a fight to be won. Magic sparked off her fingertips, fueled by rage and determination. The voices shouted their encouragements, strangely in agreement for once, but Alex didn't bother focusing on them. She listened to the sloshing of the water and searched with her magic as a guide. Reaching out, Alex connected what power she still had to the strands. Faint lines stretched out towards her.

Not far away then. The collapsed tunnel hadn't taken her far. Strands of magic rang with a sweet note as she reached for them. Alex's fingers brushed over a pale gray line. Then she found it, a dark spot not far away, a shimmering hole where the magic faded.

Magic shifted in the water. The portal, it was deep in the water, but it was there. The Demon King hadn't been lying. Wrongness seeped into her world, like oil into water and she felt the Iron Realm generating tiny sparks of magic around it. There was a focal point, both of the magic and of the portal. It nagged at her, taunted her even as the world began to turn black. Reaching out her hand, Alex pulled. She pulled on the magic, all of it that stretched out.

The portal collapsed. Deep in the water, there was a shift. A change. Something hit her hand. On reflex, her fingers tightened around the shape. It was a hilt. Magic swept through her, but this time warm and familiar. Everything tingled, and she pulled it out of the swirling water. Opening her eyes, Alex looked down and gasped. The water almost collapsed around her, but she recovered enough to push it back. In her hand was a familiar blade with a golden hilt. Cathanáil. More magic pulsed into her body as the blade offered up its power. Alex smiled, her eyes moistening with grateful tears. Arto cheered in victory, and the other voices joined in for a moment.

Then she pushed them away, putting them back into the farther reaches of her mind. Alex held the Sword tightly and released more magic into the water. The trembling tunnel widened around her, releasing her freezing feet. Sloshing loudly, the tunnel started to stabilize, and Alex looked forward. The water was spinning faster and faster ahead. The magic swept around her and tugged her further along the tunnel. It was working.

Stumbling out onto a shore, Alex inhaled greedily. The air stung to her abused lungs. Dizziness and euphoria made her stumble. Her fingers remained tight around the hilt of Cathanáil, and she opened her eyes. The others were there, spread out on the beach and fighting Demons. Their faces were awash with shock in the low illumination of Morgana's light orbs. Merlin was up, but not fighting with Shiva looming protectively nearby the old mage.

"Alex!" Morgana cried. "You're-"

Her words were cut off by the roar of the Demon King. He'd been attacking Morgana but turned away from her. Morgana sent a wave of silver sparks at his back. He flinched but stormed towards Alex.

Shaking the water from her hair, Alex glared at the Demon and only vaguely heard Shiva's cry of relief. She didn't take her eyes away from the dark ones of the Demon and slowly brought up Cathanáil. There was a collective gasp from her fellow mages. Alex smiled. A few feet away, where it had fallen, Mjǫllnir hummed. The sound filled the whole beach and Alex reached out with her magic. A dark gray stream grabbed the Hammer's handle and Alex pulled. It flung itself into the air. She caught it, the Hammer slamming to an impossible stop in her palm.

"The Sword!" The Demon King yelled. "You took the Sword! My portal!"

"This Sword is mine, and it exists to protect this world, not to serve those who would harm it." Alex lifted the blade, pointing the tip at the Demon King. "Stop this fight. The portal is closed."

"My kind will die."

"Maybe not," Alex said. The rush of power was fading just enough for guilt and worry to push through. "We can still look at a peaceful solution. Work with me and we can-"

He didn't let her finish. Swinging a huge, long sword, the Demon King lunged for her. His roar thundered in her ears, and Alex stumbled to the side. She tried to swing Mjǫllnir, but her left arm couldn't manage the motion. Lightning sparked off the metal, but it was in the wrong position. Instead, she focused her efforts and energy into her right hand and Cathanáil. The Sword hummed, slicing through the air and Alex could see wisps of magic flowing off the metal. The Demon King jumped back, but the tip of Cathanáil caught one fleshy arm.

Beneath her feet, the ground hummed. As the Demon King withdrew and hissed in pain, Alex toed off her tennis shoes. Her wet socks stuck to her skin, and she sank into the sand. Energy crept up her legs. It was slow, but she adjusted her grip on Mjǫllnir and braced herself. Speaking and cheering, the voices blended together. Stronger now, Alex pushed through the ache and readied herself as the Demon King snarled and Demons swarmed forth.

She moved. The Sword moved with her, humming in tandem with the Hammer. Tiny bolts of magic arched from them both, forming a bubble of pure energy around her. Each step shifted the magic, rippling it outward to catch any Demon that came too close. Her heartbeat joined the steady rhythm. Slash, smash, step. Repeat. Slice, crush, and walk forward. The pattern continued. Everything else fell away.

No longer did she see the Demons. The magic grew thick, clouding the world, but illuminating every form, every curve perfectly. She knew the red, blue, and yellow outlines. Shiva's brilliant blue form wasn't as it appeared to human eyes, but Alex made no hostile move towards it.

Strands of magic reached out. They twisted and turned across each other, weaving into a tapestry across the island.

Beneath her feet, magic flowed up through her legs, renewing the spark in her chest. It grew, expanding through her lungs and heart until Alex thought she might burst. She didn't. It made her stronger. Stab, smash, and step. Dark silver sparks rolled through the air surrounded by a soft halo of white. Overhead thunder began to roll once more. Alex didn't look towards the others. Their magical outlines of brilliant colors assured her that they were alright.

Demons fell, and now none were coming to take their places. Dark blood spilled across the sand only to fade away quickly. Alex kept swinging. The tide had changed, and she pushed. Fire erupted over one group of Demons while others were hurled into the sea by a wave of yellow.

Then the Demon King came forward. His sword glinted in the low light, too long and too heavy for any human. It slammed down, and Alex jumped. The sand made it difficult, but she avoided the blade. It buried itself in the sand, and the Demon King tugged as Alex jumped towards him.

Swinging Mjǫllnir, Alex heard the crack of the Demon King's armor. The dark material crumpled at the blow. There were shouts of alarm from the Demons, but Aiden and Bran rallied from behind her. Flashes of red and yellow lit up the shore and Demons shrieked. In the corner of her eye, Alex saw the Iron Trishula slice through the air with sparks of magic flying off it. Demons were thrown back by the wave of power without even being touched. Her fingers itched. Want for the magic contained there pushed forward, but the hum of the Sword and Hammer kept it at bay. She had but two hands.

The voices weren't loud. They were still. Silent. Or maybe they were all speaking at once with her own thoughts. No dissent. No distraction.

Another Demon tried to charge. The bubble of energy caught it. Burned flesh. Alex's nose wrinkled, and she stabbed Cathanáil forward, cutting into the Demon King's gut. Whatever alien metal had formed the armor gave away and crumbled as it fell from the Demon's body.

They didn't belong. Their bodies were dark in the tapestry of magic. Shiva's was wrong. The tone of his hum was different, but it tried to harmonize with the soft melody beginning to chime. Each thread of magic quivered like a plucked string, making a soft sound as the creatures moved. It was sweet when the mages moved through it, slightly off-key when Shiva hit them, but sour when the Demons came too close.

A Demon lashed at her. Alex pulled Cathanáil out of the Demon King and slashed the chest of her attacker. More were coming. Their king was roaring in rage. He struggled to stand, holding his wound. Darkness seeped off him, pushing at the strands of magic. Glaring, Alex pushed more power into Cathanáil. The Sword shuddered in her grasp and sparks leapt from the Sword onto the strands. She turned the Sword, twisting the strands around the blade, but they did not cut. They never would, not these strands.

Another Demon came too close. Mjǫllnir moved fast, faster than she should have been able to swing it with only one hand. The strands of light flashed and shifted, pulling aside for the Hammer just before it crushed the side of the Demon. It fell, and another blow crushed the body. Magic flared up from the ground, surrounding the unraveling form. The other magic, the additional power in them, gave way and was consumed.

The Demon King reached for the hilt of his sword. Alex slammed Mjǫllnir into his arm. Cracking snapped through the air, drowning out even the crash of the waves. The Demon King bellowed and fell forward, grasping its arm in pain. The armor was falling off, exposing dark skin above its spine as the Demon King fell forward.

She slammed Cathanáil into the flesh. The Sword's blade slid down. There was resistance from the sand. In her left hand, Mjǫllnir flashed with magic, a bolt of lightning striking the golden hilt of Cathanáil. Power hit Alex's chest, wrapping around her heart. It blasted around her, throwing back the Demons. The voices exploded in confusion only to turn into one voice and blend with her shock. She focused on the Demon King's flesh as it began to gray and collapse into itself like a brittle, hollow statue.

Gasping for air, Alex's body finally gave out. Mjǫllnir fell onto the sand once more amongst the vanishing dark blood of the Demon King. A pair of strong hands guided her down, so she was kneeling on the sand. She looked up to find Shiva smiling down at her though three of his arms were using the Trishula and his bow and arrow to kill Demons as they fled the battlefield. Her eyes dropped to Cathanáil, still clutched in her right hand, and now laid across her lap. It glowed in the light of the moon as her storm clouds rolled away. Alex couldn't help it. A rough exhausted laugh escaped her.

33

Rise of Shiva

620 B.C.E. Mazagaon, India

Lokpal didn't move. His lungs were tight and frozen as the Demon King lunged. The tip of the spear glittered in the sunlight. That cruel sneer was going to be the last thing he ever saw. Lokpal just hoped, prayed that they'd done enough damage to the Demon forces. The Trident hummed weakly against his skin, but he had no more magic to give it.

Then the Demon King was grabbed by two strong arms and two more grabbed the spear. There was a cry of alarm from the Demon King as he was wrestled backward. Lokpal blinked. The Old One was dragging the Demon King away from him. With two strong arms, the Old One snapped the spear and twisted the Demon King's hands, forcing him to let it go.

With a roar, the Demon King elbowed the Old One in his side. The Old One didn't let go. His remaining two free arms continued to shoot arrows at the Demons. The Demon King was much smaller than him, and the Old One's extra arms tightened their grip around him. More snarls and shouts from the Demon King drew the attention of the surviving Demons. There were flashes of green and silver that cut down a group that came rushing towards him. Lokpal flinched as their bodies crumbled to the ground.

His ears were ringing. He tightened his hand against his side. It was just slowing it down. Blood was still seeping between his fingers. Another Demon came running towards him, but a sharp point of earth blasted up from the ground and impaled the creature. Suddenly, his knees gave out, and even the Trident couldn't hold him up. Lokpal grunted as he hit the ground. Pain radiated out from his side and back. Gasping for air, he swallowed desperately as thirst hit him. Black spots appeared in his sight, but he tried to sit up.

"Lokpal," Morgana called. She knelt next to him and carefully reached for his wounds. He pulled away on instinct and Morgana made a soft shushing sound, the sort that he himself made for his children. "It's alright," she said. "Stay still. I can stop the bleeding. Just stay still."

"You can heal?" Speaking made his side throb.

"Yes, I haven't the magic to heal all the wound, but I can make sure that you don't die. Stay still." He did as she said. It was hard. Her hands began to glow silver, and she reached towards his wound. "This will feel strange," she cautioned him. "I'm going to focus on closing the wound and healing some damage. You'll still hurt a bit."

Lokpal didn't understand. Was she healing him or not? There must be limits. A strange tickling sensation spread over his side. It was cold and warm at the same time. He struggled not to pull away and took shallow breaths. Turning his eyes to the Old One, he tried to focus on what was happening. Making sense of the noise was hard. Morgana's hands were gentle as she carefully pulled the fabric of his tunic away from his side.

"Stay calm," Morgana said again.

The Old One punched a Demon in the face as it tried to free its leader. Another charged with a spear that the Old One wrestled from it before tossing it into one of his right hands. The Old One stabbed the Demon and twirled the spear to stab another that came too close. The Demon King was clawing at the Old One's face, long nails trying to slice into the flesh. The Old One's arms had adjusted themselves and were crushing the Demon King's body. Two hands moved to the Demon King's neck and were twisting it. Screams from the Demon King turned frantic. Lokpal's heart raced. The Demons were running, tumbling over themselves to flee now.

Then the Demon King's neck cracked, and the body trembled. Were these things similar enough to his own kind that such a wound was fatal? The Demon King was still moving, but weakly. The Old One suddenly released it, dropping the Demon on the ground. It hit with a soft thunk and groaned. A hissing sound escaped it, and the Demon King tried to crawl away. The Old One stepped forward, putting a foot on the back of the Demon King, pinning him to the ground. Then he turned the spear and raised it above his head before crashing it down into the Demon King's skull.

"Destroyer!" One of the Demons shrieked. It had been trying to attack Merlin, but suddenly turned and started to run. "Destroyer."

The Demon King's body was beginning to harden and crack. The Old One slammed his foot down, shattering the corpse which dissolved into dust. Lokpal stared at the pile in disbelief. His side tingled, but he didn't look down. He was too busy watching the wind carry the dust away. Then his eyes jumped up to the Old One's face. He was panting, but looked pleased, smiling a little before turning to look towards the fleeing Demons. The last of the Demon King's body vanished on a strong burst of wind and Lokpal allowed himself to sigh in relief.

He tried to move, but a firm grip from Morgana kept him still. "Don't move," she snapped. "I'm almost done…" Her voice was weaker than normal, and Lokpal carefully turned to look down.

Silver magic was fading into his skin. Gone was the slashed flesh and blood and instead the skin was a pale red but knitting back together. Lokpal gasped in shock and awe causing Morgana's lips to quirk into a smile. There was a layer of sweat on her face, and her right hand that hovered just above his skin was shaking.

"How is he?" the Old One asked, walking over to them. "Lokpal, how do you feel?"

"He'll be alright," Morgana said. Her expression was cautious and curious as she looked at the Old One. "I've sealed up the wound. He'll be sore, but he's in no danger." Morgana turned her eyes back to him and frowned. "You're lucky he didn't puncture any internal organs, Lokpal, I wouldn't have been able to fix that."

"You healed me? I didn't know that you could do that."

Morgana's expression softened, and she nodded. "You can, but it is exhausting and dangerous. A mage can die from the effort." Then she looked back at the Old One. "Dare I ask what happened to you?"

"Indeed," Merlin said. He walked over with a deep frown. "Are you to be trusted?"

"Lokpal helped purify me of the corruption in the water," the Old One said. "It washed away the… effects of being in this world. Even the ache has mostly eased greatly. I owe him greatly."

Merlin hummed thoughtfully, and Lokpal was certain that the mage wasn't confident that it was the truth. But then, Merlin's eyes dropped to the Trident as Lokpal pulled it across his lap. Merlin and Morgana shared a look, and Merlin extended his hand to Morgana.

"We will see to the village," Merlin said. "I have enough magic to help with the fires, and hopefully the villagers will return soon."

"I will stay with Lokpal," the Old One offered. "And slay any Demons that I come across."

"Good." Merlin nodded to him, giving the Old One a long searching look before he and Morgana hurried off to a nearby fire.

Lokpal exhaled as they left. "That went better than I thought it would," he said.

"Yes," the Old One agreed. "Can you stand?"

"Yes," Lokpal agreed. "I want to." He shifted his legs and carefully eased his body onto his knees. The Old One knelt next to him to Lokpal's shock and offered his arm. "Uh, thank you."

The Old One stood slowly, helping to leverage Lokpal to his feet. His side ached as he leaned too much on it, but it was more comfortable once he was standing. Inhaling slowly, he focused on the odd stretch of his skin. It felt tender, but nothing compared to the raw pain of before.

"It's strange," he said. "But I'm grateful that Morgana was there." He paused and looked towards the pair of mages. "I didn't think that they liked me much."

"I think they like you more than they care to admit," the Old One said. He chuckled slightly. "You have a good heart. Saving me was a gamble, and yet you did it anyway."

"Of course, Rud-" he cut himself off. "Sorry."

"I'll need to decide a new name," the Old One said. He looked up the road where the Demons had fled. "Though, it is not a priority. Not while there are still Demons nearby." The Old One looked towards the docks. "Do you wish to stay here?"

"No, my family... I didn't see them. We live out of the village a ways," he said. He nodded towards the proper road. "That way, please. I need to see them, need to make sure that they're alright."

"Of course." If the Old One heard the fear in his voice, he said nothing about it. They began to walk with Lokpal shifting the Trident to his left hand while The Old One kept a grip on his right arm. "I do not sense any Demons that way. Most have fled to the shores. No doubt they are using boats to escape."

"Good." Lokpal breathed a little easier. "Good. That's good to hear." He stepped wrong, and his foot slipped on the pathway making him hiss.

"Lokpal?" The Old One stopped, his grip on Lokpal's arm tightening. "You are alright, aren't you?"

"Sore," Lokpal said. "Morgana... her healing worked, but it is still sore." He shook his head and forced a smile. "I'll take being sore over the alternative."

"I am glad." The Old One shook his head. "I was angry when I saw you fall. Rage like that..." He began carefully guiding Lokpal forward once more. "It would seem that I am still the destroyer, still a warrior. Even the Demons called me that as they fled."

His expression was uneasy, and Lokpal's chest tightened in response. "That isn't always a bad thing," he said. Lokpal gave the Old One a smile. "It can be a kindness to others. An act of benevolence. Auspicious even as sometimes the old has to be removed for anything new to grow. You destroying those Demons saved the lives of those in my village. Saved me."

"Auspicious?" The Old One chuckled. "You have much faith in me, my friend."

"You helped me, even when you were in pain."

"That was for the fight."

"Then why welcome death?" Lokpal asked. The Old One gave no answer. "Even poisoned and in pain, you sought to protect. Sought to be good."

"Maybe, but Rudra is no longer the right name."

"What will you choose?"

"Perhaps I shouldn't." The Old One looked at him and smiled. "I seek to aid the Iron Realm; maybe I should be named by the Iron Soul who protects it."

"I... uh?" Lokpal floundered and looked over his shoulder. They were out of sight of Merlin and Morgana, and he could see the pillars of smoke lightening. So they were putting out the fires. He thought he heard cheering coming from the docks, but none of that helped him right now. "I can't. I mean surely-"

"You called my destruction a good thing, a kindness," the Old One pressed. "Is there a name that means kind?"

"I-yes." Lokpal nodded and studied the Old One. Then he slowly smiled. "Shiva."

"Shiva," the Old One said. "Yes, I shall be Shiva."

"Shiva." Lokpal let the name linger on his lips as he studied the Old One. Nodding, he smiled once more and leaned on the Trident for support. "I think it suits you."

Then his legs trembled, and Lokpal almost fell over. One of Shiva's arms grabbed the Trident, and another steadied his shoulder. Shiva smiled kindly at him and then chuckled.

"I fear, my friend, that you are exhausted," Shiva said.

They didn't speak anymore after that. Walking up the path, Lokpal urged his body to move faster, but he couldn't. None of the trees were burned here. There were no strew weapons about or signs of chaos. Perhaps the Demons had not come so far. Hope bloomed in his chest. It was dangerous, but he welcomed it and frantically prayed that his family was alright. Shiva kept a steady hand on his arm and said nothing as Lokpal put more and more of his weight against the Old One. Another hand came up to support his shoulder. If he had asked Shiva to carry him, Lokpal suspected that the Old One would have.

It was difficult to contain his urgent need to get home. A few times he considered just asking Shiva to leave him and go on ahead. But he didn't. They stayed together and soon they were climbing the last hill. His home was intact. There was no sign of fire. Even the outer fence was fine, and he released a sigh of relief. He tried to call to his family, but his mouth was too dry.

"Hello?" Shiva called. "The Demons have been driven back. Lokpal is here. He is weak."

Ananta appeared in the doorway moments later, her expression was guarded and suspicious. Her eyes widened as she spotted Shiva, but her attention quickly jumped to Lokpal. Rushing forward, she made a soft cry of relief. Thankfully, she didn't try to hug him, but stopped right in front of him and reached out to touch his face.

"You're alright," he said. "Ananta."

"I'm fine," she said. "Heema has the children inside. We heard the commotion in the village. We were packing supplies to slip down the back of the island if the Demons came here."

"I'm glad you're alright." Tears were gathering in his eyes as relief crashed through him. "Ananta."

"May I take him inside?" Shiva asked Anata.

"No," Lokpal said. He shook his head. "Not inside. Just let me sit on the porch. If Merlin and Morgana come to see me, I need..." He trailed off, and his knees trembled. "Just the porch. I want to be able to hear."

Shiva nodded in understanding and Ananta bit her lower lip but didn't object. Instead, she rushed back into the house and returned a moment later with a blanket. She laid it out on the porch, all the while looking his way with worry in her eyes. Shiva knelt and guided Lokpal onto the blanket with his back against the wall of the house. Ananta went inside and came back with a pillow that she placed behind him with Shiva's help.

"Do you need anything?" she asked.

"No." Lokpal smiled and relaxed. The ache was slowly fading. "I'm fine, thank you." He looked to Shiva. "Thank you for bringing me home."

"You are welcome." Shiva smiled at him but looked a little lost. "Is there anything more I can do?"

"Are there Demons nearby?"

"None that I sense."

"That's good." He closed his eyes. "That's good."

"Lokpal?" Heema's voice called.

Turning his head, he opened his eyes and looked up at his second wife. Daksha was in her arms and reaching towards him. Lokpal grinned and opened his arms, signaling to give him the girl. Heema smiled warmly at him, kneeling to kiss his cheek and carefully handing Daksha to him. Lokpal took his daughter with tender hands and smiled. The little girl snuggled against him.

"They're both tired," Heema said. "We were worried and stressed… it affected them."

"I'm glad to see you too, little one," Lokpal whispered.

He doubted that the child understood what had happened today. Heema glanced at Shiva but said nothing. He'd have to explain everything to them tonight, but for now, he just wanted to rest. It took him a few minutes to realize that Shiva was still next to him and watching Daksha curiously. A strange idea popped into Lokpal's head, but it made him smile. He shifted just enough to carefully roll Daksha off his lap and set her into Shiva's. The little girl made a small sound, and her eyes flew open.

Shiva blinked in alarm, opening his mouth to protest, but no sound came out of it. Lokpal stretched. "She was a bit heavy on my side," he said.

Shiva blinked at the small child in his hands. She was looked back at him with equal confusion, and Lokpal laughed. The sight of the little girl in the arms of the deity was too much after the strain of the day. Even the worried and nervous looks from his wives didn't stop the laughter. His sides ached, but whatever magic Morgana had used was strong, and his wound did not reopen.

"You are a strange creature, Lokpal," Shiva said. "You are very unwise."

"Unwise?"

"You fought to save me when you shouldn't have."

He absorbed the words and stared up at the clouds. They were thick and soft without the heavy hue of rain. Birds were singing once again, and he inhaled the air. The smell of smoke was fading away. Merlin and Morgana surely had things in the village under control. He felt lazy, coming home with Shiva rather than seeing to the village. But the exhaustion was overwhelming.

"I don't completely understand it," Lokpal said. "But... Merlin and Morgana say that I have a soul that will return to the world again and again. I have been a warrior for the realm before and will be again."

"Yes, I have heard of the Iron Soul," Shiva said. He nodded and shifted Daksha carefully. "Other Old Ones informed me of him and the mages soon after I arrived in this world. What force formed such a being, I do not know, but it- you are here to defend this world."

"The Demons are still out there," Lokpal said.

"Yes," Shiva agreed. "They are. Their leader is dead, and many were destroyed. I doubt that they will try anything too dramatic."

"If they do, we'll have to stop them."

"Yes."

"You'll help?" He turned his head to look at Shiva. Daksha had fallen asleep in Shiva's lap, and the Old One was gently running his hand over her dark head without even seeming to notice. "Won't you?"

"I will," Shiva said. He was smiling a little now. In the bright sunlight, the contrast between his face and his hands was far more intense, and yet Lokpal thought it suited him. Shiva looked down at the little girl in his lap and smiled. "I will protect this realm. It is my home."

"Thank you," Lokpal said. He truly meant the words. "Thank you, Shiva."

The Old One smiled at him, a warm look that reached his eyes. They fell into silence, and Lokpal watched the world pass by. Birds were singing and flying between trees. He could hear the ocean and voices were echoing up to his home from the village below. There were still Demons in the world. There would be more fights, but now the world had Shiva. Lokpal didn't understand what it meant to have the Iron Soul; he honestly didn't. Perhaps in time, he would, but for now, he was content, and his family was safe.

34

Memory of Family

There was a lot to think about, but Alex's mind wouldn't settle. Even having Cathanáil and Mjǫllnir at her side didn't help. The voices were loud now. Everyone was trying to make themselves heard and thus, Alex couldn't understand any of it. A few of her past lives were comforting, creating a warm understanding calm at the back of her mind while others were a mess of chaos. It was tempting to try and locate Arto, but Alex wasn't ready to confront the noise just yet.

Alex closed her eyes and reached for the spark of magic in her chest. For something that had once eluded her, it jumped at a mere whispered wish to come forth. She flexed her fingers and didn't need to look down to know that dark silver sparks were surrounding her hand. Even on the second-floor balcony, Alex was aware of the pulse of energy traveling through the ground below. Like a heartbeat, pushing and shifting all the tiny invisible aspects of their world.

Bran might understand it all. Alex had a hint of regret that she'd never been scientifically minded. If she had been, then maybe understanding all of this would be easier. The others had taken it all on faith. They'd felt the magic and seen what it could do. That was enough. It was magic, but Alex was on the fence. She knew enough science to understand that there were reasons. Everything that happened had some basis in the physical laws. All the prior Iron Souls had just lived in times that lacked the understanding of those laws. And to be fair, she thought her own time still did.

Merlin and Morgana were still mages of faith. Sure, they learned here and there in order to articulate the situation, but Alex doubted that they really wondered about the why. Initially, she hadn't either. Dealing with magic alone had been enough, especially when there wasn't an owl with a letter inviting her to a special magical school. The thought made her chuckle. Back then, she'd been afraid of being disappointed if magic wasn't real even after their visions had convinced the others.

Maybe she'd been the smart one. Perhaps some warning instinct had been trying to keep her from being pulled into this mess. She didn't know. It didn't matter. She was neck deep in all of it. Just a few gasps away from drowning, but now it was starting to seem like maybe she at least had something beneath her. The voices weren't so bad now. Things had settled.

Pushing out her magic, Alex opened her eyes and watched the strands stretch out. The world darkened as her eyes honed in on the magic, rejecting the visual spectrum. It was one more thing that she didn't understand. This was an act of faith. Rather than recognizing that Nicki pulled hydrogen and oxygen from the air to create her water or that Aiden's magic vibrated the atmosphere so much that it ignited or that Bran probably controlled opposing electrical charges to move objects, this was all faith. She didn't understand it.

The strands twisted. Like spider silk when a fly caught in the web. Something had moved too close. Alex tensed, but there was a warm yellow glow. That was familiar and she relaxed. Pulling on the magic,

Alex let the strands snap, and they flung back to her, filling her chest with a rush of power. Her fingers tightened around the railing.

"Hey," Bran called.

Turning around, Alex looked towards the doorway and found Bran lingering. He was smiling, but it didn't reach his eyes. Instead, he looked uneasy and unsure of if she wanted him there. Holding back a sigh, Alex nodded to him and forced a small smile. It was enough and Bran walked forward to join her in looking out over the city.

"It's beautiful," Bran said. "In a way. I'm not one for big cities, but Mumbai has quite a view."

"You're from a pretty good-sized city," Alex said.

"Are you kidding? Eugene has under 200,000 people while Mumbai is into the double-digit millions. Huge difference there, Alex."

"Okay, okay, valid point."

"You okay?"

"Fine," Alex said. "Just thinking."

"Please tell me that you got some sleep," Bran said. "After last night-"

"I slept," she promised. "I did. Not long, but I did sleep." Then she shook her head and lowered her hand to where Cathanáil was hanging on her hip. The Desai's didn't have a scabbard for it, but Nicki had wrangled up a pair of leather loops that had been fitted to her belt. "Last night was exciting."

"It was," Bran agreed. "But that doesn't explain why you're up here by yourself."

"I keep looking for things that are familiar," Alex confessed. "I keep waiting for something that I know, but there isn't anything. It's been too long, and the city is too old." She chuckled a little. "Lokpal lived here when Mumbai was still a fishing village and a bunch of different islands. He's ancient history." Looking back at the doorway, she shook her head.

"I still can't believe that they've kept that history alive. I certainly don't know my ancestors from two thousand years ago."

"Well, you also don't have an Old One keeping in touch with your family." Bran's voice was cautious at the mention of her family, and Alex held back a retort. "That changes things a bit."

"Yeah, it does."

They fell into silence, and Alex focused on the hum of the city. There were cars, hints of music, and the general clamor that came with a city so large. It put her on edge, and Alex reminded herself that she would have been one of the first lives to see a city this large. Even Gottfried's Germany wouldn't have been so crowded.

"Nothing here is familiar," Alex said. She didn't mean to say the words, but Bran came up to stand beside her and leaned against the railing. "I know it was silly, but I expected that Lokpal would recognize something."

"Does it bother you?" Bran asked. His voice was gentle and calm. Soothing. "Not feeling connected to this place."

"It's not that." Alex wrinkled up her nose. "There's magic here; I'm aware of that every moment. But there's this family that is supposed to be mine in a way, and I don't care about them. No more than I would anyone else."

"Nothing at all?"

"Well, I don't love them or anything." Alex shrugged.

"That's not surprising, no reason you should. The only one of us who has a real reason to love the Desai is Nicki, and we all know her reason."

"Avani would be lucky to have her."

"Yes, she would be, and I get the sense that Avani might be interested."

"That's good. I've never seen Nicki gone on someone like that."

"To be fair, dating is hard for us. We have so many secrets and may have to run out on dates, that it makes it hard to consider anyone seriously. Avani is the first person that Nicki can consider as a serious potential partner in a long time, and I think it is short-circuiting her brain."

Alex laughed, remembering the vivid red blush she'd last seen on Nicki's face. "Yeah." She tapped the railing with her fingertips and looked down at the leaves of a bush below them. "I hope Avani likes her too. I'd like one of us to have a win."

"Lance and Jenny are doing fine."

"Which makes me happy, but I was referring to those of us who don't have a reincarnation romance."

"Fair point," Bran agreed. "But it doesn't matter. We're young. We might meet someone down the road that we can trust with our secrets or meet other magicians."

"Maybe." Alex brushed her thumb over the smooth metal head of Mjǫllnir on her left hip. "My parents met during college, well, undergraduate school for my mom. Dad followed her to her residency and then they got married. I guess I always figured I'd meet someone in college."

"Hey, we're only going into junior year."

"Seems silly to worry about college at all," Alex said.

"No, it isn't, there'll still be a life to live when all this passes. And if it doesn't for a long time, then we'll need something else in our lives. Something else to focus on or we'll go mad. Even Merlin and Morgana are maintaining their university professor jobs. Probably because they know that from experience." Bran paused and looked over at her. "Besides, I'm sure your parents would have wanted you to finish college. I didn't know them well, but it seems like the sort of thing they would have wanted for you."

"It was, college was never a question in our house. Mom and Dad worried that so many jobs require a college degree just to be considered." Alex tried to smile and nudged Bran's shoulder. "Course, I'm not studying anything as useful as you, Mister Physics."

"Hey now, English literature can be useful, especially with the lives we lead. Besides, I'm the one who is standing in the middle of information and data that would probably ensure a Nobel Prize and yet I have to keep my mouth shut!"

Laughing, Alex let herself lean against Bran's shoulder for a moment. "Alright, you win, it does sound horrible when you put it that way."

"It is."

"You're being dramatic, usually that's Nicki or Aiden's job."

"They can't have all the fun."

They fell silent for a moment, and Alex wondered if she should move. Bran didn't seem to mind her using him as a pillow as they looked out over the city. Magic tickled lightly at her senses, and the strange smells mixed into the car exhaust tickled her nose.

"The Desai are good people," Bran said. "I'm sure that Lokpal is proud."

"We are," Alex said. Bran tensed slightly but didn't say anything about her pronoun choice. "We don't love them; there isn't enough of a connection for that. They're from too long ago, but we are proud. They've held onto something ancient and honored us while remaining loyal to the realm. We can't ask for more than that."

"Do you think about your other families?"

Alex let the question hang in the air for a long moment. "Sometimes," she admitted. "I see their faces in my dreams. It's not as confusing now, but it hurts sometimes." Alex shifted away from Bran and leaned forward to rest her arms on the railing before lowering her head. "Not knowing.

Galath is hard because I know he was miserable over our death. Morgana is hard too. We love her and most of the time we're grateful that she is there, but also sad that she's never been able to have a human life."

"I'm pretty sure that's on the Queen, not you."

"Maybe, we really don't know why those two are the way they are. Maybe it is because they are hybrids, but maybe not." Alex sighed out loud and focused her gaze on a distant skyscraper. "As I said, not knowing is the hard part."

"Well, that's a good a lead in as I'm going to get. Morgana gave me something for you," Bran said. He reached into his pocket and pulled out a small black moleskine notepad. "She said that you might want it at some time. I... uh meant to do this earlier, but it never seemed like the right time."

"What is it?" Alex plucked the small book from Bran's hand and considered it. "Lists of spells to learn?" She asked with a smile. "Homework for the summer? She's downstairs at breakfast. She could have given that to me herself."

"No... it's information on Captain Eckstein's family. While it was hard to find information on him... Morgana was able to find some things about his kids."

Alex's whole body froze. She would have sworn that even her heart stopped beating. One of the voices was suddenly too loud and too pained for her to even dare listen to. On impulse, her fingers tightened around the small notebook as if afraid that it would be taken from her. Finally, she managed to swallow. Her heart started working again, and Alex was too aware of how fast it was suddenly beating.

"Alex, you don't have to look at it-"

"It's fine, Bran," Alex said. "Thank you." Looking up at him, she didn't try to smile and didn't look at the book. "I mean it, thank you.

I've… I've tried not to wonder but being here with Avani and her family. It's making some of the others wonder." She swallowed again. "And Gottfried… well, there was always a good chance of finding out."

"Yeah, he was recent enough," Bran agreed. He was looking down at the book. "Alex, do you want to read it yourself or would you like me to read it to you?"

It should have been a ridiculous question, and yet the moment he asked it, Alex felt relief. She wanted to know but didn't want to open the small book herself. Nodding, Alex moved her hand closer to Bran with a jerky motion. Her joints didn't seem to be working, and she barely managed to loosen her grip. Bran said nothing about it as he pried the notebook out of her hand. He opened the small black moleskine book with a quick flick of his thumb and cleared his throat. Alex tried to brace herself and gripped the railings behind her.

"Well, after Captain Eckstein vanished and was declared missing in action, his family received some benefits," Bran said. His eyes kept jumping from the page to Alex's face. "Apparently, the SS figured he'd been captured and killed by the French Underground."

There was a rush of relief. Gottfried sobbed in her head, his voice broken and full of gratitude that his rushed plan had worked, that at least his family hadn't been harassed. Something must have shown on Alex's face because Bran gave her a moment.

"I'm afraid that Enrich Eckstein was killed in action during the Battle of Berlin," Bran said. "April 1945, when the Soviet army made it to Berlin."

"Enrich would have been nineteen," Alex whispered. "And he was… so caught up in the Nazi regime." She blinked back tears at the faint memory of Gottfried's son who'd been so eager to join the Hitler Youth Program. Who Ilse and Gottfried had been afraid to talk in front of.

"It isn't a surprise that he would have joined the army." Gottfried was completely silent. "Uh, what about Ilse and the others."

Bran didn't react to Alex's use of Gottfried's wife's name. "Mrs. Eckstein returned to work after the war, receiving some support due to her deceased husband and son. It wasn't a lot in the post-war, but she maintained ownership of the house outside of Cologne until her death in 1982." Another rush of relief, Ilse died at the age of 81 years old rather than in the war or the aftermath. "Thanks to being in Cologne, the Eckstein family was in West Germany," Bran added.

"Good. And the children?"

"Reinhold went on to become a doctor," Bran said with a slight smile. "He was married twice and had three children with his first wife before she passed. His second marriage was later in life. He lived in Cologne until his death in 2008. Morgana confirmed five grandchildren and recently one great-grandchild."

The tears were back, and Alex closed her eyes as her chest tightened and eased at the same time. "Good," she whispered.

"Gisela moved to Munich when she was twenty and married a musician. She worked part-time as a secretary but seemed to be a homemaker mostly. Had three children, died in 1997 shortly after her husband. Six known grandchildren and two great-grandchildren. Elsa was the youngest, and she came to the United States in 1965. She was an engineer." Alex could hear the smile in Bran's voice. "Married later in life, but never had any children. Became a university professor in Philadelphia until 2000 when she finally retired. She passed away in 2010."

Her knees shook, and it was Alex's grip on the railing that kept her upright. Then Bran held the notebook out to her. His jaw was tight, and he licked his lips nervously. Pulling one hand off the railing, Alex took the notebook.

"There's more in there. Names and birthdates of the grandchildren if you want it."

"Thanks. I'll... have to thank Morgana too."

"Are you okay?"

"Gottfried is in a bit of a state right now." Alex almost chuckled. "My memories of his family are... difficult. They were happy but living in horrible times. There was a lot of fear. I carry that with me now. I have his memories."

"I think that you're-" Bran cut himself off. "Alex, memory isn't what people think it is." Bran's tone was too soft and cautious like he was afraid she was going to bolt. Maybe he was right to worry. "People are under the mistaken assumption that memories are stored in the brain like small movies, but that isn't how it works at all."

"Oh?" Alex smiled a little and looked over at Bran. "Is the science geek going to tell me how it works?"

"If you like." Bran waited a moment to let her argue, but Alex just smiled. "Okay, memories aren't stored because they aren't physical. Memories are signals, specifically a pattern of signals in your brain. A memory starts as an electric potential created by ions moving in and out of the cells at the end of a neuron. That signal triggers a chemical signal that moves the ions to another neuron which causes a change in that neuron. It's a chain reaction between the neurons, and it forms a special pattern that is different from any other memory. I think that this is what was passed onto you, that electrical signal pattern."

"And I think my head hurts." Alex rubbed the sides of the head, trying to understand the science that Bran had just dumped. "Visual aids would have been a good idea."

"Sorry, I wasn't planning on doing a lecture."

"And to think that Aiden's the one with the professor father."

"I might be a professor someday," Bran said. "I think I'd enjoy it. Though I've got a lot of years of university left if that's the track I want to follow."

"You'd be good at it." Alex ran her thumb over the surface of the notebook. "So, I got the electrical patterns of the others' memories. I guess that sort of makes sense."

"Yes, but that's not my whole point. The thing is that these signals obviously are just patterns. The brain takes this pattern and uses it to rebuild a memory, but there isn't enough just in those signals, so the brain fills in the gaps. It helps you reconstruct your memory based on other things that it knows. Researchers have found that because of this, you can actually tell someone a story and their brain will create a visual of it, and even make them believe that that story is an actual memory. You can implant even rich memories in others through suggestion because of how the brain latches on and fills in the gaps. Memory is a puzzle, not a movie, and your brain will use any puzzle pieces it has to make sense of what you are trying to understand."

"What's your point, Bran? Thus far, all I'm getting here is a headache."

"My point Alex is that what you think you remember may not be totally accurate. Yes, when you touched Arto's skull, you seem to have gained or maybe just unlocked the neuron mapping of Arto's brain or at least of some of his memories. The others followed, but those electrical impulses aren't happening in Arto or Gottfried's brain. The brain in that skull is still yours. Those signals and the memories that they help build are being shaped by your own mind as well."

"I'm not sure what you want me to take from this," Alex said.

"You are still you. It's your brain, and no matter how many memories are in it please try to keep that in mind. Even the things that you got from the others are still reforming and connecting in a brain that developed with you. Your memory signals and experiences have become part of the way you remember Arto."

"I'm not sure you're right about that," Alex said. "It's overwhelming sometimes. Like fighting to keep my head above water before I learned to swim."

"I can believe that." Bran hesitated for a moment before putting a hand on her shoulder. "But that may be because of all the new electrical signals in your brain. It was a huge influx, but it's getting easier, isn't it?"

"A bit." Alex nodded slowly. "I suppose it is. But a person is also the sum of their memories, Bran. These things are a part of me now. I... remember things and have emotions that aren't from things this body ever experienced."

"But you own them now."

"I'm not sure what your point is. Are you saying that I'm still me? Because that doesn't feel true." She dropped her eyes to the notebook. "Alex Adams who started college with no idea about magic wouldn't care this much about the family of a Nazi. She would have been dismissive."

"But even if this had never happened, you would have changed in other ways. I'm just... I guess I'm trying to reassure you that even if these memories change you that you have changed them too. You offer a different context to them. A different way of understanding them. You own them, not the other way around and in that, you're still Alex Adams."

Alex wasn't sure if he was right. The logic was sound, and he wasn't wrong that things were getting easier. Maybe he was right. Maybe he was wrong and grasping at straws. Alex wished, not for the first time, that she understood the science around her better; that she wasn't hanging by faith and experience. But she was. Her fingers closed around the notebook, and she inhaled slowly, focusing on the beat of her own heart.

"I think that it's time to go home," Alex said. She managed a smile for Bran and then looked out over Mumbai. "The Demon King is dead, and Cathanáil isn't holding open a portal anymore. Shiva can take it from here."

"You sure?"

"No," Alex admitted. She tapped the hilt of Cathanáil. "But we've got enough problems back at Ravenslake. As much as I might like to, we can't hide here."

Bran nodded in understanding. "I'll let Merlin and Morgana know."

He stepped away from her and reentered the house. Turning her attention back to the city, Alex let her magic stretch out around her. Below was the hum of the city, colorful outlines of her fellow mages, and the dull gold shapes of the Desai magicians. Nothing dark tugged at the threads. Mumbai and Lokpal's family was safe, at least for the time being.

35

To Keep on Living

Packing to leave was easy. Alex liked the Desai family, but nagging worries about what Arthur was up to were pushing their way forward. Shiva could deal with the Demons, and she had faith that Lokpal's family would continue long after she was gone and reborn again. It was the issue of the Darkness that was the worst. Those images of dying worlds and the frantic fears of the Demons needed to be addressed.

Cathanáil hummed gently at her side and Alex touched her hand to the hilt. All the Iron artifacts called to her, but the sword was special. Maybe it was because it had been the first made, but something had settled in Alex thanks to having it back. Which was odd. Arthur had run her through with it, nearly killed her with her own sword. Yet, she was glad to have it back.

"Maybe because you can't get into trouble if I'm keeping an eye on you," Alex said. Then she laughed. "I'm talking to a Sword. Oh boy, it's official. I've lost it. I suppose it was only a matter of time."

Her clothes were all in her backpack, not that she'd brought much, and Alex glanced around to make sure that she had everything else. They hadn't gone shopping or really any kind of sightseeing, so the only new thing going back with her was the Sword. The Sword and the moleskine notebook. She picked it up from the nightstand and studied it for a long moment. Without thinking about it, Alex opened the small notebook and scanned through the notes. Morgana's handwriting wasn't the easiest to read, but there were dates and names scrawled over dozens of pages.

Alex wondered how long it had taken her to track all this down. There were notes on the children's lives from their births to their deaths with years they were in schools marked down, their marriages, and other significant events. There were pages on Gottfried's grandchildren and great-grandchildren. Running her fingers over the words, Alex gave into the ebb and flow of emotions from Gottfried, letting his grief, joy, and regret wash over her. Tears stung her eyes, but it was also happy in a strange way.

A knock on the door made her snap the book closed. Sniffing, she gathered her composure and called from them to enter. It was Morgana, her hair still damp from her morning shower, but otherwise as calm as ever. Morgana's eyes dropped to the moleskine notebook still in Alex's hand.

"Bran did give you the information I see," she said.

"He just did," Alex said. She looked down at the notebook, unsure if she was happy or not. "There really hasn't been a quiet moment lately."

"No," Morgana agreed. "I hope that I didn't overstep."

"You didn't." Giving Morgana a soft smile, she nodded to her former sister. "I think... I think it helped. After what happened with Matt and Eddy."

"They'll be fine. I was able to make the arrangements you requested. I set them up in-"

"Don't," Alex said. "It's better if I don't know. I don't want to lead Arthur to them in a moment of weakness."

"As you wish." Morgana seemed lost for words. "I did my best to make sure that they'll be happy. They don't remember that they had a sister but remember your parents and are starting over in a new city due to Matt's schooling as far as they know."

"Good." Alex nodded. "Uh, is Anne still with them?"

"Yes, they have the dog. I didn't alter her memories. She seemed very sad, but I'm sure that she'll be a source of comfort to your brothers."

Oddly enough, it made Alex feel better to know that at least the family dog remembered her. "I hate to ask, but what about my college expenses and loans," Alex said. "Are there records I need to help you change?"

"I took care of it. Your parents' life insurance has been dealt with."

There was something Morgana wasn't telling her; Alex could hear it in her voice. She could guess. Morgana had probably given all the money to her brothers and arranged to pay for Alex's school herself. It was the sort of thing Alex could see her doing.

"Thank you," Alex said. "That helps. Let me know if I need to take care of anything."

"I will, but I'll do what I can to keep it from burdening you."

"Should I keep bothering with school? It seems silly at this point. I could live in Ravenslake and train full time."

"No," Morgana said. She shook her head and gripped Alex's shoulder. "No, Alex. You need something else. If you only want to go to school part time, then that is fine, but you'll need a degree. I still live in hope that you'll see all these crises through and be able to have a real life in the future." Gesturing around them at the Desai home, Morgana smiled. "After all, Lokpal did. He had his family before and after the Demons came. Thor married Sif, and while she didn't age like him, they were happy. Don't write yourself off. Besides, you'd get tired of just spending time worrying about magic."

"Yes, but that's not the point." Alex toyed with the corner of the moleskine book. "There's a lot to worry about. We have things to do."

"That's true," Morgana said. She moved her hand to brush a strand of hair from Alex's face. "But there always will be. Don't worry about India. Shiva can handle it. His loyalty to you seems as strong as ever."

"What did Lokpal do?"

"Lokpal had faith in him." Morgana shook her head, smiling fondly. "Not as a god, but as a good being. I'm under the impression that it was something new for Shiva at the time."

Nodding, Alex turned back to her backpack and slipped the moleskine notebook inside the small front pocket. "Thank you, for the information," she said. "It... I really do think it helped."

"I was hoping that it would." Morgana licked her lips and shifted nervously. "I debated giving it to you myself but thought that Bran giving it to you would be better."

Blinking, Alex considered the words. "Maybe," she finally said. "Bran's pretty good at stuff like that." She zipped up her backpack, checking one more time for the shape of the Iron Chalice. It was there, snug amongst her spare t-shirts.

"Yes, he is." Morgana looked at the backpack. "Ready?"

"As I ever am," Alex said.

"Well, you'll be glad to know that you and the others can move into the house I arranged. It's a nice place," Morgana said. "Very private, near my home."

"Sounds good," Alex said. The words were vague. At the moment that wasn't what she was really worried about. It would be nice not to have to worry about drawing Sídhe, their hounds, and whatever else was going to come after them to their college campus. "Thanks for taking care of that while we ran off here."

"It was hardly a vacation. I'm just grateful that everyone is alright." Morgana studied Alex as she pulled her backpack off the bed. "You are sure you're ready-"

"It's fine," Alex said. "We have the contact information of the Desais, including video call information. They've agreed to help with research using their library. Staying would just be lingering, and there's a lot of other things to do."

Morgana stayed with Alex on the way downstairs. She wasn't sure if Morgana was worried or had missed her or wanted to stay near the Sword. Alex didn't mention it and smiled as the others came into view. Everyone was gathered in the main hall, chatting with smiles on their faces. Nicki was eating some kind of rice dish off a plate with her hands while Gita smiled warmly at her. Aiden stole a bit of his own and got his hand slapped by Nicki.

"Rude! This is mine! You had yours!"

"It's tasty," Aiden whined. "I don't get authentic Indian food in Ravenslake. You have to go to like Portland for the good stuff."

"I'll send you some recipes," Gita promised. She patted the side of his head as he pouted. "You mages need to eat well if you're going to stay strong."

Holding back a smile, Alex quietly moved down to join the others. But she stopped on the last stair. There was something just at the edge of her senses. Frowning slightly, Alex squinted her eyes and tried to get a lock on it. Then she recognized the tightly bound mass of energy as Shiva. He was outside the house, near the water pool, Alex realized.

Gita spotted them and her smile widened further. She hurried over to Morgana, eagerly examining the woman and asking questions. Morgana looked stunned but recovered quickly to answer Gita's rushed inquiries. A sound behind her made Alex look towards one of the doors where she found Merlin talking with Lochan. Judging from the indulgent smile on Merlin's face, he didn't mind the magician's questions.

Pulling on her backpack, Alex slipped away from Morgana and headed for the back door. Oddly enough, she'd managed to learn the layout of the house in their brief time here. Alex wondered, almost sadly, if she'd ever return to the Desai home. She paused to look at a collection of photos, tracing the faces. Lokpal's voice fluttered at the back of her mind, pushing some of Gottfried's sadness aside. The band around her lungs eased, and Alex was able to inhale and smile.

It made her think of something Morgana had said to her once. Back before she had control of her powers. The exact words were lost in her memory, but it had been about how people, ordinary people just keep going with their lives. That history might be made up of significant events, but that the past was all people. People looking after each other, trying to survive, and doing their best. Maybe as the Iron Soul, she hadn't always stopped the invaders forever, but they'd made an impact. This family was here, alive, and happy because of Lokpal. And there were people alive and living peaceful lives because of Gottfried. And her brothers could now have a peaceful life and recover from the loss of their parents.

"I'm going to be okay," Alex said. She was still looking at the photos, but the words were meant for her parents. "I'll be okay."

It settled into her bones. There was a lingering fear of the Sídhe, Arthur, and the Darkness, of course, but there was a change. It was easier to move. With a new or rather returned lightness, she went out the side door of the house and followed the pathway to the pool house.

Shiva was waiting for her, sitting on the floor, and meditating with the Trishula across his lap. Alex's fingers itched to touch the Iron Trishula, but less so now that the Sword and Hammer were with her. Shiva's eyes opened, and a small smile appeared on his face as he took in the weapons hanging at her sides. He even raised an eyebrow.

"We don't all have extra arms," Alex said. She shrugged off her backpack and sat down on the floor across from Shiva. "Why do you have extra arms anyway? Don't your kind largely decide what you look like?"

"Mostly," Shiva said. "I gave myself extra arms because the myths of this land had deities with multiple arms when I arrived here. It sounded useful, and I wasn't interested in passing as human."

"Fair enough." Alex hesitated but plowed on. "What about your skin?"

"The blue skin," Shiva said. "That is left over from when I was slipping into madness. Lokpal rescued me, but my skin still shows signs of corruption. I suppose that I could reform my body, but that is a difficult process and I..." Shiva shook his head. "It is a reminder. It reminds me to be careful and return to the waters periodically and to value humans."

"You still care about Lokpal, don't you?"

"He was a good friend," Shiva said. "A good man who cared about others and showed compassion even when he shouldn't have. He entrusted the Trishula to me so that I could fight to protect the Iron Realm and help other Old Ones if necessary." Then Shiva's smile widened as he looked at her. "You remind me of him a great deal."

"Merlin has said something similar."

Shiva laughed and nodded. "Yes, I suppose they would see it too. I'm a bit surprised that they let you come to India alone, they can be very protective of the Iron Soul."

"Not sure why," Alex said. "It's not like I won't come back." She shrugged, but Shiva's expression turned sad.

"No, you don't 'come back,' you are reborn. There is a difference, Alex. You may have the Iron Soul, but you are distinct, as was Lokpal."

"People keep telling me that," Alex admitted. "But it doesn't always seem true."

"I'm sorry. You are a human bearing a very inhuman burden."

Shiva's gaze was soft and patient. She could remember those eyes being very different. It was a flicker of memory, but she trusted it. Awareness of Shiva's past washed over her. She couldn't remember it in detail, but she knew it and was grateful for his willingness to become Shiva. Alex didn't know what to say.

"I hope that you will find peace with this," Shiva added.

Exhaling slowly, Alex nodded. "I'm getting there... slowly, but I think that day may come." Then she looked towards the water. "But I'm going back to Ravenslake with more questions than answers."

"I will see what I can learn," Shiva promised. "I will deal with the remaining new Demons and see what I can learn from them."

"Thanks."

"Thank you for coming to India," Shiva said. He shook his head. "I can't believe that I didn't sense the Sword." His eyes dropped to Cathanáil, and he chuckled. "I met Cyrridven when she carried it once. I had the Trishula then. It was an interesting conversation."

"I can imagine."

They lapsed into silence. Alex searched for what else to say, but the silence with Shiva was comfortable. It wasn't tense or awkward. She thought that she heard people talking outside. The others would join them soon.

"Thank you," Alex said. "For all your help. For watching over India."

"You are most welcome, old friend." Shiva looked at her, a small smile on his face. "You may not remember all of it, Alex, but I see glimmers of understanding in your eyes. You saved me once. As Lokpal you had compassion for a being very different than you. Even now, after all these years, I still do not understand it." Then he unfolded his legs and stood up. "But I am grateful for it."

Standing up, Alex picked up her backpack. "It was good to meet you, Shiva."

He nodded and shifted his hands, bringing the Trishula forward once again. He didn't need to say that it was hers to take. It was and she knew it, and yet it wasn't. Holding back a sigh, Alex reached out and touched the metal shaft. Flickers of magic rose up in the metal to meet her fingertips. It was warm and familiar with a comforting hum. She lowered her hand and smiled at Shiva.

"Please keep it," Alex said. "You have done good things with the Trishula and besides, some of us only have two hands."

Laughing, Shiva shook his head fondly and grasped the Trishula tighter. "You have a better sense of humor than you did then. Lokpal was always very... critical isn't the right word nor is frightened and worried. I suppose even before he learned of magic, he carried a position of great importance. He never shied away from it though he doubted what he could do throughout his life."

"When did he die? Was it in battle?"

"In battle? No, Lokpal died an old man. His eldest son Ojos, while not a mage, did learn some small ways to channel magic and is the ancestor of the Desai family. He had several children who all managed to live to adulthood and start families of their own. Lokpal gave the Trishula to me, to my surprise, later in his life when he could no longer fight. Not that there were many Demons to fight here then. Many had fled to other parts of India by then."

"And you followed?"

"To an extent. I went and fought those Demons who caused trouble. At Lokpal's insistence, I left those who lived in peace alone. But I found myself always returning here. Rudra faded away and Shiva was born in these waters. My first true friend in this world lived and died here. It is home."

Tears stung her eyes. If they were from her own emotions or Lokpal's, Alex didn't know. It didn't matter. Giving Shiva a watery smile, she nodded. While magic flowed around them, filling the world, it was different around Shiva. It shifted slightly like he was a rock in a river, but it didn't seek to attack. He was a friend of the Iron Realm.

"Thank you," she said. "Once more. For Lokpal, for his children, and for me."

"Once more, you are welcome." Shiva flexed his fingers around the shaft of the Trishula. "And should you need it, you have but to call."

"Depending on what is happening.... I may take you up on that," Alex said. "Should I just call the Desai family?"

"You may call me directly." Shiva smiled once more. "It may take me some time, but I always seem to hear you when you call me."

"I'll keep that in mind."

There was a soft knock on the door, tentative and cautious. Blinking back tears and swallowing the new lump in her throat, Alex reached over to open the door. Nicki was in front of it with the others behind her. She looked a bit nervous and apologetic.

"Uh... ready to go?" Nicki asked.

"I'm ready." Alex stepped to the side to let the others in. "Finish your breakfast?"

"Yes, and I have the recipe," Nicki said. "Not sure if I'll be able to find everything in Ravenslake, but I'm willing to try. Besides, I could always water travel to-"

"No," Morgana said. She gave Nicki a stern look, though she looked a touch amused. "No water tunnels for trivial matters."

"You are no fun," Nicki said. She pouted a little, but there was a spark of happiness in her eyes. Alex wasn't sure what to make of it and wondered if she'd missed something between Avani and Nicki. "Well, let's blow this popsicle stand, then."

"I'll open the tunnel to Ravenslake," Merlin said. He was smiling and more relaxed than Alex had seen him in a while. Green sparks flared off his fingertips as he turned towards the pool.

"No," Alex said. "Wait, let's go to San Francisco instead." Everyone looked at her, but Jenny's eyes lit up. Smiling, Alex nodded to her friend before looking back at Merlin. "I still owe Jenny a blood protection spell around her father. Let's take care of that and then get back to work figuring out how to take Arthur down."

Nodding in agreement, Merlin waved his hand, and the green sparks swept up a wave of water into the air. As it spun into a whirlpool and began to form their tunnel, Alex let herself sigh. The Demons had been knocked down enough that Shiva could deal with them. Arthur hadn't caused any urgent crisis in the past week, and some part of her felt a little better. The voices in her head were still there, and questions about the strange Darkness remained unanswered, but the dull ache in her heart had eased. The source of it was in every life, every lost person, but maybe she really could live with that.

www.ingramcontent.com/pod-product-compliance
Lightning Source LLC
Chambersburg PA
CBHW060931120726

47910CB00002B/281